STAR STRUCK DEAD

A Lauren Atwill Mystery

SHEILA YORK

POCKET BOOKS

New York   London   Toronto   Sydney   Singapore

This book is a work of fiction. Names, characters, places and incidents are products of the author's imagination or are used fictitiously. Any resemblance to actual events or locales or persons, living or dead, is entirely coincidental.

An *Original* Publication of POCKET BOOKS

POCKET BOOKS, a division of Simon & Schuster, Inc.
1230 Avenue of the Americas, New York, NY 10020

ISBN: 0-7434-7046-X

First Pocket Books printing October 2003

10 9 8 7 6 5 4 3 2 1

POCKET and colophon are registered trademarks of
Simon & Schuster, Inc.

Front cover illustration by Mark Thomas

For information regarding special discounts for bulk purchases,
please contact Simon & Schuster Special Sales at 1-800-456-6798
or business@simonandschuster.com

Manufactured in the United States of America

GAL AS A GUMSHOE . . .

I opened the center drawer. There was nothing I wouldn't have expected to find: a writing tablet, whose sheets however did not match the note Maritski had sent me, a bottle of ink, a roll of stamps, some pencils, a checkbook, and a bankbook. I flipped through them. There were no large deposits. Winslow had about four thousand in his savings account. In the right-hand drawer were a box of stationery, a new typewriter ribbon, a bank-wrapped stack of new one-dollar bills, and a long white envelope. I picked it up. Inside were a dozen negatives the size of those for amateur photographs, each about three by two inches.

I took one out, holding it by the corner. I raised it to the window, but I couldn't make out anything. I switched on the desk lamp and held it close to the shade.

"Hello," said a voice behind me.

I cried out and spun around. The negatives flew out of my hand. He didn't look at them. He was looking at me. Very hard. I was looking at the gun. . . .

For my mother, Mabel Mayhew,
and in memory of my father, Walter Mayhew, Jr.
And especially for my husband, David F. Nighbert.

Chapter 1

I was having a wonderful dream. Then I woke up.

I was in the hospital. I didn't remember how I got there.

It was a private room. That much I could make out. But somewhere off to my right, an enormous window was letting in entirely too much light. I rolled away from it, flinching and groaning—making the sounds a person makes when her head is pounding and her stomach is lurching. I buried my face in the pillow and reached for the nurse call button.

While I was still groping for it, the nurse came in.

"You're awake," she said cheerfully. It seemed like the best news she'd had in a week. "Good morning."

"Not so far."

She chuckled indulgently as she passed the foot of the bed, a brisk blur of white to my one exposed eye. I heard her snap the window shade down. The room got a bit darker.

"Thanks," I said.

"How are you feeling?"

"My head hurts, and I think I might be sick."

She pulled a bedpan out of the bedside cabinet and set it on top beside the water carafe. "Use this if you need to. When the doctor comes, we can give you something for the pain."

I made a few more groaning noises to indicate that I thought that would be a good idea.

"Now that you're awake," she said, "I'll go call the police."

I brought my other eye out of the pillow. "What?"

"Don't you remember what happened last night?"

"I couldn't have been hit by anything smaller than a truck."

She chuckled again. "I heard you were a movie writer."

"I think I'm usually funnier. What time is it?"

"About seven-thirty. A Mrs. Ross called and said she'd come by later to pick you up." She started for the door.

"Nurse, this might sound like a strange question, but where am I?"

"At County," she said proudly. "Now try to get some rest."

There was something else I wanted to ask her. Or was it a hundred things? I couldn't remember what any of them were, so I let her go and concentrated on my groaning.

After a while, though, I got tired of it and rolled over and looked around. The window turned out to be only regulation size. Beneath it was a silver radiator and a wide-planked, dark-varnished wooden floor, well scrubbed and hard-used. Almost everything else—the walls, the chairs, the bedside cabinet—was the same unfortunate shade of yellow, somewhere between mustard and jaundice. It was just the sort of color the government liked to paint the insides of public buildings, the sort of color no actual member of the public would be caught dead with in his own home. Now that the war was over, and we could get paint again easily, the hospital was apparently repainting with a vengeance.

Even a good color would not have helped much: the room would still look as if it had lived through too many years with too little money. The enamel on the slats at the end of the bed was chipped. On the ceiling, there was a faint veining of cracks spreading from the corners and from the edges of the white metal fan. As the breeze lifted the window shade, I could see that the screen was sagging and patched.

County. What was I doing at County? Why had I been brought all the way back into Los Angeles? Surely there had been a hospital closer. Maybe the thieves had taken my identification, and County was the only hospital that would accept what might be a charity case. I wondered who had found me all the way out there in Topanga Canyon. I would like to say thank you.

I lifted the sheet and examined my body. There were assorted bruises on my forearms, a half dozen stitches across my knee, and a nasty scrape on my hip where I'd fallen in the gravel. On the whole, I thought it would have been simpler if the bastards had just pulled guns. Of course, if they had, they might have shot me before they robbed me. There was that to consider. I could imagine the story in the papers—on the front page, of course, because of Franklin—STAR'S WIFE FOUND DEAD IN DITCH. A couple of men standing in line to see *The Blue Dahlia* would read it.

"Hey, you see this about Frank Atwill's wife?"

"What she do?"

"Found her dead out in Topanga."

"No kidding. What happened?"

"Don't know. Says she was shot."

"That her? Huh. Thought he'd have a better-looking wife than that."

"Says she used to write movies. Lauren Atwill. Ever heard of her?"

"Nope. Which ones?"

"Some of the Phil Marsh mysteries, says here."

"Yeah? I liked them okay."

A shrug. A grunt. The line starts to move.

My epitaph. Here lies a hack. Maybe a dozen people would care. I wasn't depressed. No, not me.

I went back to my groaning. It seemed more useful than thinking.

The doctor came in twenty minutes later, making as much noise as a person can make wearing soft-soled shoes and not dragging any chains. He was a dapper little man with a crisp, energetic moustache and a bony nose. He set a tiny paper cup with two tiny white pills in it on the bedside cabinet.

"I understand you have a headache this morning."

"Yes. Thanks."

He snapped my chart out of the rack at the foot of the bed and read it. I took the pills.

"You're very lucky," he pronounced rather loudly when he'd finished reading. "They gave you a few stitches last night, but otherwise, you're fine." He dropped the chart back into the rack with more clatter than I thought was absolutely necessary, then raised his eyebrows and gave me a reproving look. "You're very lucky."

I didn't need a lecture on how women should never drive alone at night. "How long does chloroform last?" I asked.

He blinked at me a couple of times. "I beg your pardon?"

"When I was robbed last night, I was chloroformed."

He raised his eyebrows again, this time in skepticism.

I said, "It only lasts a few minutes, doesn't it? Unless you continue to administer it?"

"Yes," he agreed cautiously.

"I thought so." I had researched it once for a script. In the early days. Before I realized that Hollywood wasn't much interested in accuracy. "Would you look at these?" I raised the droopy sleeve of my hospital gown to show him the two tiny red dots on my upper arm. "Did they give me any shots last night?"

"There's no mention of shots on your chart. These could be insect bites."

"I've been unconscious for six hours. How do you explain that?"

He raised those skeptical brows again. "I believe, Mrs. Atwill, that there was some alcohol involved."

"What?" I said so loudly that my head started pounding again.

"I understand from the emergency room staff that you were drinking last night."

"I was not drunk. I have not been unconscious for six hours because I was drunk. I was robbed and drugged."

He looked at me. If he raised those eyebrows one more time, I was going to hit him with the bedpan.

"Did they do a blood test?" I asked.

"They would have drawn blood from the vein."

"I know that. Did they do one?"

"Yes. The results aren't back yet. It is Sunday, you know."

"I was not drunk."

He stretched the skin around on my upper arm and examined the dots. "Hmmm," he said.

"I need to ask you something else. Last night . . . Did anything happen to me that . . . that I should know about?"

He let go of my arm and stared at me, then he swallowed so hard that his Adam's apple bobbed up like a fishing cork. "I . . . uh. I understand that, well, of course, under the circumstances, you were examined. You would be. Of course. Under the circumstances."

"And?"

"There are ways to tell if, well, if . . ."

"And?"

"You were not."

"They were sure?"

"Yes. You don't feel that . . . ?"

"No. Not at all. I just wanted to make sure."

"Yes. Well, then. Yes. I think you can go home as soon as you're feeling up to it." He turned and hurried out.

When he had gone, I punched the pillow around and snarled at the door. He—and apparently everybody else at the hospital—thought that I was pie-eyed last night and probably picked up some hitchhiker, who lifted my purse and my car after I passed out. And no one would ever tell them the truth, even after the blood test came back.

Despite what he had said about the thoroughness of last night's examination, I lay there for a while, running over and over what I remembered of the dream I'd been having when I woke up, looking for any detail that would indicate that it was not a dream. I didn't find one. There was a soft bed, not a car seat or the choking dust of a canyon road. There was no fear, only pleasure. The face of the dark-haired man was vague and blurred, as faces so often are in dreams, but the sensation was still warm. The smooth, bare skin of a tall, strong body. I rolled onto my side and snuggled into the pillow and closed my eyes. I slept, but the dream did not come back.

About ten, while I was moving a spoon around in some Cream of Wheat, my best friend, Helen Ross, showed up.

"Well, you look like hell," she said amiably as she tossed a garment bag across the foot of the bed. She, however, looked nearly perfect, as she always did. Her pink two-piece linen day dress was smooth and crisp, despite the car ride. Her carefully dyed blond hair was pinned up flawlessly beneath her straw picture hat. Once she had been a Ziegfeld Girl, and—now past forty—she still looked thirty-five. From ten feet away. Closer, the powder was maybe a little too thick, the rouge a little too heavy, and the China Cherry Blossom lipstick a little too vivid. She set the bedpan on the floor and dropped her bag, gloves, and a small pearl-colored overnight case on the bedside cabinet. "You okay?"

"Oh, yeah, I'm fine. I landed on my head."

"Anything left of your clothes?" Before I could answer, she opened the closet door. "God, it smells like a brewery in here." She pulled out my white satin evening gown and examined the dribbling booze stains down the front.

I said, "Now I know why everyone around here thinks I was drunk."

"Well, this is ruined. It's just as well. I don't think either one of us looked all that great in white." She rolled the gown into a ball and tossed it into the trash can. "Where's your wrap?"

"Gone with the car, I guess."

"Did they hurt you?"

"Not much."

"You know what I mean."

"No."

"Well, thank God for that. Do you mind if I smoke?"

"Go ahead."

She slipped a slim, silver case out of her envelope bag and took out a cigarette. "Juanita called me last night about three, just after I got in. She said you weren't home yet and wanted to know if you were with me. The first thing I did was call all the hospitals, then all the police departments. They didn't pay any attention to me. Apparently, Saturday nights are full of women who don't come home when they're supposed to."

She lit the cigarette with an engraved silver lighter and turned her head away from me to exhale. She scooted the trash can over beside the chair with her foot and sat down. "Then about five, the L.A. police called and asked if my friend was a tall blonde with long hair and a white dress. So I drove over here as fast as I could, and there you were on one of those—what do they call them, the stretchers with wheels?"

"Gurneys."

"You were laying there, unconscious, all scraped up, and the policeman started asking me how much you'd had to drink. I told him that, the last time I saw you, you had a car, a necklace, and an evening bag, all of which were now gone and that never, in the whole time I'd known you, had I ever seen you drunk. Of course, he didn't believe me. The police are idiots."

There was a knock on the door, and the police came in.

First, there was a young patrolman, who was wearing his hat pushed back on his head and was working hard on a hard look. He wasn't having much luck with it. He had a round, boyish face with red cheeks and pale lashes. There was a rash on the side of his neck from shaving—or trying to. Behind him, chewing on a wooden matchstick, was the man who was probably teaching him the hard look. He was about fifty and wearing a suit over plenty of bulk, but plenty of that bulk was still muscle. He had thick, unruly eyebrows and stormy jowls, but when he removed his hat, his matchstick, and his sneer, he looked more like a big, furry uncle. "Mrs. Atwill?" he asked.

"Yes."

"Sergeant Barty. This is Officer McHugh."

"How do you do?"

"Are you really married to Frank Atwill?" McHugh asked, trying to keep his eyes from getting too big.

"Yes, I am. And this is Mrs. Samuel Ross. You might have heard of her husband. He's a producer at Marathon. He's producing my husband's new movie."

"Oh, yeah, sure," he said politely. If he was going to make it as a cop, he was going to have to work on his lying.

Barty said, "I only brought him along because he doesn't get to see many Hollywood people. The report said you're a screenwriter."

"Yes."

"Which movies did you write?" McHugh asked eagerly.

"*Summer Eagle, That Girl Next Door, The Brantley Case.*" He looked blank. "Some of the Phil Marsh mysteries."

"I love those. Especially *The Candlestick Murders*. The way the candle was always burned down after one of them got killed."

"I'm glad."

Barty concentrated on the matchstick in his hand, but I could see him roll his eyes. I didn't blame him. He sat down in the other chair and hung his hat on his knee. He took a notebook out of the inside pocket of his well-used suit. "What can you tell me about last night?"

"She was not drunk," said Helen.

"That's why I'm here, Mrs. Ross. To get the story."

"Just so you understand that."

"Why don't you tell me what happened, Mrs. Atwill?"

I told him everything I could remember. I had driven out to Ramon Elizondo's nightclub up in Topanga Canyon. Usually my escort drove me, but he'd fallen ill the day before, so I went alone. I met Helen there and a small group of friends. About one o'clock, I left. Coruna, the road that runs between the club and Topanga Canyon Road, was almost deserted. After I'd gone about a mile, I came across two sawhorses in the middle of the road with an official-looking sign hung between them that said, TEMPORARY DETOUR. I turned off onto a road barely wide enough for two cars. At the first bend, there was a car stopped diagonally in the road. The driver's door was open. In its interior light, I could see someone slumped over the wheel. I got out and went over to help. Then I could see that it wasn't a person at all, but a dummy.

I told Barty about the dummy, but I didn't tell him what that moment of cold horror had felt like as I stood there, struggling to make sense of it, all the time knowing that something terrible was about to happen. A man grabbed me from behind. I fought, but he was too strong. We slipped in the gravel and fell, then I smelled chloroform.

I showed Barty the needle marks. "I only woke up about seven. They must have shot me full of dope and poured booze on me. I don't know why."

"And all this happened way out in Topanga?"

"Yes."

"So how'd you get back downtown? That's got to be twenty miles from where they found you."

"What?"

"A couple of our guys found you laid out in an alley off Broadway. You don't remember anything after the chloroform?"

"Not a thing."

He chewed on the matchstick a while, then he asked about the thieves' car. Dark. Coupe. A tall grille. I didn't remember any of the license number.

"What about the man who grabbed you?"

"He was wearing a mask. Actually, a hood. He was tall. Over six feet. That's all I know."

"Did you see anyone else?"

"No, but I've been thinking." I sat forward. "There had to be more than one. There had to be at least three. One to grab me. Another to move the phony detour sign out of the road quickly. And there had to be a lookout somewhere to make sure there weren't any cars following me."

He grinned around his matchstick at my efforts at deduction.

"Would it be very hard to find detour signs?" I asked.

"Not with all the roadwork going on these days."

"Still, it seems like a lot of trouble to go to. They would have needed a radio."

"That road, that time of night, their chances of getting a high roller with a nice car were pretty good. And there are plenty of army surplus radios around these days. How much did they get?"

"Not much money. But there was a necklace and some earrings. Emeralds and diamonds. I can give you pictures. I had them taken for the insurance. And my wedding ring."

"I'm sorry," he said, and meant it.

"Thank you," I said. "Is there any hope for my car?"

He consulted his notebook. "Forty-one, white, Lincoln Continental cabriolet. Aren't many of those around."

"No, they didn't make very many before Pearl Harbor."

"During the war, a thief could get five, six thousand for one of them. Some folks in Mexico'd probably still pay that much."

"Maybe that's why they drugged me. So I wouldn't wake up and get help before they could get the car over the border. And they poured booze on me so if I did wake up, no one would take me seriously."

"Why didn't they leave you up in Topanga? That'd make more sense."

I couldn't argue with that.

He stood up. "I'll run this past the county boys. See if anything else like this has happened." He handed me a card with the address and telephone number of Central Division.

"I'll bring you the photographs of the jewelry."

"Anytime tomorrow'll be fine. Just ask for me."

"Thank you." We shook hands. Barty's face didn't give much away. I couldn't tell if he'd believed one word I'd said.

When they'd gone, Helen said, "Don't worry about a thing. Sam'll take care of it."

"Of what?"

She slid a copy of the *Examiner* out from under the garment bag and tossed it into my lap. "It made the second edition."

"Jesus." I stared at the headline.

STAR'S WIFE FOUND UNCONSCIOUS NEAR SOLDIERS' BAR

"Jesus." I scanned the short article. " 'According to police, Mrs. Atwill, who had apparently been drinking . . .' Jesus."

"I know. I'm sorry."

" 'At press time, Mrs. Atwill had not been able to explain why . . .' How could I explain? I was unconscious! It doesn't even mention that I was robbed."

"It does. But on the next page."

" 'Frank Atwill separated from his wife last year . . .' Jesus. It makes it sound like he walked out on a drunk. Are all the papers like this?"

"I'm afraid so."

"Jesus."

"Sam'll take care of it. He's already got Morty Engler making calls. Come on. Let's get you out of here."

I lived in Pasadena, where a lot of Old Money and millionaire tourists from back East had barricaded themselves when the movie colony sprang up almost forty years ago. The house had been part of my inheritance from my maternal uncle, Bennett Lauren, who had made a fortune in oil and in selling land to those same movie people.

During the war, Pasadena had been a military headquarters: it was a quiet town, with big houses and hotels that had never filled back up after the Depression, and the Arroyo Seco—I couldn't get used to calling it the Pasadena Parkway—made it easy to get back and forth to Los Angeles.

When Franklin and I separated, the general who had been living in my house had just moved out, so I had moved in. It was a nice house, a dark brick with a green tile roof. But it looked rather dull next to its Arts and Crafts mansion neighbors. Only Juanita and I lived there.

She looked after me, did the cooking, and oversaw the maids and the gardeners who came in. The house was too big for just us, but I didn't have the energy to look for anything else in the chronic housing shortage that was the result of the population boom of the last few years. And the isolation of Pasadena suited my state of mind.

There were a half dozen reporters parked in front of the house. Helen pulled quickly past them to the end of the drive, so I could hop out and dash in through the back door before they were out of their cars. Then she walked casually back down to meet them and told them that her husband's office would have a full statement. They could go over to Marathon and get all the details or they could wait in their cars and get nothing because Mrs. Atwill needed to rest.

Inside, Juanita let me phone my insurance agent, then she took me upstairs, calling the thieves and reporters everything I wanted to—and in two languages. I told her to have the locks changed. She said she'd already called the locksmith. She had already turned down the bed, too, and closed the drapes. She gave me two aspirin and tucked me into the cool darkness.

I slept through the afternoon.

Franklin showed up in the evening.

We met seven years ago when he was the star of a movie I wrote called *The Brantley Case*. It was full of snappy chatter and proved he could be more than a pretty face. He asked me out, and we became lovers. I fell like a ton of bricks. When we married, I was absolutely, unbelievably happy. And incredibly naive.

Eventually, I discovered that he was having regular flings with his costars. Not to mention the starlets, extragirls, script assistants, secretaries, and waitresses in the studio cafeteria. When I confronted him, it went the predictable way. He was sorry. They didn't mean anything to him. He loved me.

I assumed that meant he wouldn't do it again.

I cut back on my work to devote more time to being his wife. And trying to have a baby. For the next few years, the assignments I accepted were mostly rewrites. I didn't have trouble getting the work with so many writers being drafted. And it turned out that I was very good at it. I became known as a great script doctor. Some people said it was a waste.

I like to think he tried to change, but it's just too damn easy to stray in Hollywood, where marriages dissolve on schedule, and adultery—even promiscuity—is almost expected, especially of the men. There were beautiful, available women around him every day, and his career depended on his being attractive to women, and his confidence depended on his knowing that he was. To his credit, he never once even implied that I was in any way to blame for his behavior, but finally, I couldn't take it anymore. I asked him to leave—and I didn't throw more than a dozen pairs of his shoes into the pool while I was doing it.

Juanita tells me I have a temper.

I left Marathon and moved out to Pasadena to write a novel. So far, that wasn't working out either.

I was sitting in the study in my dressing gown, reading, the pile of script paper beside the typewriter reminding me how little writing I'd done lately, when he came in. He was wearing crisply pleated cocoa-colored linen slacks and a starched white shirt open at the neck and rolled up over his forearms. His skin was glowing with a fresh tan, and a lock of his black wavy hair had settled roguishly on his forehead. He was breathtaking.

I stood up and, over his shoulder, saw Juanita make a face before she went out.

He put his arms around me and kissed my hair. "Are you all right?"

"I'm fine."

"I was out sailing. When I got back, there were reporters all over the marina."

"Don't say one word about the newspaper stories."

"I called Sam. He said he was taking care of it."

"Helen said Morty Engler was on it."

"It'll be all right. Come on, sit down. Let me get you something to drink." He went off to the dining room and came back with a brandy for me and a Scotch and soda on the rocks for himself. He sat down on the other end of the sofa. "What the hell happened?"

I told him the story. "I think the detective believed me. Maybe. I don't know. Parts of it don't make any sense."

"Here, why don't you lay down?"

"Why?" I asked suspiciously.

"I'm going to rub your feet for you. You know it always makes you feel better." He reached down, took hold of my ankles, and put my feet in his lap. My dressing gown fell open. I smoothed it back over my legs.

"I promise not to look. Unless you want me to," he said, a bit hopefully.

I didn't know what to say, so I didn't say anything. When I didn't, he smiled briefly, then he took off my slippers and dropped them on the carpet. He started on the heels and worked his way up the arch with a firm, familiar pressure. I sank back into the cushions with a long sigh.

After several pleasurable minutes, I asked, "How are rehearsals going?"

He shrugged. "The script needs help. Don asked me if I thought you'd take a look."

"How bad is it?"

"Bad enough."

"Has he told Joan and Newly that he might call me in?"

"I don't know. Would working on their script bother you?"

I repositioned my dressing gown even though it hadn't moved. "Why should it?"

"No reason. I just wondered."

"Tell Don to give me a call."

"I wouldn't ask if it weren't important."

"You didn't ask. Don did. Why didn't you?"

"I thought you'd tell me to go jump in the lake."

"Why would I do that?"

He shrugged again and took another sip of Scotch.

"Franklin, is there something you want to tell me?"

"What do you mean?"

"Are you in love with her?"

"Are you sure you want to talk about this?"

"I think I should know before I read in Louella's column that you're going to marry Alex Harris."

"There's not much sense holding on. You don't want me back."

"I couldn't go through that again," I said, but gently. I took my feet out of his lap and sat up Indian-style to face him. "Then you're going to marry her?"

"I've thought about it. You know I like being married." I laughed, and after a moment, so did he. "I didn't say I was any good at it. I just like it. I'm no good on my own."

I looked down at my feet. At how the veins were beginning to show behind the ankle bones. Suddenly, I felt very old. "What is it? Six weeks in Reno?"

"Something like that." He took another pull on his Scotch, then swirled the liquid, watching the ice cubes melting.

"Is there something else?" I asked.

"We can discuss it some other time."

"Dammit, Franklin, what is it?"

"All right. Look, the Harrises aren't Hollywood. They're very old-line, very old-fashioned. They don't approve of divorce. At all. Ever."

"I'm not going to die so you can be a widower."

He smiled faintly. "Old man Harris is a real bastard. It's a long story, but I think he always favored Christina. You remember? Alex's sister? The one who committed suicide? I was thinking, since you're working on your book, you might want to go back East. New York's a great place for writers."

"So the press releases can say you tried to patch it up, but I ran off. And you can charge me with desertion."

"It would only be for appearances."

"How can you ask me to take the blame?"

"Nobody's blaming you."

"I'm not leaving town so you can protect your spotless reputation."

"Okay. There's no need to lose your temper."

"Why should I get upset? I got married to have a husband. You got married so your girlfriends wouldn't get serious. Does Alex know what she's got to look forward to?"

"Are you going to tell her?"

"Half the women in Hollywood could tell her."

"Dammit, I didn't come here to fight. But if you want to start talking about who was sleeping with who, we can talk about you and Forrest Barlowe. You want to talk about that?"

I stared at him. I just stared at him.

He went on. "Did you think I didn't know what was going on? The whole time you were writing that spy movie, whatever the hell it was called. And who knows how long before that. And after. You even put him in your goddam will!"

"How dare you go through my things! You knew about Forrest, and you still asked me to fix Joan's script?"

"She doesn't know what happened."

"She most certainly does. They were married at the time. But that would have made it all right? If she didn't know, and I didn't know that you knew, then it would be okay?"

"This is a stupid argument. You do what you want." He stalked to the door and threw it open. "If you want to work on the movie, fine. I don't care. It was Don's idea, not mine." He stormed across the foyer and out the front door, slamming it after him.

I wanted to throw something. I wanted to cry. I waited until I heard his car start up in the drive before I did both.

Chapter 2

Don Deegan, the director of Franklin's movie, called me the next morning full of concern and good humor about the robbery. "Honey, looks like we're gonna have to find you somethin' to do to keep you off the streets at night."

"Such as working on a script?" I asked.

"Well, now, that's an idea."

"Franklin mentioned something about it."

"He said you two'd had a fight, and you might not be feelin' too kindly toward him today. If you work on this, I'll keep him away from you."

"Would you shoot him for me?"

"Aw, hell. You know Frank can't see shit without his glasses. Wouldn't be any challenge."

I laughed. Don had been born Donald Geisenberg and grown up in Coney Island. I wasn't sure how he had acquired his Southern drawl. I'd heard that, when he was playing The Young Stranger in *Magnolia* on Broadway, he had fallen in love with the style and imagery of the South and never left the role. I could see how it would appeal to his flamboyant nature. And he certainly wouldn't be the first person to come to Hollywood with a different name and accent.

"Wha'd you two fight about?" he asked.

"Nothing important."

"Nothin' to do with Joan, then?"

"What?"

"Well, now, let's see," he mused happily. "Joan wrote the script. Joan used to be married to Forrest Barlowe—"

"Good Lord! Does everybody know?"

"Don't worry, honey. I only know 'cause I was workin' with her at the time. She got crocked one night, an' it sorta slipped out. I don't reckon she told too many other folks that ole Forrest—the man she used to call the Dry Stick—had got himself a sweet young babe. An' you know I don't talk outta school."

"The hell you don't."

He chuckled. "I don't gossip. I just like to share a good story when I hear it. Joan's workin' on a script for Stanwyck over at Paramount. She doesn't give a rat's ass about this one. Will you do it?"

"When can I see a script?"

"Come see me later today, after lunch, 'bout two?"

"Don, can I ask you something? Was it your idea to ask me, or Franklin's?"

"Does it matter? We both want you." He hung up before I could tell him to answer the question.

I waited until I'd had a few cups of strong coffee before I opened the *Times*. Marathon's publicity staff had done a good job.

POLICE SEARCH FOR GANG OF THIEVES IN ATWILL CASE

According to the paper, earlier reports that Mrs. Frank Atwill, the wife of the Marathon Studios star, had been drunk were apparently erroneous. The article didn't mention that the *Times* had published those reports. It did mention that I'd been drugged and that the police believed that the thieves had probably used the time to get my car over the Mexican border. There was a quote from the assistant police chief promising to find the culprits and make sure nothing like this happened to any other women in Los Angeles.

I called Franklin's tobacconist and had two dozen Cuban cigars sent over to Sam Ross.

A few reporters called. I told Juanita to say that I was still resting. If they wanted to know if Franklin had been over, tell them, yes, of course, he'd been very kind and to call his agent if they wanted to get any more information.

There might be some energetic reporters out there who wanted more than a quote delivered through the housekeeper, who were curious about why thieves would dump me where I would be easier to find, but their editors weren't going to let them waste effort on someone as unimportant as I was. Especially when their publishers said to kill the story.

I'd probably avoided scandal, but I didn't have the truth. Why *was* I dumped downtown?

Helen picked me up about eleven in her Lincoln, which made me miss mine even more. She'd liked mine so much, she'd bought one, too, only in a creamy pale yellow. She was excited about my going back to work.

"I think it's great. You've been living too damn much alone."

I changed the subject before she could tell me once again how much I needed a man in my life.

It took about a half hour to get me a new driver's license, then Helen drove me over to a car dealer on Colorado, who had told me over the phone that he had several quality cars that could be made available for long-term lease. What he had not said was that "several" meant eight, and that he wanted a small fortune for six of them. Rather than be robbed again, I ended up with a choice between a gray '41 Pontiac Torpedo with a scuffed interior and a navy blue '41 Hudson with nothing visibly wrong with it. I took the Hudson. In the fall, I would join the rest of America looking at new cars for the first time in almost five years. If Detroit didn't change the body designs too much, maybe I could get my Lincoln back.

We had lunch at my house. I wasn't up to facing any gossipy glances.

Afterward, I drove my new Hudson into Los Angeles to the Central Police Station, where I found Sergeant Barty on the second floor in a cramped, airless office that he shared with three other detectives. He'd talked to the other city police divisions and to the L.A. and Ventura County sheriffs. There had been no robberies like mine during the last year. I gave him the insurance pictures and read over my statement; I didn't have anything new to add to it. I still couldn't tell if he believed my story.

I took Beverly out to Vine, then drove north past the country club up to Melrose and on out to the studio.

I pulled up to Marathon's gate and gave the guard my name. He consulted his list and told me where the visitors' lot was. He gave me a small visitor's button to wear. I didn't know him, and if he'd ever heard of me, he hid it well.

Inside, the road ran back between the soundstages. Fifty yards along it, sitting alone on a few acres of landscaped lawn, was the Ice House—a square, modern, ugly, white stucco office building that was cut down the center by a wall of glass. Through it, I could see the white marble lobby, the white marble staircase, and the white oleander in the building's white marble interior garden. I drove past and pulled into the visitors' lot.

The last time I'd parked there, I'd been fresh from college—lanky, awkward, and intense—trading on my uncle Bennett's connections to get a job in Hollywood. But what the studio let me do could hardly be called exciting. In the early thirties, Hollywood was full of famous playwrights and novelists who had chosen between staying East and earning maybe four thousand a year or coming to Hollywood, writing for the new talking pictures, and earning four thousand a month.

I started at forty dollars a week.

First, I cranked out story lines for pictures that were never made, then I wrote first drafts from little-known books and plays the studio had bought, drafts that—if the producers liked them—would be turned over to the topline writers. Later, I was tossed a few script assignments, but never for big stars.

If it hadn't been for Don Deegan, I don't know what I might have ended up doing. One night, while he was holding court at the Avalon Café, the restaurant he had once owned—and mired in debt—he had, in a brutal analysis of writing talent at the various studios, declared that there was only one person at Marathon who could write comic dialogue, and that was "that Tanner gal." As luck would have it, eavesdropping at the next table was Walt Weinhaus, who had been in charge of production at Marathon before the war. That screwy, backhanded compliment gave me the chance to write *The Brantley Case*.

Don had come out to Hollywood after making his reputation as the producer-writer-director and general boy wonder of a New York theater group. He took the cameras from their static, predictable angles and gave them a point of view that was sometimes wonderfully original and sometimes merely eccentric, but he put his stamp on a picture and always drew out top-notch performances. He had no patience with studio executives, calling them "artistic frauds," sometimes to their faces, but they tolerated his abuse because his films were successful. Within a five-year period, he had directed three of the most critically successful films ever made: *Turn of the Century*, *The Traveler*, and *Some Kind of Luck*. And unlike most critical triumphs, his movies had been box-office hits as well.

But he became too enamored of his own skewed view of the world and squandered money on pictures that were simply awful. He set up a small, independent studio, but he didn't have the money or the business sense to see projects through properly. It failed. Now he worked at Marathon, turning out tidy pictures from mostly uninspired scripts. But actors still loved to work with him despite his prickly, sometimes snappish, temper. It was hard to tell where it came from, and it would disappear as quickly as it came. Then Don would once again be his charming, disarming self.

At the rear of the Ice House, there was a line of golf carts with eager young men standing beside them, waiting—hoping—to drive people more important than I was. During the war, the drivers had all been young women in short skirts and white gloves. They'd all been fired after V-J Day, their jobs given to returning veterans.

The farther your bungalow was from the Ice House, the lower you were on the ladder. Don's wasn't quite halfway to the back of the lot, in a row of identical salmon-colored bungalows with red tile roofs and steep wooden steps. There was just enough space between them for one bushy oleander and behind each of them for a patio with one lime tree. Over their back fences, there was a nice view of the side of a soundstage.

His secretary brought in coffee and cake, and we scattered crumbs across his cluttered desk while we read through the script.

Don was a large, soft man whose pale, freckled, New York complexion had defied years of California sun. His wiry, carroty hair was going prematurely white, and since he had a habit of running a hand through it, shoots of it usually sat up like little Hydras. He tossed his copy of the script on top of a nearby pile and leaned back in his chair. He took off his wire-edged glasses, letting them dangle on his Hawaiian shirt by their beaded chain. "Shit, huh?"

I grunted. *The Final Line* was trite, to be sure. A bright, brash attorney is led to the edge of disaster by a crooked politician and his sultry daughter. In the end, he's saved by his scruples and the love of a good woman.

"I get some real shit nowadays." He didn't sound particularly depressed by it. "So, what can you do with it?"

"Well, I don't buy that he'd sell his soul for a beautiful woman. Unless you can get Hayworth. Let's dirty him up a little. Give him some ambitions that would drive him over the edge. And let's make the girls sisters. That should complicate things nicely. And I don't think he should get off scot-free. He's finally done the right thing, but he's going to have to pay for it—maybe even jail. In the end, I see him and the good girl. He says he'll call. She says he better not wait too long. And she means it. Maybe he'll get her, maybe he won't. Let's leave it up in the air."

"What the hell made you want to write a book? This is what you're good at."

"Rewriting other people's work?"

"I direct it. What's the difference? What can you give me by next Monday?"

"Not all of it."

"We have to start shootin' right after the Fourth. There's a thirty-day truce with the union, but when that's over, who knows? Sorrell could pull the stagehands out."

"I can give you half."

"Good enough." He stood up and lobbed a fresh copy of the script across the desk to me. "Now get the hell outta here. I gotta work." He came around and took my hand. "Always a pleasure, Laurie." He bowed over my hand and kissed it, then he said, "Don't let Sam Ross dick you around."

Sam's office was on the fifth floor of the Ice House, one floor below the studio heads. The office was paneled in mahogany, carpeted in Persian, and had a full bar built into one corner. But its view wasn't much better than Don's.

Sam was short and broad-chested; his expensive suit was cut to help conceal the breadth of his stomach. His hair was coarse, tightly curled, and thinning rapidly from the crown, but it was thick on his face, giving him a near-perpetual five o'clock shadow. Behind round horn-rimmed glasses, he had gentle eyes.

He greeted me, as he always did, with the aggressive bonhomie of a man who's used to managing people and who's not entirely comfortable when he's not.

"Good to see you. You look great. How are you? You okay?"

"Much better, thanks. I appreciate what you did."

"Hey, no problem, glad to help. Those were nice cigars you sent. Can I get you something to drink?"

"No, thanks."

"Sit down, sit down." He waved me into a leather chair and went back to his desk, which sat on a six-inch riser so his visitors always had to look up to him. He dropped into his chair and let out a short bark of laughter. "Should've heard Morty Engler working the cops. When he was through, there was a gang of dope fiends out there just waiting to pounce on every virgin daughter in the county."

"How much did you have to give up?"

"A few premiere parties. The chief, assistant chief, the wives. Anybody they owe."

"And what about publishers?"

"Bunch of bloodsuckers. Cops come a lot cheaper. Always have."

"I appreciate it."

"Glad to help. Glad to do it. So what do you think of the script? What do you want to do with this?"

"Why don't we settle the money first?"

"I got to know what we're talking about. Fix a little dialogue, or start all over?"

"Somewhere in between."

"What are you thinking?"

"Five thousand."

"Five grand! That's nuts. I got actors not making five."

"Not in the leads."

"No way I can do that."

"Your script's a mess, Sam, and you've got to start shooting. You can make that back in five minutes if it's a hit. It won't be, the way it is now."

"I can't justify that upstairs. No way. I can do twenty-five. Maybe."

"I'm grateful, but I'm not working for free. I'll give you a good script within two weeks and all the rewrites you need during shooting."

"What if we don't need rewrites?"

"Then I'm definitely worth five grand."

"We'll go over budget with Don. Always do."

"Five, Sam."

"I got a lot full of writers out there making three hundred a week."

"Then let them take a crack at it. Five."

"Three."

"Forty-five."

"Thirty-five."

"Forty-two."

"Four."

"Done."

"I can't believe I'm doing this. Don't you tell anyone I gave you four grand."

"Not a word."

"And no screen credit. I don't want any trouble with Joan and Newly."

"Fine."

He made a few grumping noises and picked up a copy of the script. "Police find anything yet?"

"I don't think they will. The car's probably in Mexico."

"Who the hell were you with, let you leave by yourself?"

"Bill Linden was—"

"That daisy, no wonder."

"He was supposed to come, but he was sick with that summer flu that's going around, so Jerry Vick escorted me and Helen."

"Not much better, still lives with his mother."

"You know, you could come with us more often."

"Clubs bore the hell out of me. Who else was there?"

"The usual crowd. Millie and Tad Elliot, Slim and Dal Crandall."

"That Elizondo come around?"

"No."

"I got the idea from Helen that he was hanging around."

"We didn't see him."

"Hmm." He bent the script open and creased the cover back. He kept his eyes on the page. "Grant Cummings's kid, what's his name?"

"Dean?"

"Yeah. I'm thinking about using him, next picture. What do you think? What's he like?"

"I hardly know him."

"I remember, last few times we were there, he came around the table."

"I'm sure it was to see you. I must seem ancient to him and his friends. Take a look at page ten. I think this is where we need to start. Do you have Morty Engler's address? I'd like to send him some cigars, too."

"Don't send him too many. Make him think he deserves a raise. I can't afford it, what I'm paying writers."

When we were finished, I walked back to the visitors' lot and scanned for my Lincoln before I remembered that it was gone. Then I heard someone call my name. The man came toward me at a half run—lean, elegant, silver-haired, and dressed in an admiral's uniform.

"Forrest!"

He put his arms around me and held me tightly to him. It felt great.

"I saw the papers," he said. "Are you all right?"

"I'm fine."

"I was out of town this weekend. I didn't know. I would have called."

"I sort of wondered why you hadn't."

"What happened?"

While I told him, he pulled my arm through his, and we strolled into an alley that ran between two sound-stages, dodging groups of wide-skirted, high-breasted Louis XIV courtesans who were headed back to Wardrobe, scratching their wigs and chewing gum.

Forrest had made his career as the fourth or fifth fea-tured man, mostly playing politicians, executives, and mil-itary leaders. He had been famous, for about six months, back in the thirties, after playing Ambassador Ellison in *The Little Ambassador* with Shirley Temple. An orphan "adopted" a lonely ambassador, who was estranged from his own daughter.

When I met him, however, he was playing the flus-tered father of the bride in a mindless little comedy that I was supposed to provide with fresh laughs. Both our mar-riages weren't working. Joan loved hard drinking, hard partying, and hard gossip. Forrest liked solitude, music, and books. She thought he was weak and dull. I thought he was wonderful. But he was of another generation; he was looking for someone to share his later years. There was too much I still wanted to do. And I was still in love with my husband.

"What are you doing at Marathon?" he asked when I finished my story. I told him. The line between his brows deepened. "You're not doing this for Frank, are you?"

"No."

He cocked his head to one side.

"All right," I said. "But it won't hurt me any. The book's stalled, and I've been leading a pretty dull life lately. Bar-ring the occasional robbery."

He took me onto the set of *Gates of Glory*, and I watched him stand and stand and stand while a new star who was playing the young commander blew line after line even though they were written on the map directly in front of him. Finally, Forrest groaned off the set and took me to dinner at MacKenzie's, where people went when they got tired of the people at Musso and Frank's—or the people at Musso and Frank's got tired of them.

I was grazed by a few raised eyebrows, but not many.

We took a booth in the rear and ordered steaks.

"Tell me," Forrest said with his clear, beautiful diction as he poured me some wine, "when are you going to get over The Jerk?"

"Soon. He's getting married."

"Not to the Harris girl?"

"Yes."

"No moss grows on our Frank. She's the only heir now, isn't she, since her sister died?"

"I think so." I changed the subject. "How are Lizzie and Tim?"

"Great. Doing great." He gave me a smile, but there was a brief spasm of pain beneath it. Lizzie and Tim were his grandchildren from his daughter, Stella. From everything I knew, he had doted on her. Briefly, she had tried acting, then gave it up happily for marriage to a wonderful young man, who had dropped dead of a heart attack at thirty-five. She had tried to start up her career again. Then, just before Pearl Harbor, she had been killed in a car wreck. Their children lived with the husband's parents—who were retired schoolteachers—but Forrest saw them every chance he had.

He went on. "I was lucky with the shooting schedule, so I'll be able to take them down to the house in La Jolla over the Fourth. They love it down there. So do I, of course. No papers, no radio, no phone."

"I remember. It's beautiful."

He picked up his wineglass. His hand was shaking ever so slightly. I concentrated on my baked potato until he had set the glass back down. The skin at his temples was more transparent than I remembered; around his eyes, it was more crepelike and shadowed. He didn't seem in any way ill, but I wondered how much longer he would be able to keep working at the pace demanded of character actors by a studio. Although he'd had a long career, he had never commanded a star's salary. He was still supporting a far-distant first wife (Stella's mother) and a widowed sister. He was more than generous with his grandchildren. And there was the second home in La Jolla. I wondered how much he had put away for the day the studio would not renew his contract.

He insisted on following me home. He had an early call, so I didn't ask him in. It was just as well. I was feeling a little relaxed from the wine, and I might have asked him to stay. He might have. It would have been a mistake.

The next morning, glad to be rid of my relentlessly boring hero, I dumped my novel into a deep drawer and rolled fresh paper into the typewriter. In fact, so glad was I to be doing something else, the ideas flowed. I had to admit that, on closer inspection, the script had more punch than I'd thought. Feeling as I did about Joan, I'd sold her short.

I buried myself in the study and worked happily through the week. The newspapers seemed to have forgotten all about me. My bruises faded, my scrapes healed, and my doctor stopped by on his way to a tennis match to remove the stitches from my knee. By Sunday, after I sent the new pages to the studio to be typed and mimeographed, I was ready for a break. I did fifty laps in the pool, then collapsed on a lounge chair and listened to the recorded broadcast of the Yankees/Philadelphia Athletics game on KLAC. Most of the other stations were broadcasting live reports of the A-bomb test off Bikini Island. I didn't want to listen. I was in too good a mood.

On Monday afternoon, we had our first read-through—after we congratulated each other on still being alive. Despite some predictions, no freak chain reaction from the bomb had caused the end of the world.

The actors did a cold reading through the first half of the script, and I took some notes as they went. Then I told them where the rest would be going. Franklin sat across the table from me and kept winking in approval.

When we broke, he took my arm and guided me out into the hallway. "You've pulled my rear out of the fire. I don't deserve it, after the other night."

"You were right. It was a stupid argument. Not that that's ever stopped me."

"I shouldn't have asked you to go away."

"Is her father really that bad?"

"Worse. I didn't want to give him anything else to complain about. She's a sweet kid."

Remembering—often far too vividly—Franklin's enthusiastic pleasure in bed, I thought the "sweet kid" must have hidden fires. "About Forrest . . ."

"You don't owe me any explanation," he said softly. "And I wasn't going through your things. I found the envelope in the safe. I didn't know what it was, so I just opened it."

"It was over by then. I don't know why I made that will."

"Maybe so you could leave it where I'd find it. It's your money. You can give it to whoever you want."

"I'm not going to cut you out of my will."

"That's not what I meant."

"I know."

He laid his hand on my arm. His fingers were hot on my bare skin. He said, "We'll be rehearsing till about six, but we could go someplace for dinner."

"Won't Alex be upset?"

"Of course not."

"I don't know."

"Please." His hand slid up my arm.

"Lauren, could I buy you a drink?" Kim Wagner, the movie's female lead, was standing in the rehearsal room doorway with my script and my handbag in her arms. "We have time."

"Yes. I'd like that. I'm sorry, Franklin, but I have to work tonight."

Kim gave me my stuff and bustled me outside.

"Thanks," I said, when we reached the sidewalk.

"Yeah, you were beginning to stall out. A girl's got to be careful with Frank. If your engine idles too long, it's likely to overheat."

She took me to Madison's, the bar across the street from the studio gates. Behind its glass-tile walls was a cool, dark oasis. The glossy ebony bar seemed to float up on the left as we came in. Anthony, in a starched white shirt and black vest, raised his hand. "Well, now, Miss Lauren, are you back with us?"

"Nice to see you, too, Anthony."

There wasn't much of a crowd yet. A few former Grandes Dames of the Theater, now working as bit players, were holding court by themselves, lifting long, slender cigarette holders more and more precisely to their lips with each Manhattan. We went down into the back room, which was empty and even darker, but where we were not likely to have to endure too many leers when the men started arriving. We took a booth. I had a gin and tonic. Kim ordered a stinger.

"I really want to thank you for working on this," she said. "I won't lie to you. I need it."

"I saw you in *King Mike*. You were wonderful."

"And I got suspended right after that. I told them I wouldn't do any more of those peroxide floozies. My agent says I'm crazy, but if I'm going to hang around, I've got to do more than that. I'm not getting any younger." She slapped her left hip. "Or any thinner. What I wouldn't give to be your height."

Kim was a talented comedienne, so when Carole Lombard died, the studio had tried to set her up as a replacement. It had been a disaster, and although she was hardly to blame, her career had suffered.

"Don wanted me for this," she went on. "The studio said I couldn't play the good girl, couldn't do a serious role, but he stuck up for me. Look, I wanted to ask you about that first scene, the first scene between the sisters."

"Yes."

"I think it's great."

"Thank you."

"Don does, too. If the studio told you to change it, you and Don would stick up for it."

"Why would the studio want it changed?"

"Well, if they didn't like it."

"Or Franklin didn't like it. I think that's what you mean."

She looked down at the table. Even in the gloom, I could see the color rising in her cheeks. She flicked at some beads of water on the tabletop. "I know what actors can be like if they think somebody else's part is getting bigger at their expense."

"I think you underestimate Franklin."

"I guess I lost my head a little. I'm sorry. I need this. More than you know."

I didn't say anything, just sat quietly while she recovered herself. Then we talked about the script some more before she paid for the drinks and said good-bye. She was smiling when she left.

I sat there smiling, too, feeling pleased with myself. Feeling like a fairy godmother.

"Mrs. Atwill?" a voice said beside me.

He was small and dark with black hair slicked back tightly from a narrow forehead. At first, he appeared to be well dressed, but when he leaned forward, I could see it was illusion. The cream-colored suit was old and the tie cheap, but he wore them with flair. I sat there with a bright, frozen smile on my face—the sort one gets when trying to place somebody.

"Mrs. Atwill. It *is* you. I thought so." He spoke with a slurred accent that greatly softened the plosive consonants and laid emphasis on the vowels. One of the Eastern European countries? The Balkans?

"Forgive me," I said, "but I've forgotten your name."

"Paul Maritski," he said, but the accent was definitely not Russian. "You do not know me, but I am a great admirer of yours."

"I'm flattered. Most people don't recognize writers."

"I have seen you many times."

"You have? Where?"

Smoothly, he slid into the seat opposite me and laid his hat and a shabby portfolio on the table.

"I was sorry when you left Marathon. Are you perhaps working there again? Perhaps on your husband's movie?"

There are rules about who you tell when you're doctoring a script. "I'm just visiting."

"I, too, am a writer. But it is difficult to start a career, especially when one is no longer young."

"You mustn't give up. Maturity will only make your writing stronger."

"I won't, then," he said, and smiled, showing me some sharp little nicotine-stained teeth. I was afraid he was about to ask for my help, but instead he said, "Recently, however, I have found another talent that I have."

"How nice. What is it?"

"I do likenesses."

"Portraits?"

"Perfect likenesses. People have paid me great sums for them."

He didn't look like he had been paid any great sums, but maybe he was only trying to impress me.

"It is very nice for me and for them," he continued.

"I'm sure."

"I have done yours."

So this was it. He was trying to make a sale.

"Would you like to see it?"

"All right," I agreed. Then I'd get Anthony to show this guy the door.

Out of his portfolio, he drew a brand-new Manila folder. With precise attention, he placed it before me. He smoothed his hands along its edges, making certain it was perfectly squared. He opened it.

I did not scream. I did not throw myself against the back of the booth. I wanted to. I tried to. But I was absolutely, completely paralyzed.

"As you can see, it is a perfect likeness," he oozed. His fingers with their bitten nails caressed the top of the photograph, then he brushed it aside to reveal the edge of another and another. "Perhaps, you would care to purchase them." Then, quickly, he scooped the pictures back into the portfolio. "I will call you. Tomorrow at noon." He snatched up his hat and scuttled out, disappearing toward the rear exit.

I sat there in the dark, deserted room, still unable to move, unable to do anything except breathe in shallow gasps. Then something cold began spreading across my lap. I moaned and slapped at it wildly. It was only my gin and tonic streaming across the table, dripping over the edge. I had no idea how or when it had been knocked over.

I grabbed my bag and stumbled out of the room, past the bar, and out into the sudden, bright sunlight. I started to run and did not stop running until I had reached my car. As I ripped open my bag for my keys, it fell to the pavement, the contents spilling onto the concrete. I crouched beside the car, grabbing for my things, sobbing without sound, without tears.

When I got home, I ran upstairs, yanking off my clothes as if something had begun to seep through them. For twenty minutes, I stood in the shower, scrubbing myself over and over. When I finished, I didn't feel any cleaner. I wrapped myself in a thick robe and lay down on the bed, curled into a ball.

Now I knew why I hadn't been left on the side of the road in Topanga Canyon. After they had shot me full of dope, they had tossed me into my car and driven me somewhere. Somewhere with a bed. They had removed my torn gown and my underwear and laid me on suitably tangled sheets.

I barely made it to the bathroom before I threw up.

I soaked a washcloth in cold water and sat down on the tile floor with the cloth pressed to my face, my hands shaking. I had only seen the one photograph. In it, I appeared to be lingering in the ecstasy of just-completed passion, my head tilted back on a pillow, my eyes closed, my lips parted. The man lay on top of me, his body half-covered with a sheet. His face was buried in my loose hair.

Had I seen that face?

There had been *two* needle marks on my arm. Had I begun to come around and been given another shot? But not before I'd seen the face beside me?

I sat there cursing myself for letting Maritski get away. Now I had nothing. No pictures, no description of his car. Nothing to give to the police.

Would they ever believe how the pictures were taken? The story was preposterous. Why would anyone fake lewd pictures? The police might believe there was blackmail, but they'd never believe the rest. I could imagine the talk around the DA's office. "Hey, don't let the boss know you saw these, okay? It's Frank Atwill's wife. Can you believe it? Pretty hot stuff, huh? Says it happened to her the night she was robbed. Hey, I'm only telling you what she said."

If they caught the blackmailers, there would be a trial. A very public trial. What if the man turned out to be someone I knew? A former gardener? A mechanic at the garage? Someone involved in this had to know my routine. His lawyer could claim we'd had an affair, that the pictures had been taken with my approval, and that I'd set up the blackmail story to punish him for breaking up with me.

I remembered the Margaret Kinsey rape case. I remembered what the defense attorney had said about her. How the newspapers had reveled luridly in her past, her lovers. She'd ended up in Morgan Valley with a nervous breakdown.

At least I hadn't been raped.

Why had they picked me? Of all the women in Los Angeles County, why would they pick me?

That night, my dreams were haunted by the shadow of a face I would have welcomed the night before.

Chapter 3

When I woke up the next morning, my brain started working again.

Juanita brought me my usual cup of coffee, and I stuffed the pillows behind me and lay there, frowning at the wallpaper, sipping, and thinking. If the blackmailers had chosen their victim in advance, they would never have picked me. I had money, true. A lot of money. But any planning would have told them that I didn't depend on a rich husband who would toss me out if he saw those pictures. There were far too many other women to choose from who would be far more likely to pay off. So Maritski and his friends had not planned for a particular victim. They had been after *any* woman coming down that road from the club alone in an expensive car, figuring almost any well-heeled woman would have someone she wouldn't want to see those kinds of pictures. Whether she was a cheater or not, she'd pay to keep them secret. They'd get her address from her driver's license and wait for an opportunity to make their pitch.

A car. Jewelry. Cash. And maybe several thousand in blackmail. Like Sergeant Barty said, not a bad night's work.

Well, they could damn well whistle for their money.

I finished the coffee and thought some more about the police. I wanted these men to pay. Besides that, Maritski must have been following me, looking for the chance to get me alone. That didn't make me feel particularly safe, although I doubted he and his friends would resort to violence to make me pay. They wouldn't want to force me to go to the police.

And what about other women? Sergeant Barty said there had been no other robberies like mine. But that didn't mean there wouldn't be. How would I feel if they did this to someone else, and I could have prevented it?

Then I saw the mob of photographers surging toward me. And a lawyer, his hands open in appeal to the jury. "As you can see from these pictures—despite what she might say now—Mrs. Atwill was more than willing to participate."

I shut myself in the study and worked through the rest of the week. Although Thursday was the first peacetime Fourth of July in five years, I didn't go to the party Helen was giving to celebrate it. I wasn't ready to face anyone yet.

Maritski called when he said he would, and several more times during the week. Every time, he told Juanita he had business to discuss with me, and every time—as I had told her to do—she said I was not available and hung up.

Friday morning, the fifth, I was posing by the fireplace in the study, pretending my pencil was a cigarette holder, trying to think of a really acid line to give to the bad sister, when Juanita tapped on the door. She never disturbed me when I was working unless it was important.

"There is a man who says he is Sergeant Barty on the phone."

"I'll take it in here."

"Mrs. Ross called, too."

"I'll call her back." I picked up the study phone. "Sergeant?"

"I got some good news," he said. "We found your car. Some uniforms picked up a couple of guys cruising Sunset in the Fourth crowd last night. We found your thieves." My stomach did a slow dance of panic. "Can you take a look at a lineup? We'll get the Hollywood boys to bring them over here. I know you didn't see anyone, but sometimes it scares them."

I didn't give myself time to think about it. "I can be there in an hour."

He laughed. "I wish everybody was as cooperative as you. You know where to find me."

I wore a suit because it covered more of my body.

I forgot to call Helen back.

All the way into L.A., I kept looking in my rearview mirror for Maritski or one of his partners following me. If there was anyone there, I didn't see them.

The lineup room had a dozen hard chairs scattered in the dark, separated from a low stage by a wooden rail, twenty feet of cracked linoleum, and a cop who looked like he could put a headlock on a tank. He opened a door, and the men filed into the light. There were six of them. All small. All dark. All about nineteen years old.

"You can't ID any of them, right?" Barty whispered.

"No."

"Then let's make them think you did. See where it gets us." He stood up and said with satisfaction, "Fine. Okay, Snider, take 'em back out." He turned to me and hitched his trousers. "Come on. I'll buy you a cup of station house coffee. Let these guys stew."

Someone had brought a fan and set it on a rickety table by the window in his office. Barty's papers were anchored to his desk with small chunks of concrete. The coffee was terrible.

"Makes a guy glad to go on stakeout," he said, and set down his mug. I held on to mine, even though I wasn't drinking. He leaned back in his chair. "First, these guys tell me they won the car in some dice game, from some Mexican named José. They just forgot to get the title. Sure, I say. And the Pirates are moving to L.A. It's in all the papers. I can't wait to see that Kiner kid hit. Then I tell them they're in big trouble. You're Frank Atwill's wife, and he's going to see to it that they get about twenty years each for kidnapping. We didn't let them talk to each other, but they pretty much tell the same story. They say they were cruising around that morning you were grabbed, about 4 A.M., when they see your car parked in that alley we found you in. Being curious types, they get out, probably admiring your hubcaps. They find you slumped in the front seat, smelling like booze. Then they decide that, if you're going to drive drunk, you don't deserve such a nice car."

"I don't understand. If they confessed to stealing the car, why did you want me to look at the lineup?"

"Because if we convince them you ID'd them as the guys who grabbed you, you never know how many other neighborhood bad boys they'll rat on to keep from getting charged with kidnapping. They say they didn't see any jewelry or money. They just laid you down on the ground and took the car. They say they called to tell us where you were so you wouldn't get hurt. Funny thing, there was an anonymous call. That's how we found you."

"Maybe they have consciences."

"What they don't have is brains. Driving around a car like that. I don't think these guys are smart enough to have waylaid you."

"No." I almost told him. I looked at his solid, reliable face and almost told him. But another detective came in, a ropy-muscled man with the leathery, blotched skin of the naturally fair who spend too much time in the sun. His neck had deep creases above his loosened collar.

Barty introduced us. "This is Detective Sergeant Tolen."

The man nodded to me. "I heard about your robbery," he said with perfunctory concern. "Anything turn up yet?"

Barty told him about the car.

"Well, I hope we can get your jewelry back for you, too." He turned to Barty. "You get a chance to look at my report on Swing Eddie?"

"Pork's steamed. Your guy pulled that gun on his mother."

"I got a homicide, Phil."

"Okay," Barty said wearily, "I'll see what I can do."

The other man grunted, nodded to me, and walked away.

Barty said, "Tolen's working the homicide table. My snitch and his snitch got a feud, goes way back. My snitch wants to put his away on a violation of parole rap. But his snitch's got something Tolen needs in a case. Guess I'll have to talk to Pork." He shook his head. "The guys I end up protecting in this business." He stood up. "Let's go get your car. We'll get someone to drive it home for you."

"Is it all right?"

He coughed and hitched his trousers. "They painted it."

"Oh, dear. What color?" I asked with creeping horror.

"Red. Not too smart, these guys."

It was no shabby paint job, either. They had spent some time on it. The car had been washed and polished. The chrome gleamed. I felt a little sorry for them.

Helen called me again about five. "Where the hell have you been?" she asked cheerfully.

I told her about the car and the new color. "It looks pretty good. Maybe I'll keep it this way."

"Don't you dare. You missed a hell of a party last night."

"I'm sorry."

"Why don't you bring your fire engine out to Elizondo's?"

My heart started doing a little tap step. "Not tonight. I've got to finish a scene."

"I was thinking about tomorrow. Sam's flying to New York in the morning for a week. I thought I'd spend the evening with him. Not that he'll notice. Is Elizondo's okay? We could go somewhere else."

Even if I didn't have the courage to tell the police yet, I'd be damned if the blackmailers were going to scare me anymore. "It's fine. Tomorrow sounds good."

"About eight. Sorry, but I have to bring the Camlics. I owe them. I think I can get Jake Farrell." I groaned. "You have to have an escort. I've fixed you up with plenty of nice men, and you don't give them the time of day."

"I know," I said humbly.

"Jake'll come get you."

"No. I want to drive myself. Get back on the horse."

"Okay. Oh, and wear something delectable. What about that green shantung?"

"Why?"

"The word is, Mr. E is interested."

"That's ridiculous. Where did you hear that?"

"Would you give yourself some credit?"

"For goodness sake, Helen. He's a gangster."

"We call them 'sportsmen.' Don't you read the papers? And I notice it doesn't keep you away from his club. You could use a good man in your bed, and I hear Mr. E is sensational."

Elizondo's was what everybody ~~called it,~~ but it didn't really have a name. It was tucked away up in the north end of Topanga Canyon, which made it just far enough away so that, after the payoffs, it was easier for the policemen and politicians to look the other way. And probably easier to cut deals with the other sportsmen, who wouldn't want their territories trespassed.

During Prohibition, Ramon Elizondo had "imported" booze. Afterward, he maintained three gambling ships beyond the three-mile limit in Santa Monica Bay until the new state attorney general, Earl Warren, put them out of business. Elizondo dropped out of sight, but the day gas rationing ended a year ago, he resurfaced and opened his club.

The club sat along a dusty stretch of Coruna Road, whose dry earth was mottled by scrub grass, twisted manzanita, and stunted, wind-hewn cypress. When the club appeared, it was a sudden, startling jewel: a piece of alabaster set on glistening, sodded lawns and bordered by perfectly trimmed hedges of gleaming boxwood and eucalyptus.

It was a Hollywood version of a gangster's nightclub. Most gambling dens were hardly more than roadhouses, with pine-paneled walls, sticky floors, and the lingering scent of old beer and watered whiskey. But then Hollywood had taught gangsters how to dress and how to think they had class. Why shouldn't it teach one of them how to build a club?

Elizondo had built his as a sprawling hacienda of white stucco and red tiles. The side of the club that faced Coruna was a blank wall. There were no windows, not even on the second floor. There were no lamps on it and no address. The long, crushed-gravel drive rose from Coruna toward the blank wall, then curved smoothly to the left, again to the right and around the side of the building to the entrance. It was a wide drive: most of the people who used it expected to be given as much room on the road as they were in the rest of their lives. When you got to the entrance, slim, crisp young men opened your door and did all they could not to sneer if your car was anything less than a Buick. From the tiled portico, you could smell the manzanita, the eucalyptus, and the bored money.

The lobby was carpeted in deep, plush mauve accented with white magnolias. The walls were covered in a slightly paler shade of raw silk. The sconces were wide saucers of frosted, beveled glass. Broad chrome-edged steps swept up to the casino, which was concealed behind upholstered doors. A stone-faced man in a black tux stood beside them ready to admit "members." Below, on either side of the stairs, wide arches opened into the dining room. The band was playing "Where or When."

I handed my wrap to a sugary redhead who was saving her smiles for anyone who looked like a producer, then I gave my name to the maître d'. None of my party had arrived yet, so I sat down on one of the tufted velvet benches outside the bar to wait.

"Mrs. Atwill."

The man was standing on the bottom step, wearing exquisitely tailored evening clothes and holding a cigarette in a long, elegant hand. The lines on his face, the knowledge in his dark eyes, and the confidence in his movements were all just deep enough to give him an intense aura of masculine experience. Ramon Elizondo came over and sat down beside me.

"I was sorry to hear about your robbery," he said. "I'm glad it hasn't dissuaded you from visiting us again."

"Not at all. I understand that Jeannie Lee is back with the band."

He smiled. "You're one of the few people who doesn't come here for the gambling."

"I'm afraid I'm very conventional."

"Perhaps if you come to us more often, we can cure you of this affliction."

There was nothing blatant in it. There was nothing blatant about him. Nevertheless, remembering what Helen had said, I blushed all the way to the neckline of my gown. I looked away and saw Helen and the Camlics coming in. Helen wiggled her fingers and eyebrows at me. We went over to them.

Art Camlic owned a new development north of Laguna, where a few hundred fishermen were being pushed out so he could build a marina. His jaws had almost forgotten to grow a chin, and his protruding lower lip nearly covered what little there was. His wife, B. J., was a full, blowsy woman whose considerable figure was trying to escape from her orange taffeta dress in several directions. She reached under her wrap and tugged the dress higher on her freckled shoulder, tottering a little with the effort.

"What a way to start the evening!" she said so loudly that I stepped back involuntarily. "Would you look at this?" She held out a portion of the skirt over her thigh. "Helen's damn Scotch bottle sprang a leak."

"It doesn't show, Beej," her husband said wearily. "I keep telling her it doesn't show."

"Have to wear my damn wrap all night."

"It doesn't show," said Helen.

"What a beautiful dress," I said.

"Well, I hope I have better luck with the dice," She laughed harshly and hitched at her dress again.

"I certainly hope so," Elizondo said with grace, and de livered us to the maître d'. "If you do not mind, may I join you later?"

"Of course," Helen said quickly.

Elizondo bowed and went back up the stairs.

Our table was halfway around the dance floor, along the rail of the first gallery. Almost immediately, our waiter appeared with two bottles of champagne, compliments of Mr. Elizondo.

"Now," Helen whispered as she pushed my glass toward me, "promise me you'll forget Frankie-boy and the script for one night."

"There's nothing I'd rather do than forget this past week."

"Good."

Jake Farrell arrived just as B. J. was emptying the last of the champagne. He made polite conversation with me through dinner, giving me as much attention as he was going to give a lost cause. As the waiter cleared, he sat back, crossed his legs, and lit a cigarette. Languidly, he exhaled the smoke through his nostrils and surveyed the crowd below through the blue haze. On the far side of the dance floor, Mary Astor came in with a man I didn't recognize. With them was John Darnell, one of MGM's music directors, and his widowed sister. I knew her because her late husband had been the president of my uncle Bennett's real estate company. She was small and soft and rich. Jake's eyes narrowed. Apparently, he knew her, too.

He waited until the coffee arrived, then he crushed his cigarette thoroughly in the ashtray, and said, "Excuse me for a minute. I see John Darnell over there. I have some business I need to discuss with him."

"Of course." He went off, smoothing his jacket. "Don't bother," I said to the waiter as he started to pour Jake's coffee. "I don't think he's coming back."

"Mrs. Ross!" A lean, breezy, sandy-haired young man appeared beside the table. "What a pleasant surprise!"

Helen's eyes lit up, too much for mere pleasant surprise. "Dean! What are you doing here?"

"Came with some friends. We just got here." He gestured to a table where several other young people were settling in. "They kept me on the set till almost nine." Dean said hello to me and the Camlics, and we nodded our good health.

"Sit down for a minute," Helen said.

"Sure. Glad to." He sat down in the empty sixth chair at the table, which happened to be next to Helen. "I hope you're okay," he said to me. "I heard about the robbery."

I said I was. "How have you been?" I asked.

"I had that flu a couple of weeks ago. Doctor almost put me in the hospital. Half the cast is sick with it."

Dean's father was an executive at Marathon and his mother a society power from a very old family. He had been given a contract just before the war, and when he got out of the army, the studio had honored it. I thought his father must still support him because he lived far above what a first-year contract paid. He wasn't a bad actor. He just didn't like to work too hard. He preferred parties, clubs, and women. He was just the sort of dashing, shallow young man that Helen always got involved with.

I thought about the questions Sam had asked me about Dean.

Elizondo came in, making his way slowly between the tables beside the dance floor, greeting patrons, remembering every important face and name. He came up the short flight of stairs beside our table and sat down in Jake's chair.

"Mrs. Atwill," he said, after we had thanked him for the champagne, "I wanted to tell you earlier that I have spoken to certain parties in the police department in case thieves are beginning to prey upon my guests."

"Under the impression that your guests are leaving here with money?"

He laughed, warm and golden, then said with serious dark eyes, "I would like to assure you that I will do everything in my power to prevent such a thing from ever happening again, even if I must hire my own guards to patrol the canyon."

"Thank you," I said, trying to ignore Helen nudging me under the table.

A large shadow fell across us. A swarthy, pockmarked man, bulging in his evening clothes, loomed up beside us. He had a thick wave of steel-gray hair and a right eye that was permanently half-closed, its lid white. There were two strong lines of muscle on either side of his neck, and his arms rested a few inches away from his body, either from overdevelopment of the trapezius or from long habit of being ready to reach for a gun. It was George Scarano, Elizondo's assistant. In the old days, he'd been called his bodyguard.

I said good evening to him. His head nodded slowly. Once. Then he leaned over and whispered to Elizondo.

Elizondo said, "Please excuse me. I must attend to some business in the casino." He bowed and went out ahead of George across the gallery.

"Whew," said B. J. "I wouldn't want to meet that one in a dark alley. I hear he still carries a gun all the time."

Art stretched to his feet. "Well, I guess we'll head on up to the tables. You coming?"

"Not just yet," Helen said. "We'll see you up there."

He took B. J. firmly under the arm and guided her toward the lobby. Despite his navigating, she managed to bump into most of the young men coming in.

"This is the last time I invite Jake Farrell anywhere," Helen said with disgust. On the other side of the dance floor, he was whispering to the widow. She was finding it interesting.

"Don't blame him too much," I said. "I'm not very good company."

Below us, a couple was being shown to one of the floorside tables. The girl was short, slender, and pretty but with a nervy, high-strung look that only generations of money can produce. She was wearing a flowing gown of lavender organza, with her long, black, waving hair held back softly with pearl combs. The man with her glanced up and saw us.

"Shit," said Helen.

Taking the woman by the elbow, he led her up to our table. "Hello, Lauren, Helen. Cummings."

"Hi, Frankie," said Helen. He hated being called Frankie.

"Hello, Mrs. Atwill," the girl said shyly. Her nostrils flared and quivered.

"Hello, Miss Harris. How are you?" I said.

Franklin said, "I got the new rewrites today. They're great."

"Isn't that great?" said Helen.

"It was very nice of you to do this for Franklin," Alex said. No one called him Franklin but me.

"Have you heard anything from the police?" he asked.

"I got my car back," I said.

"You did? Did they catch the guys?"

"They caught the ones who stole the car."

"What do you mean?"

Just beyond the railing, a light flashed the sudden, blinding flare of a flashbulb. I jumped and let out a little yelp. Through the glaring ball of white that dominated my field of vision, I saw the photographer turn and shoulder his way quickly through the couples on the floor, headed for the lobby.

"Damn," said Franklin. "He got all of us."

"Papa will be furious," Alex said urgently. "I promised him I wouldn't go anywhere too public."

Franklin started down the stairs after the man.

At the arch, George Scarano appeared and covered the man's forearm with his hand. After a brief, indignant, hopeless tug-of-war, the man gave up. Holding his camera protectively against his stomach, he was led away.

Franklin came back up to us. "George'll take care of it," he said. "Well, I guess we'll go back to our table. Have a good evening."

Alex took a deep, shivering breath, smiled, and said good night.

"Inbreeding," Helen said, when they had gone.

The band struck up a conga, and there were groans of protest from some of the men on the floor. George came back through the gallery to our table, blotting out most of the available light.

"Mr. Elizondo," he said, in a rumbling, raspy voice that was, however, free of any accent that I associated with bodyguards. It wasn't Ivy League, but it wasn't stevedore, either. "Mr. Elizondo asked me to tell you he was sorry about the photographer. We don't let them in here. Unless the customer wants them in."

"It couldn't be helped."

"It turned out he wasn't much of a photographer. He opened up his camera and ruined all his film."

"Did he? I saw you warning him to be careful."

There was some movement at the edges of his mouth that might have been a smile, but I couldn't be sure. I moved my lips around a little, too. "Thank you. Very much."

"Mr. Elizondo wanted you to know he took care of it." He nodded stiffly again, turned, and went back out.

Helen said, "Do you really think he wears a gun?"

"I don't think there's room in there for his body *and* a gun."

The band segued into a rhumba. "Would you like to dance?" Dean asked Helen.

"We shouldn't—"

"Oh, go on," I said. "I'll be fine. Really."

"Are you sure?"

"Of course."

Dean led her onto the floor. I watched them go and heaved a sigh for her. And for myself because no one, gigolo or otherwise, had asked me to dance.

At the end of the number, the lights came up just a little, just enough to remind the patrons that there was more to do at Elizondo's than eat and dance. Many of them responded to the subtle encouragement and made their way toward the casino with new purpose in their eyes. A man came in around them out of the lobby and stood between the arches, taking some time to get a cigarette out of his case. He took out his lighter and flicked the wheel. The flame flared in front of his eyes.

"Well, well, well," Helen said appreciatively, following my stare as she and Dean sat down at the table. "Who's that? Do you know him?"

"No. No, I don't." I started breathing in tight little gasps. I could hear them, but I couldn't stop them.

"I think I've seen him in here before. François!" she hailed the walter as he passed. "That man—the one at the door—do you know him? The one with the cigarette?"

"Yes, ma'am. That's Mr. Winslow."

"Does he come here often?"

"Once a month, perhaps."

"If his party hasn't arrived yet, would you ask him if he'd like to join us for a drink?"

"No!" I cried, barely able to control my voice. "That's all right, François. Don't bother." He bowed and left. Nothing showed on his face, but then nothing would.

"What's the matter with you?" Helen complained. "He's gorgeous. He's alone."

"I don't want to," I snapped. "I just don't want to, all right?"

"Okay."

"I'm sorry, I didn't mean it to sound that way. I'm not feeling well all of a sudden. I think I should go home."

"You don't look too well. Do you want me to take you?"

I almost said yes. I almost clung to her and let her take me home where I would lie on my bed, sick and shaken. And helpless.

"I'll be all right. Really. Tell Mr. Elizondo I'm sorry I couldn't stay. I'll be fine. You two go dance."

"Lauren—"

"Oh, stop acting like my mother. It's only a headache. Go on. Go." I shooed them off.

The man was still standing by the far arch, smoking. I watched him. Logically, rationally, what were the chances of his being the man in that picture? He resembled the face that I remembered from what I had thought was a dream, but so could a hundred other good-looking, dark-haired men. The face had never been anything but a blurred memory.

And yet, if it wasn't him, why had my body had such a strong, almost overwhelming, reaction to seeing him?

He turned and went back out into the lobby. I picked up my bag and made my way along the gallery. There was a knot of people at the first arch: a woman and her escort were stooping to gather scattered pearls from a broken necklace. I turned and started toward the other arch. And stopped abruptly. Winslow was standing just on the other side of the opening, not ten feet away. I retreated, squeezed past the crouching couple, and darted down a short passage into the ladies' lounge.

"Lauren Atwill! I haven't seen you in ages!"

Just what I needed. Louella Parsons was descending upon me rapidly from the line of vanity tables, her stout body rolling perilously from side to side on very high heels, black glass beads swinging frantically from her dress. She had her hands up in front of her shoulders as if she were incredibly delighted to see me—or her nail polish was still wet.

"I just saw Frank with little Alex Harris. How does she feel about you working with Frank again? I heard he's been flirting outrageously with you at rehearsals."

"Not at all. I haven't even been to rehearsals."

"Reconciliation on the way?"

"I don't think so."

"Let me know if anything happens. I'd like to see you two back together. Remember how nice I was to you in the column when you two separated."

I didn't, but said I did. I was spared any further intrusion. Gene Tierney came in, and Lolly swept off to accost her without even saying good-bye to me.

I sat down at one of the vanities and examined my face. It was pale, but there was a curious energy in the eyes. I looked down at my hands. They were remarkably steady.

I waited until several women were ready to leave at once and, using them as a shield, went back to the lobby. Winslow was gone.

The redhead was still saving her smiles, but she retrieved my wrap promptly.

"I'll get my car," I told the attendant as I slipped him a dollar with my ticket. "I need the air." He didn't argue. There were a half dozen cars waiting to be parked in the lot beyond. The serious gamblers had begun to arrive. I was counting on that. No one would pay any attention to me. I went off across the drive into the deep shadows of the hedge-lined lot, tiptoeing to keep my satin heels out of the gravel.

The Lincoln was parked in the second row, sandwiched between a couple of Packards. I was reaching for the door when I realized that the window was rolled down. I had rolled it up when I arrived. I was sure that I had. My heart jerked around for a second before I realized that it was not my car. The upholstery was darker, and there was a discarded lace handkerchief on the passenger's side. And, of course, it wasn't red. I'd forgotten my car was no longer white. I craned my head until I could read the registration on the steering column. It was Helen's car.

I found mine in the next row, parked so close to a coupe that I couldn't open the driver's door more than a foot. I went around and climbed in through the passenger's door.

I scooted across to the wheel, started the engine, and backed carefully out of the space. At the end of the row, I turned, not toward the portico but toward the rear of the lot. I swung into the last row and parked opposite a nice, wide Chrysler.

I slid down behind the wheel.

Time passed.

It turned out not to be the best of arrangements. The lot had a natural rise in it between me and the club, so I couldn't see the entire portico for the roofs of other cars. Besides that, the portico was dimly lit. Flattering to the patrons, no doubt, but difficult for surveillance. Every time a tall, dark-haired man came out, I sat up. I almost mistook Jake for Winslow when he came out with the widow. I thought about moving closer, but I didn't want to be noticed.

At midnight, Helen came out alone. The attendant brought her Lincoln around. She and the Camlics had apparently driven out in separate cars.

Twenty minutes later, Dean came out and waited for his car. He stayed in the shadows close to the doors and it took me a while to recognize him. He got into a Cord convertible and drove off.

I sat there, marveling that—given the amount of fairly flagrant sin going on at the club—the blackmailers had ended up with me. I didn't feel particularly sorry for them.

More time passed.

I began talking to myself as characters from *The Final Line*, taking notes on the pad I kept in the glove compartment. I finished the entire resolution scene in Elizondo's parking lot.

At one-twenty, I sat bolt upright. Winslow came out, alone, helpfully waiting for his car directly beneath one of the lamps so I could get a good look. He did not give the attendant a ticket. Despite what the waiter had said about his being an infrequent visitor, they knew his car, a very ordinary-looking coupe. And they didn't sneer at it. I started my engine and backed out of the space. His car disappeared over the top of the drive, and I followed.

At the bottom, he turned right onto Coruna, headed back toward Topanga Canyon. Almost immediately, the road began to twist, so that only occasionally on a brief straight stretch—could I see his taillights through the churned dust before they would disappear into the next turn. For a while, it didn't matter, because the chance that he was turning off onto one of the few side roads was remote, but as we got near Topanga, I had to make up some distance.

We came out of the final plunging curve, and he disappeared behind an outcropping that hid the intersection. I slowed down and crept around it just in time to see him turning right. There was a car coming up Topanga from the left. I waited and let it get between us before I pulled out.

Tailing, I was discovering, was damn hard work. I had the other car as a shield, but now I could barely see Winslow's taillights. If he got too far ahead, I might have to risk passing on a curve to catch up.

When he reached 101, he turned toward the city. The car between us did the same. We stayed together until we reached Sepulveda, then Winslow turned south. The other car went on.

I made the turn, and followed, holding back as far as I dared. After a couple of miles, I came out of a curve in time to see him turn onto Mulholland. Just my luck, I thought, one of those Mulholland speed jockeys. I was right. He laid his foot on the accelerator and shot away. Almost immediately, his taillights became dim, distant points in the black.

I did my damnedest to keep up. For miles and miles, we swept through the sweet air on the crest of the mountain, with him hugging the tight, terrifying curves expertly and me doing the best I could. In the thick black of the night, my headlights illuminated no more than the next curve. Thirty would be the highest safe speed. We were doing forty.

My palms started to sweat, and my stomach shuddered.

As we approached the city, the traffic got thicker, but it made little difference to him. He slowed down only until there was a stretch long enough to pass, then flowed easily around the other cars and kept going. I began to wonder where the hell the police were.

Finally, blessedly, the traffic and the turns became too much even for him, and as we dropped toward Cahuenga, I had gained enough ground until there was only a cab between us.

We drove south, now at a saner pace, past the reservoir and the Hollywood Bowl. When we came out of the hills, he turned east.

My heart stuffed itself into my throat. The light at the end of the block turned red. Winslow stopped. The cab pulled up beside him. Rapidly, in the space I had left, I calculated how much Winslow could see in his side and rearview mirrors. I pulled up behind the cab in what I hoped was Winslow's blind spot.

The light changed, and the cab turned right. Winslow and I continued on, with me hanging back in the right lane. When we reached Canyon Drive, he turned into the labyrinthine streets that lined the edge of the hills southeast of Griffith Park. I cut across the lane and made the turn as well.

I had to stay back; yet if he turned into one of the twisting side streets, I could lose him instantly. I chewed my lip.

He made a right on Valley Oak, and by the time I reached the corner, he was gone. I slapped the steering wheel in fury and stomped on the accelerator, not that I could go very fast on the winding, narrow street. I looped up to Verde Oak and continued north, now much slower, so that I could snap my head into the short side streets, hoping to catch sight of him. I didn't find him in Holly Oak or Live Oak, or Hill Oak, Mountain Oak, Spreading Oak, or Canyon Oak.

Finally, at Park Oak Drive, I found him again. Down in the middle of the block, he was just turning into a driveway. I went on past the intersection, cut the headlights, and made a U-turn. I crept onto Park Oak and coasted over to the curb. He had left his car parked in his driveway and was strolling up the slight incline, his hands in his pockets, stopping only long enough to take a breath of the cool wind before he turned and walked across the small yard into the house. The lights went on. I eased along the curb until I was satisfied that the blinds were drawn, then glided past the house, checking the number that was hung on the gray stucco under the porch light. So deep was I in my thoughts that I ran the stop sign at the end of the block.

When I got home, the light was on in the kitchen. Juanita was sitting at the table, a cup of dark, sweet Mexican chocolate in front of her.

"What are you doing up?" I asked.

"I wanted to see you got home all right. You want some? It's hot."

"I'll get it." I poured myself a cup.

When I looked up, she was examining me, her chubby face cocked to one side. "You look very nice. Excited. You meet a nice man?"

"I met a man."

"That's no good. We've already had a not-nice man."

I laughed and slipped a napkin under my saucer. "He won't be coming here. Now, go to bed."

I went into the study, set the chocolate on the desk, and tossed my wrap on the sofa. I sat down at the desk and pulled out the phone book. I flipped to the back, going through the tail end of the alphabet to remind myself where W came.

Wa— We— Wi— Wilson. Wingate. Winslow.

There it was. Winslow, Peter. 84 Park Oak Drive.

At the bottom of the drawer was last year's edition of the city directory. I got it out and looked up Park Oak Drive. Winslow, Peter was listed at 84. Below his name was his occupation.

Private Investigator.

Chapter 4

I spent Sunday with my typewriter out by the pool, polishing dialogue. And falling back on a few clichés because I couldn't concentrate.

Unlike almost every detective movie ever written—some by me—private eyes were not hard-drinking romantics with sterling codes of ethics. And they did a lot of divorce work. Winslow would be right at home with a camera.

Of course, I didn't have anything that remotely resembled evidence. As for my reaction to him . . . Helen said that she thought she had seen him at the club before. It was possible that I had, too, and had held his face somewhere in the back of my mind. I didn't have to be Freud to figure out that, given what had happened, I might have taken a dark, handsome face and substituted it for one I could not bear to recall. He could actually be the face in my memory/dream, and it wouldn't mean a thing.

And the more I thought about it, the more I doubted that a private detective would use himself in blackmail pictures, even with his face hidden. Or let Maritski show me *his* face. That seemed like a stupid—and dangerous—thing to do. What if I hadn't been paralyzed with shock?

What if I'd called for help? What if I'd had a gun in my bag?

I gave up on Winslow and started thinking about Maritski. The frayed suit, slicked hair, and accent could all have been part of a disguise. If they were, he played the role well. He had mastered the alternately fawning and boastful manner I had seen so frequently in Hollywood's outcasts, thousands who—without skill, beauty, or luck—were drawn to a business that demanded all three. The seedy boarding-houses and transient hotels were full of them. If Maritski wasn't playing a part, I'd start looking for him there.

Or maybe there was somewhere else I would look first.

Monday morning, I went to the studio for the first day of shooting and made a few notes for the scenes I hadn't finished yet. Mostly, I watched Don work, goading and praising, helping Franklin crack open the polished exterior of his character to reveal both the ruthless ambition and the deep wounds of poverty that had created it. It was going to be Franklin's best work in years.

Afterward, I borrowed a phone on a desk left empty by the lunch hour and made a call to Central Casting Corporation. I asked for Myrna Pearl.

I'd met Myrna when she was a contract player at Marathon—at the end of a limited career. Her curvaceous form was seen on the lap of the hapless hero when the heroine walked into the room in several of the low-budget comedies I had written in the days before Walt Weinhaus overheard Don praising me in the Avalon Café. Now, I'd heard that she was divorced and supporting herself and her three children by casting actors herself.

"Hey, kid," she said, through a bit of lunch. "Sorry. Busy today, had to eat at my desk. It's been ages. What have you been up to?"

"I don't want to interrupt, but I was wondering if you could spare me a couple of minutes this afternoon?"

"Have to be before four."

"How about now?"

"Sure. Know where we are?"

"Yes. Thanks."

I bought a ham sandwich from a coffee wagon making its way back toward the soundstages and ate while I drove.

Central Casting had offices on the third floor of the Producers Association Building on the corner of Hollywood and Western. It was supported by the association to supply extras to fill out crowd scenes, dance floors, country clubs, train stations, and army platoons. Whenever "background artists" were needed, the picture's casting director would send over specifications, and Central Casting would find them, no matter how many.

Just inside the building's Art Deco white stone entry arch was a wall of glass-backed brass filigree and a set of double doors. Just inside them, in the small lobby, were a half dozen extras hoping to remind someone from Central Casting who they were. They were all women. Three were extremely thin, no longer young, and wearing their finest, one complete with an ancient wrap of martens; two were well-fed character types, dressed as "mamas" in house dresses and aprons; and one, with a sun-creased face, was arrayed in full cowgirl regalia, a lariat looped in her belt. They all gave me fairly natural smiles and said their names, on the chance I was a new casting director.

I took the elevator to the third floor with another half dozen. These were all young and nervous and far too hopeful, on their way to see if they could register. They all probably still thought they could break into the movies by starting as an extra.

Myrna had left my name at the front desk, so the receptionist called her immediately. The others had to sit on the hard chairs and wait.

Since I had last seen her, Myrna's brunette hair had turned a vivid shade of red not found in nature. It was swept up in the back and arranged in Betty Grable curls above her forehead. She was wearing white-rimmed glasses and a white, double-breasted, shawl-collared blouse that gaped a bit over the cleavage that had grown even more ample over the years.

"I don't believe it!" she cried. "It's been forever! Come on back to the office." She waved her hand toward the end of the hallway, scattering ash from her cigarette over the carpet. "You ever been here before?"

"No."

"Well, then, you're in for a treat."

The room at the end of the hall was a large rectangle, with two rows of pine tables at our end. Four women and two men sat at the first table, four women at the one behind them. They were all facing a room divider that reached almost to the ceiling and looked like it was made up of library card cabinets. It was lit from above with a long fluorescent tube; the rest of the room had white glass-shaded lamps that hung from the ceiling to about five feet above the tables.

The long sides of the room were lined with small offices behind half-wood, half-window walls. In one of the offices on the far side, I could see five operators plugging cords into switchboards and snapping them back out rapidly. About half the lines were lit up.

Behind me, above my head, a woman's voice called out from a loudspeaker, "Sybil Riley."

A man sitting in the front row punched one of a line of buttons on the tabletop in front of him and picked up the receiver to his telephone. He spoke into it crisply. "Paramount, tomorrow, 8 A.M. Sports clothes." He waited for a few seconds, then he said, "Right," and punched the button again. He hung up.

"Herman Loomis," a different woman's voice announced on the loudspeaker.

The woman at the far end of the first table punched a button. I couldn't hear what she said, but it didn't take her any longer to complete her business.

Myrna said, "The casting directors are in the front there. They handle the extras. The girls here in the back, they handle the requests that come in from the studios over the phone or the teletype. They take down the specifications and give them to the casting directors. The casting directors go over them, figure out how many they'll need from the types they cover, and wait for the extras to call in."

"Daphne Henson," the loudspeaker squawked, on cue.

"Like that," Myrna said. "The extras who are registered with us call in, the switchboard girls call out their names. If one of the directors wants him, he picks up the phone, punches one of those buttons, and connects himself to the switchboard line. Then he tells the extra where to be and what to wear."

"And if there's nothing?"

"Nobody out here picks up. The switchboard girls tell them, 'No work.' "

"Do they call back?"

"Oh, Lord, do they. Every fifteen minutes, some of them. We don't let them call back more than that. Drive you crazy. On quiet days, we tell them not to call back till after four. That's when the studios start sending over most of their work."

"Ruth Custer," squawked the box.

"Let's go into my office," Myrna said.

We went into one of the small glass-partitioned offices on the opposite side of the room from the switchboards.

"Welcome to Paradise," she said, and closed the door. The litany of names continued outside, but more quietly. "You should hear it from four till about seven. It never lets up. The switchboard girls probably answer a few thousand calls. Each. Sit down." She gestured toward the chair opposite her desk and scattered some more ash over her blotter and the waxed paper that held the crusts of her lunch. "Want some coffee?"

"No, thanks." There was hardly enough room for the chair between her desk and the wall. I squeezed myself into what space there was, and we caught up on the last few years. I clucked appropriately over pictures of her children.

"And not one of them ever wanted to be in pictures," she said, "thank God. Five years I've been here, interviewing new registrants. You wouldn't believe some of the mothers who drag their kids in here, the next Margaret O'Brien, the next Mickey Rooney. Can't dance, can't read a line to save his life, but he's going to be a star. The way they treat those kids. I want to take half of them home with me." She shook her head.

"You interview everyone who comes in here?"

"Me and another girl take care of it. We talk to them, see if they have any special talents, see if they fit a special type. We decide which ones we'll register." She sat back in her chair and regarded me. "So," she said, "what's the big mystery?"

I smiled casually. I hoped. "I need a little help."

"Writing a script about us?"

"That's not a bad idea. But right now, I'm trying to find

a man who might have done some extra work. His name's Paul Maritski."

"Not one of our regulars."

"You have their names memorized?"

"Most of them."

"There must be thousands."

"About seven, give or take, in the files. If you work here, you've got to have a good memory. After I pick the ones I want to register, I call in the casting directors to take a look at them. Then one of the office boys glues the pictures onto cards." She shuffled into a pile of papers on her desk and pulled out a blank card about four by seven inches. "Like this. They have to bring us some pictures, no bigger than what could fit on half this card. Then I transfer my notes to the cards: experience, talents, height, weight, approximate age. They all lie about that one, one way or another. Then the casting directors get the cards for the types they specialize in so they can memorize them. When a name comes over the loudspeaker, they have to know whether they can use him."

She stood up and opened the office door. The room outside had fallen quiet. She called out, "Anybody recognize the name Paul Maritski? Maritski, anybody?"

A couple of them glanced over at her, but nobody answered. "Sorry," she said to me.

"He might have used a stage name. He's maybe forty-five. Fifty. Short, dark. Oily-looking."

"Doesn't sound like a romance."

I laughed. "He was in a writing seminar I did at UCLA. He wrote a story I want to work on, but I can't find him. I seem to remember he mentioned that he did extra work." If my excuse sounded a bit thin, Myrna didn't seem to notice.

"How long ago was this that you think he worked here?"

"I'm not sure."

"The reason I ask, we purge the files every six months or so. They all have to reregister every six months. If we don't think we can use them anymore, we usually carry them for a while, and hope they get the message when we tell them 'no work' day after day. If they don't, we'll tell them face-to-face when they come back next time. It's not fair to lead them on. But let's see what we've got out here. Come on."

She led me back out into the main room to the wall of library cabinets. The drawers were slightly larger than those of a card catalog would be, big enough to hold the picture cards. The stacks were divided into four sections, with a category name above in five-inch letters: MEN, WOMEN, CHILDREN, RACIALS.

"Racials?" I asked.

"Negro, Mexican. Could this guy look Mexican?"

"I think more Eastern European."

"You're welcome to what we've got here. I don't think anybody's going to need these drawers this afternoon. There's an empty office down there at the end. We use it if any of the studio casting directors come over, wanting to look for special types. You can take the drawers in there. Just stay out of the way. And keep the cards in order."

"I will. Thanks."

She found me a short, wobbly stepladder, and I went to work. I pulled out the drawer marked MABARRY–MORSE, although I didn't think Maritski was dumb enough to have given me his real name. I took it into the office Myrna had indicated, which was just a room with a couple of chairs and another pine table. I set the drawer down and flipped through all the cards. Maritski wasn't there. I put it back and dragged out the top drawer under MEN.

For the next two hours, I flipped through every card in the section and every one in the Racials files as well, just in case. I didn't find him.

I wiped the dust off my hands with a handkerchief and went back to Myrna's office. She was lighting a fresh cigarette and looking over the faces in a small stack of cards. The new registrants, I assumed.

"No luck?" she asked.

"No, but thanks a lot. I appreciate your help."

"Hey, you're not through yet." She stood up.

On the other side of the room divider, there were shorter stacks of cabinets.

She said, "This is where we keep cards for people with special talents. We've got it all: Western, which means they can ride, dancers, musicians, weight lifters, skaters, circus acts, all kinds of things. We might get a call for somebody with a wooden leg who can play the accordion and walk on his hands. Most of these are duplicates, but there might be some you haven't seen. We have some special categories, like midgets and animal handlers, Arabs who can handle camels, things like that, and—Wait! Wait a minute! You said this guy could look Eastern European?"

"Yes."

"Small, dark? Could he look like one of those weasely spy types? Could he look sinister?"

"Yes," I said, maybe a bit too vehemently.

"We needed a bunch of those during the war and before. Not much now, but we've still got a 'spy' drawer around here somewhere. Here." She stuck her cigarette into her mouth and grunted down into a crouch. She pulled out one of the bottom drawers. I took it from her, and she groaned to her feet, exhaling a cloud of smoke. "Try that."

She went back to her desk. I took the drawer into the empty office, sat down, and flipped through the cards. They were filled with the sorts of faces that had populated the thieves' dens and spy hangouts for the last decade of European-intrigue movies. The style of pictures had changed considerably since most of them had been taken. These poses were much less natural, the lighting starker. Many of the men were wearing heavy stage makeup. You could see the eyeliner and the brow pencil. My hand stopped flipping.

Myrna's head appeared around the corner, wisps of smoke curling around her face. "It's almost four. It might get hectic out here, so— What? Did you find him?"

"I think I did."

Even then, he had worn his hair the same way, slicked back tightly. He was sporting a thin moustache and an expression that shouted Latin Lover.

Myrna came around behind me and read the name. "Raoul Ricardo." She laughed and shook her head. "I remember this guy. He had no idea what type he was. But he had a good spy look, when he wasn't trying to look like that. So we took him on. Let me get you his casting sheet from bookkeeping. It'll have his address on it."

When she returned, she handed me four carbon copies stapled together. At the top of the first page was the name Raoul Ricardo, then below it "a.k.a. Paul Kovak." There was an address, ironically on Hope Street, and a phone number.

Below that was a list of movies, the studio names, the dates worked, and the amounts paid for each engagement. I flipped to the last page.

"He hasn't worked in a while," Myrna observed, reading over my shoulder. The last movie listed was *A Spy Among Us* for Paramount in July of '45. I ran my finger back up the list and came to one I recognized. *The Scarlet Spy.* "Say, didn't you write that?" Myrna said.

"Don't remind me." It was one of the few original scripts I'd done during the last few years. What I had submitted bore almost no resemblance to what had ended up on the screen. The script had gone through two other writers. Our names appeared together in the credits, looking as if we had at least spoken to each other. We hadn't.

I glanced over the rest of the list. Maritski/Ricardo/Kovak had worked on over fifty films at various studios. Only six at Marathon. I had not worked on the other five.

"You're lucky he's still here," she said. "Take a look at the front of the card. See the date there and the X." Next to his name, there was "Oct 45" written in pencil and a black X in ink. "That's what we do when we've decided to drop somebody. We just don't need much of that look anymore. That card would have been thrown out in another couple of months."

I copied the address and the phone number into my notepad.

"I owe you lunch," I said as I handed the casting sheets back.

"Sounds good. I'll take it."

She reached for the drawer.

"Don't bother. I'll put it back," I offered. "You've done enough."

She left me alone. I tucked Maritski's card into my handbag before I put the drawer back.

I gave her a wave good-bye as I passed her office. She returned it, scattering ash over the desk top.

I went home and changed into a simple cotton dress and low-heeled sandals and got out the Hudson. With the Arroyo Seco, I was back in Los Angeles in an hour and a half, even in the late-afternoon traffic.

Most of Maritski's neighborhood was still a well-kept lower-middle-class part of town, but some of the blocks were showing signs of slow decline, and many of the wasting, spacious homes had been converted to rooming houses and apartments.

The west side of Hope Street was a steep slope with a head-high concrete wall at the bottom, over which ragged arms of ivy dangled. A long flight of stairs with a pipe railing climbed up Bunker Hill. Halfway up, hugging the stairs, was Maritski's apartment house, a sagging clapboard that looked like it had just exhaled. The house was turned sideways on the lot so that the front door was separated from the stairs only by the narrow porch and about three feet of sidewalk.

I parked around the corner, took a wide-brimmed straw hat off the seat, and got out. Watching the house wouldn't make much sense if he didn't live there anymore. I tugged the hat down, trying to decide if it concealed my face or only made me look more conspicuous.

The front door of the apartment house was warped and standing open. Inside, the foyer smelled of cabbage and damp, its pale gray wallpaper powdery with age. The floorboards were rutted and worn in a path to the stairs. To the left was a row of dented, rust-red mailboxes. I went over and examined the names on them.

"Can I help you, doll?"

I whipped around. He was halfway down the stairs, leaned nonchalantly against the rail, wearing a short-sleeved black shirt over some very good muscles. There was plenty of chiseled chin under a day-old scrub of beard.

I threw my hand onto my hip and started cracking some imaginary gum. I didn't have the slightest idea why.

"Geez," I said, "you could scare a girl to death."

"That'd be a waste, doll." He gave me a hard leer. I tried to picture the sort of girl who would find it exciting. "Something I can do for you?"

"Maybe. I was lookin' for a guy used to work for my uncle. We got a bar down on Ninth. He quit, but he's still got some money comin'. I say, the hell with him. He wants his money, let him come get it, but my uncle's got a soft heart, so I say, okay, I'll come look the guy up."

"What's his name?"

I dug into my bag. "Geez, I can't remember. Got the check here somewhere. He left this address. Little oily guy. Got an accent."

"Kovak. Used to live in 2-B."

I stopped searching. "Used to?"

"Yeah, he skipped out last week. Owed me a couple months' rent, too, so why don't I just take that check off your hands?"

"I don't know," I said slowly. "You look like a guy who might not always tell a girl the truth." He liked that. "Don't suppose you know where he went?"

"Wish I did. Nobody here seems to know. It looks like he left owing most of them money, too."

"You wouldn't know where he worked, would you?"

"I thought you said he worked for your uncle."

"Yeah. Sure. He did. But only part-time."

"Last year, I know he was cleaning up some building downtown at night. If he comes around looking for that check, let me know. I'll make it worth your while if I get the back rent out of him. Why don't you let me buy you a drink so it shouldn't be a wasted trip?"

"I gotta get to work, but if you're ever down at the Palomino, ask for Sally. Everybody knows me."

"Not everybody."

"Maybe we can fix that. See ya, big fella. Don't hurt yourself." I undulated out.

I hadn't found out a thing. Nonetheless, I felt light-headed with a vibrating sense of elation. Everything around me—the cracked surface of the sidewalk, the sooted pits in the concrete wall, the fleshy stalks of the hanging vines—all seemed magnified and intensely real. I wondered if this exhilaration at having put something over was why most criminals couldn't go straight. Or why policemen did undercover work. Or why men became private detectives.

I got back in the car and took a few deep, calming breaths. When I could think of a better cover story, I'd come back and ask the tenants and the neighbors some questions. Anyone who knew Maritski/Ricardo/Kovak well enough to know where he was now would also know he hadn't worked in a bar.

I put the car in gear and drove out to Topanga Canyon. I didn't think I was going to remember anything else by going back to the scene of the crime. I didn't think I was going to find Maritski wandering along the side of the road, but I went anyway.

There wasn't much more traffic on Coruna Road in the daytime than there was late at night. I met only two cars, each churning up plenty of dust.

I turned off Coruna onto the road where I had been attacked. Not far beyond where I had been forced to stop my car, the road ended in a half-built glass-and-stucco house that was creeping to the edge of the canyon. This was probably where my attackers had picked up the saw-horses.

Carefully, I turned the Hudson around and went back out onto Coruna. I pulled over onto the shoulder and sat gazing up the glaring, dusty, climbing stretch of road in the direction of the club. Two of the gang had hidden somewhere around here, one ready to drag out the detour sign, the other out to pounce on whichever poor woman came along.

It was a perfect place—and, behind me, there was one of the few long straight stretches of Coruna, so they could see the distant headlights of any potential-witness customers coming up from Topanga.

Where had their lookout been? Far enough up the road toward the club to give them adequate warning that a woman alone was on the way. I put the car in gear.

Very soon, the road began to twist. If the lookout had been hiding anywhere along here, I would have come upon him too quickly, and with the top up—I always rode with the top up at night—he would not have been able to see that I was by myself. Maybe the lookout had not been beside the road at all.

I parked the car in a fire road fifty yards from the club's drive and walked the rest of the way on the gritty shoulder. Very quickly, the dust turned to dabbles of mud between my sweating toes.

Outside the lawn's border of eight-foot-high hedges, the ground was covered in brown, brittle grass and squatty shrubs, stunted and twisted from the wind and lack of water. They didn't look happy about it. As a path up to the club, it wasn't exactly inviting, but I started climbing. I didn't want to use the drive. I didn't want to be seen and have to explain what I was doing. The way up was even hotter and dustier than the road had been, and my ankles were soon covered in tiny, bleeding scrapes. I began to think this was a very silly thing to do.

I stopped twice to take a look at the drive through the hedges. At night, it was lit only by carriage lamps. I decided that it would have been difficult, maybe impossible, for a lookout to see inside any of the cars, even with binoculars.

At the top of the slope, the hedge cut away sharply to the left to border the customer parking lot. I followed it around, searching the ground as I went. I didn't know exactly what I was looking for. I didn't find Maritski's wallet with his new address in it. I turned the corner and began making my way along the hedge at the rear of the lot. Not far ahead, a large square of grass was laid back flat as if someone had spread a blanket out on it. I went over and crouched beside the spot. Something had definitely been laid down there. The grass was broken and crushed. Then I saw, beneath the hedge, covered in a fine layer of windswept grit, a half dozen cigarette butts, all neatly ground out till they were flat. They would have to be. No one would want to risk starting a fire in the parched field. I dusted a bit of dirt aside and examined the butts. They had started to disintegrate: the paper had cracked in places, and the tobacco was showing through. How long would it take for that to happen?

I stood up and looked through the hedge. It was thick, but there were spaces wide enough to see most of the portico, although the rise in the middle of the lot would obscure the view as it had mine. Was this the spot where the blackmailers' lookout had stood watch? Or where a couple of eager clubgoers had consummated a few too many drinks?

Carefully, I picked up the longest stub and wrapped it gently in my handkerchief, then I finished the complete circuit of the club. I didn't find anything else. I went back to my car and drove slowly back down Coruna.

At the intersection with Topanga, I sat for a moment, trying to decide if there was anything else to take a look at before I went home.

A strong flash of light from the scrub-covered hillside across from me caused me to flinch. Instinctively, I reached for the visor, but it was already down. I looked across at the narrow strip of land that I could see between the edge of the visor and the rearview mirror. I didn't see anything made out of glass or metal, and I didn't think the grass was high enough to conceal anything that could have made such a flash. Where had it come from?

Then I realized I was facing west. The sun was in front of me. It couldn't reflect off anything on the opposite slope. It could only reflect off something behind me. A flash that would then be reflected in my rearview mirror.

I whipped around, my heart vibrating. There was nothing behind me but the outcropping of rock twenty-five yards away. The same outcropping that I had crept around Saturday night when I followed Winslow. It was plenty big enough for a car to hide behind. A car that could have edged around the curve just far enough to see me still stopped, then backed up. But not before its grille had thrown off a burst of sun.

I sat there, watching the road behind me. No car appeared.

Geez, I was getting jumpy.

Still, what had caused that flash?

I didn't go back around the corner to investigate.

I drove home, exceeding the speed limit, watching all the way for a car that stayed with me. None did.

Juanita was gone, spending her day off visiting her sister, who had just had a baby. I made sure all the doors were locked.

I put the cigarette butt away in my desk, and after I took a shower, I pulled out the phone book and found all the Ricardos and Kovaks (other than the Paul Kovak on Hope) in the county. And anything close to Maritski. I called Information to see if there were any listings not in the phone book. Then I called all the numbers I had, ready to identify myself as Central Casting, but I came up empty.

Now what?

I stared at the typewriter and the script and the steno pad sitting beside it that contained the notes I had taken that morning on the set. I dragged my attention back to my job. I read through the scenes Don was shooting over the next week, to see if there was anything else I wanted to do to them.

About three, I remembered that I'd never eaten lunch. I went into the kitchen to make myself something to eat, which consisted of taking the chicken salad and iced tea that Juanita had left for me out of the refrigerator and dropping a couple of pieces of bread into the toaster.

The phone rang. I went out into the hall and answered it.

"Mrs. Atwill," the voice said, "you have been very hard to reach. We have business to discuss."

"No, we don't."

There was a pause. He had not expected me to refuse him.

"Mrs. Atwill, please consider what will happen if you do not pay. I would be forced to offer them to Mr. Atwill."

"You little creep!"

"I think it would be worth something to you if he did not see them."

"I don't give a damn what you think."

"I will sell them to him, if you do not pay. Believe that I will. Why don't I send you one, Mrs. Atwill, and you can imagine your husband seeing it." He hung up.

I was shaking so hard with rage that I could hardly replace the receiver. The moment I did, the phone rang again. After three rings, I picked it up. And listened.

There were a few seconds of silence, then a woman's voice said, "Hello?"

"Helen."

"I didn't hear you say hello. I thought there was something wrong with the phone."

"I had something caught in my throat." I made a few vague coughing noises.

"Need some company?"

"Sure. How about some lemonade by the pool?"

"I'll be over in an hour."

"Fine."

Maritski had killed my appetite, so I went upstairs and changed into a swimsuit, then made a pitcher of lemonade, rolling the lemons back and forth methodically on the board before cutting them, calming myself with the thought that pretty soon Maritski and his friends were bound to catch on that they were not going to get paid.

Would he really go to Franklin?

Helen looked stunning, as usual, in white slacks and a sea-green shirt. She changed into her swimsuit, and we went out to the pool. She lay back on one of the lounge chairs, stretching out her long, perfect legs.

"Sam wants to have a party for the cast and crew on

Sunday," she said. "After he gets back from New York. He thinks it'll be good for morale, especially with all the union trouble. Just a few steaks on the grill. Will you come? Joan won't be there. She already told Sam."

"I don't have anyone to bring."

"That's all right."

"Maybe I could invite Mr. Elizondo."

She didn't laugh. She didn't make any salacious comments. There was no sound at all except for the soft whoosh of the sprinklers in the shade at the foot of the garden. I turned to her. She was lying with her face to the sun, her eyes closed behind her sunglasses.

"Is something wrong?" I asked.

She said, "I'm being blackmailed," the same as if she'd been asking for the suntan lotion.

I stared at her.

"They have pictures. They said they'd show them to Sam if I didn't pay."

I kept staring. I think my mouth was open. Finally, I managed to speak. "What happened?"

"It was Saturday. After you left the club. I went over to Dean's. We were— Oh, hell, you know what we were doing. And suddenly, there was a flash at the window. It filled up the whole room. Then there was another one. I couldn't believe it. Dean pulled on his pants and ran and got his gun out of his desk. His gun, for God's sake. The guy had a car waiting. There's a lot of construction out there, and the pavement's torn up. I guess that's what it was because the guy with the camera tripped and fell down. Another guy got out of the car and started toward him. I thought Dean was going to catch up, but the first guy jumped up and got into the car, and they took off.

"Of course, I thought it was Sam. That he'd hired

someone to follow me. Then yesterday, a guy called—on my private number—and said he had the pictures, and if I didn't give him five thousand dollars, he'd show them to Sam." Her face twisted in pain, and tears rolled down her cheeks. "I don't know what to do. They'll show them to Sam. I couldn't stand it. I love him so much. Isn't that funny?"

I sat down on the edge of her chaise and put my arms around her. I said, "How did they know about you and Dean? Do you have any idea?"

"No. We didn't think anyone knew."

"How long has it been going on?"

"Three, no, four months now."

"Have you told him?"

"Yes. He said he could get his hands on maybe a thousand and that I could have it all."

"Don't worry about the money."

"I'm sorry, but I don't know what else to do. I can't get that much without Sam knowing."

"It's all right." I fished a handkerchief out of the pocket of my wrap that was hanging on the back of my chair and gave it to her. "What did the man on the phone sound like?"

"Like he meant it."

"No, I mean, did he have an accent?"

"No."

"Was one of them dark and ratlike?"

She frowned at me. "They were wearing masks. Hoods. Why?"

"Because," I said, "I'm being blackmailed, too."

I told her what had really happened the night I was attacked.

"Oh, Lauren! Oh, dear God! Why didn't you tell me?"

"I think I was too ashamed."

"What on earth have you got to be ashamed of?"

"Nothing, I guess. Nothing at all."

"Do you think it's the same people?"

"I don't know. Mine wore hoods, too. Tell me about the men. Was one of them short?"

"No. The one with the camera was about average. Thin. The other one . . . I only saw him for a second. When he got out of the car." She thought about it. "The roof only came up to his chest, so he must have been pretty tall. Over six feet."

"What time was it?"

"Two-thirty or so."

Damn. If I'd stayed outside Winslow's house Saturday night, I'd know whether he was the tall man. "When they call back, tell them you have to see the pictures."

"I don't want to make them mad."

"They want money. They don't want to go to Sam. For all they know, he could throw them out on their behinds, so tell them you have to see what they have."

"What are you going to do?"

"Let's just make sure they have a picture with your *face* in it, then take it from there."

Chapter 5

By seven the next morning, I had the Hudson parked at the corner of Park Oak Drive, hidden behind another car. All the way over, I watched for cars with shiny grilles. I noticed a green coupe that ran a stop light behind me coming off the parkway. It followed me through two turns, then I cut into an alley and waited. I thought it slowed down when it reached the alley opening, but it could have only been traffic. I didn't see it again.

At seven-thirty, Winslow came out and got into his car. Hanging back as far as I could, I followed, one eye on him, one eye in my rearview mirror. He parked his car in a lot on Fourth and went directly into a prosperous-looking office building at the corner of Fourth and Hill.

I was lucky that it was still so early. I was able to find a space on Hill, diagonally across from the building, with a good view of the entrance. In another hour, the curbs would have been full of people looking for free parking, since the downtown lots were getting more and more expensive, some now charging seventy-five cents just to park your car for the day.

I put on my straw hat, climbed out of the Hudson, and

crossed the street. By the time I got to the building, I was
breathing as if I had been running.

The lobby was green-and-black marble. Its chrome
stairway led up to a mezzanine whose balustrade was
made of chrome panels with scenes from the history of
California on them in bas-relief. Winslow's name wasn't
on the directory. It didn't list any detective agencies, either, but there was a Paxton Security in Suite 302. I went
into one of the phone booths by the newsstand and got
Paxton's number from the phone book. I dialed it.

I was still breathing hard. The receptionist probably
thought I had asthma.

In a crisp voice, I said that I was calling from First National Bank's loan office, and I simply wished to confirm
that Mr. Peter Winslow was employed there. Yes, he was,
the receptionist assured me. Did I wish to speak with him?
No, I did not wish to. I went back to the car, rolled down
all the windows, and unfolded the newspaper against the
steering wheel. I waited.

Howard Hughes was all over the headlines, having
crashed his experimental plane into a street in Beverly
Hills while attempting an emergency landing on the golf
course. He was not expected to live. No one on the
ground had been hurt.

Secretary of State Byrnes was pledging to dismiss all
communists and "their fellow travelers" from his department.

On page three, I saw that the estate of Christina Harris
Winnack, Alex Harris's older sister, had been settled, four
months after her suicide. The bulk of her fortune had
been left in trust to her two young daughters.

I waited. I watched Winslow's building fill up with office girls, nurses, dental technicians, and the people who

hired them. I didn't know what I was waiting for. Maybe for Winslow to come out with a sign on his back that said, THIS WAY TO THE NEGATIVES. I went back to the paper.

The army was putting six hundred Quonset huts on sale to California veterans for housing. Half of them had windows.

Now that price controls had been lifted, the mayor was predicting that more meat would appear in grocery stores. The Meat Fair Play Committee was demanding that past gougers be prosecuted.

The traffic got heavier. The car got hotter.

I knew one thing. The police in movie stakeouts didn't look half miserable enough. I crawled out, stretched my stiff back, and flexed my aching knees. What was I doing this for?

The answer was standing down on the corner, waiting for the light, wearing the same cream-colored suit and carrying the same portfolio he had at Madison's. Maritski crossed Hill and turned smartly into Winslow's building. I slammed the car door and raced down to the corner and across the intersection without paying any attention to the light.

After I grabbed a few breaths, I eased into the lobby behind a couple of well-fed businessmen just in time to see the doors to one of the elevators closing. Maritski was not in the lobby. I took the stairs two at a time to the mezzanine. Down to the right was the door to the fire stairs. I pushed it open and dashed up to the second floor landing, then crept toward the third floor. Someone had propped open the hallway door to let some breeze in from the stairwell windows, so I could see the door to suite 300. RUNYON IMPORTERS. PLEASE WALK IN. Thirty feet down the hall were double doors of frosted glass. PAXTON SECURITY. No invitation to come in.

Maritski came down the hall and went in anyway.

I hotfooted it back to my car and waited, the engine idling. Ten minutes later, he came out and cut back down Fourth. I put the car in gear and shoved the Hudson's nose into traffic, but no one would stop. In the movies, when someone was tailing a suspect, he *never* had to wait for a break. Finally, a space-hungry Ford let me out. Before I could get to the corner, the light turned red. The "stop" arm came up beside it.

I pounded the wheel in aggravation and strained to see into Fourth. Finally, the light changed. The arm dropped. I gunned the car around the corner between startled pedestrians and searched the sidewalks along Fourth. He was gone. I kept driving, kept looking, kept cursing. Then I went home and threw a few unbreakable things around the study.

When I had cooled down, I called my lawyer, Harned Chalmers.

"Hullo, Lauren," he said with his usual starched precision. "What may I do for you?"

"Have you ever heard of Paxton Security?"

He cleared his throat. "This isn't about Frank, is it?"

"No. I take it you've heard of them. Ever hired them?"

"Well . . ."

"I only want to know if they're reputable."

"Reputable," he repeated and savored the word. "I don't suppose private investigators are ever truly held in esteem."

"But you have no reason to believe they're not honest."

"No, none at all."

"It's a big firm? Expensive?"

"Oh, yes, very expensive."

"Do you know an investigator there named Peter Winslow?"

"I have never met any of their staff. I have always dealt with Mr. Paxton personally."

"Thank you."

"Lauren, I'm Frank's attorney, too. I must ask again—"

"Harned, if I were going to have Franklin followed, I wouldn't call his lawyer for a recommendation. Thanks."

I sat, drumming my fingers on the blotter. Paxton was a big outfit, making plenty of money. The owner wouldn't get involved in sordid schemes like mine or Helen's. Too dangerous. Maybe it was just one operator doing a little dirty business on the side. And he couldn't keep his dirty business in the company safe.

I kept drumming my fingers. And thinking.

There was a knock on the door, and Juanita came in. "Mrs. Ross is on the phone," she said.

"Thanks."

She offered the small stack of envelopes and advertising circulars in her hand. "The mail is here." She set it down on the corner of the desk and went out.

I picked up the extension.

"They called," Helen said, her voice full of breath. "I told him I—"

"Let's wait till Juanita hangs up," I said quickly.

After a moment, I heard Juanita pick up the hall phone and then the click of the receiver dropping back into the cradle.

"Okay," I said, "go on. What happened?"

"They called. A man called. I told him I had to see the pictures. I told him I couldn't pay unless I knew he had something worth buying. Just like you said to do it. I was pretty brave. Then. Now, I'm a mess. He said he'd mail me one. I think they know Sam's not home."

"You could be right."

"Do you think they're watching the house?"

"The Bel Air police wouldn't let anyone hang around your street."

"I guess not."

"It's going to be all right. I swear."

"Yeah." She hung up.

I heaved a big sigh and picked up the mail. There wasn't much. A few bills, an invitation to a charity benefit for war amputees, and a catalog of new Kent radios. Caught in its pages was a Manila envelope with no return address. I opened it. There was only one picture, the one I had seen in Madison's. Clipped to it was a sheet of cheap notepaper with block letters printed on it.

$3,000 IS VERY REASONABLE FOR PEACE OF MIND.
I WILL CALL THURSDAY AT NOON.

Carefully, I put the picture and the note back into the envelope. I took out some paper and began to make notes of my own, as thoroughly, as meticulously as if I had been plotting a pivotal scene. I had to. I was about to commit a crime.

When I was finished, I picked up the phone again and set my plan in motion. I called Paxton Security and asked for an appointment with Winslow the following day. I was put through to his secretary, who said she was sorry, Mr. Winslow would not be available all day on Wednesday. Could one of the—? No, I said, I wanted to see Mr. Winslow. It was important. He had been rec-ommended to me. She went away for a full minute.

When she came back, she said that she could give me an appointment at nine. Would I please be prompt? I promised that I would. I told her my name was Mrs. David Morris.

I got out the Hudson and drove over to Winslow's neighborhood, using a few more alleys to check for company. I didn't have any. I stopped to call his house from a market not far away. No one answered.

Park Oak Court was a short arc of road that ran almost parallel to Park Oak Drive. It was a cul-de-sac with only six houses on it. I parked in the middle of the block and marched up the narrow concrete path between two of them, straight up the slope of Winslow's backyard, and onto his service porch, trying to look like I belonged there. I stayed only long enough to get a look at his lock, but it was long enough to lose all the strength in my legs.

My next stop was a hardware store, where I bought a lock exactly like it. Then I went home and shut myself in the study. I unwrapped the lock and set it on the blotter. Out of the desk, I took a scuffed chamois pouch and carefully removed the delicate tools inside it. For a moment, I sat there, contemplating the enormity of the step I was about to take. Some of that unappreciated research I'd done in my early days at Marathon was about to pay off: I could pick locks.

Wednesday promised to be a blazing day. By seven, the air was already thick and heavy, unrelieved by the wind, which was hot and restless and gnawed my nerves. I sat in the Hudson at the top of Winslow's street and watched. Men began to come out of their houses, adjusting their hats to the glare. A few of them stopped to clip bill payments to the mailboxes. Then Winslow came out. He didn't touch his hat. It was already pulled down to the regulation private eye position. He scooped the newspaper from the yard, tossed it into the front seat of his car, and drove off in the other direction.

I drove back down to the market and called his home number. No one answered.

Nothing stirred on Park Oak Court except the grass. I retraced my path from the day before, climbed Winslow's service porch steps, and shut the screen door.

Out of the pouch in my handbag, I took three picks and put them between my teeth. One was a thin, strong wire that came to a U-shape at the end; the second, another wire with two Y-shaped extensions close together along the side; the third, a thin, filelike strip. I inserted the first one into the lock and began to feel for the tumblers, but I hadn't practiced working with shaking, sweat-soaked fingers. Out of my bag, I took a pair of cotton gloves and put them on. I had less dexterity, but at least my hands stayed dry. Finally, they stopped shaking as well, and I managed to find the first tumbler. Maintaining a firm pressure on it, I inserted the second wire and moved it gently back and forth until I had fitted the hooks to the other tumblers. When I had them, I held both wires firmly with one hand, inserted the strip, and turned. The lock clicked, and the door swung open. I blinked at it and thought, bizarrely, that Peter Winslow really ought to get himself a better lock.

I went in, put everything back into my handbag, and closed the door. My blood began to stampede through my body.

The kitchen was old-fashioned, with glass-fronted cabinets and counters of small octagonal black and white tiles. There were clean breakfast dishes on the drainboard. I hoped that didn't mean a wife who didn't answer the phone. No, there was no wife. There were no ruffled curtains or bright pot holders or gingham aprons. Breathlessly, I crept into the living room and listened long enough to make sure there was no maid moving around either.

The room was plainly furnished, with a dark green and beige tattersall sofa and a wood-trimmed side chair covered in a nubby, dark brown fabric. There was a glass-fronted bookcase, a heavy mahogany desk, and a floor-model Zenith radio. But there was no evidence that anyone spent much time there. There was no clutter of any kind, no magazines dropped beside the rack, no slippers tossed in front of the sofa, no half-finished crossword puzzle thrown onto the chair.

Through a wide, flat arch was the entry foyer, which led to a hallway and two bedrooms. The first one did not appear to be used. The single bed was covered in a chenille spread, but there was nothing on the dresser and only a lamp on the nightstand. Winslow's bedroom was at the back of the house. His bed was neatly made, but there was the vague reminder of a cheap scent in the air. On the bedside table, there was a green glass ashtray with two crushed cigarettes, one with lipstick on it—a garish tangerine shade. There was an empty pack of Chesterfields in the trash can.

I looked through his small closet. There were three unexceptional summer suits and, beneath a protective covering of sheeting, one very expensive one and his evening clothes. There were four pairs of lightweight slacks, hung from their cuffs on special hangers, two sports coats, and three short-sleeved sports shirts. In the shelf above were two hats, an empty shaving travel kit, a folded blanket, and several boxes of ammunition for a .45 handgun. On the floor were three pairs of shoes with shoe trees and a typewriter case with only a typewriter inside. There were no mysterious boxes and no safe hidden in the wall behind the clothes.

In the chest of drawers, the underwear, socks, handkerchiefs, and starched dress shirts were precisely arranged. I was careful not to move anything out of place as I looked for negatives between the boxer shorts. There weren't any.

I decided to try his desk. I went back to the living room.

Beside the green leather blotter was a framed photograph, fifteen or twenty years old, of five children lined up beside a Model T. The little girls wore patched dresses; the only boy—who was about six—wore overalls that were much too big for him. Tucked into the corner of the blotter was a sealed envelope addressed to Miss Jennifer Winslow in San Francisco.

I opened the center drawer. There was nothing I wouldn't have expected to find: a writing tablet, whose sheets, however, did not match the note Maritski had sent me, a bottle of ink, a roll of stamps, some pencils, a checkbook, and a bankbook for a savings account. I flipped through both books. There were no large deposits. Winslow had about four thousand in his savings account. I put the books back exactly where I had found them. In the right-hand drawer were a box of stationery, a new typewriter ribbon, a bank-wrapped stack of new one-dollar bills, and a long white envelope. I picked it up. Inside were a dozen negatives the size of those for average amateur photographs, each about three by two inches.

I took one out, holding it by the corner. I raised it to the window, but I couldn't make out anything. I switched on the desk lamp and held it close to the shade.

"Hello," said a voice behind me.

I cried out and spun around. The negatives flew out of my hand. He didn't look at them. He was looking at me. Very hard. I was looking at the gun.

He came out of the kitchen, eased over to the arch, and jerked his chin toward the bedrooms. "If you got any help back there, he better come out." I didn't say anything. "Come here."

"No."

"Come *here*," he said roughly. "If I have to come get you, it won't be pleasant."

Stiffly, I walked over to him. "Let's go," he ordered. "You first."

I led the way down the hall and stood where he told me while he searched both bedrooms and the bathroom.

"Okay," he said then, "back outside."

I went back into the living room and over to the desk with its completely useless telephone.

"Funny how things happen," he said. "I forgot a letter I had to mail. I came back and heard you in the bedroom." He came toward me, looking me up and down with frank appraisal. "My secretary said there was a Mrs. Morris who wanted to see me this morning. Had to be me. You wouldn't be Mrs. Morris, would you?" I backed out of his way. He dumped the contents of my bag onto the desk and shook the tools from their pouch. "Very nice," he said approvingly. He flipped through my wallet to my new driver's license and read the name and marital status. "Find what you were looking for, Mrs. Atwill?"

"You know what I was looking for," I said, trying to sound like I didn't give a damn that I was staring down the barrel of a gun. "I'm not paying for them. Not one penny. And you can tell your friends that, too." It was a stupid thing to do, tell an angry blackmailer with a gun that he wasn't going to get his money, but I was frightened and furious. I started for the door. The room was very warm.

He cut me off at the arch. "Not yet. I want some answers."

"To hell with you." I marched back to the phone and yanked it out of the cradle. When the operator answered, I said, "I need the police. Central Division." It began to ring.

He started toward me.

I stepped back, but there was nowhere to go. I backed into the wall. He reached out with his left hand. His fingers edged into my hair against my scalp and moved the receiver an inch away from my ear. When the phone rang again, he was close enough to hear it. I don't know how many times the voice said, "Central Division."

My own voice was dry and whispered. "Sergeant Barty, please."

It rang twice. "Homicide. Barty."

"Sergeant Barty?"

"Yeah. Who's this?"

"Mrs. Atwill."

"Oh, hi. How are you?"

Winslow was still standing over me. "I need some help," I said.

"What can I do for you?"

"Do you— Have you ever heard of a private detective named Peter Winslow?"

"Pete Winslow? Sure. You thinking about bringing him in on your case?" He sounded a little hurt.

"No, it's something else. For a friend. Do you know him well?"

"About ten years, maybe."

"What's he like?"

"A pain in the— A real pain in the neck sometimes, but he's good. Don't tell him I said so."

"Would you say he's honest?"

"Don't worry about Pete."

"Oh."

"I've been reassigned to the homicide table for a while. Somebody else'll be on your case. Name's Haskell, if you want to check with him."

"Thank you, Sergeant." Winslow stepped back just far enough to let me hang up. I stared at my hand, still wrapped around the receiver. "I was looking for some pictures."

"I figured that out. Those are pictures of my nieces and nephews if you want to check."

"I saw a man go into Paxton's yesterday. His name's Maritski."

"I don't know anybody named Maritski."

"He also calls himself Kovak. Sometimes Ricardo. He's small, dark, with his hair slicked back. He was wearing a white suit."

"Nobody like that came to see me, but it's a big agency. We get plenty of people. Sometimes those people aren't too nice. Is he the one with the pictures?"

"Yes." I let go of the phone. He was still standing over me. I didn't look up. "I thought you might have the pictures. Because of Maritski. And because— I don't know what to say except that I'm very sorry. Of course, I'll pay you for the appointment. For your time." I fumbled with my wallet. "Will ten dollars be enough?" I laid the money

on the desk and scooped my belongings back into my bag.
I edged past him, and in a very straight line, I walked to
the front door. It wouldn't open. He had thrown the bolt. I
gave the bolt a sharp tug, but it didn't move. I gave it another one, harder, then another. My bag slipped from
under my arm and fell to the floor.

Smoothly, he picked it up and handed it back to me.
Somewhere, he had gotten rid of the gun. He slid the bolt
back easily, but he didn't open the door. "I'd say you don't
do this for a living."

"No."

"I'd say you never did this before."

"No."

"Are you all right?"

"Yes, of course."

"Are you sure? Maybe you should sit down. I usually
offer a lady a drink after I pull a gun on her."

"No, thank you."

"Mrs. Atwill, can I ask you something? Do you drive a
Lincoln? A Lincoln that followed me from Elizondo's Saturday night?"

"Yes. It's my car."

"Then it wasn't Maritski you were following yesterday.
It was me."

"Yes."

"I'd like to know why."

"I'm sorry. I can't. I'm not the only one involved."

"Look, if somebody's setting me up, I want to know."

"It's nothing like that. It was entirely my mistake.
You're not in any trouble. I give you my word. Not that it's
worth much just now."

After a second, he said, "You know I'm a private detective. That means I can hear a story and keep it to myself."

"I can't. Not yet."

Finally, he opened the door, and I went out, not swaying very much. Not so much that I fell down. Determinedly, I walked through the thick, heavy sunlight to my car. I opened the door, slid behind the wheel, and set my bag on the seat. Then I laid my head against the steering wheel and cried.

Chapter 6

It took me a couple of hours to put myself back together enough to see Helen; I wasn't about to tell her what a great detective I'd turned out to be. Especially since I wanted her to trust my judgment a while longer.

Her picture came in the afternoon mail. The printing on the envelope didn't look anything like what had been on the one that Maritski had sent me. We went upstairs to her sitting room—what some people still called a morning room. She took the envelope into the bathroom to open it. I don't know what she did with it. Tore everything into pieces and flushed it all down the toilet probably. I didn't ask.

"I guess we pay," she said hollowly when she came out.

"Helen, I know a policeman we could talk to."

"No. I can't have the police."

"Then what about a private detective? He could take them the money. It would be safer, and he might know how to make sure we get everything back. We have to think about that."

"I know," she said, low and tormented.

The call came an hour later on her private line, which only rang in the sitting room. I was standing close beside her when she picked up the phone. The voice sounded harsh and raspy, like someone snarling to prove he was tough. And maybe to disguise his voice.

"We want small bills. Old bills. Nothing bigger than a twenty. Got that?"

"I can't get that much without my husband knowing."

"You take a good picture. He might like to see how good."

"I'm not lying. I can give you three."

"This is not a goddam auction! You think your husband'd pay five thousand to keep from paying you alimony?"

I put my hand on her shoulder and nodded. "All right," she said miserably.

"That's better. You got till tomorrow afternoon. We'll call at five. Five o'clock."

He hung up.

"I can get a thousand myself," she said to me. "I'll pay you back. I will."

"Whenever you can. Please don't worry about it."

I wanted to stay with her, but I also wanted to make sure that I wouldn't have any trouble getting the money. I called my bank in Pasadena from her house and told them how much I intended to withdraw, then I went home to retrieve my bankbook from the study safe, which was concealed, not very cleverly, behind six volumes of Shakespeare in the bookcase. I hadn't gone through its contents in a long time, opening it only when I needed to get out some of my jewelry. Beneath the velvet boxes were copies of deeds to property I owned, the originals being with my lawyer. There were copies of insurance policies as well—on the property and my life—along with lists of stocks and bonds, and some emergency cash. At the back, in a long, thin envelope, I found the copy of my will. After reading it, I tried to remember what state of mind I had been in when I wrote it. And what Freud would have said about my having left it in that other safe where Franklin could find it.

Franklin and Forrest were the chief beneficiaries. Franklin got the real estate and some other investments that together were probably worth almost three million; Forrest's share was about a quarter of that. After some gifts to charity, I had left Juanita and Helen a hundred thousand each in stocks. Helen got my jewelry as well. Sometimes I forgot—or maybe had never truly been able to comprehend—just how well-off Uncle Bennett had left me.

My bankbook showed that I had enough in my savings account to cover the payoff and a bit extra in case the blackmailers tried to up the ante at the last minute.

The bank manager scurried over to make sure I was absolutely certain I wanted to withdraw such a large sum in cash. I assured him I knew what I was doing. On the way back to the car, the muscles along my spine started crawling, and I kept darting looks over my shoulder. All the way home, the doors stayed locked and the windows cracked only a couple of inches.

Sam was coming back from New York that night, so Helen asked me to call Dean from my house after he finished shooting for the day and tell him what had happened.

He said, "I'd go to my father, but we've been having some trouble about money lately."

"Do you have any idea who these men could be?"

"We can't go to the police. You know that."

"I know. But was there anything familiar about them? Or their car?"

"No. But I'll find them after this," he said fiercely, "and I'll make them pay."

I hoped his desire for vengeance—and his gun—weren't going to cause more trouble than we already had.

I waited at home the next morning to see if Maritski would call. He did, promptly, as promised, at noon. I had Juanita give him a message, which she delivered while watching me through narrowed eyes. I had been called out of town, she told him, to work on a script. He should call back Tuesday. I would talk to him then.

I wasn't sure what I was going to do about him, but I needed some time to take care of Helen first.

I doubted that he was watching the house. There was no point. But just in case, I called the Pasadena police from my study. I told them that I had seen a suspicious car cruising around the neighborhood. No, I didn't know what kind, but if they could just swing by a few times a day, I'd feel so much better. They promised they would.

I took the money out of the safe and went over to Helen's.

We pretended to eat lunch. Then we pretended to read. Finally, at five-thirty, the man called. I stood close to her, to offer support.

"You got the money?" I heard him say.

"I don't want to deliver this alone."

"You bring anybody with you, and we make a phone call. Got that?"

"I'm not going down any dark roads."

"Don't worry. It'll be nice and public. Now, wrap the money up in a nice package. Real plain. Brown paper. Got that?"

"Yes."

"Then stay by the phone. Next time I call, be ready to leave."

"When do I get the pictures back?"

"We get the money tonight, you get the pictures tomorrow. So you be a good girl." He hung up.

Sam was working late, watching early rushes from *The Final Line*. We wrapped the money and waited. During a break in his shooting, Dean called on her listed phone number, leaving the private line free for the blackmailers. I answered in the bedroom. I told him we were waiting to hear where to leave the money.

"I'm coming over," he said. "I'll find a way to get out of here. I'll handle the drop. I've got my gun."

"No. We're going to do it their way. We're going to deliver the money, then go to my house." I heard the private phone ringing in the sitting room. "You can come over there, if you want. I have to go to Helen now."

She was standing by the phone, a pad of paper in her hand. On it was an address. "I'm supposed to go to the phone booth at this corner and wait for another call. They said it might take a while."

"They have to make sure no one is following you."

"I have to go now."

I followed her as far as Pershing Square, then turned around and went home. Dean arrived about an hour later. I took him into the study and poured him a drink. His street clothes looked as if he had thrown them on. His makeup was still streaked across his face.

Helen arrived just after ten, white as a sheet. I gave her a brandy and refilled Dean's Scotch. She had left the money. She had gone to several phone booths and finally ended up in a coffee shop just after dark. They told her to go straight into the ladies' room and throw the package out the window. She didn't want to talk about it anymore.

They took their sweet time calling, of course. It was after seven the next evening, which was Friday, before she heard from them. The address, she told me over the phone, was in Venice. The pictures and negatives would be taped under the seat of a phone booth in a drugstore near the pier. "Dean's going to get them. He insisted. I gave him the address. He'll take them to his place. We can meet him there about nine. Do you mind driving out there?"

"Of course not."

It seemed to get dark very fast, so that by the time I got the car out, the daylight had been wiped away, leaving only a rind of moon and a few crumbs of early stars. As I pulled the Hudson into her drive, Helen came out. She slipped into the seat and clasped her bag tightly on her knees. "It's almost over," I said. She gave me a little smile. However, except for her navigating, it was a silent trip.

Dean lived in Laurel Canyon on the far side of Mulholland, where the canyon road began its drop into the valley, on one of the streets that washed up into the hills.

The cream-colored stucco bungalows were set close together, no more than fifteen feet apart, in what had once been a cul-de-sac but had now been sliced open by a newly bulldozed road. At its corner, a streetlamp leaned drunkenly over the pavement, the victim of a plundering truck. Beyond it, I could see faint outlines of heavy equipment and the shells of new houses.

I pulled into the empty driveway. Dean had left the porch light on for us and the lights in the living room. Helen took a key out of her bag and let us in.

The living room was stiff and modern, expensively decorated in black and cream, with a geometric pattern in the carpet. The chairs were hard and angular; the tables had splayed legs. The only real warmth came from tall golden spikes of gladioli on the table behind the sofa. I had never known a bachelor who kept flowers in his house. At least not one who dated women. Maybe one of the women Dean entertained had suggested it. And maybe paid for it.

"I need a drink," Helen said.

I dropped my gloves and bag in a chair. "I'll get it. Sit down."

"In the dining room," she said, and gestured to a set of French doors.

In the far corner of the dining room was a black glass bar cart with a skyline of liquor bottles. Sitting next to the creme de menthe were two highball glasses half-full of amber-colored liquid that had tiny, dying ice cubes floating in it. I took two snifters from the lower shelf and poured us brandies.

Quickly, we ran out of meaningless things to say, so we thumbed through magazines, listening to the ticking of the black marble clock on the mantel. We finished our drinks.

She flung the magazine away. "They didn't leave them."

"Maybe they kept him late on the set. There's probably some windbag in the phone booth." I tried not to think about Dean doing something stupid, like pulling his gun on the windbag to get him out of there.

"I have to use the bathroom," I said lightly.

"It's just through there," she said. "Watch out for the faucet. The water comes out pretty strong."

Off the dining room was a short hallway with a bathroom straight ahead and a room on either side. The door on the left was open wide enough for me to see a desk by the light in the hallway. Helen said that, the night the pictures were taken, Dean went after the gun he kept in his desk. I went in and turned on the lamp.

Silently, I opened the drawers and lifted enough paper aside to determine that Dean's gun was not there. It didn't mean that he had taken it. Maybe he had moved it into his night table. I crossed the hall and pushed open the bedroom door.

The hall light fanned gently across the carpet. The room was still. Very, very still. The windows were open, but no breeze rustled the blinds. No breath of summer air lifted the curtains.

The bed had a pale gold, tufted headboard and a coverlet of a slightly darker shade. Beside that were a night table and a lamp with a bronze statue for a base. Beside that was a chair with a gold-and-green stripe. Beside that was a body. It was lying curled on its side. The shoes were new, the soles hardly worn, the ankles, politely crossed. A stain spread from the shirtfront out onto the carpet.

I might have run, if I'd been able to. Instead, I stood there with my muscles locked, staring even though I wanted to look away. Anywhere. Even if it meant looking into the shadows where someone might be waiting, raising a gun. My insides shrunk.

In the living room, Helen switched on the radio. If she hadn't done it, I don't know how long I might have stayed there, frozen.

Haltingly, I went over and crouched at his head, well out of the blood. There was no doubt that he was dead: his eyes were open. I reached out and closed them. The skin was cold and thick.

Below the seeped pool of blood was a smeared line that

ran down below his feet. After he had been shot, he had tried to crawl away.

A dull thudding began in the back of my brain, pushing out the horror, warning me that we could not be found there. I had to get Helen out.

She glanced up from her magazine. "I thought I'd lost you."

I took our glasses to the kitchen and washed them. Holding them in a kitchen towel, I took them back to the bar cart and put them away on the lower shelf. I wiped the brandy bottle. Then I realized it would be impossible to wipe off every print she had ever left in the house without wiping away evidence. I looked at the glasses of amber-colored liquid. The ice cubes were gone. I leaned over and sniffed. It was Scotch.

"What are you doing?" Helen asked.

I went over and knelt in front of her. "Something's happened." She frowned at me, baffled. "Something terrible. Dean's been hurt. He's— He's been killed."

The frown got only a little deeper. "Dean's gone to get my pictures."

"He never went. He's in the bedroom. I just found him. He's—Helen, no!" She jumped up and pushed past me so hard that I fell over. "Wait!" I scrambled after her. She threw open the bedroom door. "Helen, don't!"

"Oh, God! Oh, dear God!"

She stumbled forward and dropped to her knees beside him. I dived for her. "Don't! You can't get blood on you!"

"Let me go! He's hurt! Can't you see he's hurt!"

She struggled, but my hands, wrapped around her wrists, were stronger.

I dropped my voice to a calm, rational intensity. Hysteria would only bring it out in her. "Helen, stop. Please.

The windows are open. Someone will hear you. There's nothing we can do."

"No!"

"I wouldn't leave him if there was anything we could do. You know I wouldn't leave him." Finally, she stopped fighting. "I'm so sorry," I said softly.

"What happened?"

"I don't know. We have to call the police. But we can't be here when they come. You know we can't. He wouldn't want that. We have to go."

After a moment, I released her and stood up. I waited quietly with my hand out to her and let her decide. There was no way I could force her to leave.

Slowly, very gently, she laid her fingers on Dean's cheek. Then she let me take her arm and guide her back into the living room. "Put on your gloves," I said. Mechanically, she obeyed. I put her bag in her arms. "Is there anything here that belongs to you? Clothes? A picture? Something with your name on it?"

"No. No, I don't think so," she said dully.

"Are you sure? Think."

"Yes, I'm sure. We're always careful."

I put on my gloves and switched off the radio. I put the magazines back where we found them. I took her arm and steered her out to the car.

I pulled halfway down the street before I turned on the headlights. "Do you own a gun?"

"What?"

"I just want to make sure someone didn't steal your gun. To blame you or Sam for this. Do you own a gun?"

"Sam does."

"What kind?"

"What do you mean?"

"An automatic? A revolver? Does it have a cylinder for the bullets?"

"I think so. A cylinder?"

Shock was setting in.

Fortunately, Juanita had gone to bed. Upstairs, I went into my bathroom and, using a nailbrush, washed my hands thoroughly, then I got a couple of tranquilizers out of the medicine cabinet and filled a glass with water.

Helen was sitting on my bed, still in her hat. She took the pills without question.

"Are we going to call the police?"

"In a minute. Anonymously."

"Did the blackmailers do this?"

"I don't know."

There was nothing more I could say. I kept seeing those untouched glasses on the bar cart and the dying ice cubes. If they melted away in the half hour or so that we were in Dean's house, the drinks could not have been there for very long before we arrived. Dean had poured drinks, had entertained someone when he was supposed to be in Venice. It almost certainly meant he had poured a drink for his killer. Did it also mean he knew there were no pictures in that drugstore in Venice?

Winslow looked a little surprised to see me, almost as if he hadn't expected me to keep my appointment. I sat down in one of the chairs opposite his desk, gripping the Manila envelope. The secretary went out and closed the office door.

"Thank you for seeing me so quickly. And on a Saturday," I said.

Winslow sat down and leaned back in his chair. "I take it you haven't found your pictures."

"No."

He waited. I didn't say anything. "It is blackmail, isn't it?" he asked finally.

"Yes."

"Have you paid them?"

"No."

"Do you want me to do it for you?"

"No."

"Do you want me to try to get the pictures back? You know, you might have to give me some help here."

"I could be in trouble," I said. "A man's been killed."

"Did you kill him?"

"Of course not," I said indignantly.

"Good. Do you mind if I smoke?"

"What?"

"Do you mind if I smoke?"

"No."

He opened a small hammered-silver box on the desk and took out a cigarette. He turned the box to me; I shook my head. He said, "I think this would go faster if you did some of the talking." There was a pocket lighter next to his ashtray; he lit the cigarette and sat back again. "Just start at the beginning."

I did. I told him about being attacked and about thinking I had only been robbed. He listened, the smallest of frowns between his brows. I told him about how Maritski had approached me. "I was in Madison's bar with Kim Wagner. The actress. I'm a writer. I'm working on a movie at Marathon."

"I know."

"You do?"

"You worked there for twelve years. You left eighteen months ago when you and your husband, Frank Atwill, separated. You were born in L.A. in 1910. Mabel Lauren Tanner. Your father was a professor at UCLA, respected but not rich. Your maternal uncle was Bennett Lauren, who *was* rich and left you plenty when he died. But it doesn't seem to have spoiled you too much since you went to work and you do your own breaking and entering."

"Mr. Winslow, I think you're showing off."

He laughed. It was a good laugh. I liked it.

"Did you talk to Sergeant Barty?" I asked.

"I didn't get that from him."

"No. But did you talk to him about my robbery?"

"Phil would ask too many questions. I found out about your case from someone else. I was curious."

"I can imagine." I finished telling him about what happened at Madison's, then I took the Central Casting picture of Maritski out of my bag and gave it to him. I told him where I'd found it. "He doesn't wear the moustache anymore, but otherwise, he looks about the same."

"He didn't leave a name when he was here, but one of our men remembered him from your description. He was looking for protection, someone to go with him when he picked up a package. It didn't sound too legal. Our man told him our fee—and that we'd have to have it up front. He never came back."

"When I saw him come in here . . ."

"With the courthouse and the law offices around here, there must be a dozen agencies within a few blocks. He was probably making the rounds. Taking a look at what he could hire and for how much. Mrs. Atwill, under the circumstances, I think you should tell me why you were following me."

"Yes." I took an audible gulp. "When I saw you at Elizondo's, I thought you were the man in the picture."

He stared at me.

"I thought it was you."

"Why?"

"It looked like you."

"Can I see it?"

I stared back at him.

"May I see the picture?"

There was a sick dread in my stomach, and a tiny of sweat broke out along my hairline. "I know you have to," I said, but I couldn't bring myself to hand over the envelope.

He stood up and opened a cabinet in the bookcase. He took out a decanter and a glass and poured out about an inch. "Here. Drink this."

The brandy sheathed my nerves a little.

"I've been in this business a long time," he said. "Long enough not to be shocked anymore."

"It wasn't *your* feelings I was thinking about."

He laughed. It was as good as the last time, and it made me feel better. I gave him the envelope: it was damp and wrinkled where I'd been gripping it. He sat down and opened it. Out of the tops of my eyes, I watched him. There was a momentary frown, but that was all, then he put the picture back inside. I was glad he didn't whip out a magnifying glass and examine it for clues with me sitting there.

"Is this the only one you have?" he asked.

"Yes."

"Then why did you think it was me? You can't see this man's face."

I took another sip of the brandy. "After the attack, I had a dream. I thought it was only a dream. When I saw the pictures, I realized what had caused it. The man had a face something like yours, and when I saw you, I felt . . . I don't know why. My friend Helen thought she'd seen you at the club before. I guess I had, too, and maybe I substituted your face. I can't explain why I thought it was you."

"This man has a scar."

"Yes. On his left shoulder blade."

"I don't."

"I know it's not you."

"Phil Barty's word must carry a lot of weight."

"It wasn't only that. Now that I've had a chance to think about it, it's all wrong. If you wanted to blackmail someone, you'd know plenty of people who'd have to pay up. You wouldn't need to take phony pictures. And you wouldn't meet Maritski here, where your boss might ask questions."

"No, but it's interesting that you came to me, considering."

"Sergeant Barty said you were good. And I knew there were people here who'd seen Maritski."

"Unfortunately, he didn't leave an address."

"He used to live on Hope, but he's gone now."

"So it was *that* Kovak."

"I'm sorry?"

"You told me the names he'd been using. I did look them all up in the phone book, even though I figured they were all phonies. You've been busy. What else have you been up to?"

I told him about my other feeble attempts at investigation. He took some notes. I gave him the cigarette butt I'd found near Elizondo's.

"It probably doesn't mean anything," I said.

"It might. It's an odd place to find cigarettes. No lipstick. We can probably find out what brand this is." He held up what was left of his cigarette for inspection. "Mine are Chesterfields." I didn't mention that I already knew that from finding the pack in his house.

"Tell me about the dead man," he said.

I told him about Dean and Helen and everything else I could remember that had happened in the two weeks since Maritski had confronted me in Madison's. He took more notes. Then I told him about finding the body and finding the glasses on the bar cart.

"Do the glasses prove anything?" I asked.

"They prove he was pouring drinks when he should have been in Venice."

"Before I came here this morning, I drove out to the drugstore. It has a phone booth, but there weren't any pictures under the seat."

Winslow reached into his wastepaper can and retrieved his newspaper. There was a studio picture of Dean on the front page under the headline: ACTOR FOUND MURDERED. He scanned the story.

"Not much here. Does your friend own a gun?"

"Sam does. Her husband. But I think it's a revolver, and chances are the gun that killed Dean was an automatic."

"Did you find casings?"

"No, but the houses on that street are close together, all with their windows open on a summer night. No one heard a gunshot. You can't use a silencer on a revolver."

"You can, but it wouldn't do much good. You know a lot about guns?"

"My uncle was a collector. Do you think my blackmailers and Helen's are the same? They both wore hoods."

"There could be two gangs at work. This town's got plenty of secrets and plenty of people willing to take advantage of them. Right now, nothing about your bunch and hers looks the same, except the hoods. Her bunch makes contact over the phone. Your bunch is hard to figure out. The guy who grabbed you wears a mask, but Maritski shows you his face. He's got partners. But he comes to us looking for protection for the payoff. That doesn't make sense."

"Nothing about blackmailing me makes much sense. They must have been after any woman who left the club alone."

He shook his head. "Next to kidnapping, blackmail's the most dangerous game a guy can play because he has to go get the money. If you don't pick the right victim, you might as well make an appointment with the cops."

"They can't have been after me."

"Who would profit from pictures like this?"

"No one."

"Maritski threatened to show them to your husband. Would your husband think he could use them to force you into a divorce?"

"Of course not."

"Does he want a divorce?"

"We talked about it, yes."

"And what did you tell him?"

"I said yes. Well, I did tell him I wouldn't be the guilty party. He asked me to go away so he could use desertion. But Franklin would never do something like this. Besides, he didn't even ask me about the divorce until after the attack. He didn't know I was going to be stubborn."

"Or maybe he did. When did Maritski show you the pictures? Before or after you told your husband you wouldn't do it his way?"

"After. It doesn't matter. Those pictures are not going to make me do anything I don't want to do."

"That's not what I'm asking, Mrs. Atwill. I want to know if there's someone who might *think* they could use them."

"Franklin would never do something like this to me."

"Is there another woman? Someone he wants to marry?"

"Yes. Alex Harris. Ronald Harris's daughter."

"The Ronald Harris who owns half the county?"

"Yes. But I don't think the pictures would be of any use to her. I've already said I'd divorce him. Her parents are conservative, but it's not as if they'd threatened to disinherit her if Franklin had to be the guilty party. He would have told me if that were the case. Besides, she has a fortune in her own right."

"You can't see enough of this man to tell who he is, except for the scar. You're sure this man wasn't meant to look like someone you've been seeing? Someone you've . . ."

"No."

He looked at me.

"No, Mr. Winslow. There isn't anyone. There hasn't been anyone since my husband and I separated." In spite of myself, a flush crept over my face.

"It's nothing to be ashamed of."

"I know."

For a moment, we were just looking at each other. My flush got deeper.

He said, "What about a personal grudge? Someone who might enjoy scaring you?"

"There might be people who don't like me, but no one who'd go this far. They weren't after me."

"It doesn't look like it. But it's hard to believe they were after just any woman who came down that road." He sat for a few moments, frowning at the envelope, then he said, "Do you know where Cummings was the night you were attacked?"

"He said he had that summer flu that's going around."

"We can check that. Did you leave his house the way you found it?"

"Yes. Helen says there's nothing there that can be traced to her, but I don't know."

"Any signs of a struggle?"

"No. And no signs of a search. If Dean were part of the gang blackmailing Helen, wouldn't they have searched for anything he had that would implicate them?"

"If the killing was planned, they'd have already made sure he didn't have anything on them."

"Mr. Winslow, I have to ask you— Maybe I should have asked you before—"

"Have I ever investigated a murder?"

"Have you?"

"I don't spend all my time creeping around under bedroom windows."

"I know that."

"Most people think we don't know how to do anything else."

"When Sergeant Barty said you were good, he didn't mean at that."

"Sometimes I find embezzlers for companies who don't want to attract public attention. Sometimes I run checks for investors so they know some guy's clean before they give him a few million for a land deal. Sometimes I work for defense lawyers. Find witnesses. Check alibis. Do the work the cops won't do when they think they've got a case. They don't always care too much about the guy who's sitting in jail swearing he's innocent."

"And some of those men were accused of murder?"

"A few."

"Can you find out who did this?"

"I'd say the cops have a better chance. They have the body, the evidence, and the muscle to make people talk."

"That's encouraging."

"It's the truth. But if you want me to take this, here's what I can do. I can find out what Cummings's friends and coworkers know. I can send someone over to Maritski's old apartment to start tracing him. I can check with other private investigators, see if he tried to hire any of them, see if we can get a lead on where he is. If we find him, we can find out if your blackmailers and Mrs. Ross's are the same. If they are, I can try to get both sets of pictures back and find out who Maritski's boss is. Maybe— maybe—if I do all that, I can find out who killed Cummings. But you should know right now that it won't be cheap. We have to move fast and cover a lot of ground. That means men. With expenses, it's going to run you over a hundred a day."

"Would a thousand be enough retainer?"

His brows lifted a little. "That'll be fine. I'm going to have to talk to Mrs. Ross—the sooner, the better."

"If her husband finds out—"

"There are plenty of places we can talk without worrying about him. And when you see her, try to get a look at that gun."

"I will."

"Mrs. Atwill, there's something we should get straight. There's no such thing as client confidentiality for private investigators."

"Meaning that you're supposed to tell the police everything I just told you?"

"You've hired me to look into an attempted blackmail. And you have knowledge of another one that might be connected. You found a dead man. You called the police. You didn't disturb the evidence."

"But I have information the police would want. Can you get into trouble?"

He smiled. "It's not often I get a client who worries about me. If I was Philip Marlowe, working out of a couple of cheap rooms, maybe. But Ed Paxton's got lawyers with muscle, and he knows plenty of the right people. And a few of their secrets. This wouldn't be the first time we've kept something from the cops. But I want you to understand that, if I find out who killed Cummings, I will go to the cops. No matter who it is."

"I understand."

"If the cops come to see you, and it looks like they know something, call your lawyer. You're a loyal friend, but don't get yourself into trouble you can't get out of."

"I won't."

"From now on, I want you to keep an eye out. When you go anywhere, cut through a few alleys."

"I have been." I told him what I'd been doing and that, so far, I had only seen one car that could possibly be suspicious.

"Keep it up. If you spot anyone, I want to know right away."

"Yes."

"But spotting a tail is as far as I want you to go. No more detective work. It's my job now. And from now on, don't tell anyone anything I tell you about this case."

"What about Helen?"

"You're my client, not Mrs. Ross. And this is murder. Whatever we get, we keep to ourselves. That's the way it has to be. We don't want the cops or the killers to find out what we're up to by accident."

I nodded.

"I want you to stay home as much as you can. We have to hope Maritski calls again. If he does, tell him you'll pay. Then let him set up a drop. That's all you do."

"All right."

"Good." He smiled at me briefly. "You said that Mrs Ross has seen me before at Elizondo's."

"Yes."

"How are you going to explain hiring me?"

"I told her that, when I saw you last week, I thought you looked interesting, so on my way out, I asked one of the staff what you did for a living. Then, when I thought we might need help delivering the payoff, I checked you out with Sergeant Barty. She has no idea that I thought it was you in the pictures. Or that I broke into your house."

"Does she know you can pick locks?"

I laughed. "No."

"Where did you learn to do that?"

"Research. For the first Phil Marsh movie. But the studio thought it was a bad idea to show people how to do it correctly. They just give all the detectives skeleton keys."

"Wish I knew where to find one of those. Where did you get the picks?"

"From the locksmith I interviewed. He was retired, and he gave me a set as a present. As a joke, really. I might use them in the book I'm writing. It's a mystery."

"Is there a surly detective in it?"

"I don't think you're surly."

"And you don't think that's me in your pictures."

"No."

"You sure?"

"Of course," I said, but there must have been something in my eyes.

"I think we'd both feel better if you were." He stood up. He took off his jacket and loosened his tie.

"Mr. Winslow, I—"

"Don't worry. I'm not going to embarrass either one of us more than necessary."

I didn't tell him to stop. He was right. I wanted to be sure. I sat there. My hands and face got very hot. He took off the tie and began to unbutton his shirt. He fumbled with the third button. And the fourth.

"This is— This is—" I stammered.

"It's all right," he said softly.

He slid the shirt back. It was a very nice chest, a very nice shoulder. The very nice shoulder didn't have any scars on it.

"I'm sorry," I said.

"Well, now you know." He rebuttoned his shirt, sat down, and got a contract out of his desk.

Chapter 7

There were no police cars in Helen's driveway.

She was upstairs in her sitting room, still in her dressing gown, an untouched breakfast tray beside her. "Sam's in the study. He didn't go in. He always goes in on Saturdays when he has a movie shooting. Do you think he knows?"

"He couldn't possibly."

"I told him I thought I was coming down with the flu. To help explain the red eyes. What did the detective say? Do you think he can help?"

"It won't hurt to have him in our corner." I told her about Winslow's wanting to see her. "He knows some places where we won't be seen."

"I can't go today. Sam thinks I'm sick."

"Pretend to go to the doctor."

"He already called the doctor. He's coming over later."

"Then we'll have to work something out for tomorrow."

"Tomorrow's the party."

"I forgot."

"Could he come with you?"

"I guess nobody who's coming would know him. I hope."

"I'll tell Sam he works in insurance. He's someone you met at Elizondo's."

We found Sam's gun in the top drawer of the chest in his dressing room. It was a revolver, a Webley .320. I remembered it was a top break, but I forgot about the automatic ejector. When I broke it open, the bullets tumbled out into the drawer. Meekly, I fished them out of the handkerchiefs. Before I reloaded the gun, I looked down the barrel. It was immaculate. I didn't think the killer would have cleaned it. Unless the killer was Sam.

There were no police cars in my driveway either.

But there was a black Buick, polished to gleaming, sitting in the curve that ran in front of the house. I didn't recognize it.

There was no one waiting in the living room.

Back in the kitchen, Juanita was examining a sorry-looking hen, shaking her head forlornly. Sitting at the table was a young Negro man in a chauffeur's uniform, finishing coffee and a piece of her famous cherry cobbler. He stood up sharply when I came in.

"Mrs. Atwill," he said, with a crispness that sounded former military.

"Yes."

"A delivery, ma'am. From Cartier's." He handed me a package about nine by five, wrapped in thick, cream-colored paper and gold ribbon. In his other hand, he held a leather-bound notebook opened to a receipt that did indeed have Cartier's across the top. "Would you sign here, please?" He offered me a black-enameled fountain pen.

I signed. I reached into my bag and gave him a dollar. "Thank you."

"Thank you, ma'am." He thanked Juanita as well, and tucked his hat under his arm. She showed him out.

I took the package into the study and unwrapped it.

Inside the paper was a small square vellum envelope. I opened it and took out the card.

Allow me to say once again how sorry I am.
                                    R. Elizondo

I lifted the lid.

It was gorgeous. Of course. It was Cartier's. And it had been selected with a sure eye for simplicity and perfection. Lying on the thick velvet was a narrow line of diamonds dropping to, and encircling, a square-cut emerald pendant.

It was not the necklace I had lost. Nor was it a copy. But it would have done. Very nicely.

If I could have kept it.

I called Winslow to tell him about my meeting with Helen, but he was out. I waited through the afternoon in case Maritski called. He didn't. But then, I was supposed to be out of town until Tuesday.

I had no idea what time Elizondo arrived at his club. Helen always made the reservations, so I didn't have the unlisted phone number to call and find out. I didn't want to call Helen and have to explain why I wanted it. I waited until seven and drove out to Topanga Canyon. Before I left, I told Juanita that, if Maritski called, to tell him I'd be back before nine. And if a Mr. Winslow called, to tell him the same thing.

The attendants at Elizondo's gave me surreptitious once-overs when I got out of the Hudson in my blue suit, but I gave one of them a dollar to keep the car handy.

I asked the redhead at the coat check where I could find Mr. Elizondo. She stared at me as if she had never been asked such a difficult question.

I went upstairs and asked the man guarding the casino. He nodded toward the door at the end of the hallway. I half expected him to tell me I couldn't go back there, but he didn't.

I knocked on the door. When it opened, George Scarano filled up the frame.

"Excuse me," I said. "I'd like to see Mr. Elizondo for a minute." He stepped back to let me in.

The room did a good job of looking like something from an exclusive men's club: mahogany paneling, worn leather sofas and chairs, and overlapping Turkish carpets. At the far end, beyond the bar, was a round, felt-topped table where a high-stakes private poker game could be played. The room was immaculate, and all the windows were open, but the air still hinted of the cigar smoke that had soaked into every surface.

On the other side of the room, George knocked on a door and went in. Almost immediately, the door reopened, and he ushered me inside.

Ramon Elizondo was standing beside his desk, in his perfect evening clothes, pulsing male potency.

George went out and closed the door.

"I've come to return the necklace," I said. "It's beautiful, and I thank you for wanting to replace mine. But I can't keep it."

"No," he said quietly, and took the box from me.

I regarded him steadily. "I don't think you expected me to keep it."

"I would like you to. However, if you were the sort of woman who would, I probably wouldn't have wanted to give it to you."

"I thank you for that as well."

He smiled. His eyes got darker. "Might I offer you

something since you've had to come all this way? A brandy perhaps? Or some cognac?"

"Thank you, but I have an appointment."

"I understand." Still, he took a while before he crossed the room and opened the door. "Have you heard anything from the police? Do they have any leads in your robbery?"

"I think you'd know more about that than I would."

He laughed. "May I walk you to the stairs?"

"I think my reputation can stand it."

He did not go all the way to the top, however, but left me with a handshake and a final smile while we were still out of sight of the patrons in the foyer below.

One of them was Forrest Barlowe.

He was standing at the top of the passage that led to the ladies' lounge, glancing down it, a cigarette in his hand. I came up behind him, and said, "How long can it possibly take a woman to put on a little lipstick?"

"Lauren!" he exclaimed happily. He crushed his cigarette in the chrome stand nearby and took both my hands. He smiled warmly down at me and gave me a light kiss on the cheek. He glanced back down the hallway after he did it. I couldn't decide how I felt about that.

"Who is she?" I asked.

"Maude Townsend."

"Hmm," I said. Mrs. Frederick Townsend was a very well preserved society lady, dedicated to spending the fortunes her husband and her father had left her on charity and an art collection that made museums genuflect.

"A bit out of my league, I think," he said.

"Not if she's interested in class, charm, and sex appeal." He flushed.

Before he could say anything, a voice behind me called out, very loudly, "I know you! I know you!"

B. J. Camlic, whom I had last seen a week ago, the night I'd followed Winslow, was rounding the end of the staircase, a bit unsteadily, pointing at Forrest with blurry certainty. Her husband Art was trying to take her elbow. She pulled it away and kept pointing.

"I *know* you!"

"Forrest Barlowe," I supplied, and introduced them.

"No," she insisted adamantly, waving a dismissive hand at me. "You're . . . You're that guy."

"Yes," I said, "he's—"

"The guy in that movie. What's your name?"

"Ellison," Forrest said graciously. "Ambassador Ellison. How do you do, madam?"

"Ooh," she simpered. "I loved you."

"Huh?" Art said, incisively.

I said, "Forrest starred in a very popular movie with Shirley Temple a few years ago. *The Little Ambassador.*"

B. J. sighed, almost as loud as she talked. "What a shame she doesn't make movies anymore."

"She does," Forrest said. "She's just older now."

"I loved her."

"We all did."

I took Forrest's arm. "I'm sorry to drag him away, but we're meeting friends in the bar." After a hurried good night, I steered him away. Art and B. J. disappeared into the dining room.

"I don't know how you stand that," I said.

"I don't mind. It's not like with Frank, where women get so excited they might hurt him. Won't you stay and have a drink with us?"

"Thanks, but I have to be somewhere."

I didn't think it would be a good idea for me to have drinks with him and his new love. He didn't either, but he was a gentleman. I kissed him on the cheek and went home.

Winslow called back about nine.

He said, "One of our contacts at the studio gave me the names of the cast and crew working on Cummings's movie. They've shut down production for a few days, so we made some calls and caught them at home."

"Pretending to be the police?"

"Don't ask too many questions. Cummings left the studio about seven last night. Earlier, after lunch, one of the assistants went to call him back to the set. Just as she started to knock on his dressing room door, she heard him yelling. At first, she thought he was rehearsing a scene from another movie because it sounded like movie dialogue. No offense. He was saying something about a letter. How he had put it in a safe place. She knocked and stuck her head in. He was on the phone and looked angry, so she told him he was wanted on the set and ducked back out. She didn't hear anything else."

"Has she told all this to the real police?"

"They haven't talked to her yet. It looks like he couldn't have been in on your attack—at least not in person. He was too sick to get out of bed. His maid says he was so sick the doctor almost put him in the hospital. He had a private duty nurse that night.

"The cops are telling reporters he was shot once in the chest. A .380. Probably a Remington automatic. You were right about that. He wasn't shot with his own gun. That was a .32, Smith & Wesson. They found it in the bedroom."

"It couldn't have been Sam's gun, either," I said. "I saw it this afternoon. It's a Webley revolver. A .320."

"The coroner's report will be out Monday. It probably

won't tell us much more. We called a few of the neighbors. One of them remembered seeing a car in his driveway about nine-thirty. Must have been yours. But he couldn't remember anything about it. Cumming's car was in the garage. Nobody remembers seeing any other cars near his house, but the killer could have easily parked somewhere else and come up through the backyard in the dark."

"What about the letter Dean mentioned?"

"I'd say they've already found it. But not in his house. He never would have hidden it there. Tomorrow morning, I'm sending a man over to Hope Street to start asking questions at Maritski's apartment house. We'll have a better chance of finding them home on a Sunday morning. We got the make and license number of his car, '38 Chevy, registered under Paul Kovak. He doesn't sound like a guy with much cash, so if he's still in town, he's holed up in a cheap hotel or rooming house. He has to park his car. We know where the cheapest lots are. We'll check them out, drop a couple of bucks on the attendants to keep an eye out for the license plate. We'll start downtown and move out. Funny thing about people who go into hiding, people who've never done it before. They pick places where they're comfortable. He might not have gone too far away."

I told him about Helen's party. "I'll have to start calling you by your first name. Do you prefer Pete or Peter?"

"Peter."

"Me, too. I met you at Elizondo's. You're in insurance."

"Did you come up with that?"

"No."

"I didn't think so. Who else is going to be there?"

"Why?"

"I don't want to run into any former clients."

"Or former victims."

"That, too."

The maid showed us out to the terrace, which was not quite as big as Nebraska. From there, the lawn sloped to the pool, the cabanas, and—behind a row of palms and rhododendron—the tennis courts.

Most of the guests were already there—at least a hundred people—separated into casual groups at the bar, the wrought-iron tables, or the clusters of lawn chairs. From what I could see, Sam's best efforts were for nothing. The crew, the designers, and the actors had segregated themselves nicely.

Helen came over to greet us, wearing bright orange, her hair pulled back with a matching scarf. There was a brittle cheerfulness about her that stung my heart.

She took us over to the far end of the pool, where Sam was standing under a green-striped canopy, sporting a long apron and busily rearranging the steaks that the cooks had just carefully laid out on waxed paper.

"Great to meet you, Pete. Make yourself at home. We've got rackets if you want to try some tennis and some extra suits if you want to swim."

Peter thanked him and, the perfect guest, congratulated him on his most recent picture. He was impeccably dressed, too, in well-tailored tan slacks and a teal blue shirt, neither one of which I had seen in his closet.

Sam said, "We'll have to fix you up for the premiere of this one. Lauren's done a great job on the script. Why don't you get yourselves some drinks? Need anything else, just let someone know."

There was plenty of activity around the bar, which had

been set up under another canopy not far from the barbecue. Embarrassed stagehands were getting fancy, brightly colored drinks for their wives.

We moved on past them and strolled around the pool. I said hello to the actors and crew whom I knew. No one shouted that Peter was the cheap private eye who had ruined his life.

Don Deegan was sitting alone, stretched out on a lounge chair on the far side, a large drink in his hand. "Hey there, honey," he hailed loudly without getting up. "Come on over here."

I made the introductions. Don squinted up at Peter. "Dammit, Laurie, when're you gonna give up these pretty boys an' find yourself a man with some character? I've got an idea. This party's duller'n shit. Wha'd' you say we fight over her? Might liven things up." He set his glass down hard on the small table beside him. "I mean it. I was Golden Gloves champ in school. Thirty-two and three. Bet I can still beat the shit out of a pretty boy. Wha'd' you say?"

"I'm afraid not," Peter said gravely. "I can't afford to bruise my face."

A smile sneaked across Don's lips, and he chuckled dryly. "This one's not bad. Not too bad. Wha'did you say his name was?" I told him. "Well, dammit, sit down."

As we sat, I glanced across the pool. Franklin and Alex were coming down the lawn toward us. He was resplendent in crisp white. She was wearing a simple blue linen dress with her hair lying on her shoulders. She looked about eighteen.

I have to admit that I took some pleasure in the expression on Franklin's face when he realized Peter was with me. And I thought Peter took full advantage of the moment, although I wasn't sure why, taking some time to rise to his full height, which was a good five inches more than Franklin's. I heard Don chortling behind me.

Peter turned to Alex and, for all his posturing with Franklin, he greeted her gently, seeming to sense her nervousness. Her face hardly quivered at all. He had great technique with women. How smoothly he had coaxed my picture from me. Then, suddenly, I remembered his fumbling with his buttons, and I remembered his chest, and I began to concentrate very hard on the toes of my sandals.

"You work for one of the studios?" Franklin was asking.

"I'm in insurance."

"You sell insurance?"

"My family owns a small underwriting firm."

Franklin said, "Oh."

"We haven't said hello to Helen yet," Alex ventured softly.

"Yes, must say hello to our hostess." He didn't say it had been nice to meet Peter, but Peter didn't say it had been nice to meet him, either.

There was a moment of silence as they moved off, then Peter turned to me. "Can I get you a drink, Lauren?" It was the first time he'd used my first name, and I stared at him stupidly. "A drink?" he repeated.

"Uh, just some lemonade."

"Anything for you?" he asked Don. "What are you drinking?"

"Scotch. Think I'll come along. Gotta make a trip indoors, anyway." They went off together, talking companionably.

I sat down and rolled my lips around a little to suppress the smile. *My family owns a small underwriting firm.*

Water splashed up onto the edge of the pool, and Kim

Wagner, her hair tucked under a bathing cap, surfaced and dragged herself up. "Hi," she said cheerfully.

"I didn't know you were here yet. Come sit down."

She took off the cap and shook out her platinum hair. She sat down beside me, dripping and breathless. "I did thirty laps. Good news: I've lost five pounds since we started shooting. Of course, most of it's in my tits. So, who's your friend?" I told her the lie. "Well, it's about time, kiddo."

"How's the shoot going?"

"Great. Don let me bring my agent in to see some rushes. I told him to get off his ass and get me out of the bimbo roles, or he'd get his walking papers."

"Whew!"

She laughed. "Yeah, I'm one tough cookie. Don't look now, but Frank keeps shooting glances over this way. Good for you. Give him some of his own back." She lifted her hair and lay back in the chair. After a moment, she said, "I guess everybody's talking about Dean Cummings."

"Yes, I guess so."

"That stupid kid," she said with sad vehemence. "I never thought he'd get into any real trouble. It'll probably turn out to be somebody's husband."

"Is that what everybody's saying?"

"I guess. Of course, he liked to gamble, too, and always had plenty of zip powder for anybody who wanted it, so maybe he owed the wrong people. I don't know. I always liked Dean. He—" She stopped, her eyes directed across the pool. "Oh, shit," she said with feeling. "Just shit."

"What? What is it?" I followed her stare.

Joan Trent, Forrest Barlowe's ex-wife, was just leaving the terrace, taking the last step very carefully. She leaned on the arm of her companion, a small, diffident man with a moustache and an ascot: Newlin Gardner, called Newly, her longtime writing partner. They started down the lawn.

"She's snockered," Kim said. "Christ, it isn't even six o'clock yet."

I could not escape. Newly tried to stop her, but she slung his hand off and headed straight for me.

"Well, well, Lauren Atwill!" she said with cheerful venom. Newly hurried up and hovered at her elbow.

"Hello, Joan," I said.

Her short silver hair was brushed back from her face, and she was wearing hardly any makeup. The bones were still good, but the skin was thick and coarse from too much sun, smoke, and booze. "There's not a damn thing to do in this town on Sunday, so we decided to drop by. How's the script going?"

"It's finished. I had a lot to work with."

"Aren't you sweet? If I put anything of mine in your hands, I know you'll take good care of it."

"Lauren," Kim announced loudly, "I'm going to the little girls' room. Want to come along?"

"Yes. Yes, I would. Excuse me," I said, and hurried away with her.

"This'll be a fun night," Kim said. "She always gets a real mouth on her when she's had a few. I think I'll go get into some armor. Watch your back." Shaking her head, she went off toward the cabanas.

When I reached the canopy, Peter materialized with my lemonade. "Who's that woman? She doesn't seem to like you very much."

"Joan Trent. She wrote the original script." I told him what Kim had said about Dean, the cocaine, and the gambling.

"Keep your ears open. I'm going to talk to Mrs. Ross now," he said. "I'll have to tell her what we found out about Cummings, so don't wander off in case she needs you later." He shouldered his way through the knot of people who had gathered around the grill to offer unsolicited cooking advice. In another minute, I saw him go off with Helen toward the tennis courts, quite open and innocent. Nevertheless, when Sam looked up and saw them, there was a momentary twitch of the muscle along his jaw. Then, just as quickly, he was ordering the cooks around again.

"All right!" he boomed. "Who wants their steak rare?"

After dinner, Helen, looking drained, pleaded her recent bout with the flu and went to her room. Kim and I wandered down to the courts, took off our shoes, and lobbed the ball back and forth—and more often into the net—until dusk, then strolled back between the high borders of rhododendron, congratulating ourselves that our games had not improved one iota since we had each last played.

Halfway up the path, we met Franklin, waiting beneath a palm, smoking, one hand in his trouser pocket. "Could I talk to you for a moment?" he asked me. He dropped his cigarette and crushed it methodically underfoot.

"Of course."

Kim turned to me, crossed her eyes, and scampered away into the settling darkness.

"So, how long have you been seeing this Winslow?"

"Not long."

"Where did you meet him?"

"At Elizondo's."

"Gambling with the family money?"

"He doesn't gamble."

"Then what was he doing at Elizondo's?"

"Having dinner."

"You seem to go out there a lot."

"What does that mean?" I tried to get around him, but he barred the way.

"Wait! I'm sorry. Look, don't go. I didn't mean it like that. It's only because I care what happens to you."

"It's a little late for that."

"Don't be angry. Can't you see I'm jealous?"

"Franklin, don't."

"I miss you."

"Which is no doubt why you asked for a divorce."

"If I wanted one, I'd have got it by now."

"Stop it, Franklin."

"Couldn't we talk? Please."

"Stop it! Wasn't breaking my heart once enough for you? You see me with another man, and, suddenly, you can't decide if you want a divorce? Wasn't once enough?"

I pushed past him and ran up the path, my face hot. I hated myself for still caring, for still wanting him. Ahead, in the lights by the pool, I saw Peter sitting with a group of people. He saw me and stood up. I went straight to him.

I was immediately sorry.

Joan was sitting with her back to me. When I came up beside Peter, she turned and smiled broadly. "How nice of you to join us. Is something the matter?"

"No, of course not," I said, more sharply than I meant, angered at being so transparent to her.

"We've been talking about poor Dean Cummings," she said, and arched a brow at me.

"Have you?"

"Miss Trent thinks it might have been communists,"

Peter said, with a degree of seriousness that I found disturbing. I hoped he was only working.

"Get it right, loverboy," she said. "I said that's what I heard."

"This is great stuff," said one of the actors eagerly. "Go on."

"Well, Dean's father runs one of those groups that're making lists of the commies out here. Sometime while he and his wife were out of town last week, somebody broke into their house. When they came back today, after they heard about Dean, they found the safe was empty. That's where the lists were. Grant Cummings told the police he thinks it was a revenge killing."

I didn't say that didn't make much sense. Everyone else seemed to think it was fascinating.

Except for Don, who had wandered up behind us.

"That's a crock o' shit," he said.

"The police don't think so."

"Then they're full o' shit."

"For Christ's sake, Don, keep your mouth shut for once. Everybody knows you're a goddam Red."

"That's not funny, Joan."

"It sure as hell isn't. Your name'd be right at the top."

"Go on," the actor prompted her, breathlessly. "What else have you heard?"

"Dean spent a lot of time out at Elizondo's. That guy's slick, but I bet nobody ever welshed on him. He doesn't keep that Georgie-boy around for his looks."

I said, "Gamblers don't usually shoot people who owe them money. It's hard to collect from a corpse."

"Know a lot about gamblers, do you?" she asked with an acid smile. "Oh, but I forgot, you do. How'd you like the necklace? I heard Mr. E gave you one worth about ten grand. Have the police talked to you yet? I heard you and Helen were out there with Dean just last week."

"You hear a lot."

She looked back and forth between Peter and me, and said with mock concern, "I'm not speaking out of turn, am I?"

I said, "Do you usually wait your turn?"

"What?"

"I hope you'll take this in the spirit it was intended. You're a crude, petty woman who shouldn't drink so much."

"You little shit!"

"And never at a loss for words."

"You goddam shit!"

Peter took my elbow and drew me away. "Let's go. Now."

Joan tried to get up, but her sandal slipped in the grass, and she sat back down hard. We started up the lawn.

"You shit!"

A glass and a stream of liquid flew past my shoulder.

"Hey, loverboy!" she shouted. "You want to hear some good words?"

Newly was saying, "Joan. Now, Joan," very uncomfortably.

"Hey, you want to hear some good words? Ask her about fucking my husband!"

Peter's hand tightened on my arm.

"Ask her about fucking my husband!"

He supported me until we got into the house, but as soon as we were inside, he let me go. I couldn't look at him.

I shrugged. I tried to. "I should know better with drunks after all these years. I guess we should go."

"I guess so."

"I'd like to say good-bye to Helen."

"I'll wait here."

I went upstairs and found Helen lying on her bed, wrapped in her dressing gown and covered with an afghan. She had taken off her makeup.

"The windows are open," she said. "I heard Joan screeching. I'm so sorry."

"It's not your fault."

"What set her off?" I told her. "You said that? Good for you." She smiled wanly. "I like your Mr. Winslow."

"So do I."

"Oh?"

"But I think he likes his women a little cheap."

"What makes you think so?"

"I'll tell you sometime. Are you feeling better?"

"He told me what he found out about Dean."

"It means he wasn't part of what happened to you. It means he wanted out."

She struggled with some tears. I held her hand.

"Mr. Winslow says I have to put on a brave face. For the police. And Sam."

"We'll get though this. I promise. Try to rest."

"Yes. I think I'd rather be alone, if you don't mind."

"Of course. Get some sleep. I'll call you tomorrow."

"I'm sorry about Joan."

"Don't worry about it." I kissed her on the forehead and slipped out.

I stood just outside her door for a while, not quite ready to face Peter. Finally, I didn't have any choice and started back toward the stairs. Before I reached them, a door on my right opened. Alex was standing in it, her hand to her face. Her eyes were very red. When she saw me, she leaped back, startled.

"Mrs. Atwill! I was—I was just going over to the bathroom."

"Is something wrong?"

"No. No, of course not," she said quickly, her head turned away from me.

"What is it?"

"Nothing. Really." I didn't block her way, but I didn't stand aside. "I'm all right, I just need . . ." Her face crumpled, and she collapsed into harsh little sobs, made worse by her effort to control them.

I steered her back into the empty bedroom and sat her down in a chair, then I fetched a cold cloth from the bathroom across the hall and shut the door. "Did Franklin upset you?" I hoped she hadn't overheard our argument. She shook her head. I pulled a footstool over and sat down. "Are you sure? He can do that sometimes."

"No, it's not him."

"Do you want to talk about it?"

"I can't. I really can't. It's just that I . . ." She broke down again and cried into the cloth. "I don't know what to do. I can't pretend anymore."

"Pretend what?"

"That I'm not going crazy."

After a while, I said, "If you feel this bad, maybe you should see a doctor."

"It won't help. Nothing will help."

"Isn't there anyone you can talk to?"

"No."

"Not your friends? Or your family?"

"No."

"Surely you can talk to your friends."

"No. Not about this."

"Is it so terrible?"

"Yes."

"What is it? What's happened?" I sat there, looking at her. "Alex. Alex, are you being blackmailed?"

Her head whipped up, terror studded in her eyes. She gripped the cloth to her lips and drew back into the chair, her face quivering.

"I won't tell anyone," I said quickly.

"I don't know what you're talking about!"

"I won't tell anyone. I swear. Alex, listen to me. Please," I said, while my mind was racing for some explanation of how I could possibly know. "A policeman. A policeman I met after my robbery. He told me there was a gang of blackmailers working in Los Angeles. He thought maybe I'd been waylaid because I wouldn't pay up." It was a ludicrous story, but fortunately, she was too upset to notice. "Is it blackmail? I swear I'll never say a word to Franklin. I wouldn't do that."

"Please don't tell him. It's not what you think."

"What I think is that someone's done something terrible to you. Alex, we've all done things we wouldn't want on the front page of the paper. I guess you heard what Joan Trent said about me."

"No."

"Oh. You must have been up here. I had an affair with her husband several years ago, and she just told the entire party. It was a long time ago, wasn't it? What you did?"

"Yes."

"Does it still matter so much?"

She stared at her hands, stifling sobs. I waited and let her make up her mind. Finally, she said, "It was years ago, when I first moved into my own apartment. My parents hated it, but I had my own money, and they couldn't stop me. Some of the girls I knew at school were living here, too. They were older, and they seemed to be so free—the way I wanted to be. But they were pretty wild. I mean with men."

"I understand. Go on."

"It was only one party. I swear. I got drunk. And things started to happen. Somebody had a camera," she said miserably. "The next morning, I felt awful. I felt so dirty. I never saw any of them again. Never. But then, a couple of months ago, I got an envelope in the mail." She started to tremble again.

"But you don't do things like that now."

"It would make a difference. You know it would."

I thought she was probably right. Franklin might be able to tolerate the thought of her having been with another man before she met him, but the fact of it—an orgy recorded on eight-by-ten glossies—would be something else.

"I don't know what I'm going to do," she said. "I've already given them ten thousand dollars."

"Oh, Alex."

"I know."

"Do you have any idea who it might be?"

"No."

"Who was at that party?"

"Why? Please, you won't tell that policeman?"

"I won't. I won't tell anyone. Not unless you say it's all right. I swear."

Peter was waiting at the foot of the stairs. He didn't say anything about how long I'd been. When we got in the car, I said, "Do you think the police will believe it was communists?"

"I hope so. If they go off in that direction, it'll buy us

some time. I'll check out what she said about the robbery at Cummings's parents' house. That could be where he was keeping the letter the studio assistant overheard him talking about. Mrs. Atwill, for the future, when I'm working, trying to get information out of people, try not to pick fights with them."

"I'm sorry. It won't happen again."

We drove silently the rest of the way to Pasadena. I kept looking out the window so he wouldn't see my face.

I knew I should tell him about Alex. At the very least, I should tell him another woman was being blackmailed. And yet, I'd given her my word. Tomorrow, I'd talk to her. Tomorrow, maybe she'd trust me because I hadn't told Franklin.

"Do you want to come in for some coffee?" I asked, as we pulled into the drive.

"Am I still in insurance?"

"I didn't tell Juanita anything. It's hard enough keeping track of the lies I'm telling everyone else. She's gone to spend the night with her sister. She just had a baby. The sister, not Juanita."

She had left the terrace lights on for us.

"Go on out," I said. "I'll bring the coffee."

Instead, he followed me into the kitchen. I took out the percolator. He leaned his hips on the counter and folded his arms. I concentrated on filling the percolator with water, but I could tell he was watching me.

I pulled the canister toward me and opened it.

"How well did you know Dean Cummings?" he asked.

"Not very well."

"Is that the truth?"

"Yes," I said, and tried to sound offended, but it came off evasive. Between Alex's secret and Joan's announcement, I couldn't look at him.

"Has Mrs. Ross had many boyfriends?"

"Let's get one thing straight. Helen Ross is not a tramp."

"I didn't say she was. You haven't answered my question."

"A few."

"Who were they?"

"Why don't you ask her?"

"I'm asking you."

"I don't know. She never told me."

"Never once?"

"No. She wouldn't want me to feel I had to cover for her."

"So you have no idea."

"There were some I suspected, but I don't know. Do you think I'm lying?"

"I know you're not telling me everything. You neglected to mention that Joan Trent has a pretty big grudge against you. Did it just slip your mind?"

"That was years ago."

"So it doesn't matter?"

"It's not that kind of grudge."

"Really? When you broke up her marriage?"

"I did not break up her marriage. It was over."

"According to who?"

"They were practically separated. I do not have to—"

"What else are you keeping from me?"

"Nothing."

"I don't believe you. You're holding out on me, and I want to know what the hell's going on."

"Nothing."

"There's a man dead, and you knew him. You were seen with him at Elizondo's. For all we know, you might have been seen at his house. You were being blackmailed, and he might have been doing it. Dammit! Do you want my help or not?"

"Don't yell at me!"

"Then don't lie to me! How much do you know about this blackmail?"

"Nothing!"

"Do you know who shot Cummings?"

"How dare you!"

"I want the truth!"

"Get out!"

He reached out and grabbed my wrist. "Do you know who killed him?"

"Get out of my house!"

His other arm was around me before I knew it. He pulled me to him, hard against his chest, hard against his hips. My fingers clutched at his shoulders, and my head fell back.

His eyes searched my face. "Why are you lying to me?"

"I'm not. I won't."

"Do you still love him?"

"I don't know."

His mouth came down on mine with enough passion to make my bones soft, but not nearly as much as I wanted. I arched my back and pressed my breasts and my hips against him, answering every movement of his body and his mouth. A deep, hungry need filled me, one I had not felt in such a long time that it nearly overwhelmed me. It wouldn't have taken more than a word, and I would have gone straight upstairs.

But he didn't say the word. Instead, after a breathless minute, he released my mouth, if not my body.

"Jesus," he said softly against my temple.

"Is this how you get your clients to tell you the truth?" I asked shakily. "It's a pretty good trick."

It took him another minute to let me go, then he pulled out a chair for me and one for himself. He set his close to mine. "All right," he said. "Now, tell me about Joan Trent." I told him about my affair with Forrest. "Why didn't you tell me this at the office?"

"I didn't think it could have anything to do with this. And I was embarrassed."

"Was there ever anything between you and Deegan?"

"Don?"

"He's carrying a big torch for you."

"He is not. He was just needling you."

"Hmm," he said, unconvinced. "What else? What did she mean about Elizondo giving you a necklace?"

"He tried to replace the one that was stolen, but I returned it to him. Helen told me she'd heard he was interested. I didn't believe her at the time."

"What do you think about him now?"

"I'm going to be insulted in a minute, Winslow."

"I didn't mean because he gave you the necklace. I meant now that you know he's interested."

"I'm not."

"Okay. What else is there? There's something you're not telling me."

"Nothing. That is, nothing I kept from you before tonight."

"But tonight?" he encouraged.

"I found out there's someone else being blackmailed."

He stared at me.

"I can't tell you who. Please, I gave her my word."

"Lauren—"

"I gave her my word. Tomorrow, I'll go see her."

"Listen to me. What if she makes you promise never to talk? What are you going to do then? Will you keep quiet?"

"No."

"Then what difference does it make if you tell me now? You want to give her back her peace of mind? Then help me. Now."

"Alex Harris."

Something passed over his face. Something like pain. "She doesn't seem like the sort of person who could handle it."

"No."

He took my hand. "Tell me what she said."

I did, then I said, "They waited a long time."

"She didn't have much to lose before. Now, she's about to marry Frank Atwill. We have to get her to tell us who was at that party, who ended up with those pictures. Go see her tomorrow."

"I will. I'm sorry I didn't tell you about her. It's important that you know other women are being blackmailed."

"I already knew there were others."

"What?" I asked, astounded.

"While I was checking with the other investigators, looking for a lead on Maritski, I asked them about blackmail payoffs they'd handled. Nobody was going to give out names, but every one of them had handled at least one payoff in the last three years. None of the clients wanted to go to the cops. They just wanted some advice or someone to go with them, for protection, while they dropped off the money. The victims didn't all go to the same place, so no one realized it was the same operation. Or how big it was."

"How big is it?"

"Over the last three years, at least a dozen women. And those are just the ones we know about."

"*We* didn't know about them at all."

"Okay, don't get hot. I didn't have all the information till just before I came to pick you up. I didn't want that on your mind tonight with everything else you had to play. I told you the first chance I had."

"Are you sure it's the same gang?"

"All the same MO. The couple's surprised somewhere. Then a tough voice calls, offers to sell the pictures. The money had to be wrapped in brown paper, and the victim had to follow a trail to different phone booths. Finally, she'd end up downtown somewhere and be told to go straight to the ladies' room and throw the package out the window."

"Wouldn't it be dangerous to do it the same way every time?"

"The gang had plenty of time while they were following the victim to check for a trap. But I'd say someone in this gang knows this town well, knows the gossip, and knows who can't afford to go to the cops."

"Dean might have had that sort of knowledge. He was always at the clubs, at parties. He knew a lot of women."

"It looks like all this started about three years ago. Where was he during the war?"

"Here. He was a liaison for the army. Scheduling stars for bond drives. That sort of thing. His father got him the job. Were any of the other women set up like I was?"

"No. Not one of them."

"Then there are two gangs."

"I don't think so. I've got an idea. It's just an idea, but it starts to make some sense of all this, and it never made sense that your bunch was waiting on that road for just any woman who happened along. It's not the way black-mailers work. They have to know they've got a victim who won't go to the cops. I couldn't figure it out. Then tonight, I found out something else you forgot to tell me."

"I told you everything," I protested indignantly.

"You didn't tell me that you and Mrs. Ross have identical Lincolns. Hers is yellow; yours was white, but at night, they're the same car. And you didn't tell me how much you two look alike."

"Helen and I look nothing alike."

"You're both tall blondes, about the same build. She told me you were both wearing white satin gowns that night."

"I guess we were. I remember now that she said something about how the color didn't suit either one of us when she threw my dress away at the hospital." And I remembered that the night I had followed Peter, I had mistaken her car for mine.

"It would be hard to tell you apart from a distance. You said yourself you had a hard time spotting me from your car the night you followed me from the club."

"Wouldn't they have had binoculars?"

"Yes. But it wouldn't make much difference if the shadows were dark enough. The night you were waylaid, Mrs. Ross drove out to the club alone. It was also the night the gang was sure Cummings wouldn't be following her when she left. He was too sick to get out of bed. Someone with a radio was waiting, probably where you found those cigarettes. He radioed ahead to the others, who were waiting with the detour sign.

"Cummings wanted out, and he had a letter, some sort of hard evidence that would make the gang let him out and leave him alone. The gang wanted it back. If they got compromising pictures of Mrs. Ross, they could be sure he wouldn't use the letter against them until they could find it. As soon as they cleaned out his parents' safe, they killed him to make sure he never talked."

"Two weeks later, somebody got pictures of Helen just by sticking a camera up to a window. That's a heck of a lot easier than trying to waylay her on a dark road."

"But a lot more dangerous. Remember, Cummings had a gun. They wouldn't want to risk that unless they had to."

"If they were after Helen, they would have known they had the wrong woman right after they chlorotormed me."

"Yes, so they'd have to stash you and your car and wait for Mrs. Ross. But when she left, there must have been another car too close behind her."

"Then why take pictures of me?"

"They're blackmailers. It's what they do. Even if they didn't recognize you right away, they'd know you were rich from the car and the jewelry. They'd have to figure there might be some money in pictures of you."

"But they'd find out fast that the pictures were useless. They never would have gone through with the blackmail."

"I don't think they did. A bunch who wears hoods isn't going to make contact in person. Maritski showed you his face. A stupid move, but just the sort of thing a rank amateur might do. And you've seen how he lived. He's not part of this gang. He's not part of any gang. I don't know how he got your pictures, but I'll bet they don't belong to him. Look, it's just an idea. Let's wait and see what our man found out at Maritski's apartment house today. Tomorrow, I want you to go see Miss Harris."

"I'll have to tell her I'm being blackmailed, too. And

I'll have to tell her who you really are. I can't stay with that stupid police story. And she might feel more like talking if she knows the police aren't involved."

"Okay, but tell her your pictures were mailed to you, and some guy has been calling you, so you hired me. Don't tell her anything we know about Maritski or Cummings. We don't know who else she might confide in. She's probably being blackmailed by somebody she knows. Maybe somebody you know."

"I understand."

"Be careful."

"You, too."

"And get back here as soon as you can in case Maritski calls."

"I will."

He stood up to go.

"Winslow. About that kiss . . ."

"It won't happen again."

"That's too bad." I stood up and leaned toward him, and after a moment, he pulled me to him again, this time much more gently. He kissed me again. His mouth was just as nice when it lingered as it had been in hot passion. After a while, I said, "This might be a good time to ask. You're not married, are you?"

"No."

"What about your girlfriend?"

"What girlfriend?"

"The one with the orange lipstick. I saw it on the cigarette by the bed in your house."

He blushed. He actually blushed.

"She's not my girlfriend."

"Oh?"

"I don't see her much."

"Hmm."

"Hardly at all."

"Good."

We looked at each other for a while longer.

"I think I'd better go," he said quietly.

"Are you sure?"

He didn't pretend to misunderstand. "There are rules about sleeping with clients."

"I could fire you."

He laughed. He kissed me again. But he went home.

Chapter 8

The next morning, after Juanita came back, I drove the Hudson over to Alex's, pulling through a few alleys on the way. I didn't see anyone following me.

Alex lived in one of the overblown apartment buildings north of Wilshire, this one designed to look like a moor's palace, with Mediterranean arches and embellished minarets, an effect somewhat spoiled by the salmon color of the stucco and the picture windows. Inside, the lobby had gold-veined marble columns, a muraled vaulted ceiling, and a dozen empty chairs covered in Oriental silk. The desk was nearly buried behind potted palms. I waded through the carpet and found the clerk between the fronds. When I asked for Alex, he picked up a cream-and-gold phone and whispered my name.

The elevator boy had a short red jacket and black harem pants. He didn't look at me as he whisked me up to the penthouse. If I had to wear that outfit, I wouldn't make eye contact either. A maid answered the door and showed me into the living room. Alex was sitting in an overstuffed fan-backed chair, her hands in her lap: Alice waiting for the Mad Hatter.

I sat in the chair she offered, and the maid went out.

"You didn't tell Franklin," she said. "Thank you."

"I have no reason to hurt you," I said, but she looked skeptical. "My marriage was over long before he met you."

"Sometimes, I think he still loves you."

"My marriage is over, Alex. Franklin is going to marry you," I said, maybe a little too strongly, worried as I was that I couldn't get her to talk. "I have a confession to make," I said then. "I didn't exactly tell you the truth yesterday. I didn't guess that you were being blackmailed because of a policeman." I told her my story. I told her how I'd been waylaid. A picture had come to me in the mail, I said, and a blackmailer had been calling. She looked about twice as skeptical as before. "You don't entirely believe me, do you?"

"Please don't think that. It's just that— Why would anyone do such an awful thing? It's bad enough, what they did to me. But to someone who hasn't done anything . . ."

"I think it must have been some sort of mistake."

"Mistake?"

Damn, I thought. I can't tell her that the gang might have mistaken me for Helen. Once again, I was proving to be a great detective. "I mean they must have thought I'd pay to keep the pictures out of Franklin's hands. Perhaps they didn't know I wouldn't be asking for alimony." Before she could examine the flaws in that, I told her about Peter. I remembered not to tell her about Maritski or Dean.

"I've hired a private detective. I certainly can't go to the police. I'm hoping he can find a way to get my pictures back and make those people leave me alone. You met him yesterday. Mr. Winslow."

"The man who was with you?"

"Yes. I asked him to come. I'm nervous about being out

alone when it starts to get dark. Would you be willing to talk to him? If you don't want to, you could give me the names of the people at that party. No one would have to know where I got them."

"If he talks to them, my name is going to come up. Maybe they've forgotten all about it. About me. I don't want them to remember."

"Whoever is doing this was probably at the party."

"I know. I want to help. I do. But there's no way of knowing if these people are the same ones you're looking for."

"Mr. Winslow has already found out that there are other women this is happening to. Maybe a lot of them. The people we're looking for make you go from phone booth to phone booth, then throw the money out a window. Did you have to do that?"

"Please," she said, suffering. "I have to think it over."

"Of course." I gave her a card with my number on it.

The police came to see me in the afternoon. They called first to see if I would be in. I remembered to ask them what it was about.

There were two of them, homicide detectives with good gray suits and good manners. One of them was tall and thin, his face made even thinner by long ears with long lobes. The shorter one wore glasses and took notes. Juanita served coffee and cake, and I handed the cups across to them with what I fondly hoped was an innocent smile.

They said they understood that I knew Mr. Cummings and that I had spent some time with him at Elizondo's a few days before he died. I explained that I had only run into him there. He had come with others. They wanted to know if he seemed worried that night. Did he say anything that would indicate he was in trouble? They wanted to know who his friends were, his enemies. On the latter, I could claim ignorance with perfect honesty.

"I don't know how to put this exactly," the tall one said delicately, although I had the feeling he had decided exactly how to put it, "but we've been told that he had a lot of women friends."

"Yes."

"Very good friends. And that some of them were married."

"Dean was a popular escort. He was attractive and a bachelor. There are plenty of women—married and single—who have places they want to go and no one to take them. Sometimes, things might have gone further. I don't know."

"Did he ever escort Mrs. Ross?"

"I don't think so. A woman doesn't usually choose an escort who's much younger than she is unless she's elderly."

They asked me to call if I remembered anything that might help. I said that I would, and I walked them to the door.

I called Helen to make sure we had our stories straight. The police had called her, too. She had agreed to see them the next day. Dean's body had been released to his family. The funeral would be Wednesday. I promised to come. She said Sam would take care of getting me into the service.

I left a message for Peter at the office. The secretary said he would be gone all day. If it was urgent, she could reach him. I told her no.

Maritski didn't call. But then Juanita had told him Tuesday. At eleven, I took a book to bed.

Just before midnight, the phone rang. I turned on the lamp I had just switched off.

"Lauren?"

"Peter. Where are you?"

"In a phone booth. I wanted to make sure you'd be home in the morning. I'll pick you up at eight."

"Why? What's going on?"

"I'll tell you then."

"The police were here today." I told him what happened.

"Did they ask about the Hudson? Or take a look at it?"

"No. I went to see Alex. She wants more time. Maritski didn't call."

"We'll talk about it tomorrow. Get some sleep."

He arrived ten minutes early. Although his shirt was fresh, he didn't look as if he'd slept. When Juanita offered him breakfast, he didn't argue with her. She set it in front of him, her eyes full of speculation.

When we got into his car, I asked, "Am I allowed to know what this is about?"

He didn't answer right away. He didn't slide over and kiss me either. There was no indication at all of what had passed between us Sunday night.

As he pulled out of the drive, he said, "We might have found a blackmailer."

"Who?"

"I'd rather not say till we get there. The autopsy report on Cummings is out. Nothing much new. He was shot in the chest, from maybe ten feet away. It definitely looks like a Remington .380. And we checked on that robbery at Cummings's parents' house. It turns out Joan Trent was right. The thieves cleaned out the safe, including lists of communists. But they didn't touch anything else in the room. The detectives think the communist story is hooey, but the brass like it, so we might get some more time."

We stayed on Figueroa until we reached Venice Boulevard, then took that into Venice toward the now shuttered and deserted pier. The city fathers had decided to close it down, hoping that, without the garish strip and the garish crowd it attracted, property values would climb as wildly as they had in the rest of L.A. I didn't think that was likely, as long as L.A. kept dumping its sewage where it regularly washed up onto Venice's beaches.

About a mile from the shore, we turned into a neighborhood where the landlords weren't spending any more on upkeep than they had to, and with the housing shortage, that wasn't much. The "Venetian cottages" that had been intended to be middle-class seaside retreats thirty years ago sat crammed together and wasting on their twenty-five-foot-wide lots. Even the larger lots had yards that were mostly sand, stripped palms, and rusty clotheslines. The roofs were bleached by the sun and salt until they looked chalky. In the store windows, hand-painted signs announced DISCOUNTS TO VETERANS, EASY CREDIT, GOVERNMENT CHECKS CASHED.

We turned into a dismal little street.

"This is it," Peter said, and gestured ahead. It was called the San Marcos Courts. Through the wrought-iron gate, I could see a weedy courtyard, surrounded by neglected bungalows of chipped, rose-colored stucco. When Venice of America was going to be the town of dreams, they might have been something to see. A sign on the gate said NO VACANCIES. We drove to the end of the next block and turned. The sun glared on the crumbled sidewalks and on the chrome of a rattletrap gray Studebaker parked just around the corner, hidden from the main street by a huge bougainvillea. When we had pulled alongside the hood, Peter leaned across me. "Need some help?" he called down at the pavement.

I hadn't seen the feet sticking out from under the bumper. The body started wiggling itself out. It was wearing hard-used dungarees and an undershirt that had been under many cars. Greasy hands grabbed the bumper and pulled, and the face finally appeared. The man got to his feet awkwardly and limped over to my window, swinging a stiff left leg.

"This is my brother, Johnny," Peter said.

He was younger, somewhere in his early twenties, with many of the same features: the line of the jaw, the shape of the nose, and the color of the hair, but together, they didn't make his brother's face. The eyes were still far too innocent.

"Anything happen?" Peter asked.

"Not yet. He's still inside."

"Good. Get back to work."

Johnny pulled out a handkerchief and mopped his face. "Thanks a lot." He stepped back, and we pulled down to the end of the street, turned around, and parked under a tree. Johnny was sliding back under the car.

"We tried to rent a bungalow," Peter said, "but they didn't have any vacancies. Johnny slipped the clerk a bribe to hold the next one that comes empty. He might get in. Maybe not. He couldn't look too eager. We don't want to tip anything."

"How long has he been under there?"

"Since about six. Don't worry about Johnny. He's put up with worse than this."

"Did you watch until six?"

"Not from under the car. Don't worry about me, either. I can take care of myself."

"Peter, is something wrong?"

"No."

I slid across the seat and slipped my arms around his neck. I kissed him. He didn't fight it. In fact, he didn't seem to mind at all. In an appropriate pause, I said, "I just wanted to make sure you still felt the way you did on Sunday. You were acting sort of funny."

"I thought you might have changed your mind."

"Why would I do that?"

He took a deep breath. "Look, Lauren. I'm not exactly the kind of man you're used to."

"That's good news."

"I mean it. I come from the wrong side of the tracks in about every way you can imagine. I get to know the worst kind of people, and, a lot of the time, I don't act any better than they do. I make my living digging into private lives and lying to get what I need. I've helped ruin people, and some of them never did anything worse than fall in love with someone they weren't married to."

"Geez, Winslow, you don't have to sugarcoat it for me. What happened to all those innocent men with only you between them and the Big House?"

"I've led a very different kind of life than you have."

"You'll have me swooning on my bustle in a minute."

He laughed and seemed to relax a little. I laid my hand on his thigh. "However," he said, "there are rules about—"

"Rules? Careful, Winslow, you'll have me believing you have a shred of decency after all. Okay, you're right. We shouldn't be doing this while you're trying to work." I scooted back to my side and arranged my skirt over my knees. He watched while I did it. "So, what do we do now?"

"Wait." He handed me a *Harper's Bazaar* and a *Woman's Home Companion* from the backseat, then took off his hat and leaned his elbow on the windowsill. We waited. I opened the *Harper's* and resisted the temptation to slip my skirt up again and test his resolve. It had been a long time since I'd wanted to entice a man. I'd almost forgotten how much fun it was.

The sun started to climb. I read. Johnny got out from under the Studebaker, lifted the hood, and started replacing spark plugs.

"May I ask what happened to him?" I said. "Was he injured in the war?"

"His jeep hit a mine in Germany two weeks after V-E Day. He was lucky. The other guy was killed. He's been looking forward to meeting you."

"Why?" I asked anxiously.

"Don't worry. No one has seen your picture but me, and no one will. I told him that, when I pulled my gun on you, you hardly blinked."

"My eyelids were too scared to move. That picture on your desk? Is that him?"

"Him and my sisters."

"Are your parents still alive?"

"My mother died right after Johnny was born, when I was thirteen."

"Your father took care of six children?"

"No. He couldn't do that and work all day. So I mostly took care of them."

"How did you go to school?"

"I didn't very much."

"And your father?"

"He's still around," he said, and turned back to watch Johnny.

I waited. After a full minute, he said, "I told you where I come from."

"Yes."

He kept looking out the window. "All right. After a couple of years, Dad got married again. Natalie was good to the kids, and they liked her. It was all right for a while, but after the Crash, he wasn't working, and he started drinking more than ever. Mostly, he'd take it out on her, but sometimes the kids, and I'd break it up.

"One night he came home and started throwing her around. I was about eighteen then, and I was finally bigger than he was, so I threw him out and told him to stay away from us."

"I see."

"He and Natalie made it up after about a year, but the kids never went to live with them."

"How did you survive?"

"I got a job."

"A kid during the Depression? Doing what?"

"Delivering stuff."

"For Ramon Elizondo?"

I can't say that I didn't enjoy the amazed expression on his face. "How the hell did you know that?"

I said, I think modestly, "I thought you might be a friend of his. The waiter said you didn't come there often, but he knew your name. The attendants knew your car. You were either a very big tipper or a friend of the boss."

"I went over to see him one day. I knew who he was, of course. I said I needed a job."

"Just like that."

"I was too young and stupid to know any better. I just said I had to have a job, and I'd do anything."

"So long as you didn't have to hurt anybody."

"No, I would've done that, too, if it meant a job. But he never asked me to. So I delivered booze for him, and he taught me how to dress, how to act, and how to talk to people. Any polish I've got comes from Ray."

"How did you end up at Paxton's?"

"He knew Ed. I think he'd hired the agency to follow one of his wives around. When Prohibition ended, he sent me over. Ed gave me the worst assignments, mostly stakeouts. He only took me on as a favor. I think he wanted me to quit."

Remembering my own stakeout experience, I said, "I couldn't have done it. I'm not very patient."

"You must be, or you never would have stayed married to Frank Atwill."

"Winslow, you know, if this is going to work out between us, you might not want to take every opportunity to insult him."

Johnny took a red rag out of his hip pocket.

"That's it," Peter said, and started the car. As we pulled past Johnny, he called out, "Stay here in case he gets visitors while he's gone."

We spotted the car—a caramel-colored Ford—stopped at the first intersection. All I could see through the oval rear window was a man wearing a hat. "Who is it?"

"Not yet." The Ford moved on. Peter let him gain some ground on us. "Tailing isn't easy. If you don't want to get spotted."

"I remember," I said dryly.

We followed him back north on Venice, dodging around the streetcars, letting them run interference for us.

Just past a high school, the Ford pulled over to the curb. A tall man got out, his straw fedora pulled low on his forehead. He went into a drugstore. We passed the Ford and parked at the end of the block. Two minutes later, the man came back out with a pack of cigarettes, unwrapped them, and dropped the cellophane on the sidewalk. His head was bent forward, concentrating on unfolding the foil. A wide-hipped girl in a tight yellow dress came out of the flower shop next door and started toward us with a full, undulating sway. He raised his face and gave her behind a hard leer.

"My God!" I cried. "It's Maritski's landlord."

"You sure?" Peter said.

"Of course I'm sure. That's the man who told me Maritski had skipped out."

The man got back into his car and slowly pulled into traffic. As he passed us, we turned our faces away, then followed. I said, "Are you going to tell me what this is all about now?"

"Sunday morning, Johnny went over to Maritski's old apartment house. He's got a great face for that part of the business. Wounded veteran looking for the guy who sold his mother a set of encyclopedias and never delivered. Turns out, Maritski didn't have a landlord, he had a land*lady*, who's about seventy and loves to keep an eye on her tenants. Maritski lived there for eight years as Paul Kovak. As far as we know, that's his real name. He worked in a photography lab. Recently, he'd told her he was thinking about buying his own camera shop. He was coming into some money. She hadn't set much store by it. She liked him well enough. He was always polite, kept his apartment clean, and paid the rent on time. But he was always talking about the plans he had, all the famous people he'd met working in pictures. Every time there was a picture of an actor or actress in the paper or in a magazine, he would claim to have met them. But she thought maybe he'd come into money after all, because he went on vacation three weeks ago and hasn't come back."

"When did he leave?"

"July third."

"That's two days after he showed me the pictures. If I hadn't waited a week to go to Central Casting . . ."

"Don't kick yourself. You did all right finding that address. Besides, if he'd still been there, what would you have done? You couldn't go to the police. We checked Maritski's bank. He's closed his accounts."

"Does the landlady have any idea where he is now?"

"No. Neither does the post office. We checked."

"So who's this we're following?"

"The name's Jack Hochauser. When Johnny asked the landlady about family and friends Maritski had, she mentioned a man who'd come to see him a couple of days before he disappeared. She heard the man yelling, and she almost called the cops. She made sure she got a look at him when he came out of Maritski's apartment. Then the same man came back a couple of days later, and when he found out Maritski was gone, she said he got real upset. He's been checking with her and the other tenants, claiming to be worried about his friend, but he wouldn't leave a phone number. She didn't trust him. Her description sounded like the guy you'd seen.

"We checked out the photo lab where Maritski worked. He'd been there for about ten years, except for the days when he was working on a movie. Too old for the service. The day before he disappeared, he told his boss he'd like to take his vacation. The boss was a little put out that he didn't get much notice, but Maritski was good at his job, so he said okay and let him go. He was supposed to be back last week. I asked his boss if he knew anyone who fit the description of the man you'd talked to at the apartment house. He said it sounded like a guy who worked for him part-time. A guy named Jack Hochauser. I got an address and went over to his house."

He chuckled his fingers out on the steering wheel

"Well?" I said.

"Jack cut out Sunday night. I found a girlfriend there, throwing some china around. Seems that Sunday night about nine, when they got back from a date, he got a call. All he said was hello and whoever was on the other end talked for a couple of minutes, then Jack hung up and told her something had come up, he'd have to send her home in a cab. He was pretty upset, so she went over there yesterday to see how he was. He was gone. The place was rented furnished, but he'd cleared out everything that belonged to him."

"I don't understand. Jack stayed in his house even after I saw him at Maritski's, but Sunday night, suddenly, he disappeared?"

His eyes cut to me. "Does that suggest anything to you?"

There was a cold stab in the pit of my stomach. "That someone at Helen's party recognized you as a private detective and warned him to clear out."

"We're tracing any police sheet or service record he might have for leads. His neighbors say he kept to himself, but always had girlfriends going in and out. And a nice little green Mercury coupe, which he seems to have gotten rid of."

"I thought there was a green coupe following me the day I went to watch your office."

"I remember."

"I wonder if he has a scar on his left shoulder."

Peter looked over at me, and I tried to smile.

At Figueroa, Jack cut up to Olympic and continued east.

Peter said, "The lab owner says Jack worked for him since '43, when he got out of the service on a medical discharge. His references say he worked as a photographer at some nightclubs before the war. That could be where he met someone who was at the Rosses' party. If he ever worked in pictures himself, he never mentioned it to anyone at the lab. But we'll run his name and picture past our contacts at the studios and the places that cast extras just in case. His girlfriend had one she hadn't torn up yet."

"How on earth did you find him?"

"I talked to the girlfriend a long time, trying to find out where he might have gone. She didn't know much, but she mentioned that he was a big fight fan. Went every week. So, I had some men stake out the Ocean Park Arena last night with copies of his picture, and there he was."

"Why didn't you tell me this last night?"

"I didn't want to plant anything in your mind in case we had the wrong man."

"Did you think I wouldn't remember what he looked like?"

"You'd be surprised how many people can't remember the face of someone they met yesterday."

"It looks like Maritski stole the pictures from the gang."

"Jack must have suspected him and confronted him, and Maritski ran, still thinking he could collect from you."

We passed Los Angeles Street, and the neighborhood

turned more industrial—small factories, warehouses, and distributing companies against a backdrop of oil storage tanks on the other side of the river.

I said, "Do you want me to get a list of the people who were at Helen's party?"

"No. I don't want anyone—even Mrs. Ross—to know we suspect someone who was there. But write down as many names as you can remember."

"There must have been a hundred people there."

"Get started." He took a notebook out of the pocket in his door and tossed it to me.

"Thanks."

I started jotting down names. We went north on Alameda, through the garment factories and into the produce district. Just before Sixth, Jack turned again, toward the river. The air was heavy with exhaust fumes and, beneath them, on a steady southerly breeze, the aroma of the meatpacking plants in Vernon.

Cautiously, we followed, easing around the trucks that were backing into and leaving the docks, using them as shields. Jack turned right. Before we got to the corner, a large truck swung around it toward us, taking up both lanes. Peter had to tuck the car against a loading dock to make enough room. As it passed, it layered us with dust.

When we took the right, there was no sign of the Ford. At the next intersection, we stopped. The road looped around an empty lot—an overgrown two acres that served as a parking lot for the warehouses' workers and a dumping ground. In the middle of the lot was a fifty-foot-high pile of coarse sand, which was surrounded by parked cars and the junk that the warehouses hadn't bothered to have hauled away: enormous wooden spools that had once held wire, rusting attic fans, some unidentifiable broken metal, and twisted axles. Bottles, cans, and melting cardboard littered the rest of the visible land.

Along the right side of the road were three small, two-story warehouses, dark red brick and a half-century old. Each had a couple of arches that opened into loading areas recessed beneath their upper floors. The arches didn't look tall enough for bigger, modern trucks. On the other side of the field was a sprawling brickyard surrounded by a chain fence. Off to our left was another road, which ran to the Kerry Pottery Factory, whose name I could see easily on the side of the grimy gray brick just beneath its belching chimneys.

I didn't see the Ford. We started around the loop.

As we passed the third warehouse, Peter suddenly grabbed my arm and yanked me down across the seat. "Get down!" He turned his face away, and we kept going around till we reached the road that led to the factory.

"Okay, come on up," he said. He turned the car around and drove back to the intersection. It was a good spot for surveillance: the pile of sand partially concealed us. Peter reached across me, took a pair of binoculars out of the glove compartment, and trained them on the warehouse.

After a minute, he handed them to me. I practically had to sit in his lap to see around the sand. He didn't seem to mind. It was too dark beneath the arches to see anything but the rear end of the Ford. All the warehouse windows had been boarded up. Except for the car, there was no sign of occupation.

Reluctantly, I went back to my side of the car. He watched the warehouse. I watched the sand.

Ten minutes later, Jack came back out. Peter handed me the binoculars and put the car in gear. We followed him, staying far back now. Before we reached Olympic again, we were caught by a red light and lost him.

We drove slowly back into Venice and pulled into a gas station at the corner of the street that led to the San Marcos Courts. Peter got out and made a wide arc around the front end of the car, wide enough to see down the street, then he came over to my side and bent down to the open window. "He's home."

"What do we do now?"

"I try to find out about that warehouse. I'm going to make a call." While he did, I used the ladies' room, then I got a couple of Coca-Colas out of the chest and put two nickels in the slot. When Peter came out of the booth, I gave him his. He took a long swallow, then said, "I've got somebody to watch the warehouse, and I set up a tail on Jack. To do it right, we should have two men each in two cars."

"Why?"

"We need the extra man in case we have to suddenly tail him on foot. And two cars so they can trade off and be harder to spot. We're going to go through your retainer fast."

"I'll give you another check."

He looked at me. I wondered if his research had told him exactly how much Uncle Bennett had left me.

"What do I do?" I asked.

"Stay home and wait for Maritski to call."

I knew that was all I could do, but I didn't like it.

Chapter 9

As soon as I got home, I called Helen. The police had been there and gone. They were very polite, she said, seeming surprised, but I thought they weren't about to antagonize Sam Ross's wife without good reason. "But, God, I don't know how I got through it. I'm going to take a ride up the coast. I've got to get out of here."

I told her I thought that sounded like a good idea.

As I was running a bath, Juanita came in. Her sister's new baby had colic. Her sister wasn't getting any sleep, and her brother-in-law was trying to hold down two jobs. I told her to go stay with them as long as she needed to. Although I wasn't too crazy about sleeping in that big house alone, I knew, logically, that she wasn't exactly protection. She said she would come back tomorrow to cook dinner. I told her to go ahead and take her regular day off. She ignored me.

Before she left, she set out my only black suit for Dean's funeral the next day.

I climbed into the tub, rolled a hand towel behind my neck, and rested my head back on the tiles, thinking about Jack Hochauser and his Sunday night phone call. Just hours after I showed up in public with a private detective, Jack got a phone call telling him to disappear.

I spent a half hour in the tub in profitless thought with the hot water tap drizzling to keep the water warm, then I put on some shorts and was headed downstairs for a glass of lemonade. The phone rang. I sat down on the edge of the bed and picked it up. "Hello."

"Mrs. Atwill?"

A line of ice ran up my spine. "Yes."

"Do you know who this is?"

"Yes."

"Is there anyone there with you?"

"Do you think I'd tell you if I were alone?"

"I do not mean you any harm. I only wish to conclude our business." He was trying to be smooth, but his voice was drier and higher-pitched than I remembered.

"Very well," I said, trying to sound resigned. "You win."

There was a pause. "You will pay me the money?"

"I don't have any choice, do I?"

His voice was even drier. "You have made the right decision. You will get the money. Three thousand dollars. And I will call and tell you where to leave it."

"When? When will you call?"

"You will have to wait," he said, now with a trace of smugness.

"I can't sit by the phone twenty-four hours a day."

"Very well. I will call tomorrow at noon."

"Why wait? I want the pictures. You want the money."

"The banks have already closed, Mrs. Atwill."

"Yes, but I could get the money today," I said slowly, letting the words sink in, despite Peter's telling me to do no more than set up the drop. "I know people. I know people who would lend me money. I can call them."

He went off, just as I had hoped he would. "No! Do not tell anyone!"

"Why?"

"Do not tell anyone!"

"All right. I won't. I won't tell anyone."

"No one."

"All right. Whatever you say."

"You will get the money from your bank tomorrow. If you tell anyone, you will not get the pictures. I will call you at noon."

"Wait! Don't hang up. Are you in Los Angeles?"

"It does not matter where I am."

"Yes, it does. Are you in a safe place?"

"Why?"

"I want those pictures. I'm ready to pay your price. Do you understand? You'll get the money. But you have to be careful. There could be people looking for you."

I held my breath. I heard nothing on the other end of the line. For a horrible moment, I thought he'd hung up. Then he said, "What makes you think people are looking for me?"

"I've been over to Central Casting. I thought I remembered seeing you on the set of a movie I wrote. *The Scarlet Spy*. You have a very memorable face, Mr. Kovak. I went over to your apartment house. Your landlady said you were gone, but that there had been a man there asking questions, angry, trying to find out where you were. Are you in a safe place?"

"Do not try to trick me, Mrs. Atwill."

"I'm not."

"You have no proof that I have done anything."

"No."

"I will not talk to the police. "

"Why would I tell the police? Do you think I want them to see those pictures? But I do want to know who did this to me. I don't think it was you. But you know who they are. I can get your money. All of it. Tonight. Without calling anyone. Tell me who they are, then I'll decide what to do to them. You can disappear."

There was a pause while he thought it over. "I must have the money first."

"Of course. But convince me you know something worth three thousand dollars. Who was this man asking questions?"

Something clinked against the receiver. Liquid sloshed, and I heard him swallow. He said, "His name is Jack."

"That's not worth much. How did you get those pictures? Three thousand dollars, and you get out of town."

There was a longer slosh and bigger swallow. And another long pause. "Jack and I worked at a photography lab. Many of the people who worked there were photographers themselves. Our boss would let us use the darkrooms on Mondays, after the shop closed. One night, I went into one of them. The red light was off. I thought it was empty. But Jack was in there. He tried to hide what he had been doing, but I saw that the pictures were of a man and woman. In bed. He was angry at first, but then he laughed. He said that he was doing it for lawyers. For divorces. And he gave me twenty dollars not to tell the boss."

"That's a lot of money."

"Yes. I began to wonder." As he told his story, the fear in his voice began to be replaced by an oozing pride. "I thought lawyers would know places to send such film where no one would have to hide what he was doing. I followed him home. I saw the car he drove and the house he lived in. I did not think he could afford them on what we were paid, even if he was paid extra money from lawyers.

And he only worked at the shop three days a week. He did not work the next day, so I called my boss and told him I was sick, and I followed Jack. He did not go to a lawyer's office. He went to a warehouse. I waited there where he could not see me. Two people came later. I recognized them. Not many people would have, but I did."

"How could you tell who they were if you were far enough away that he couldn't see you?"

"I am a photographer, Mrs. Atwill. I took their pictures and enlarged them."

"Very clever. Were they people from the movies?"

"I will not tell you that."

"Why? Because they were people I know?"

"I will not tell you until I have the money."

"Was one of them Dean Cummings?"

There was a sharp intake of breath.

"Listen to me, Paul. These people were blackmailing a friend of mine. They had pictures of her and Dean Cummings. After she paid them, we found him dead in his house. And we found some things that made us think he was part of the blackmail. Was one of the people Dean Cummings?"

"I did not kill him."

"I know that. I know you're not a killer."

"Who have you told about this?"

"No one. And my friend's married. I have to protect her. She wouldn't tell anyone either. How did you figure out it was blackmail? You couldn't have known that from just seeing a set of pictures."

The liquid sloshed again, then he said, "They went into the warehouse, and later, one of them drove to a library."

"Who? Jack? Dean? Or the other man?"

"I will not tell you."

"All right. Go on."

"I followed him inside. He had a large envelope and he took it into a row of books. I could not see what he did with it. I had to be careful. But he left without it. I stayed there for hours. Finally, a woman came. She was the woman in the photograph. I could tell from her jewelry and her furs that she was rich. She took the envelope out of a large book. She was crying."

"How did you get my pictures? Jack must have been very careful after you caught him."

"Maybe I will tell you how I did it. Later."

"Tell me now. Or you can stay where you are and wait for him to find you."

"Do you want me to disappear?"

"No. But let's not kid each other. I need information and you need money. So convince me that you were never part of this gang. How did you get my pictures?"

He took a dry little breath, and then said, "For a long time, I waited for him to reserve a darkroom. I thought perhaps I was wrong about what he was doing. Then one day, I saw his name on the list. I stayed as well, but he locked the door this time. When he left, I saw him put the envelope in his car. I followed him again. He went into a bar. He did not have the envelope."

"So you broke into his car."

"No one locks his car in Los Angeles. I found the envelope under the front seat. There were many pictures. I recognized you."

"And you took some of them. It's all right. I don't care if you don't have all the prints and the negatives."

There was a pause, then he said, "I took only one of the negatives. He had the pictures and the rest of the negatives. I did not think he would notice."

"But he did. And he suspected you."

"He knew that I was at the shop that night. He came to my apartment. He accused me. He was very angry. I denied it, but I could see that he did not believe me."

"And you decided to go away?"

"Just for a while. Until he was not so angry. I told my boss that I was going on my vacation."

"And you could spend a couple of weeks trying to get money out of me. Then Dean Cummings was murdered."

"Yes."

"Whoever else you saw at the warehouse, have you seen them since?"

"I do not think that I will tell you any more until I have been paid."

"It's someone I know, isn't it?"

"I will not tell you anything else."

"Dammit! Why shouldn't I call my friends for money? Is it someone I know?"

"Yes."

"How do you know that?"

"I know! Do not talk to anyone!"

"Okay, okay. I won't. But you have to tell me everything."

"Three thousand. I must have three thousand."

"I can get it. Without making any phone calls."

"If you bring anyone else, I will not come. You have nothing to fear from me. I only want the money. Bring no one. I will know if you do, and I will not come."

"I understand."

"Neither of us wishes to end up like Mr. Cummings."

"No."

I heard a tapping on the other end, four solid knocks on glass. A rough, muffled voice said, "Hey, buddy, you gonna let someone else use the phone?"

"I will call you back," Maritski said hurridely. "You will wait for me to call."

Immediately, I phoned Paxton. The receptionist put me through to Johnny.

"I have to talk to Peter. Where is he?"

"Trying to find out who owns that warehouse. Why?"

"Maritski called."

"I'll find Pete. Stay put."

I didn't think there was much chance of Maritski's showing up with a gun for his money, but I double-checked all the doors anyway and, despite the heat, closed the windows. I didn't have a gun, so I settled for a knife. I put it on the table beside the chair in the study and got out a book. I never opened it.

It was someone I knew.

How would Maritski know who my friends were?

No, it couldn't be a friend. Once they'd realized that they'd grabbed me instead of Helen, they wouldn't bother to take pictures. They would know it was highly unlikely that I would pay up.

Maybe it was only someone he *thought* was a friend. Someone he'd seen me with on the Marathon lot when he was working as an extra.

But he had last worked at Marathon three years ago. Could his memory be that good?

Maybe it was someone he'd seen me with in a magazine or newspaper? Again, it would have been a long time ago.

Someone he'd seen me with during the time he'd been following me?

Peter called back an hour later.

"Where have you been?" I demanded.

"It's all right. I'm here now," he said soothingly. "What happened?"

"You were right. My blackmailers and Helen's are the same. I found the connection between Dean and Jack and *my* blackmail. It's someone I know."

"Slow down. What are you talking about?"

I filled him in.

"Dammit, Lauren! You were just supposed to set up a drop!"

"It's someone I know."

"We had a pretty good idea of that already. And we still don't have a name. What if he has second thoughts about how much he told you?"

"He wants the money."

"Enough to risk you calling the cops?"

"I was afraid he didn't realize he was in danger."

"I told you not to play detective!"

He was right. I couldn't admit it, so I didn't say anything.

"Now we have to wait and see if he'll call," he snapped. "Will you be all right alone?"

"Yes," I snapped back.

"I'm at the office. When he calls, take the Hudson. Make sure you're not followed and call me here from a pay phone. I'll have the switchboard operator put this number through to me. Don't call from your house just in case he calls back to see if your line is busy." He hung up.

I went to the study, feeling like an idiot, and dug into my safe past my insurance papers, my will, and my jewelry, and found the emergency cash I kept there. It wasn't three thousand, but it would do if I had to flash some money. I took it upstairs and put on a dress that had a long matching jacket with patch pockets big enough to hold the money, then I went down to the kitchen and made an omelet. I didn't eat it.

Was it someone I knew?

I waited.

At eight-thirty, Maritski called back. "I will meet you at the Whately Hotel." He gave me the address. "Room sixteen. The door will be unlocked. Do you understand?"

"Yes. It might take me an hour to get there. I'm going to make sure I'm not followed."

"If you bring anyone, I will know. I will not come."

"I understand."

"Leave now. Bring the money." He hung up.

Thirty seconds later, the phone rang again. Maritski was checking up, just as Peter said he would. I didn't answer.

I looped around the neighborhood until I was sure there was no one behind me, then I called Peter from a gas station while the attendant filled up the car. He picked up the phone on the first ring. I told him about the rendezvous. "Let me check my map. Okay. It's near Seventh and San Pedro. Meet me at the corner of Twelfth and Towne. That's a safe enough distance. Can you find it?" He didn't sound angry anymore.

"Yes. I've got a map."

"It's not the best of neighborhoods at night, so stay in the car."

It took almost the full hour to get there. The late-evening traffic was light, but I took plenty of detours.

When I had parked the Hudson not far from the rendezvous corner, I turned off the engine and rolled down the window a little more. But not much.

On either side of the street, on tiny lots, there were small, worn-out clapboard houses that had been thrown up in the twenties during that decade's population boom to provide housing for factory workers, and probably hadn't been touched by a paintbrush or nail since. The sound of a radio floated out of the new darkness, the Spanish sharp and smooth at the same time. On the porch of the house next to me, two stout women sat open-legged on a gutted sofa, fanning themselves.

There was a knock on my window. I jumped so hard, I struck my thighs on the steering wheel.

"Good God! You scared me to death!"

"Sorry." He went around the car and got in. He was wearing an old, shiny suit with frayed lapels; his hat was stained and misshapen. I looked for the bulge of his gun in his coat. I didn't see it.

"I had to check out the hotel," he said. "It's easier if I look like I belong in the neighborhood. There's some bad news. We lost Jack."

"He's gone?"

"No. Our man Lou lost him this afternoon. We had two cars on him, but I told you how hard it is to tail someone." His jaw bunched. I felt sorry for Lou. "Lou's gone back to the San Marcos Courts to wait. Johnny and the other car that was tailing Jack are cruising around here, trying to spot Maritski or his car. There wasn't much time to set anything up, and the last thing we want to do is scare him off. There are two ways out of the hotel—the front door and a side door into the alley. The alley door can't be opened from the outside. I tried it."

"What are we going to do?"

"He's not going to be in the room. He's not that stupid. He probably left you a note with instructions. He's around the hotel somewhere, watching to see if you bring anyone. Park your car at the far end of the alley that's next to the hotel, but come around on the sidewalk to get to the front door, just to be safe. When you get the instructions from his room, make sure you're not followed, and drive back here. Don't worry. If Maritski shows himself, we'll step in."

I nodded. I would have said all right, but I was trying to swallow.

He got out and disappeared into the dark down a rutted path between the houses. The women on the porch watched him, a little fearful. I put my bag in the glove compartment and slipped the envelope of money and my keys into the pocket of my jacket.

The Whately Hotel was a dingy gray brick building that had once been prouder. It had columns of bay windows with some fancy stonework above them. But that was about all that was left. It was one of the many small, inexpensive hotels that had once attracted commercial travelers and the city's new residents, but had slipped into decay with the continuing decline in railroad passengers and civilization's move to the western part of L.A. Three semicircular concrete steps, their white paint chipped, led up to sagging screen doors. Above the doors was a rusty, sputtering neon sign.

On one side of the hotel was the windowless front of a dance hall. Western music blared through the open doors; the band already sounded tired. Soldiers, sailors, factory workers and their dates wandered in and out. A few women wearing short skirts and very high heels were walking in pairs up and down the pavement. They were probably just waiting for their husbands.

On the other side, across the alley, was a coffee shop with its windows painted halfway up in blistered, flaking green. A hand-lettered sign by the door said, PLATE LUNCH

35¢. I could see a few customers hunched over the counter enjoying the plate dinner.

Two men with beer bottles were sitting on the steps of the Whately. They both looked at my legs, and one of them made a not-too-generous offer for the temporary use of the rest of me. Inside was a dim lobby that had probably once had wicker furniture and magazine racks and potted palms beneath its white-bladed ceiling fan. Now there were sunken, sprung chairs and battered red metal smoking stands scattered around on faded, peeling linoleum.

The main stairs were set against the left-hand wall and had a heavy railing and balustrade of dark mahogany. A wide strip in the center of each step was paler than the edges. Someone had torn up the carpet when it became too threadbare. Or maybe there had been a rubber runner, sacrificed to one of the rubber drives during the war.

The front desk faced me at the far end of the lobby. Behind it, next to the key slots, was a door open far enough that I could see what looked like a small office. Off to the right, running parallel to the front of the hotel, was a narrow hallway that must have led to the alley door, and possibly some back service stairs.

I started up the main stairs.

"Whoa. Whoa there, honey." The clerk came out of the office. "Yeah, you, sweety. Come on back down here." He was wearing a pale blue short-sleeved shirt open over an undershirt. He was lumpy and puffy-eyed from too many fights in too many bars. "Where do you think you're going?"

"Upstairs. I have an appointment."

"An appointment. I like that." He opened the half door

at the end of the front desk and propped his bulk against it. The door protested. "Not till I see a cut of the action, you don't, doll." He looked me up and down and ran his heavy-jointed fingers across his belly just below his belt. His tongue showed between his teeth. "I ain't seen you before, have I? Come on over here, and let me have a look."

Peter came out of the phone booth in the far corner behind me and walked toward us. "I see this place is real careful about its clientele."

The clerk gave him a slow, contemptuous once-over. "What's it to you, buddy?"

"We've got business here, and it isn't that kind of business, so why don't you just leer at me for a while?"

"Who the hell are you?" He stepped back behind the desk and slammed the half door. He turned and reached for a drawer. In an instant, Peter was across the room and over the door. He kicked the drawer shut. When the clerk jerked his hand away, Peter grabbed it and yanked it up between the man's shoulder blades. With the other hand, he snatched a fistful of collar and walked the man straight into the wall. His cheek spread out on the plaster.

Peter said, "I can take my time with you, or we can be friendly. You decide."

"All right. All right," the clerk said, but it sounded more like "Aw vride. Aw vride," with his lips splayed in front of his nose.

"Good." Peter loosened his grip on the man's collar. "What's your name?"

"Gus."

"Gus, we're looking for a guy. Small, dark. Wears his hair slicked back. Got an accent."

"Yeah, yeah. Little wop. Bertelli. Sixteen."

"Is that the only room he has?"

"Yeah."

"How long's he been here?"

"Maybe three weeks."

"Got any friends with him? Any visitors?"

"None I seen."

"Anybody else ask about him?"

"Didn't ask me."

"Is he up there now?"

"I don't know."

"Come on, Gus. You never miss a cut of the action. You see everybody who goes up."

"He made a call about eight-thirty or so. Then he went back up. We been busy tonight. Bunch of sailors next door. I might've missed him. Sometimes people go out the back way, I can't see their faces. I saw two guys go out maybe nine, one of them had on a white suit. Might have been him. I don't know."

Peter released him, then took Gus's gun out of the drawer and dropped it into his jacket pocket. "Behave yourself, and I'll see you get this back." He took a five-dollar bill out of another pocket and set it on the counter. "Behave yourself, and I'll see you get another one of these on the way out." He came out from behind the desk and took me by the elbow.

I said, "You have great bedside manner, Doctor. I hope your patient doesn't have another gun."

"He could wring hookers a long time and not make ten dollars. Go on up. We don't want Maritski to spot us." He turned and went off down the hall toward the rear stairs.

Gus muttered, "Asshole," but he stuffed the bill into his shirt.

Number 16 was on the second floor in the front. I

looked both ways down the hall, but I didn't see Maritski's eyes peering out of any cracks in any of the other doors. I knocked.

"Mr. Maritski," I called softly. I knocked again. "Mr. Maritski, it's Mrs. Atwill."

No one answered. I tried the door. It wasn't locked. I went in and switched on the light. In the windows, there were puckered net curtains and yellowed shades raised a couple of feet. The apple green wallpaper was lifting at the seams. There was no body sprawled beside the single bed. No body tucked under the rusty sink or dumped behind the torn shower curtain. And there were no clothes in the closet or in the chest. A smeared glass and an empty bottle of gin sat on top of the chest. That was all. There was no note for me.

I sat down on the hard chair and waited, my hands clutched in my lap, watching the door. Nothing happened. Five minutes passed. Ten. Fifteen. Maybe he'd had second thoughts. Maybe it was just a test to see if I'd bring anyone. My back began to ache from the tension. I stood up to stretch.

A scream ripped the air apart. Then again. And again.

I flung open the door and dashed for the back stairs. Peter was below on the landing, flat against the wall beside the window, his hand on his gun. "It's coming from the alley! Get back in that room and lock the door!" He disappeared down the stairs.

I didn't pay any attention. I scrambled down and looked out the landing window. Forty feet down toward the rear of the alley, just beyond the light thrown by the lamp over the back door, a woman was huddled against the wall, her legs working on the broken pavement. She was wearing a gaudy, low-cut dress and a saucer of a hat that had been knocked over her ear. Farther down, two men in aprons and undershirts peered carefully out of the kitchen door of the coffee shop.

At the top of the alley, a couple of dozen people had already gathered, keeping safely to the sidewalk. A sailor nudged his way through them and edged forward in careful inches.

Beneath me, the door opened slowly and Peter appeared, looking like a curious patron. I went on down the stairs.

Just as I reached the bottom, Gus stormed past me carrying a baseball bat. "I should've known it was you," he yelled at Peter. "What the hell's going on out there?"

"I don't know," Peter said calmly.

The sailor appeared beside him, and together they headed down the alley. Gus caught the door as it started to close and leaned on it. I scooted out and followed Peter.

"I didn't do nothin', I didn't do nothin'," the woman was moaning hysterically. She kept trying to push herself into the wall. "I swear. I didn't do nothin'." I got close enough the see that there was a pair of red panties wrapped around one bare ankle.

Peter crouched beside her. "I believe you," he said gently. "Tell me what happened."

"*There*." Her hand flailed out across the alley into the dark to piles of empty cardboard boxes and splintered crates and a row of lidless, reeking trash cans from the coffee shop.

Peter took a small flash out of his jacket pocket. He went across the alley and raked the ground with the light.

"It's all right now, ma'am. It's all right," the sailor said, but the woman continued to wail, and covered her face with her hands.

There was nothing around the boxes. Nothing around the crates. Peter moved on, examining the pavement behind the first trash can. He grabbed the handle and dragged the can away from the wall. As he did, the flash's light danced on something metallic behind it on the ground.

"What do we have here?" he said.

"What is it?" I asked.

"Looks like a knife."

He wrapped his hand around the handle of the second can to move it out of the way. The girl shrieked. We all turned to her. She was staring at Peter, horrified. I looked back at him. He was absolutely immobile, staring at her, then he turned and shot the light down into the open can.

He jerked backward. His hand, caught in the handle, tipped the can. It tottered and fell. It seemed to take a very long time to fall, making a slow, sweeping arc before it hit.

A man's head and shoulders flopped out of it.

The woman screamed again. The rest of us stood stock still, riveted by the grotesque vision of the head lolling with the rocking of the trash can, the gray face moving in and out of the light from Peter's flash.

"Jesus Mother Christ," the sailor whispered.

Peter went down on one knee and laid his fingers on the side of the throat.

The eyes fluttered open.

"He's still alive! Get help! Now!" Instantly, the sailor dashed off past Gus into the hotel.

Peter dropped the flashlight, wedged both hands into

the can, and pulled, laying his foot against the rim to get some leverage. The can slid and rocked but wouldn't let go.

"Get over here and help me!" he shouted at Gus. Gus didn't move. I pushed off the wall and knelt at the foot of the can, leaning on it as an anchor.

"Lauren, don't!"

"Just pull!"

The knees, wedged tight, came free, and the body oozed out onto the pavement. The front of the cream-colored suit was black with blood from the spilling wound in its belly.

Gus had finally moved. To go back inside. The door was closing. I jumped up and caught it just before it locked me out. Gus was throwing up on the baseboard.

I darted down the hall and into the office, where the sailor was talking frantically into the phone. In the tiny washroom, I found a fairly clean towel, grabbed it, and ran back out. The woman had disappeared. I handed Peter the towel, and he pressed it over the bloody mess that was Maritski's abdomen. I knelt on the other side.

The eyelids fluttered open again.

"Who did this?" I asked. I took his hand. It was ice-cold. "Who did this, Paul? Tell me who did this."

He didn't turn his head. His eyes were wandering over the sky. "Who did this?" I said.

His lips moved. I put my ear in front of them. Peter brought his head down beside mine.

"Eh-"

"Yes?"

The syllables came out on short, dry, gasping, choking breaths. Final, struggling, futile breaths.

"Eh—Lih—"

"Yes."

"Eh—Lih—" The gasps became sharper. I could hear the blood. "Zon—"

"What?"

"Eh. Lih. Zon. D—D—"

The lips twitched and pink foam came out from between them. The eyes stopped wandering.

I sat back slowly. "Did he say—?"

"I heard him," Peter said roughly. He stuffed the flash into his pocket and shoved himself to his feet. "Come on!"

"We can't go."

"Come on!" He grabbed my arm and hauled me to my feet.

"Stop it!" I cried angrily.

"Where's your bag?"

"In the car. Stop it!" I kept trying to pull my arm away, but he held on and dragged me away toward my car. I dug in my heels. "We have to stay!"

He grabbed my other arm and gripped me painfully. "So the cops can make out that Ray Elizondo did this? You don't have any idea what he was trying to say."

He jerked me forward and propelled me to my car. He opened the door and put me behind the wheel, then he went around and got in.

I ripped off my bloodied gloves and threw them onto the floor. "They saw our faces!"

"Do you want to talk to the cops now? Before we've had a chance to figure out what we're going to tell them, who we're going to involve?"

I glared at him. He was right. I snatched the keys out of my pocket and started the car.

His car was parked in an alley two blocks away. "Lauren, I have to talk to you," he said when we stopped.

"Juanita's gone for the night," I said harshly. "Come to my house. You can clean up there."

He got out. He bent over and looked at me across the seat. "Lauren—"

I reached out and slammed the door out of his hand and left him standing in the middle of the sidewalk. As I got to the first light, I heard sirens wailing.

Chapter 10

He caught up with me just south of First and followed me the rest of the way to Pasadena. I opened the garage door so he could pull in, then I locked it and let us in the back door. I went into the kitchen and flipped on the light.

He had wiped his hands, but they were still red. The lines on his knuckles were dark with blood. There were wet blotches on his shirt cuffs.

I opened the basement door and took a shirt off the hook behind it. It was one of Franklin's, converted years ago. "I use this in the garden. It's stained, but it's clean." I handed it to him. "Through that door's a hallway. It'll take you out to the stairs. There's a bathroom in the bedroom at the top. You can use that."

"Thanks," he said quietly, and went out.

I took off my hat and my jacket and laid them on the table. There were bloodstains on the jacket's elbows where he had grabbed me. I sat down at the table.

We had to go to the police. The clerk had gotten a good look at both of us; Peter would be in big trouble if he waited for the police to come to him.

How much would the police make out of what Maritski had been trying to say? What *was* he trying to say? It could have been Elizondo, but he was dying—possibly delirious.

No matter what the police would think, we had to tell them.

Could we get away without telling them the whole truth? Could we say Peter had discovered a gang of blackmailers without having to tell them about anyone else?

I picked up my jacket and hat. I'd take a shower—and put off thinking about the possibility that I might not be able to protect my best friend.

I went upstairs to my bedroom.

I didn't remember having closed the dressing room door. I opened it.

It had never occurred to me that Peter might go into my bedroom instead of the guest room across the hall. It had never occurred to me that he would go into the wrong room.

He was standing in the middle of my bathroom, wearing only his trousers. His bloody shirt was lying at his bare feet beside his shoes. His jacket was folded smoothly over the toilet seat, the socks draped neatly over the sink.

How much the mind can take in in a scant three seconds.

I also believe that in those three seconds, I raced over every decision I had made since the whole affair began. Every foolish, fateful, fatal decision. All in the three seconds that it took for me to see the scar on his right shoulder blade. And for him to move.

The fear shot through me like an electric charge, the painful burst of adrenaline doing just the opposite of what it should do—making my legs weak, my balance shaky, slowing me down. Still I ran. I screamed. There was nothing else to do.

He caught up with me at the bedroom door, grabbed my arm, and whipped me back inside. He slammed the door.

I kept on screaming.

He clutched at my body, at my clothes, trying to get hold of me, trying to get his hand over my mouth, while I slapped and punched at him, dodging away desperately, searching for some means of escape, some weapon.

He snatched the shoulder pad of my dress, yanked me to him, then spun me around. His forearm locked across my breasts; his other arm wrapped around my waist. Pinioning me to him, he carried me, straining and struggling, into the dressing room. He kicked the door shut. There were no windows in the dressing room, none in the bathroom. Only old, thick, soundproof walls.

I kept fighting. I dug my fingernails into his hand at my shoulder, using all my strength to pry it loose. I bent forward. Just a few inches. It was all I needed. I slammed my head back straight into his face. I heard something pop. He groaned and staggered. His grip loosened. I struggled free.

I got one step.

He threw both arms around me, pinning my own to my sides. He kicked my feet out from under me. Helplessly, I fell as he dropped to one knee, then both. My legs raked the ground wildly. I pounded my head into him, but now it only struck his chest. His arms still tightly around me, he weighed me down onto my stomach. I could not move, but I fought anyway, enraged by my helplessness and the touch and the scent of his bare skin. I strained furiously, making unintelligible, angry, terrified sounds. It was useless.

"Stop it, Lauren. Stop it. You're only going to hurt yourself."

He was far stronger, far heavier than I was. I stopped fighting.

For an eternity, we lay still, both dragging air out of the carpet. Finally, he said, "If I let you up, will you let me explain?"

I didn't answer. He didn't move.

"Will you let me explain?"

"Yes," I snapped. It was better than lying degradingly on the floor.

Slowly, he released me. Slowly, I rolled over and sat up. He sat back on one knee and held the back of his hand against his bleeding nose, then, a little shakily, he got to his feet, which were covered in nasty red welts from the heels of my shoes. He pulled the small chair out of the corner, and said, "Sit down."

I stood up, leaning on the wall. The fear and the fighting had left me so weak that it was all I could do to make it to the chair. He took the stool out of the other corner and set it in front of the door to the bedroom. Heavily, he sat down and took a few breaths through his mouth.

"You're pretty good in a fight," he said.

I didn't say thank you.

He examined me—the rumpled dress, the torn nylons, the skinned knees, the smeared, streaked face. "Are you hurt?" I didn't answer. He took another breath. "I didn't kill Maritski, and I didn't kill Cummings."

I didn't say I didn't believe him. I kept searching the room out of the corners of my eyes for a weapon.

"I've got to get a towel," he said, and stood up.

I stayed where I was. I didn't have enough strength yet to run or fight. Watching me, he ran cold water onto a hand towel and washed most of the blood away. He soaked the towel again.

His shoulder holster was hanging from one of the hooks by the door; he came out with his gun. He sat down and, with one hand, laid the towel against the back of his neck. With the other, he held the gun on his thigh. It was a Colt M-1911, an automatic, standard military issue.

"Have you ever handled a gun?" he asked.

"Yes."

He pulled out the magazine and showed it to me. "It's loaded. I'd appreciate it if you didn't use it until you let me explain a few things."

For a moment, I was sure it was some perverse game he was playing, torturing me with hope of escape. Tentatively, I put out my hand. He snapped the magazine back in and laid the gun in my palm. I wrapped my fingers around the butt. It was a good thing I didn't have to use it. In the sudden rush of relief, my hand started shaking so badly that I probably couldn't have hit him, five feet away. I held the gun in my lap. "All right," I said, "I'm listening."

He tilted his head back against the door and took another breath through his mouth. "That was me in your pictures."

"I think we've established that."

"I didn't know there were any pictures until the day you came to my office."

I must have looked somewhat skeptical.

"Do you mind if I get that shirt?" he asked.

"Stay away from the clerk's gun."

"Anything you say." He rinsed the towel again and gingerly wiped his face, then he put on Franklin's shirt. The sleeves were too short, so he rolled them up. It was too tight through the shoulders, so he left the first buttons open. He came back and sat down. He put the towel against the back of his neck again and said, "Christina Harris Winnack was a client of mine."

I stared at him dumbly.

"Miss Harris's sister," he said. "Do you remember? She killed herself."

"I know who she is."

"She came to see me last fall. It was blackmail. She wouldn't tell me much about it. Something in her past, something her husband wouldn't understand. She didn't want to find the guys, just get the pictures back. She wanted me to go with her when she made the payoff. And pick up the pictures and negatives. After I did, I didn't hear from her again. I thought everything was fine. I should have followed up. I should have made sure. Then she turned up dead in her garage. The cops who investigated said it was an accident, but it stunk. I went to their captain and told him what I knew. He leaned on them, and they leaned on the husband. Finally, he handed over the suicide note she'd left and told the truth.

"The blackmailers hadn't given her all the pictures, of course. They must have warned her not to get any more help. They kept bleeding her. Finally, when she couldn't take it anymore, she broke down and confessed to her husband. And he left her. Told her that he would take her two little girls. Mrs. Winnack was very much like her sister— sensitive, high-strung, maybe even more so. It was too much for her.

"Her father hit the ceiling when the cops told the papers it was suicide. He made a few phone calls, and the investigation died. Except for him and the husband, I don't think anyone else in the family knew about the blackmail. The cops never got to question any of them. But I couldn't let it go. That's when I started talking to the other investigators in town and found out there'd been other victims like Mrs. Winnack, that there was a gang at work.

"Last month, a man called me. He said he thought his stepson was stealing from the business. He said he didn't want to come to the office, but could I come to his house? I didn't suspect a thing. There were lights on in the house, a car in the drive. A guy in a mask stepped out of the bushes. I wasn't wearing my gun, but it wouldn't have made any difference. I remember getting into a car, but that's all. I woke up in the trunk, tied up."

He wiped his face again. The bleeding had almost stopped.

"I keep a small knife and lock pick inside the waistband of my trousers. It's not easy to find in a frisk. Fortunately, I could get to it. I cut the rope and forced the lid. Trunk locks are practically useless. I raised it enough to see where we were. Next light, I tumbled out onto the pavement and started running.

"It turned out that the people who owned the house had been out of town. It was all a setup. I didn't know why I'd been grabbed. Then I found you in my house, found out you'd been waylaid the same night I was. Then you showed me that picture with me in it."

"Why didn't you tell me?" I asked, not very kindly.

"Because you might have believed me, but you might not have hired me. Well? Can you say for sure you would've given me the job?"

"I don't know."

"I couldn't take the chance. If I was going to find out who drove Mrs. Winnack to kill herself, I needed a client. Everything I've found these last few months, I got on my own. Between other cases. Ed Paxton's not going to pay his men to do the cops' work for them. Then you came along, willing to do something. And with the money to do it."

"And so sure of myself that it never occurred to me that Maritski might have reversed the negative. Why did you take off your shirt that day?"

"Because I could tell you weren't sure. Eventually, you might want to make sure."

"What would you have done if I'd wanted to see both shoulders?"

"I'd have told you the truth. It was a gamble. But I wanted you to trust me."

I almost hooted.

"It doesn't look too smart now," he conceded.

"Where did you get the scar?" I asked.

"Shrapnel. Guadalcanal."

"I don't suppose you bothered to tell the police what you found out from the other private detectives."

"I didn't have anything to give them."

"Let's go."

"Where?"

"To call Helen. Somebody's going to know you're here." He dragged the stool aside and led the way into the bedroom. I set the receiver down on the night table while I dialed. The bedside clock said 11:25.

"Hello?" Helen said groggily.

"Helen, are you listening?"

"Lauren?" She sniffed a few times. "What is it? What time is it? Is something wrong?"

"Is Sam there?"

"He's still at the studio. What is it?"

"Maritski's dead."

"Oh, God! Oh, dear God! What happened? Are you all right?"

"For now. Peter's here with me. Maritski called and wanted to talk, but he was dead when we got there."

"Are you in danger?"

"I don't think so," I said slowly. "Peter's here."

"Yes, I heard you."

"He's going to stay here tonight. I'll call you in the morning. If you don't hear from me by eight, call the police. Do you understand?"

"Yes," she said hesitantly. "What's going on? Why are you—? Wait. I hear Sam."

"You don't want to have to explain this call." I hung up.

"I think you could use a drink," Peter said.

"No, thanks," I said crisply.

"I think I could use one. And maybe some ice for this nose."

We went downstairs, and he got two brandies from the dining room. Then we went into the kitchen so he could get some ice to put in his towel. He sat down on one side of the table; I sat on the other. He put the towel gently against his nose and slid my glass toward me, but I didn't touch it.

"What else is there?" I asked, my hand still on the gun.

"I've told you everything."

"How did this gang find out you were onto them?"

"I asked a lot of questions. I might have asked the wrong person. I don't know who."

"Why would this gang want to put you in any pictures?"

"They couldn't use one of their own guys. They wouldn't take that chance. They needed pictures of Mrs. Ross to keep Cummings quiet. They waylaid me to use in them, but they got you instead of Mrs. Ross. They took some anyway on the chance they could get money out of you. Then they were going to take me out to the desert and shoot me. I'm sure of that. But I got away."

The phone rang. I jumped and nearly dropped the gun. I answered it before it could jangle again.

"Mrs. Atwill?"

"Yes, Johnny." Peter started to get up. I waved him back down with the gun.

"Is Pete there?"

"Not at the moment. He should be back soon."

"There are cops all over the Whately."

"Maritski's dead."

"I was afraid of that."

"Has Jack come back to the San Marcos Courts yet?"

"I don't know. I haven't heard from our man down there. Should I come over?"

"No, I'll be fine. Where are you?"

"The office."

"Go on home. If Peter wants you to do anything, he'll call. You might bring him a change of clothes in the morning. About seven."

I said good night and sat back down. Peter sipped his brandy and watched me. Finally, I said, "Do you think Christina Winnack committed suicide?"

"Yes. There was alcohol in her blood, but not enough to make her pass out. There were no other drugs and no signs of a struggle. No bruises or scratches. She left a note. It looked genuine. It doesn't matter one way or the other. They still killed her."

"We have to go to the police."

"Lauren—"

"Look, if you're telling the truth, I don't want to cost you your license. If you're lying, then I sure as hell want someone to know."

"You might have to tell them about Mrs. Ross."

"Stop it! There's nothing else I can do!"

"You can wait till we get a look inside that warehouse. There might be a way to hand this gang to the cops without involving anyone else. The desk clerk doesn't have any idea who we are. Give me one day. Then we'll go to the cops and tell them everything."

"If you want some more ice, you'd better get it."

"Lauren—"

"I can't think anymore. Do you want some ice or not?"

He got some, doing everything slowly so I could see every move. After he had folded it into the towel, I got a spool of thick twine and a pair of scissors out of a drawer and motioned him in front of me up the stairs and into the bedroom at the end of the hall.

"Go on. Lie down."

Obediently, he turned back the bedspread and got in, fully dressed.

"Take off your trousers."

"What?"

"Do it."

He pulled the spread over him and unzipped his fly. He slipped out of his trousers and handed them out to me. I squeezed along the waistband until I felt the blade he'd mentioned. He was right. It was hard to find.

"The way the lawn slopes on this side of the house," I said, "there's a drop of almost three stories. There are no sheets on the bed, and the spread won't reach. I've got your car keys, so if you don't break your leg, you'll be hitching a ride in your shorts. Good night, Mr. Winslow."

The key to the room was in the night table. I took it out and locked the door after me. I cut off a length of twine and tied one end to the doorknob and the other to the neck of the lamp on the hall table, then placed the lamp on the edge.

In the study, I typed out an abbreviated version of everything that had happened in the last month, including Peter's being in my pictures and what Maritski said before he died, then I locked it in the safe.

The lamp had not moved, but I searched my room anyway, then I locked my door and wedged a chair under the knob.

I picked up my jacket and hat off the floor, then took off my dress and hid everything in the back of the closet.

I put the envelope of money away in the chest of drawers, then turned on the taps in the bath and stood by the door to the hall, listening, while the water ran. While I soaked, the Colt lay on the floor in easy reach.

I set the alarm for six and lay on my side, staring at the clock and the gun on the night table and the door beyond. Somewhere near three, I dropped off, but I kept jolting awake, grateful I couldn't remember my dreams.

Chapter 11

At five-thirty, I got up. The muscles in my shoulders and legs ached, my knees were raw. There were bruises all over both arms. I rinsed my face over and over in cold water, but my eyes were still red and swollen. I dressed in slacks and a long-sleeved blouse, then I took Gus's gun out of Peter's jacket, unloaded it, and put the bullets in the pocket of my slacks. I shoved it into my waistband and gathered up the trousers, the scissors, and the keys. I picked up the Colt and tore down my barricade.

The lamp was still perched on the edge of the table. I cut the twine and rapped on the door.

"I'm still here," he called. He didn't sound as if I had awakened him.

He was lying on his back with both pillows shoved under his head. His nose was swollen wide and fat. Both eyes were going black.

"Does that hurt?" I asked.

"Like the devil."

"Good." I tossed his trousers on the bed and went out.

In the kitchen, I turned on all the lights, put the clerk's gun in a drawer, and started coffee. By the time Peter came down, it was ready. His face looked even worse in the full light.

The Colt at my side, I went out and pulled the newspaper out of the azaleas. The murder was on the front page, with a picture of the covered body lying beside the trash can. The story wallowed in the grotesqueness of the crime; there were few solid details. The deceased had registered as Paul Bertelli. He had been stabbed. The probable weapon had been recovered. Robbery was a possible motive since the man's wallet and possessions were missing. There was a not-very-detailed description of him. The police wanted to question a couple who had asked about the dead man just before the body was discovered. Peter was older in the description. I was called a platinum blonde.

The doorbell rang.

We were both very still, looking at each other across the table. "It's too early for Johnny," Peter said.

We went through the dining room to the living room and peered around the edges of the curtains. Sergeant Barty was standing on the porch.

Peter said, "If you have to let him in, let me do the talking." He went back toward the kitchen.

I dropped the gun into the drawer of the table in the foyer before I opened the door.

"Good morning, Mrs. Atwill," Barty said, and took off his hat. "Sorry to bother you so early."

"That's all right. I was up."

The other detective I'd seen at Central Division came around the corner of the house from the garage. "His car's there," he said gruffly.

"You remember Sergeant Tolen?" Barty said. I said I did. "We'd like to talk to Pete. He's here, isn't he?"

I stood away from the door. "Come in, gentlemen."

I took them back to the kitchen. Peter was there. The newspaper was gone.

"Nice face," Tolen sneered.

"She did it. So watch your step with her."

"We don't need any crap from you."

"Settle down, both of you," Barty said mildly. "It's too early."

"Would you like some coffee?" I asked them.

"If you don't mind," Barty said. They sat down at either end of the table. I poured the coffee and took the last chair.

While he talked, Barty loaded sugar leisurely into his cup and stirred. "Last night, we get a call about a messy stiff down at the Whately Hotel. Now, unlike most of the clerks you find in these places, this guy's real talkative. He says just before the body turned up, there's a couple in there asking about the stiff. The guy asked questions like a cop. Big guy and real tough. Roughed up our boy. The woman was a blonde, he says, tall, classy. Too classy for his joint. And I start thinking, what classy blonde has been asking me about what PI with bad manners lately?"

Tolen said to Peter, "You going to tell us about it, or do we haul you downtown for an ID?"

Peter said, "I thought this was just a social call since I don't see any Pasadena cops."

"Keep it up," Tolen said, "and we can start talking about your license."

"That won't be necessary, sergeant," I said. "We were there." I glanced at Peter. His eyes were full of caution. "I was so upset after we found the body that Mr. Winslow had to bring me home. He was coming to see you this morning. That was his intention, and I'll swear to it if I have to." I took Gus's gun out of the drawer and gave it to Barty. "Mr. Winslow only roughed up the clerk after he pulled this on us."

"Why would he do that?"

"Because the man made some lewd remarks to me, and Mr. Winslow told him it wasn't very polite."

Barty broke out the clip and tried not to smile. "Was it loaded?"

I dug the bullets out of my pocket and handed them over.

Barty put them in his coat and set the gun down on the table. "So, what was it you were coming to tell us this morning?"

Peter said, "First, Mrs. Atwill's not involved in this. She's only acting for a friend."

"Who would that be?" Barty asked.

"A client."

Tolen's fingers twitched, but he didn't say anything.

Barty picked up his cup. "Go on."

"Your stiff tried to sell my client some compromising pictures, but it looks like they weren't his to sell. It looks like he stole them from a pretty dangerous bunch. Your stiff told my client as much when he called her last night. He was scared and was going to tell what he knew in return for protection."

"What was this guy's real name?" Barty asked.

"He told my client it was Maritski. Paul Maritski. He said that, just before he stole the pictures, he followed the guy who had them, and saw him meet with somebody he claimed my client knew. He wouldn't say who."

"Who was he following?"

"He didn't say. He was going to tell us both names."

Tolen said, "And you were going to give him money for them so he could get out of town."

"That would be obstruction of justice."

"Keep pushing, hotshot. You're half a step from finding a new line of work."

"What did you find in his room?" asked Barty.

I said, "Mr. Winslow never went into his room. I did. There was nothing there but a glass and a bottle of gin."

"What time did you two get there?"

"I was there about nine-fifteen," Peter said. "Mrs. Atwill about nine-thirty." He told them how we'd ended up in the alley.

Barty said, "What did you do till Mrs. Atwill got there?"

"Watched the building. Tried to spot him."

"How'd you know what this guy looked like?"

"My client gave me a description."

"She'd seen him?"

"He was an amateur."

Tolen said, "When did your client talk to this guy last?"

"Mrs. Atwill talked to him last, about eight-thirty. He had agreed to let her handle the drop. He called here to tell her where to meet him."

"He's still alive at eight-thirty, but by nine-fifteen, when you get there, he's in a trash can, and the killers are gone?"

"That's the way it looks."

"Quite a coincidence." Tolen sneered.

"Yeah. But I don't see that it could be anything else. Mrs. Atwill didn't tell anyone we were going to the Whately. I only told my men, and by the time I did that, Maritski was probably already in the trash can. The desk clerk saw a guy in a white suit go out the back door with someone about an hour before we found him. That's got to be coincidence, unless you think somebody's got microphones running out of my house or this one, maybe sitting out in the garage right now, listening."

"You know how long we can hold you as a material witness?" Tolen snapped.

"You know how much good it'll do you? If you arrest me, it'll make the papers. Then the killers will know the cops have found out about the blackmail, and they'll go so far underground, you'll never find them. If you want to take me downtown and announce it to them, fine. And you can explain it to your captain again."

Tolen started out of his chair, but before he could get up, Barty reached out and slapped Peter hard across the face.

"You remember who you're talking to," Barty said fiercely. "Or maybe you'd like to go see the DA. He'd love to hear how you were going to help a blackmailer get out of town. He'll have your license before you can break a sweat."

There was a long, uncomfortable minute. Barty and Tolen glared at Peter. Peter, his mouth set stubbornly, stared at the tabletop.

"Sergeant," I said quietly to Barty, "there might be a way out of this."

"You don't have to tell them anything," Peter said.

"Do you want to go to jail?"

"I've been there before."

"Do you want to go back?"

Barty clinked his spoon against the rim of his cup almost as if he were only tapping coffee from it. "What do you have in mind, Mrs. Atwill?"

"Mr. Winslow's trying to make you angry at him so you won't think too much about me. He's trying to protect me. I'm the one who was being blackmailed." I told him about how Maritski had confronted me in Madison's with the faked pictures, omitting that Peter was in them. "I was too embarrassed to go the police. I was afraid you wouldn't believe me. I hired Mr. Winslow to help me."

Tolen did his best not to snarl at me. "Do you have any of these pictures?"

"Maritski was going to give them to me last night."

"Mrs. Atwill," Barty said, "if you have some, we need to see them. We're not going to give them to your husband, and we don't care how they were really taken."

"That's why she didn't want to go to the cops," Peter growled. "She knew you wouldn't believe her."

"It doesn't make sense. Some guys kidnap a woman and take dirty pictures of her on the chance they might make some money?"

"Maybe you should worry more about the gang of blackmailers you've had working your town for years. Right under your noses."

"What the hell are you talking about?"

Peter told them what he'd found out about there being other victims by questioning other investigators. "It won't do any good to talk to them. They won't give out client names without a fight, and none of their clients saw their blackmailers anyway. If you take anyone downtown, it'll make the papers, and we'll lose the gang. I'll tell you what I can, but Mrs. Atwill hasn't done anything wrong. She doesn't deserve to be dragged across the headlines."

"Now you're in trouble, you want to cooperate," Barty said.

"You can slap me around some more, if it'll make you feel better."

"You had that coming."

Peter didn't deny it. Barty and Tolen looked at each other. Tolen's face was still flushed, but he gave Barty a curt nod.

Barty stood up, and said to Peter, "I'm going home to shower and get a couple hours' sleep. Then I want to see you at my desk. Ten o'clock. Maybe you better get that face looked at." He hitched his trousers, and said to me, "Did you really give him those shiners?"

"Yes, but it was an accident."

"If you play me for a sucker, Pete, I'll make them look like mother's kisses."

I went out with them. Tolen got behind the wheel of a gray Ford, but Barty lingered beside me on the porch.

"Don't pay too much attention to Tolen today. Pete rubs him the wrong way."

"I think there's more to it than that."

"Well, mostly it's about a case a few months ago."

"Christina Winnack?"

"Yeah. Tolen did the preliminary investigation. Called it an accident. When Pete got the case reopened, Tolen wasn't too happy. It made him look bad in front of the captain."

"Was he paid off by the family?"

His head swung around to me sharply. "Most suicides get called accidents. The truth only hurts the family, and they're hurting enough already. Tolen's got a short fuse, but he's a good cop."

"I'm sorry. I shouldn't have said that. I guess all this has made me a little suspicious of everybody."

"It might be a good idea to stay that way. Be careful. This is murder, Mrs. Atwill. I like Pete, but he's not as tough as he thinks he is." He put on his hat and got into the car.

I went back inside, down the hall, and directly into the downstairs bathroom, where I splashed my face with cold water. Then I spent some time looking in the mirror at a woman on the brink of being arrested for withholding evidence. How much was I willing to risk in order to give Peter another day to clear his friend? And to preserve one woman's marriage and another's sanity?

The doorbell rang. It was Johnny.

"Were those cops in that Ford?" he asked, as he limped in, carrying a garment bag and a shaving case.

"Yes."

"I thought it looked like one of their cars, so I waited till they were gone."

"Come on into the kitchen. I'll make you some breakfast."

Peter was still sitting at the table.

"Good golly!" Johnny exclaimed. "What happened to your face?"

"I'll tell you later," his brother said shortly, and went out with his things.

"What's the matter?" Johnny asked me. "Are we in trouble with the cops?"

"Maybe."

While I fixed breakfast, I told him what had happened at the hotel. As we finished eating, Peter came back down.

"Do you want some food?" I asked.

"If it's no trouble."

I poured him some coffee. "The gun's in the hall table."

"I found it."

Johnny looked back and forth between us, confused. "I got the report on Jack. He didn't get back to the San Marcos Courts till almost four. What happened to your face?"

"She didn't tell you?"

"Only what happened at the Whately."

Peter wrapped his hands around his cup and told Johnny the truth. All of it. "Your brother's been a horse's ass."

Johnny didn't disagree with him. Some of the puppy-like adoration had gone out of his eyes, and I thought it was all for the best. After a minute, Johnny said, "Sooner or later, the cops are going to find out I was at Maritski's apartment asking questions."

"Yes," Peter said, "we don't have much time. If we can find something at that warehouse tonight, something that'll make a case for them, they're not going to care very much that I stalled them for a day."

"And if we don't?"

"We've still got Jack to hand to them."

I said, "Are you sure they're not going to care?"

He ignored my question. "Right now, besides the ware-house, our best lead is that whoever Maritski saw there with Jack and Cummings was someone he thought you knew well, well enough to call for money. And someone he was proud of recognizing. How would he know who your friends are?"

"I don't know. I don't even know how he recognized *me*. He couldn't have seen me very often at Marathon. And writers don't get much publicity. I was never in the papers—"

"Except with your husband," said Peter.

"Maritski would hardly have bragged about recogniz-ing Franklin. Most of America would have."

"Unless he was in disguise."

"Franklin did not do this."

"He didn't join up, did he? He was here during the war when the blackmail started."

"He couldn't serve. His eyesight's terrible. He did as much as he could. As soon as he finished a picture, he'd go on bond drives, visit the military hospitals. It was not Franklin."

"You've got a lot of money. He might like a chance to

get some of it. He spends almost everything he earns. Don't tell me you didn't know that."

"Have you been investigating him?"

"I'm investigating everyone. We checked out his finances. Your husband's squeezed. He didn't have to save when he was living with you. He got out of the habit. Where was he the night you were waylaid?"

"He said he was sailing, and I believe him."

"Okay, okay. Was there anyone you saw a lot of at Marathon when Maritski was there? Someone he might have seen you with?"

"He only worked on six pictures. I wrote only one of them. But he could have seen me talking to anyone for a couple of minutes on the lot and thought we were friends."

"Did you ever work at any of the other studios where he might have seen you?"

"Only rewrites. And I didn't actually go onto the lot. I'd park the car, go into the offices, talk with whoever I needed to talk to, then leave. If I ever spent any time where Maritski could have seen me, I don't remember it."

"Then we come to the time he was following you. He saw you with Miss Wagner at Madison's."

"Yes, he must have. He said that he thought I was working on the movie. He must have recognized her."

"She was at the Rosses' party and could have been the one who called Jack to tell him to disappear. If Maritski thought you were working on the movie, he'd know you were working with Deegan. Deegan was at the party, too. Who else could Maritski have seen you with while he was tailing you?"

"I spent almost all my time here, working on the script. There was Helen. And Juanita, of course. And . . ."

"Who else?"

"Well, there was Forrest. I ran into him at the studio the day I picked up the script. We went out to dinner. But he wasn't at Helen's party."

"If Joan Trent was sober enough—and mean enough—when she got home that night, she might've called him to tell him about your new boyfriend. And he could have called Jack. Do you know where he was the Saturday night you were grabbed?"

"He told me he was out of town."

"Anybody else?"

"No. Maybe we'll find something in that warehouse."

"You're not going," said Peter.

"I can pick locks."

"So can I."

"If there's anything in there that points to someone I know, I'd recognize it before you would."

"You're not going to get shot breaking into that warehouse."

"Are you planning on getting shot?"

"You're not going."

"Yes, I am."

"I said no!"

"The police know about me! I'm part of this now whether you like it or not!"

"Don't tell me how to do my job! You learn a few tricks, and you think you're Sam Spade! This is not a game, godammit! There are two men dead, and nobody's going to spare you because you're an amateur! You're not going, and if you don't like it, you can fire me!"

He slammed out of the kitchen and out of the house.

Methodically, in the silence that followed, I cleared the table. I scraped the plates and dumped Peter's untouched eggs into the trash and stacked everything beside the sink.

Finally, Johnny said, "Pete's got quite a temper sometimes. But I've never seen him lose it with a client before. I'm real sorry."

I sighed. "I should have kept my mouth shut. It cost him a lot to tell you all that. And to get slapped around by the police in front of me. He's worried about what might happen to Mrs. Ross, and especially Miss Harris and Mr. Elizondo. This isn't an ordinary case to him. Has he ever kept this much from the police before?"

"Pete knows what he's doing."

"I hope so." I turned on the taps, sprinkled some dishwashing powder under the running water, and watched it froth. I started washing the dishes. Johnny came over and stood beside me and dried them.

"You like Pete, don't you?"

"Yes."

"He likes you, too. I can tell. I'm glad. You're not like the women he usually goes out with. I mean that as a compliment."

"Not to your brother."

He laughed. "I guess not."

When we finished, I poured out the old coffee and started a fresh pot.

The phone rang. I picked it up. I could hear traffic on the other end.

"Can I speak to Johnny?" Peter said stiffly.

I handed Johnny the phone. He listened for a minute, then started to hang up. "Give it to me," I said. "Peter?"

"Yes?"

"Do you still need a client?"

"Yes."

"Then I'm in. But all the way."

"I don't want you hurt."

"I know."

"You do as I say. To the letter."

"Yes."

"Johnny's going to stay with you while I check out some alibis. All of the people you knew at the Rosses' party—and Barlowe—might have alibis for both killings. They might have still been filming both nights. We won't try the warehouse until dark. Get some sleep. And bring your tools tonight."

"I thought you could pick locks."

"I'm not as good at it as you are."

I laughed and hung up.

Johnny said, "Pete said to clean up the mess he left in your bathroom."

"There's not much. But there are sponges and ammonia in the pantry if you need them."

"I'll take care of it."

When he had gone upstairs, I went into the study and called Helen. She was nearly frantic.

"I saw the papers. Is that you they're looking for?"

I said it was and tried to calm her down, telling her as much as I could, which wasn't much. I didn't tell her that the police had already found me. I'd wait until we'd seen what was inside the warehouse. She had enough on her mind. She asked me to sit near her at the funeral. In all the commotion, I'd forgotten that Dean's funeral was that day. But I promised I would.

Chapter 12

We took Johnny's car and parked three blocks from the church because we couldn't find a space any closer. In front of the church, on both sides of the street, police were keeping the press and gawkers back. To get inside, we had to get approval from a thin-lipped man with dandruff who was planted at the top of the steps. Sam had left my name on the list.

The church was almost full—friends of Dean and his parents, executives from Marathon, and, which explained the crowd outside, plenty of stars from Marathon and the other studios, who had come out of respect for Dean's father. At each end of the family's pew were men who looked like bodyguards.

Johnny sat down alone at the rear of the church.

I found Helen and Sam halfway down the right-hand aisle. I said hello, but that was all. I could hardly say more. I didn't want to look like I was comforting her. Forrest was sitting not far away, in a group with other Marathon character actors. He scooted over to make a place for me. After the service, Helen and Sam went on to the cemetery. I didn't go with them.

Johnny hung back while I walked down the steps with

Forrest. The cordons of police were still holding the fans back, but they couldn't keep them from screaming and snapping pictures when one of their favorites appeared.

"I heard about what happened at the Rosses' party," Forrest said. "I can't tell you how sorry I am."

"You're not to blame. It's—" I stared at him. "How did you find out?"

"Newly Gardner called. He wanted to know if I had any influence with her. He says she ought to check herself into a hospital. I told him she wouldn't listen to me."

Alex came out of the church, scanned the crowd, and hurried down to us. She looked even frailer. Her face was pinched, her eyelids swollen. I introduced her to Forrest. She blinked at him a couple of times before she offered her hand, and I remembered that I had told her I had slept with him.

Since we could hardly keep talking about Joan's drinking, I asked him, "Are you wrapping soon?"

"On Friday. Then I'm headed straight for La Jolla."

"Are the grandchildren going with you?"

"Not this time. Stella's in-laws are taking them up to San Francisco to visit some cousins."

"Have a good time."

"I will." He leaned forward and kissed my cheek. "I'm sorry about Joan," he whispered. He said good-bye to Alex and went off through the crowd to find his car.

"Stella was his daughter," I explained to Alex. "She died a few years ago in a car accident."

"It must have been terrible for him, to lose a child."

"Yes, it was. His grandchildren are some comfort."

"I know. I feel the same way about my nieces. They help. A little. Mrs. Atwill, I've been thinking about what you said. Do you still need me?"

"Yes."

She started to go on, but Franklin peeled away from a group of mourners and sauntered up behind her.

"Hello, Franklin," I said.

Fear leaped into her eyes, and she snapped her mouth shut. Surreptitiously, I patted her hand at her side.

"Are you okay?" he asked her. "She felt a little dizzy."

"I'm fine now," she said softly. "I put some cold water on my face. I'm all right."

A girl in the crowd cried out Franklin's name in a shrill throb of longing. He gave her a brief wave. There was a concerted shriek of delight from the rest of the girls, and they surged forward against the stout row of uniforms.

"I guess we better go before they break through," he said. "We'll see you, Lauren. Drop by the set someday. Don won't mind." He led Alex away to their waiting limousine.

When Johnny and I returned to the car, we found a leaflet under the windshield wiper from *The Committee for a Free America*, asking that names of communists in Hollywood be sent to their post office box. Confidentiality was guaranteed.

Juanita was in the kitchen, purring over a beautiful rolled roast the butcher had sent over. I admired it, too. It was the best-looking piece of meat I'd seen outside a restaurant since before the war. I asked after her sister and introduced Johnny. I didn't explain who he was.

I called Alex from the study. She was out, so I left a message. Then I went to bed and slept through the afternoon.

At dinner, Johnny devoured three helpings of roast beef and two pieces of peach pie. When we finished, I went into the kitchen and asked Juanita if she'd like to go stay with her sister for a few more days. She crossed her arms and, for a moment, just looked at me, then she fished into her apron pocket and took out a bullet. "I found this in your slacks," she said. "First, there is this strange man Maritski calling you, then there is Mr. Winslow, then the police come to see you about Mr. Cummings. Today, I find a towel with blood on it in the garbage outside, and this man won't take off his coat because he is wearing a gun."

"Mr. Winslow and his brother are private detectives," I explained humbly. "I can't tell you anything else right now, but it has something to do with the night I was robbed."

"Can they take care of you?"

"Yes."

"They better."

After she had gone to her sister's, I dressed in dark clothes and soft-soled shoes. In a canvas carryall, I packed my tools, two Thermoses of coffee, and some sandwiches I'd made out of the leftover beef. Remembering my previous stakeouts, I tossed in a roll of toilet paper. When it was dark, we went out the back way and climbed into Johnny's car. Along the way into L.A., we pulled into side streets and waited. No one was following us. We parked three blocks from Peter's house.

At five after ten, Peter threw open the back door and jumped in. Johnny had the car moving before the door closed.

"Is there a stakeout?" Johnny asked.

"Yes. One of these days, the cops'll stop using those gray Fords."

We drove in a jigsaw pattern while Peter kept watch for a tail. When the light from the streetlamps fanned the interior, I could see his face. Although the swelling had gone down, the discoloration beneath his eyes was still dark. The doctor had put a bandage across the bridge of his nose when he reset the cartilage. I winced, thinking what that must have felt like.

"How were the police?" I asked.

"Not bad. I behaved myself, and so did they."

"Do they think we're telling them everything?"

"Not likely. They asked a lot of questions about how Maritski would know who your acquaintances are. I gave them the names of the people he probably saw you with when he was following you."

"Did they say anything about putting a sketch of him in the paper?"

"No. They want to move slowly. They don't want the gang to know anybody thinks he was important."

"I saw Alex today at the funeral," I said, "She couldn't say much, but I think she wants to help. I left a message for her."

"Good. Call her tomorrow."

I handed him a sandwich.

"Thanks," he said. "I didn't get a chance to eat. We got the report back on those cigarettes you found at Elizondo's. Raleighs. You know anyone who smokes them?"

"I'm not sure what brand anyone smokes. They use cases."

"Not even your husband?"

I shot him a look, but in the dark I don't think he could see it. "He used to smoke Camels. I guess he still does."

He unwrapped the waxed paper on the sandwich. "I talked to our contact at Marathon. *The Final Line* and Barlowe's picture both finished shooting by seven o'clock last night and last Friday when Cummings died. Nobody's got an alibi for the murders."

"Oh."

"We found out who's owned that warehouse for the last few years. A company called Santiago Imports. Based in Juarez, like a hundred other companies who want to keep their owners a secret. The real estate people say the sale was handled by a Mexican lawyer. It'll take a while to get names."

He took a bite and chewed gratefully. "We're still looking for a way that Jack could've hooked up with whoever Maritski saw at the warehouse. We haven't found any record of a Jack Hochauser at the studios, Central Casting, or any other service like the Call Bureau. We did get his service record. Drafted in '42, caught TB. Honorably discharged in '43."

"Just when the gang got started," I said.

"Yes."

I poured him some coffee from the Thermos and handed the lid carefully over the seat. "There are a couple of things I don't understand."

Johnny laughed. "Just a couple?"

"How did the gang know Maritski was at the Whately, and how did they get him out of the hotel?"

Peter said, "The cops've talked to all of the hotel's desk clerks. They say nobody came in asking questions."

"How can that be?" I asked.

"They might have found him by looking the way we were. Searching for his car near the places he could afford to stay. When they found it, they waited for him to show up and followed him back to the hotel. And they had three weeks to do it. His hotel room faced the street. They might have even been able to tell which was his room."

"But they couldn't go into the hotel and get him out," I said. "He never would have gone quietly."

"No."

"Then it seems awfully lucky that he went out into that alley and walked right into their hands."

"Too lucky. Maybe there's an answer in the trash can."

"Come again," Johnny said.

"Not in it. But in why the killer used it. It took time to put the body in there. Enough time to risk a witness. And eventually the body would be found anyway. Why not just leave him on the ground? Better yet, why not sap him and toss him into a car? Kill him later. No body. No police." He shook his head. "Why did they leave him in that can?"

None of us had any answers.

Johnny cut his lights, and we made a turn. We pulled down the block and in behind a small paneled truck that was parked on the shoulder near the spot where Peter and I had first watched the warehouse. The driver, wearing dark coveralls, got out and climbed in beside Peter, who introduced us.

Gil Hillman was a thin, stooped man with horn-rimmed glasses and wisps of hair combed neatly across a bald pate. He looked more like an accountant or an insurance adjuster, which—I suspected—were the roles he usually played during investigations.

"Nothing has happened since I arrived," he reported precisely. "Unless they have a watchman whom none of us has seen, the warehouse is empty."

"Let's take a look," Peter said. Gil covered his gleaming head with a cap.

They couldn't turn on a flashlight, so, very quickly, they disappeared into the garbage-strewn field. Johnny and I waited. It was a half hour before they came back.

Peter opened my door. "Ready?" He laughed at whatever expression was on my face.

The trip across the field took an eternity. Even though Peter kept telling me there was no one around, it was all I could do not to hang back. It was all I could do not to hide behind him.

We went in under the brick arches. A loading dock ran across the rear wall. On it, there was a regular wooden door and a long, roll-up metal one for deliveries. The regular door was solid oak and looked fairly new. We climbed onto the dock, and I dug out my tools. Peter shined the light on the keyhole until I got the first pick in place, then turned it off. The lock was a lot better than the one on Peter's door. It took a full five minutes to pick.

When the door swung open, Peter grabbed it, but the new hinges didn't squeak. We went into the dark and listened. Nothing stirred. There was no sound of a watchman's thick shoes or a radio. Peter closed the door and turned the thumb bolt on the lock. It closed us in with a soft click.

Holding the flash in his left hand, and keeping his right on his gun, he swung the light back and forth as we gingerly eased past the stairs and into the large open storage area at the rear, pausing after every creak to listen.

The room was roughly 150 feet square, with bare brick walls, shuttered windows, and the iron grille of an elevator shaft in the rear wall. The air was still, heavy, and warm. It hadn't moved in a long time. There was plenty of dust and nothing else.

Quietly, we went back out and up to the second floor. At the top of the sagging stairs was a wide hallway that cut the building horizontally. On the left-hand side was a long, wooden sliding door that I figured opened into a large storage area like the one below. Halfway down on the right side was another hallway that ran, with marks of inattentive sweeping, to the front of the warehouse. Along that hallway, there were four doors, two on either side, one with a pebbled glass panel. We tried them all. One led to a bathroom with a stained sink and a chain-pull toilet. The other three were locked.

We went back to the sliding door. Peter ran his light across the top of it. There was a long metal gutter that held the pulley mechanism that operated the door. At one end of the gutter was a thick chain with a ring handle that hung down to about six feet from the floor. Peter stepped over and gently, cautiously pulled the chain.

It jerked out of his hand. The door flashed past me, swinging from its pulley wheels with a shattering clatter of metal and wood. It raced away, unstoppable, and came to a crashing rest against the far wall. After the absolute silence, it seemed to shake the entire building.

"Christ!" Peter said between his teeth.

He went down to the door, then I heard him grunt, and the door slid toward me again, much more quietly. When it was three feet from closing, he said, "It works better if you use the handle."

I tried with little success not to laugh.

He left a small opening, and we went through. The room beyond was only slightly smaller than the one downstairs, and only slightly less dusty. Peter shot the light around the floor and up onto the bare brick walls as we made our way back toward the elevator shaft. There was only one thing in the room. At the far end of the rear wall was what looked like a shelf of extremely tall, thin books—maybe two dozen panels, side by side, each about twenty feet tall. We went over, and I laid my hand on one of them.

"What are they?" Peter asked.

"I think they're flats."

"What?"

"Flats. Fake walls. Look." I took the flash from him and directed the light into the narrow space between two of them. We could see the back of one flat, which was a frame of one-by-three pine with cross braces every four feet to keep it stable. The front of the flat beside it showed the canvas covering—made taut and hard by the sizing of glue—which had been painted to look like wallpaper. "They use them for sets. On stage and in low-budget movies. During the war, a lot of movies had to use them, because the studios couldn't get the wood to make complete walls. These—"

Peter grabbed my arm. Hard. I knew better than to speak. From below, I heard an engine. Maybe two. Peter took the flashlight from me and raced to the door on tiptoes. With aching care, he eased the sliding door shut.

There was no place to go but the rack of flats. We squeezed behind it into the narrow space between the edges of the flats and the rear wall and pressed ourselves into the corner. His flash went out. As it did, light sprayed up the elevator shaft, and above the pounding of the blood in my ears, I heard the gates open on the first floor. Peter grabbed the end of one of the flats and scraped it back against the wall, shielding us from the elevator.

Out of his waistband, he pulled the small blade hidden there. He removed its protective leather sheath and poked the blade into the canvas in front of him at eye level. Gently, he sawed back and forth until he had made an inch-long cut, then he sliced another at a ninety-degree angle. He put the knife away and peeled back the triangle with his left hand. His right went into his coat and rested on his gun.

Across the room, the sliding door rattled open, and in the next second, the room was flooded with light. Beside me, there were three-inch gaps between the flats. If anyone stood on the other side, they were bound to see us. I didn't move. I didn't breathe.

Heavy footsteps crossed the floor toward the elevator. A man yelled down the shaft in a husky snarl. "Hurry it up. I have to be back by one."

"Fuck you," a voice called back cheerfully.

Something slapped down onto the platform below.

"What the hell are you doing?" the man on our floor shouted. "You want to bust that open?" Shrill whistling came up the shaft, and something else slapped down. "You hear me?"

The motor groaned reluctantly to life, and after a minute, the elevator came to a stop with a crashing shudder, and the gate rattled open.

"I told you to be careful!"

"You know, you could lend a hand once in a while. Here!" There was a thud and a grunt. "Nice catch."

"You fucking idiot! How am I supposed to explain this?"

"Say you met up with an old whore and had to dust off her twat first."

"Don't push me, Jack." The voice was ice-cold and oddly familiar. The steps going off were slow and deliberate.

After a long moment, Jack went off down the hall, too. But he wasn't whistling anymore.

Peter let go of the triangle and took a deep, pained breath. And then I knew where I had heard the voice before. Down the hall, a door slammed. We waited.

Eventually, Jack came back, wheeling what sounded

like a loaded dolly. Peter leaned forward to the hole. While we waited, cramped and aching, Jack made a dozen trips, then he crashed the gate shut. The elevator whined, jerked, and descended. In five minutes, it returned, and Jack rolled the dolly down the hall, whistling again. A door closed, then another. There were muted voices in the hall and footsteps coming back. The overhead lights went out. The sliding door clattered and slammed shut. After another minute, the light from the shaft went out. The room was absolutely black.

An engine started up, then another. The rumbling had died away before Peter spoke.

"Stay here," he whispered. He slid the flat back and squeezed out. Soundlessly, he crossed the floor, but there was no way to open the door without making noise. After he had gone, I strained to hear something—footsteps, voices, a muffled cry, a body falling.

Nothing happened.

I saw the light from the flash.

"It's okay. They're gone," he said. I slithered out and stumbled on wobbly legs. Instantly, his arms were around me.

After a moment, he kissed my hair. "We'd better go tell Johnny we're not dead."

We had barely made it out the door to the loading dock when Johnny stepped out from behind one of the brick arches, his gun in his hand. "Jesus Christ!" he exclaimed in relief. "Jesus *Christ!* We saw those guys go in, and there was nothing we could do."

"We're okay," Peter assured him.

"The guy in the truck was Jack."

"We know. Lou and his team should've been on him."

"They were. Both of Lou's cars were tailing him. Gil

and I saw the car and the truck pull in down here. We were just getting out when Lou pulled up behind us. The three of us hotfooted it over here and saw Jack load some stuff in the truck. Lou's team's still following him. Gil went after the guy in the car. We couldn't see who it was."

I said, "George Scarano. Elizondo's bodyguard."

Peter's eyes swung around to me.

"Jesus," Johnny said.

I said to Peter, "Are you still up to some burglary?"

"Yes."

"Then let's go see what's in those offices."

We were upstairs, following the flashlight, before he spoke again. "How did you know it was Scarano? You couldn't have seen him."

"I thought I'd heard the voice before. Then I saw your reaction after you saw him. Peter, if anything, it looks better for Elizondo now. If he were involved, George wouldn't be worried about having to explain how he got his clothes dirty. And Maritski might have been trying to say, 'Elizondo's bodyguard.' "

He didn't reply. He guided the flash around until he picked up the dolly tracks in the dust. They went to only one door. My adrenaline was still flowing, keeping my senses keenly alert. It only took a few seconds to pick the lock.

The flash's beam scraped the room, revealing a bare plywood table and two hard chairs. The dolly was leaned against the wall beside wooden shelves that had two cardboard boxes on them, each about two feet long and a foot high. There was nothing else in the room.

Peter handed me the flash. For a moment, he stood with his hands resting lightly on one of the boxes, memorizing its position, then he lifted it down onto the table.

"It's sealed," I said.

"Yes, but thanks to our friend Jack, it might have sprung a leak." He turned the box over. Through the seams, I could see a layer of newspaper, but that was all. He took a full-sized pocketknife from his trouser pocket and inserted its blade carefully at the corner. When he pulled it out, he examined it, then flipped the box over and gave it a hearty shake over the center of the table. A faint dusting of white powder trickled out.

"Cocaine," I said, very hushed.

He set the box down bottom up and swept his finger through the powder. He sniffed it, then smoothed it along his gums above his front teeth. He dipped it again and held it out to me. Tentatively, I leaned forward and parted my lips. He smeared the powder on my teeth. I licked it, expecting my tongue to go numb. It didn't. The taste was bitter.

"Heroin," Peter said.

I jerked back and tried to wipe the residue off my teeth. I knew actors who doped with cocaine, but I had the lingering idea that, with heroin, you could get hooked by taking even the tiniest amount.

"Is this worth very much?" I asked.

"It depends on where it came from and how much it's been cut. Anywhere up to a quarter million."

"A quarter of a million dollars?" I said, astounded.

"This is a lot of junk for just one shipment to L.A. You could sell it, but it would take awhile. And you'd have to knock off several of the harbor boys, who control the heroin business now. I'd say this is headed somewhere else. Kansas City, Chicago. The mobs there are always looking for good pipelines out of Mexico."

Holding his hand beneath the tear, he replaced the box

on the shelf precisely, then with equal care, wiped the table clean with his handkerchief. We locked the door behind us.

The pebbled glass door looked like it might be an office, so we tried it next. I had expected to find a desk and chair, which we did. I was not surprised by the coffeepot on the spindly wooden table or by the fan. But I had not expected a Craig 16mm film editor sitting on a long wooden table or shelves above it full of empty reels and boxes of Kodachrome film.

Peter opened the desk drawers. In one of them there was a yellowed pad of paper, some pencils, a handheld sharpener, and some books of matches. Nothing else.

The door connecting the room with its neighbor was standing open. He made sure we didn't alter its position as we stepped through.

Hulking against the far wall were two ponderous cream-enameled machines, one with a deep tub that had thin, horizontal bars running several feet above it. We went over and examined them. "These things are for developing movie film, aren't they?" Peter said.

"Developing and duplicating, yes."

We turned around. There were more wooden shelves, filled with ghostly shapes covered in dusty sheeting. We lifted the edges cautiously. Underneath was film equipment—old, but good: Bell and Howell Filmo cameras, a couple of home-type projectors, boxes of movie lightbulbs, several baby keg lights, and a pile of cable, tripods, and light stands. Leaning against the wall at the far end of the shelves, draped in sheeting, was a mattress and frame. And a headboard. I recognized it from my pictures.

He said, "They couldn't very well drag two unconscious people into a hotel."

I nodded and felt a little sick.

I said, "Why didn't Jack set up a darkroom out here instead of using the photo lab?"

"It's hot in here. It's a long drive. And most hoods keep some sort of regular job, to keep the neighbors from getting suspicious. Developing film could be the only legitimate skill he has."

Carefully, he rummaged in a tall trash can and drew out a small reel of film. "Can we take a look at this? Do you know how to use that thing in there?"

"I think so."

Back in the other room, he pulled the stool out for me, first noting its original position. I hopped on, fitted the reel on the spindle of the editor, and threaded the film. I turned on the light and began to crank. It was easy to see why it had been discarded. Improperly duplicated, it was dark, although still discernible. With my inexpert touch, the images jerked like old Edisons.

There was a man sitting behind a desk, wearing a white doctor's coat. A woman was sitting in a chair across from him, her hands in her lap, her knees tightly together. A nurse came in wearing a very tight low-cut uniform with a very short skirt. She sat down in the chair beside the woman and unbuttoned the patient's dress while the doctor watched. The nurse reached down and caressed the woman's breast.

Peter switched off the viewer light.

I sucked on my cheeks to keep the grin down. I said, "What did you think it was?" He grunted and took the film out, replacing it carefully in the trash can. "Is there much money in this sort of thing?" I asked.

"Plenty of small-town boys got a look at them during the war. That hasn't hurt business any. There must be thousands of new veterans' clubs. And those all-male film clubs popping up everywhere aren't just showing their home movies."

"But with all that heroin, why on earth are they bothering with blackmail and dirty movies?"

"Crooks never think they have enough money. The junk could be a new line for them. It could be the reason Cummings got himself killed, if he didn't like it. Come on. We better get out of here."

We looked up and went back to Johnny's car to wait for Gil to come back, finishing the coffee and sandwiches.

It was almost two before he returned. He had followed George as far as Topanga, then pulled off. He had decided that George was probably going to the club, and the road was too quiet. He was afraid he would be spotted. Then he'd gone out to Venice to get Lou's report. Lou and his partners had followed Jack to a half dozen post office branches, where he had dropped off some packages, then back to the bungalows. We told him what we'd found in the warehouse.

Peter said, "We know Jack's not sending dope through the mail. It's still in the warehouse. He must be shipping out the movies. And spreading them out, so the postal authorities don't get suspicious."

I said, "If Lou's been watching Jack all night, then he knows where he got the heroin."

Gil shook his head. "I'm afraid not. Mr. Scarano arrived at the bungalows at approximately ten-thirty, Lou said. When he and Mr. Hochauser came out of the bungalow, Mr. Hochauser walked down two blocks and got into the truck. We don't know where it came from."

"Tomorrow," Peter said, "we'll try to trace it. But the plates'll probably turn out to be stolen."

"Tomorrow," I said, "we're going to the police. We've got something to give them now that has nothing to do with blackmail. Let them follow Jack and George. They'll see that Elizondo's not involved."

"Maybe they can follow them in those Fords without getting spotted. Maybe. But if somebody starts to move that junk, the cops'll have to grab them. How long will that be? Two days? Three? And the second the hired help is snatched, their boss'll be on a plane to Brazil. Somebody's running this show, and it's somebody we haven't seen. George isn't the boss, or he wouldn't take crap from a guy like Jack. The DA'll want to believe it's Ray. If George offers to nail him in return for a deal, the DA'll take it. Sending Ray Elizondo to the gas chamber could make him governor. He'd make a deal even if he knew George was lying."

"I'm sorry, Peter," I said quietly, "but we can't wait."

He didn't say anything. He sat, looking across the field at the warehouse. After a long time, he nodded.

Chapter 13

When I came down the next morning, I found Johnny standing over the stove in shirtsleeves and Juanita's apron, frying bacon. "I hope you don't mind," he said. "I thought you might sleep late. Sit down."

"It smells wonderful. Did you sleep all right?"

"Just fine."

"Peter's not up yet?"

"Would you like some coffee?"

"Yes, please. Where's Peter?"

"How do you want your eggs?"

"Johnny, where's Peter?"

"He had some things to do."

"I don't suppose talking to the police was one of them."

"He just wants to talk to the desk clerk. See if anyone who came into the hotel the night of the murder sounds like someone we know. After you went to bed, he set up a tail on George Scarano. He wants to see where he goes today, who he talks to."

"Do you know where to find him? The truth."

"He was going to see the desk clerk. That's all I know."

"Do you know the address?"

"No."

"Will he call in to the office this morning?"

"Yes."

"Then leave him a message. If I don't hear from him by one o'clock, I'm going to the police. I mean it, Johnny."

I sat down at the table and sipped my coffee while he laid the bacon out to drain. I said, "I'm sorry. I know it's not your fault."

"That's okay."

"What are you going to do today?"

"Go over to Jack's old neighborhood and ask some more questions. See if anyone remembers visitors he had."

"Especially any that sound like people I know."

The phone rang. I grabbed it. It wasn't Peter. It was Alex. She didn't even say hello.

Her voice was small and hoarse. "Could you come over? Now? Before I change my mind."

"I can be there in an hour."

"Don't bring anyone. Please. Not yet."

"Of course not. Not till you say so."

She made a little sound and hung up.

I told Johnny where I was going. He wanted to follow me over, but I said, "I have no idea how long I'll be. You have plenty to do, and we're running out of time."

He looked down at me with his brother's eyes. "Be careful. And check in with me as soon as you see her."

I went upstairs and changed quickly. At the last minute, I tossed my lock picks into my handbag. I had a vague vision of Peter's needing to open just one more door before we went to the police. Or maybe I was planning to slip him one through the bars of his cell.

*   *   *

Alex opened the door herself and took me into the living room. On the coffee table was a silver tea service and a coffee cake. "Would you like something?" she asked.

"Thank you. That would be nice."

She poured boiling water from the kettle into the silver pot, stirred the leaves and set the lid back down. "I know how to make tea. I lived in England for a year. I'm not much good at anything else, but I can do that." Beneath a layer of powder, her face was pale and blotched, and even cosmetics couldn't conceal the red around her eyes. On the table beside her was a porcelain ashtray, a silver cigarette case, and a jade holder. The tray was piled with stubs.

"Have you and Franklin had a fight?" I asked.

"You know, you have a disconcerting way of seeing right through people. Or is it only me?"

"I'm sorry."

She cut a generous wedge of coffee cake and handed me the plate with a brief smile. "Don't comfort me too much. I might change my mind."

We were silent until she had given me my cup. The tea was excellent.

"Sometimes," she said, "you want to be liked—loved—so much that you'll do almost anything. Put up with almost anything."

"Yes." I took another sip. I waited.

After a minute, she pointed to an envelope beside the tray. "I wrote down as many names as I could remember. There must have been dozens of people there at different times. It was one of those parties where people come and go all night. I don't remember very many of them."

"How long ago was this?"

"In the fall of '41. I'm not sure exactly when. Not long before Pearl Harbor, though."

I picked up the envelope and took out a single sheet of paper. There were ten names on it. Six women and four men.

The first name was Christina Winnack.

She said, "I didn't tell you the truth about not seeing any of those girls again, but she was my sister. Then later, when I started trying to remember who else was there . . . Go on. Read the other names."

Meryl Siddons	Sudsy Burns
Zoe Fredericks	Leslie Quillan
Stella Palmer	Dick Raney
Karen Verne	
Hope Davis	

At the end of the list of men was Dean Cummings.

She said, "Does this have anything to do with Dean's murder?"

"I think so."

"And my sister's death?"

"She was being blackmailed, too. The pictures probably came from this party. Her husband found out about them. It's why he left her."

She nodded. "I thought it might be that." She looked devastated nonetheless.

"Your sister hired Peter—Mr. Winslow—to help her deliver the money the first time. She never told him they came back for more. He's determined to find the people who did this."

"Poor Cissy. In those days, she had some very wild friends. She introduced me to them. But when she met

Chuck Winnack, she changed. She loved him so much, but he would never have understood. He's a hard man. Like my father, in many ways," she said bitterly. "Were they—? They couldn't have been blackmailing Dean."

"He might have been one of the blackmailers."

"No," she said firmly. "I've known Dean since we were children. He played around with married women, he didn't have a strong character, but he couldn't have done something like this."

"Whatever he was doing—and maybe because of your sister's death—he wanted out in the end. That's why he was killed. What can you tell me about the other people on this list?"

"I never even knew what Sudsy's real first name was. Everyone just called him that. He and Leslie were both killed in the war. Meryl got married and moved to New York. The other women were friends of Cissy's. Actresses I think. That's all I know. I didn't want to see any of them again after that night."

"Who took the pictures, do you recall?"

Her eyes dropped to her hands. "Everyone sort of got involved. I think it was Sudsy's camera. It was his house."

"How did your blackmail start?" I asked.

"Just after Christmas." A picture had arrived in the mail with a note printed in a childlike scrawl. She had destroyed them both. There had been a call. They had her unlisted number. She had delivered the money herself. After following a series of calls in public phone booths, she had been told to throw the money into an alley through the window of the ladies' room at Woolworth's. Then the blackmailer had wanted more. She refused, and he started reciting Franklin's private phone number. She paid again, then again, but they never returned the pictures. She had not heard from them in several weeks.

"Do you have any idea who these people are?" she asked.

"The man who tried to blackmail me was killed night before last. Unfortunately, before he could tell us anything except that Dean was involved. You might have seen the story in the paper. The man who was found in the hotel alley. We're going to find who did this, Alex. We're going to make them pay for what they did to your sister. You've done the right thing."

"I hope so," she said in a pale whisper.

When I returned to the car, I made a copy of her list on my notepad, then, as I promised, drove over to Paxton's to check in with Johnny, who had set up headquarters in Peter's office. Peter had not called in.

"Is that unusual?" I asked.

"Not necessarily," he said unconvincingly.

"Especially if he thinks there might be a message from me telling him to go to the police." I gave him Alex's list, and he locked everything away in Peter's safe. Then he opened a desk drawer and took out a few copies of the picture of Jack that Jack's girlfriend had given Peter. "I'm going over to talk to Jack's old neighbors. There's nothing else you can do. I want you to go stay with Mrs. Ross today. When Pete checks in, the secretary will give him your message. He'll call you there. Don't do anything till you've talked to him."

"I won't."

Helen loaned me some shorts, and we sat out by the pool beneath an umbrella. I told her about my visit from

Barty and Tolen and how Peter was trying to stall them. "But we've run out of time. We have to go to the police. They could put him in jail."

"And you, too. I understand, honey."

"The police will—"

"Don't tell me they can keep it quiet. I've known all along this might happen. Sometimes, I think it would almost be a relief to tell Sam."

"No, you don't."

"No."

I sat there in hot, helpless fury. So many lives were on the edge, and there was nothing I could do about it. What would happen if Jack and George started to move the heroin before we found out who Maritski had been afraid that I would call? Was the DA really so ambitious that he would send Elizondo to the gas chamber for something he didn't do?

It was, of course, possible that Elizondo *was* the boss, but he couldn't have been the person Maritski saw at the warehouse. If he had recognized Ramon Elizondo, he would have known the blackmail was too dangerous. And he would have had no reason to think I knew Elizondo.

Who had Maritski seen? For the ten thousandth time, I ran it over in my mind. He'd had my pictures a week before he approached me at Madison's and I started looking for tails. In that week, he could have seen me with only three people he might have bragged about recognizing if he had seen them at the warehouse: Kim, Forrest, and Helen. And I wasn't sure about Kim. Was she too famous? He guessed that I was working on the movie, which meant that he probably knew about Don and Sam.

Five people. And I absolutely refused to believe it could be any of them.

Perhaps the answer lay in how Maritski had recognized *me* from those pictures. Was it really likely that he could have seen me a few times on the Marathon lot or in magazines with Franklin and remembered?

What had he said at Madison's? Just before he sat down? I told him I was flattered that he recognized me. What had he said? That he had seen me many times. How was that possible?

I had a sudden, painful vision of Maritski sitting alone in his shabby, rented room with scrapbooks of photographs. Pictures that he had taken himself outside of premieres and at the studios where he'd worked. And pictures that he had cut from magazines. Pictures of stars he had worked with. I saw him spending his evenings listening to the radio and gently turning those pages, imagining that he actually knew the people whose forever friendly faces smiled back at him.

And there I would be for him to see time and time again, looking stiff and uncomfortable as I always did, while Franklin smiled easily beside me. It would be a publicity shot arranged by studio press agents to promote the stars and their projects. Often the pictures would feature several stars together congratulating one another on their latest movies. In those shots, everyone looked like friends. Sometimes, the captions said they were, even if they had never met before.

At the fabulous Perrino's restaurant, Marathon Studios star Frank Atwill and wife, Lauren, congratulate good friend Bunny Boogie on his new hit movie for Paramount.

Maritski might have saved such a picture and believed what the caption said, especially if he had worked as an extra in Bunny Boogie's new hit movie.

I stood up. "I have to go see someone."

"Who?" Helen asked.

"Someone who might be able to help. It's a long shot. A very long shot. If anyone calls, tell them I'll be back in a couple of hours."

I went upstairs and changed back into my dress.

First, I drove over to Paxton's and told the receptionist I had left my gloves when I had been in earlier. Since she knew me, she let me go back alone. I didn't need my picks. Johnny had not locked the desk drawer. I took out a copy of Jack's picture, then pulled my gloves out of my bag and waved them to the receptionist on my way out.

I went to see Myrna Pearl at Central Casting.

"Hi, kid. How're you doing?" she asked cheerily without taking the cigarette from her mouth. It bounced up and down like a cartoon diving board. "Any luck finding your man?"

I told her no. "Would it be too much trouble to see his casting sheets again?"

"Not at all. Sit down. I'll only be a minute."

She finished arranging stacks of extras' picture cards into character types. Then she went out and, a few minutes later, came back with the list of movies Maritski had done. She handed me the sheets and took her stacks out to the casting directors. They started going over the faces with her.

I pulled out my notebook and copied down the titles of all the movies Maritski had worked on from 1937 to the middle of 1944, when Franklin and I would have been photographed together. I thought about the stars and featured actors I could remember who had been in those movies, then made a very short list of the ones I could remember ever being photographed with.

Myrna came back in and sat down, "I read Louella's column. The girls'll kill me if I don't ask."

"What did she say?"

She found the *Examiner* under some files on her desk, folded it open to the column, and handed it over.

> . . . Frank is bragging that this is his best role in years. His estranged wife, the lovely screenwriter Lauren, has joined with Joan Trent and Newlin Gardner on the final script. The question is whether there's going to be a new collaboration between the Atwills.

"Joan and Newly will love this," I said, but I was thinking about Alex. "There's nothing to it. You know Louella. She gets it wrong about half the time."

"I'm sorry."

"I'm not."

"Oh?" she said wickedly. "Who is it?"

"Someone I met at a party. He's in insurance." I took Jack's picture out of my bag. "Do you know this man?"

"He's scrumptious. Is this your new boyfriend?"

"No. Do you recognize him?"

"Should I? I don't think I've— Wait a minute, you know he does look sort of familiar. Oh, gosh, I know who this is. It's Jack Logan. Is that right?"

"I'm not sure."

She narrowed her eyes and gave me a comical leer through the cigarette smoke. "Was this guy in one of your writing classes, too?"

I laughed. "No, but can you help me? Who's Jack Logan?"

"He was at Marathon years ago. Ten, maybe twelve.

Absolutely no talent, but he sure had the looks, so the studio kept hoping. They sent him to every coach in L.A., but nothing helped. Jack Logan. What do you know? I hadn't thought about him in years. That guy had some high opinion of himself, I can tell you. We worked on *The Crimson Blade* together. He made a real hard pass at me one day. I didn't have much of a costume, and he had his hands on every inch."

"When did he leave Marathon?"

"Maybe '36, '37. He didn't last long."

"How would I find out what pictures he worked on?"

"That's a tough one. It was a long time ago. The studio's probably thrown out all those files by now."

"I don't suppose he ever worked here? After he left Marathon."

"With his ego? Are you kidding? But I'll check if you want." She went out to the card catalog drawers and came back empty-handed. "Let me check bookkeeping." When she returned, she had a single page in her hand. "Well, we have a Jack Logan. Funny thing, with no picture in the file."

"Could there be two Jack Logans?"

"Sure. This probably isn't the same guy. Working as an extra after having a contract? Of course, some people can't give it up."

"How unusual is this, to have no picture on file?"

"It doesn't happen often, but sometimes one of the casting directors at a studio wants to throw a little work to his girlfriend, or his boyfriend. They add the name to the list over at the studio, they call the actor. We just handle the paperwork."

"They wouldn't have to register?"

"No. But somebody at the studio would have to make

sure the bookkeeper had all the information, so we could make out the check."

There was no picture on file and he was listed under a different name. That would explain why Peter's contacts at Central Casting had not uncovered a file on Jack Hochauser. It was possible that no one at Central Casting had ever seen Jack's face.

"Have you got a cigarette?" she asked. "I'm all out."

"I'm sorry. I don't smoke."

"Lucky you. Let me go see if I can bum one from somebody. By the way," she said casually at the doorway, "eventually, I would like to know what this is all about."

"I promise. You've been great, Myrna."

"Yeah." She gave me a wave and was gone.

I compared Jack Logan's credits with Maritski's. None of the titles was the same. Jack Logan had worked on only five movies dating back to '43—when our Jack got out of the service. I started writing the titles down. I recognized the first one. *The Family McGuiness*. Joan had been writing that when I first met Forrest. I knew the second one. *If Not for Love*. It had been Kim's first success after the Lombard fiasco. Then the third. *Turnabout*. They were all Marathon movies. *Element of Chance*. *The Woman in Question*. I stopped writing. I saw what else they had in common.

I didn't go back to Helen's. I couldn't face her. I couldn't face anybody just now. I went home and sat in the study, thinking. And not wanting to.

The doorbell rang. I checked through the curtains before I went out to answer it. It was Sergeant Barty.

"You're not answering your phone," he growled.

"I just got home. Please, come in."

He didn't. "Where's Pete?"

"I don't know."

"I told him what would happen if he played me for a sucker. He's lucky Tolen's taking a prisoner to San Diego."

"Sergeant, I—"

"Does the name Paul Kovak mean anything to you? His landlady thought she recognized his description in the papers. She's been sort of worried because he went away all of a sudden, and all these people keep coming by asking questions about him."

"Sergeant—"

"You remember Gus Barnes? The night clerk at the Whately? Well, somebody shot him dead. They found his body this morning. That's another murder, Mrs. Atwill. All because you and Pete didn't level with me. If you hear from him, I want to hear from him. I don't think I have to make that any plainer." He didn't say good-bye. He turned and marched back to his car.

I called Paxton's. Johnny was still out. I left urgent messages for both Peter and him. Johnny called back an hour later from a phone booth.

"What are you doing at home?" he demanded.

"The desk clerk from the Whately's been murdered."

There was a moment's pause while he gathered himself. "Pete was headed over to see him. He must know he's dead. Why didn't he call?"

"Because it would get you into trouble. The police can't prove how much you knew before today. But if you tried to help him now—"

"I've got to talk to Mr. Paxton. Go back to the Rosses'."

I went back to Helen's and told her what had happened. Peter wasn't going to be able to protect any of us. He couldn't even help himself. I kept thinking that, if I'd told the police everything when I had the chance, he would not be going to jail. And another man might not be dead.

Finally, I changed and went down to the tennis courts and hit some balls very hard against the backstop. It didn't make me feel any better. About five o'clock, the maid came to get me. I had a phone call. It was Johnny. Peter was under arrest.

Chapter 14

The desk officer didn't have any idea who Peter was. He called down to the holding cells. There was nobody named Winslow there. He said the suspect was probably still being questioned. I could wait if I wanted to. I asked for Sergeant Barty. The sergeant was busy. I could wait if I wanted to. I wrote a note and asked if it could be delivered to Sergeant Barty. The desk officer said he'd see. I could wait.

Johnny came in half an hour later and sat down beside me on the hard bench. "I talked to Mr. Paxton. One of our lawyers is on it."

"They won't tell me anything. They won't let me see Sergeant Barty."

Johnny asked again at the desk. The officer told him to wait, but he handed my note to another officer. At this point, I remembered the lock picks in my handbag and slipped them into the pocket of the jacket Helen had loaned me. Then I took off the jacket and folded it beside me on the bench. "If they arrest me," I told Johnny, "hide my burglary tools."

In a few minutes, Barty lumbered in through the double doors from the hallway. "Got your lawyer?" he asked me curtly.

"Do I need one?"

"We'll see. Come on." Johnny got up, too. "Not you."

"You don't have to say anything," Johnny reminded me.

"That's been real good for her so far," Barty said, and held one of the doors open for me. I left Helen's jacket and went with him.

The interrogation room was small and stuffy, barely big enough for the table and chairs. A long-chinned detective in a brown suit was sitting with his chair tilted against the wall, rolling a cigarette around in his fingers, but he didn't look very interested in it or in anything else he might have seen in the last year. Peter was sitting at the far end of the table. He wasn't wearing any new bruises.

He stood up when we came in. "What is this?"

"We can't let you two share a cell," Barty said, "so I thought you might like a few minutes. Sit down, Mrs. Atwill. You, too," he said to Peter.

Peter said, "She's a client. She didn't—"

"She knows the law. She knows about withholding evidence. You going to tell me you didn't know withholding evidence was a crime, Mrs. Atwill?"

"You don't have to say anything," Peter said.

"She just heard that from Tweedledum."

"Who?"

"Johnny's here," I said. "He called and told me you'd been arrested."

"This is a very good client," the detective on the wall said, and went back to his cigarette.

"This is Detective Evans," Barty said to me. "He's investigating the murder of the hotel clerk."

Peter said, "I'm the one who decided not to level with you. Not her. She wanted to come clean. It was my mistake."

"You've made plenty of those."

"I told you, I'll give you the story. But not till I know you're not going to drag innocent people across the front page. And not if I go to jail."

"And I told you, you're not calling the shots here. How much of the story do I get if *she* goes to jail."

"She's not going to jail."

"Why's that?"

"Because she's about as tough as you are, and she knows how to write a story. When she's through with it, the papers'll fry the department for going after the victims and letting the criminals get away."

"We can write a pretty good story ourselves. And she won't like the way it sounds. Your time's run out, but you can still keep her out of trouble." Barty looked at me. "You talk to your boy."

"I'm not going to tell him to help you send him to prison," I said bluntly. "You can threaten me all you want, Sergeant. You can put me in jail. I know that. But eventually, you'll have to let me out. By that time, the gang will be long gone. Do you want to catch them, or do you just want to take him down? I'll help you do one, but not the other."

I sat there, my lips pressed together, trying to look determined. Trying to keep my teeth from chattering. For a moment, all three men stared at me. Then Evans scraped himself off the wall and lit his cigarette.

Finally, Barty said, "How do I know I'm going to get the whole story now?"

"I can only give you my word," I said.

"I'll listen and see if I like the sound of it."

Peter said, "Not yet."

Barty stabbed the air with his finger. "I'm wearing plenty of crap because of you!"

"I never meant for that to happen."

Barty glared at him, chewing angrily on the inside of his jaw. After a moment, Evans pulled the glass ashtray toward him and dropped some ash into it.

We sat there. Then, slowly, Peter leaned his forearms on the table and stretched his fingers out on the surface. "You've got plenty of reason to want to nail me," he said quietly. "But you know nothing could have saved that desk clerk." I must have made a sound because he glanced over at me. "They found his body in his rooming house this morning, but he'd been dead for over twenty-four hours. That means he was killed a couple of hours after Maritski. Even if we'd stayed at the hotel, he would've been sent home, and he would've been killed." He turned back to Barty. "Look, Phil, we can sit here all night—all month—and I'm not going to talk, and neither is she. There are other people in this, people who don't deserve to have their lives ruined. All it takes is for somebody from the DA's office to come down here and nod. Then I'll make it up to you."

"How?"

Peter looked at him, weighing the risks, weighing his chances. "Okay," he said finally. "The guy at the Whately was killed by the same people who killed Dean Cummings."

"You're crazy!"

"Maybe. But I'm not wrong. We've got to move slow, or we'll lose everything. You've got to convince the DA. We've got to be patient if we want to get the guy behind this."

"We might have found him," I said. Suddenly, there was a raw pain in my chest. "I found something."

"Not yet," Peter cautioned. "What do you say, Phil?"

It took Paxton's lawyer, the DA, and Betts, the assistant DA, two hours to work out an agreement under which the identity of all blackmail victims would be protected as much as possible. And none of us would be prosecuted for withholding evidence. Betts and the DA tried to look unhappy about it, but their ambition kept getting in the way.

The DA, caught as he was leaving his office on the way to a party, was wearing a white dinner jacket. He was a tall, striking man with smooth, tight, flawless skin and a laboriously arranged crown of waving silver hair. He had a deep line between his pale eyes that gave him an expression of perpetual concentration. The eyes themselves, however, didn't look as if they'd had many new thoughts behind them in quite some time.

Betts was small—no more than five-four—with sharp, eager features and delicate hands. He was wearing a pearl gray suit and a daring purple tie. Not as daring as the gold watch on an assistant DA's salary.

It was crowded in the shift commander's office, with the DA, Betts, the police chief, the assistant chief, and the director of detectives all there, along with Barty, Evans, Paxton's lawyer, and the stenographer. Peter started telling our story. All of it. I looked at the faces around me, and hoped these men could be trusted to keep secrets.

When Peter came to Maritski's last word, they all sat forward as if someone had pulled a string.

"Don't get too excited," he said. "If Elizondo's guilty—and I don't think he is—you can be sure he'll have an airtight alibi."

I said, "He might have been trying to say 'Elizondo's bodyguard.'"

Betts said, "His bodyguard's involved?"

Peter went on. When he got to the heroin, the DA's mouth dropped open, and in his excitement, he actually ran a hand through his perfect hair.

When Peter finished, I took out my list of Jack Logan's movie-extra credits and gave it to the DA.

"How does this lead us to the gang's boss?" he asked.

I told him why I had gone to Central Casting. "I wanted to check all the movies Maritski had been in, to see if I could remember ever being photographed with any of the actors in them. But I took Jack's picture along with me, too, and asked Myrna if she recognized him, since we hadn't been able to find any connection that he had to the movies." I told them how she had identified him as Jack Logan and found his name in the files of extras. "There was no picture, but I think this is the same Jack we've been following. His extra work started in '43, when our Jack got out of the service."

"And?" the DA said.

"All of those pictures were done at Marathon. And all of them were directed by Don Deegan."

Beside me, Peter said softly, "Deegan?"

"Yes," I said miserably. "It would explain the quality of the equipment we found at the warehouse. Don used to have an independent studio, and he was the first to use 16mm for costume and makeup tests. It could have been Don that Maritski saw at the warehouse. A movie fan would recognize him. And he might have been afraid I would go to Don. He knew I was working on his movie."

Betts said, "Could anyone else have hired Jack for all these movies? Who hires extras?"

"The casting director assigned to the movie."

"Would Deegan have the same casting director every time?"

"I don't think it's likely."

"Who can tell a casting director to hire someone?"

"The movie's director. The producer. A star could, but only after getting approval from the director or producer."

The DA nodded profoundly. "A perfect setup. If we were tipped to what was happening, we would have to tell the head of the studio before we could get onto the lot. No studio head would let one of his directors be arrested for dope peddling. He'd see that he was warned."

"Wait a minute," Peter said. "You don't sell heroin by getting Jack onto the lot five times in three years."

The DA didn't look particularly happy to be told he was all wet.

Two new faces appeared: the homicide detectives who had come to my house to ask me about Dean. For the next few hours, surrounded by coffee mugs and smoke, Peter and I told our story again and again. We spent a lot of the time going over what Maritski said before he died. I repeated what he said, the way he said it, trying to get past the choking gasps between the syllables. I repeated it as one word, as two, as three. They tried to decide if he was saying, "L is on . . ." They tried to figure out who or what "L" might be. My head began to hurt.

The DA asked for the sixteenth time if I was sure Dean had never expressed any fear of communists. I asked for some aspirin.

Finally, they looked at each other, nodded, and told me I could wait down the hall. Detective Evans opened the door for me.

On the way out, he asked Barty, "Want me to try to get hold of Tolen again?"

"He'll probably stay the night down there. If he comes back tonight, he'll check in."

"He's going to hate missing out on this," he observed. But I thought Peter had been lucky indeed that Tolen was in San Diego. If it had been left to him, I was sure Peter would have accidentally fallen out of his chair several times before I got there.

Evans took me to another room. It looked like the interrogation room, except that it had a window and pebbled glass in the door. When he left, I tossed my bag on the table and opened the grimy blinds. There was nothing much to see through the streaked glass: it was dark. I looked at my watch. It was almost midnight. I sat down, kicked off my shoes, and put my feet up in another chair. My eyes burned. My throat ached. I hadn't eaten anything since a sandwich at Helen's, but all I wanted to do was sleep. I would have confessed to several dozen crimes in return for a bed.

A shadow moved across the glass panel. Peter came in and shut the door. There were deep lines at the corners of his mouth, and the bruises under his eyes were very dark.

He sat down beside me. "The ballistics report came back on the desk clerk. It was the same gun that killed Cummings. The Remington."

I was astounded. "The gang kept the Remington? Why? Why wouldn't they get rid of it?"

"It gives us an edge. We can tie them to the murders if we can find one of them with it. I think the DA'll keep Mrs. Ross and Miss Harris out of it. He doesn't want Sam Ross or Ronald Harris mad at him. Not when he's looking for big campaign contributors."

"I hope so."

"You saved my skin, you know."

I slipped my hand into his. "It's worth saving."

Barty came in. He wasn't that big. He wasn't that loud. Nevertheless, in that moment, he seemed to fill the entire room. Peter let go of my hand.

"Okay," Barty said. "Time to go see the DA again."

There were even more people in the office this time. I was too tired to ask who any of them were.

"You can go home now, Mrs. Atwill," Betts said. "Although Mrs. Ross knows that you're speaking with us, I remind you that you're not to discuss this case with her or anyone else. Do you understand that?"

"I understand."

"Very well."

"I'll walk her out," Peter said. "My brother's downstairs. He'll take her home."

Johnny was waiting where I had left him. He helped me into Helen's jacket.

"Take her home," Peter said, "and stay with her. The cops are going to replace our surveillance on Jack. I asked them to try to find something besides those gray Fords. On your way, go tell Lou to expect some plainclothes."

"Can't you leave?" I asked.

He smiled wearily. "They'll see I don't get out of here for a long time. Get some sleep."

Johnny took my arm, and we went out into the thick night. The lingering bitterness of Los Angeles's industrial air had never smelled so good.

"We'll take my car," he said, and patted his stiff left leg. "There's no clutch. I'll see somebody brings yours home."

"Fine."

We drove slowly toward Venice. I rested my head on the back of the seat and closed my eyes. The gentle swaying lulled me right to sleep. I didn't wake up until he pulled up beside Lou's car, which was parked among others waiting to be repaired beside the gas station where Peter had made his phone call the day we found the warehouse. Automatically, Johnny flicked the switch on the overhead light so it wouldn't come on when the door opened.

There were two men in the car. One of them got out and climbed into Johnny's backseat. Johnny introduced us. Lou Brandesi was a rock-hard man with a pugnacious jaw and soft eyes. He doffed his hat to me and held it on his knee.

Johnny told him what had happened. Lou moved it around in his mouth for a while, then said, "The cops'll have an easy night. Nothing's happening."

"Maybe," I said, "maybe not. Look."

A car had passed us and pulled to the curb in front of the San Marcos Courts. A man got out. Although he was wearing a dark jacket and hat instead of evening clothes, George Scarano's bulk was hard to miss. He passed under the light beside the iron gate and disappeared into the courtyard.

"There's no one following him now," Johnny said to me. "The tail had to back off after he went to the club. That road's too empty."

I said, "He didn't leave the club in those clothes. I'd like to know where he's been in them."

We waited. Fifteen minutes later, George came out, smoothing his jacket.

"I hope he hasn't shot our boy," Lou said casually, but seconds later, Jack came out, too, carrying a suitcase.

"Looks like he's on the move again," Johnny said to Lou. "Stay on him. We'll take George. Call the cops and tell them what's up." Lou hopped out and disappeared around the corner of the gas station to a phone booth.

George pulled away from the curb, made a U-turn, and came back toward us. We dipped down into the seat. Jack was taking his time loading his suitcase into his trunk. He had a clear view of the gas station, so when George passed us and pulled out into the intersection, we had to stay where we were.

"Damn," said Johnny.

Finally, Jack went back up the walkway into the courtyard. Johnny pulled out and floored the accelerator.

We were lucky. The lights were with us, and George wasn't breaking any speed limits. We spotted him turning north onto Venice, headed back to L.A.

"He's not going to the club," I said. If he were, he would have gone south and taken the coast road, then Topango north. "Maybe's he's headed for the warehouse."

Even late on a Thursday night, there were enough cars out so that we didn't have to stay too far back. I rolled my window all the way down and leaned my elbow on the sill. I didn't feel the least bit sleepy anymore.

As we approached downtown on Olympic, however, the traffic thinned, and we had to drop back. At Broadway, George made a left and headed north.

Johnny said, "If we can stop someplace that's safe for you to be alone, I want you to get out and call the cops. They'll send someone to pick you up."

"Peter told you not to leave me alone."

"He'll kill me if I put you in any danger."

George turned again. Cautiously, we pulled around

the corner in time to see him turn into a three-story orange brick parking garage.

"What's he up to?" Johnny said as much to himself as to me.

We drove past the garage. I didn't see George's car. Above the entry was a wide concrete lintel with PARKING painted on it. Bolted into the brick beside the entrance were two metal signs. One said OPEN 7AM TO 6PM. The other had the hourly, all-day, and weekly rates (fifteen cents, seventy-five cents, and $3.50) and a flat fee for any car left after five o'clock or for overnight (thirty-five cents). On the second and third floors were large rectangular windows, each made up of a dozen separate grimy panes. Some of the panes were opened outward like transoms.

There was a gas station at the corner, and I thought that cars left there for repairs probably accounted for the overnight business, since the station didn't have much parking space on its lot. The day business would come from a couple of large office buildings on the block, the courthouse, and the civic center.

Parking garages were rare in Los Angeles, given the availability of lots that usually could offer cheaper rates. In fact, not far beyond the garage and on the opposite side of the street, there was a small lot carved out between a bargain store and a pawnshop. But if you could afford the few cents extra, it might be worth it to have your car parked out of the sun.

Johnny turned into the parking lot, then swung around and parked the car against the wall of the bargain store so it couldn't be seen from the garage.

"Should I call the police?" I asked.

"Let's wait a minute and see if we can tell what he's

doing." He climbed out and stationed himself at the corner of the building. A few cars whooshed past, but no one had much business in this part of town at this time of night. The sidewalks were empty.

I joined him. "Do you think he spotted us?" I asked.

"I don't know why he'd go in there if he did. I'm going in to take a look."

"You're *what*?"

"I kept my head down for three years during the war. I think I can do it for five minutes in a garage." He heaved his Colt out of his holster, checked it, and replaced it.

"I don't think this is a good idea."

"If I can't find a place to hide, I'll come back. You go make the call. Tell the cops to make sure they come up through the rear of this lot."

Before I could protest further, he was moving across the street and into the shadows. He bent forward and crept into the garage with an awkward, lurching motion. My heart started beating very hard. He had kept his head down during the war, but he had also been able to run.

Quickly, I walked down to the phone booth in the next block. When I shut the door, the light came on. I opened it again. I took a nickel out of my jacket pocket and had the operator connect me. I asked for Sergeant Barty. The voice barked into the phone. "Homicide."

"Sergeant. Johnny and I are down the street from a parking garage," I said in a rush. "I don't know the exact address. It's near the corner of Broadway and—"

"Whoa, whoa. Slow down," the voice said. "Who is this?"

"Who's *this*?"

"Evans."

"This is Mrs. Atwill. I—"

"Okay. Hold on."

"No, wait!" But he couldn't hear me.

"Hey, Tolen! Call here for your partner!"

After a few seconds, Tolen said, "Yeah?"

"Sergeant Tolen," I said in relief, "we've followed George Scarano to a parking garage off Broadway. Something's up."

"Hold it. Hold it. What are you talking about? Who is this?"

"It's Mrs. Atwill," I said in sharp exasperation. "For heaven's sake, don't you know what's going on?"

"I just found out. I've been in San Diego."

"Johnny Winslow and I have been following George Scarano. He— Oh, no!"

"What? What is it?"

"He's leaving!" I whipped around in the booth so my back was to the street. George's car dipped off the ramp and turned in the opposite direction.

"What is it?" Tolen demanded. "Are you okay?"

"Yes. George just left." I watched the taillights getting smaller and smaller. "I think we've lost him."

"Look, Mrs. Atwill, don't take any chances. Where are you?"

I told him.

"You two stay put. Don't do anything stupid. We'll be right there. Understand?"

"Yes." I hung up and immediately crossed the street. Despite my promise, I was not about to stay in the car. I hadn't heard any gunshots, but neither had Dean's neighbors.

There was an attendant's box just inside the entrance. Its door was locked so no one would steal the paper coffee cups on the shelf or the newspaper on the floor beside the wooden stool.

Beyond, the first level was a concrete arcade, with three thick support columns and a dozen empty parking spaces along each side. There were lights at intervals in the middle of the ceiling, dim bulbs capped with tin shades, most of which appeared to have been turned off after closing. The center of the floor was ghostly lit; the area near the walls was black. There was no sound at all.

I took off my shoes and stood there, listening and examining what I could see. At the far end, there was a 180-degree turn, and the floor rose as a ramp to the second level. The ramp, despite its angle, seemed to be used for parking as well, because I could see a set of headlights on it peering at me out of the dark above a short wall that I supposed was a barrier to keep cars from overshooting the spaces.

I heard nothing.

Hugging the right-hand wall, I crept back toward the far end of the first floor. Finally, I could see over the barrier. There was only the one car parked on the ramp. There were painted lines for two dozen more spaces. There were plenty of shadows too thick to penetrate. I didn't see Johnny.

I kept moving.

I edged around the support column that stood at the juncture of the ramp.

I waited. Nothing happened.

Then, as my eyes grew more accustomed to the gloom, I could make out the vague glint of a door off in the corner directly to my left. I crept over and carefully, silently, opened it a couple of inches. Beyond it, there was only a narrow metal stairwell leading to the upper floors. I probably should have known what was behind the door, but I'd never been inside a parking garage before.

Very quietly, I tiptoed back the way I came, passed the solitary car, and fitted myself into the shadows along the right-hand wall. I kept climbing, listening, until I could just see the second floor above its barrier wall. There was only one car parked there as well, a dark-colored Cadillac, backed into a space in the center of the floor on the far side.

Johnny was standing beside it, calmly shining a small flash into its interior.

I put my shoes back on and stormed up the rest of the way, my heels clicking angrily on the concrete. "Just what the hell do you think you're doing?" I demanded. "You scared me to death."

"Sorry." He grinned sheepishly. "When George left, I knew I'd never make it down in time to tail him. Now, we've lost him. You were right. It was a bad idea. Did you call?"

"Yes. They're on their way. Whose car is this?"

"That's what I'd like to know. There's no ID on the steering column. Just when I got to where I could see George, he was relocking the trunk of this car. Then he got back in his own car and drove off. I hid down on the ramp behind that car."

"I think we should go back down."

"I'd sure like to get a look in the trunk. I don't know if the cops can get a search warrant."

"Okay, but let's make it fast." I took the lock picks out of my jacket.

"Great." He gave me the flash.

He positioned himself by the support pillar at the top

of the ramp so he could watch and listen for anyone coming up or coming out of the stairwell. I walked around to the driver's side where the light was slightly better and got out a pick. The Cadillac's rear bumper was almost touching the wall. There would be no way to manage the flash, the pick, and the lock's cover while leaning over the fender, so I kicked off my shoes again and squeezed myself up onto the bumper, squatting sideways, jammed into the tiny space. I set the light down on the fender and felt my way to the lock. As Peter had found out the night he escaped from the gang, trunk locks are practically useless. The lid popped open almost immediately. I wiggled around until I could get the lid up past my hips, then dropped the pick into my pocket and grabbed the flash. I moved the light around inside the trunk. A set of golf clubs in a plaid bag sat on top of the spare tire well. Scattered around that were a half dozen dog-eared science-fiction paperbacks, a small red metal first-aid kit, a yellow windbreaker, a navy blue cap with an anchor on the crown and a jack. A pile of blankets was stuffed behind the clubs.

Peeking out from beneath the blankets was a wooden, stirrup-shaped handle, the kind that belonged to a shovel.

I held on to the lid with one hand and leaned in. Using the flash, I lifted the edge of one of the blankets. Far enough to see what was under it.

I cried out and threw myself back into the wall.

"What? What is it?" Johnny ran over and came down the driver's side of the car to where I was crouched, trapped on the bumper.

"There's a hand. There's a body in there."

He reached over the fender for the blanket.

"Oh, Johnny, don't!" I tried to crawl away from him to the passenger's side.

In the next instant, a chunk of wall exploded beside my face. Before I could even register what had happened, Johnny grabbed my arm and yanked me backward toward him and off the bumper. Another piece erupted where my body had been. I hit the floor hard on my hip and my elbow, my feet still on the bumper.

"Get down!" Johnny screamed.

I scrambled down behind the rear wheel. I tried to make myself as small as I could. I tried to climb into the wheel.

Johnny was crouched beside me, his back against the car, his bad leg straight out in front of him. He already had his gun out. Silently, he eased himself down onto his stomach and searched beneath the car for something moving beyond in the dark, his back rising and falling rapidly with his breathing. Then I heard a sound. The scrape of a shoe? The brushing of a shoulder against concrete?

Suddenly, Johnny was rolling away from me, over and over and over and up onto his good knee. He slung his arms onto the hood of the car and fired twice.

For the longest time, he stayed there, frozen, his face a steel mask. Then slowly, he took one hand off the gun, laid it on the fender, and pushed himself up. I stood up, too, and moved halfway down the side of the car till I could see.

The man was lying facedown at the edge of a pool of light, the toes of his shoes pointed toward us, one arm flung wide, the other tucked neatly beneath him as if he had put his hand into his pocket. Blood began to seep out around the rib cage.

"He must have come up the stairs," Johnny said. "I

thought he was gone. Damn! I didn't see him. I didn't even hear him."

"Is he dead?"

He crossed in front of the car and slid down to one knee beside the body. I stayed where I was. He reached out to feel the pulse.

"Freeze!" a voice screamed out of the blackness of the ramp. "Police! I said freeze!"

Johnny didn't move. He shouted, "It's Winslow! John Winslow! We called you!"

"Put the gun down! Now!"

"Anything you say." Johnny laid his gun down very slowly and scooted it farther into the light.

There were gritty footsteps, and Sergeant Tolen appeared out of the dark. He edged a few feet toward Johnny. "Let's see some ID. Real careful."

I called out of the shadows, "It's all right, Sergeant. It's me. Mrs. Atwill." I stepped forward into the light at the front of the car, still in my bare feet.

He looked from me to Johnny and back, letting out a breath. "I thought I told you to stay in the car." He lowered his gun, but his eyes were still alert for danger. "Is this guy dead?"

"I think so," Johnny said.

"You want to check?"

Johnny felt for a pulse while Tolen stood guard.

"He's dead," Johnny said and stood up.

"He have any friends with him?"

"None that I saw."

"That increases the chances they'll live to testify." He went over and shouted down the ramp. "Downey! It's all right up here! Call an ambulance! Better make it the coroner, too!" He came back, not looking one bit pleased.

"So, now you want to tell me what happened?" He looked at me as I came over to them. "What happened to your face?"

Only then did I feel the sharp burning in my right cheek. I put my hand to it. I was bleeding steadily, cut by the spraying concrete.

Gently, Johnny raised my face to the light. "It's not bad. A couple of stitches, maybe," he said reassuringly. "We'll get you out of here in just a minute." He gave me a handkerchief.

Tolen knelt by the body and lifted the shoulder to get a look at the face. "Who do we have here? Hey, this is—"

"Yeah," Johnny said. "George Scarano." He picked his gun up off the floor and put it away.

Tolen said, "I hope *he* had one of those."

"It must have gone over there somewhere," Johnny said.

Tolen stood up, holstered his gun, and went off into the dark, searching in the direction Johnny had pointed. "Tell me what happened."

"I followed him up here to see what he was up to. He opened the trunk of this car. We wanted to take a look inside, but he came back."

"I can't see a thing over here," he called. "Why don't you take Mrs. Atwill down?"

"Sergeant," I said. "There's a body in the trunk."

"A what?"

"A body," Johnny said. "Where's the flashlight?"

He found it behind the rear wheel on the driver's side; it was still working. He reached into the trunk and pulled the blankets back. I retreated a couple of steps behind him. He pointed the light inside. "Jesus!"

"Who is it?" Tolen asked, coming up to the opposite side of the trunk.

"Don Deegan," Johnny said.

Tolen moved in the dark. He raised his hand and fired. Johnny stared at him, an astonished, uncomprehending expression on his face as he staggered back helplessly. Tolen fired again. As he was falling, Johnny reached into his jacket and fumbled for his gun, but it was too late.

The only thing that saved me was the trunk lid, which momentarily obscured Tolen's line of fire. By the time he pulled the trigger again, I was moving.

There was nowhere to go but up. Tolen was between me and any other chance of escape.

I turned and ran. I ran for my life.

Ahead of me were the transom windows. They were too high for me to reach and too small for me to get through anyway. If they had been large enough, if they had been low enough, I would have jumped. I would have thrown myself through and broken myself on the pavement to get away from him.

I kept running. My only hope was to make it to the third floor. To the stairs. I dashed across the eternal space of light in the center of the floor, around the support pillar at the bottom of the ramp, and into the dark of the far wall, moaning as I tried to accelerate up the incline. I had to outrun him.

Why hadn't he fired again? He could easily have cut straight across the floor and shot at me over the barrier. He must be checking to see how many bullets he had left. He had to be using George's gun. He couldn't use his service revolver. Suddenly, I heard the pounding of his shoes. My mind stopped reasoning. There was nothing else in the world but the pumping of my arms, the jarring

impact of my bare feet on the concrete, and the top of the
ramp.

When I reached it, I raced straight for the far dark corner. For the stairwell. There it was in the black: the outline of the door. The glint of a brass knob. I grabbed it. I
turned it. I pulled. I turned and pulled again. It couldn't
be locked. It must be my hands. The sweat on my hands. I
yanked at the door one last time. I wheeled away just as
the gun exploded. The roar filled my head. I staggered
against the far wall and kept running along it into the
dark.

Ahead of me, there were two cars parked side by side.
Two big, shielding cars. I scrambled over the first bumper
and dived between them. I lay there, my chest and throat
burning, searching beneath the car for his feet, trying to
breathe without sound, trying not to sob.

I didn't see him.

Where was he? Behind the pillar at the top of the
ramp? Or had he already passed it? Was he creeping down
the wall behind me in the darkness to shoot me over the
bumper? A moan of incapacitating terror rose in my
throat. It was all I could do to keep it down.

No, he could not be that close. He had only fired to
keep me out of the stairwell. He was still on the ramp.

As silently as I could, struggling with the panic and the
uncontrollable trembling, I dragged myself foot by foot
beneath the belly of the second car to the other side.

Then, looking beneath the two cars, I saw his legs appear from behind the support column at the top of the
ramp. He paused. Then cautiously, he began moving.
One step, then a stop to listen. Another step and another
stop.

I waited, breathing with my mouth open, but I

couldn't get nearly as much air as I needed. My lungs were on fire.

He took another step, then stopped. He didn't move again. He was waiting, too. Waiting for some sound, waiting for the strain and the fear to make me betray myself. He wasn't sure where I was. It was dark along the walls. Was I hiding between the cars? Under one of them? Or somewhere in the blackness beyond? He had to be careful. He couldn't let me get away.

How many shots did he have left? George had fired twice. And Tolen fired twice at Johnny—oh, Johnny—and twice at me. That was six shots. Revolver or automatic, it was not likely he had more than two left. He had to make them count.

Soon, he would get down on his knees and look under the cars. When he did, I might be able to make it to the barrier, jump down onto the ramp, and make it to the entrance.

He took another step. I could hear his ragged, raspy breathing. Then I heard a small, exhaled grunt. I saw him go up on his toes as his knees bent. With agonizing care, I pushed myself up onto the balls of my feet. I pressed my palms on the floor and pushed with all the strength I had left.

I got two steps.

"That's it!" He appeared suddenly at the end of the car, the gun pointed straight at me. "That's it!" he snarled.

He didn't fire. I stepped back, as far into the dark as I could. I kept moving away from him, sliding along the wall. There were pillars. There was darkness. There had to be something.

I was talking. My voice was shaking. I couldn't control it. "You'll never be able to explain this."

"You and the kid called me. I came to pick you up.

When I got here, I found both of you dead." He held out his gun hand. He was wearing a glove. "No powder marks. Let's go."

"No."

"Have it your way. George came back with an accomplice. The kid got George, but the accomplice got him, then chased you up here and got you, too."

I kept backing away. "Do you think Peter's going to believe you?"

"Downstairs or up here! I don't give a damn! You want it now? I don't give a damn!"

I backed into a car. I tried to squeeze past it, but the tiny front bumper was tight against the wall. My space had run out. My time had run out. I looked away at the side of the car, at the long strip of chrome, and the ballooning rear fender. Tolen took a step forward. He wasn't going to miss. I couldn't look at him, but I couldn't close my eyes. There had to be one last thing to see.

He shot me. There was the explosion of the gunshot. His hand jerked with the recoil, but there was no sense of impact. No pain. This is how it is, I thought with relief. You don't feel it. You don't feel a thing.

Tolen's knees buckled. His arms twitched like a marionette's as he staggered and fell. He flopped forward, his head and chest slamming into the rear fender. Then slowly, almost gracefully, he slid toward me and dropped to the floor. Only then did I see the spraying hole in his throat.

Peter.

He raced toward me, appearing like a ghost out of the shadows, his gun in his hand. I took a step, but my legs wouldn't hold me any longer. He caught me before I hit the ground.

"Johnny—" I said.

"I know." There was agony in his eyes. Very gently, he set me down on the floor. "Are you all right?"

"He was going to kill me."

"Are you hurt?"

There were other, slower steps, and Barty, his gun drawn, trotted up, breathing through a grimace. He came to a stunned stop at the dead man's feet.

"Take care of her, Phil," Peter said. He went back down to Johnny.

With a grunt, Barty lowered himself onto one knee and wiped the sweat out of his eyebrows. He looked at the body. There was no need to check for a pulse.

"He shot Johnny," I said.

He kept looking at his partner's body.

"He was going to kill me. He shot Johnny." I could hear the hysteria rising and put my hand over my mouth to stop it.

"Jesus," he said quietly. He let out a long breath and wiped his forehead again. "He could have answered plenty of questions. I guess Pete wasn't thinking about that after he saw his brother." He put his gun back inside his jacket and, finally, looked at me. And the blood on my face. "You're hurt."

"It's only a cut. The wall," I said, as if that explained it.

He handed me a handkerchief. "We better get it looked at." He took me by the arm and helped me gently to my feet. I leaned on him.

The ambulance arrived almost immediately, along with more police. Two officers pulled Don out of the trunk, still alive but unconscious. They untied him and pulled off the gag. The ambulance attendants loaded him in beside Johnny and sped off. Barty wouldn't let Peter go with his brother. A policeman had been killed.

Peter wrapped me in a blanket, and he and Barty took me outside. The street was covered with police cars and washed in flashing red lights. They put me in one of the cars, and I waited, numbly staring at the dashboard, aware that I was beginning to shake, but I didn't seem to care. In a few minutes, an officer got in. He spoke to me. I think he told me his name. He drove me to the hospital, although I don't remember getting there.

Chapter 15

It seemed as if I woke up in the same room where it all began. With the same oppressive, glaring light. But this time, there was no headache, no nausea. Just a deep, clutching sadness.

Juanita was sitting by the window, reading a newspaper, her handbag in her lap. She heard me stir and looked up, then she stood up and set her things in the chair. "Mr. Winslow called me," she said simply. She cranked my bed up to a sitting position, then rinsed out a washcloth and bathed my face in cool water, careful of the new stitches on my cheek.

There was a knock on the door. She opened it, and Peter came in, wearing a different suit. Johnny's blood must have been on the other one. Behind him was Betts from the DA's Office and Detective Evans.

Juanita took the blanket from the foot of the bed and wrapped it discreetly around my shoulders. Betts motioned out the door, and a rumpled, startled-looking man in a blue suit and a twisted green tie came in carrying a steno pad. A patrolman brought in two extra chairs and went back out. Betts checked his for dust before he sat down. Peter laid his hat on the windowsill, folded his arms, and leaned against the wall by the window. Evans propped himself on the opposite wall and watched him.

"Johnny," I said.

"He's holding on," Peter said. "He's a tough kid. It could take more than a cop to kill him."

Evans's look got harder.

"Mr. Winslow," Betts said, "you might want to consider whether such remarks are serving your cause."

"Thanks for the advice."

"Gentlemen," I said, "what can I do for you?"

Betts cleared his throat. "We would like to ask you a few questions about last night." He glanced at Juanita.

"Would you give us a minute?" I said to her. Gravely, she readjusted my blanket and went out.

I said, "You want to know if Sergeant Tolen tried to kill me. The answer is yes."

I told them the whole story. The steno's pencil moved over several pages.

When I finished, Betts said, "Mr. Winslow did not call out to the sergeant? He made no attempt to ascertain what was happening before he fired?"

"It was fairly obvious what was happening."

"He did not call out?"

"I don't think he had time."

"Mrs. Atwill."

"Very well. No, he did not."

"You were alone with Mr. Winslow before Sergeant Barty arrived."

"It couldn't have been more than a few seconds."

"After seeing a man killed, you would naturally be upset. It would be difficult for you to judge time."

"No, it wouldn't. I've had a lot of practice with dead bodies in the last two weeks."

"What did Mr. Winslow say to you?"

"He asked me if I was all right, then he went back to his brother."

"What did he tell you to say?"

"Nothing."

"You two have concealed evidence before."

I looked at him for a long, tight moment, then I said, "If you're trying to make a case that Sergeant Tolen was only trying to save me and Mr. Winslow shot him by some kind of horrible mistake, you'd better be able to explain why the sergeant was wearing a glove with powder marks on it. And why he had an automatic in his hand and his service revolver in his holster. And you better be ready to explain it in court because I'll tell my story to a judge, a jury, and every reporter in California if I have to."

The stenographer kept scribbling. Abruptly, Betts motioned for him to stop, then he drew some air between his teeth and looked at me. I looked back.

Finally, he got up and tapped his hat on his thigh a couple of times. "Very well." He opened the door and motioned the steno out.

"How is Don?" I asked him.

"He has a mild concussion. He's refusing to talk." He tapped his hat again and went out. With one last glare at Peter, Evans followed.

Peter shut the door.

"Does he really believe any of that?" I asked.

"If he did, he never would've let me come in here. He's talked to Phil. But they'll go a long way before they'll admit a cop was in on this."

"Peter, I'm so sorry."

"Why did he go in there?"

"He wanted to see what George was up to. I should have stopped him."

"Nobody stops Johnny when he's made his mind up. Don't blame yourself."

I did nonetheless.

"How are you feeling?" he asked.

"I'm fine. I—" I stopped and frowned at him. "How on earth did you find us?" It was a sign of the shock I had suffered that it had not occurred to me before.

"You told Evans where you were. He remembered something about a parking garage near a corner of Broadway." He pulled Betts's chair closer to the bed and sat down. He looked exhausted. "After you and Johnny left, Tolen came in, supposedly just getting back from San Diego, but the cops down there say he left about five. When we briefed him, he didn't bat an eye. After that, there wasn't much to do but wait while the cops set up the new surveillance, so Phil and I decided to go get something to eat. Tolen said he didn't want to go. I thought he was just sore because I wasn't going to jail.

"While we were gone, he must have got a call through to Jack. Lou says Jack came out of his bungalow like nothing was wrong but pulled through the first alley he came to and disappeared. He knew he was being followed. When we got back, Evans told us Tolen had gone to get you. We decided to go, too. I wanted to make sure you were okay, and, I don't know, something didn't feel right, him going by himself.

"We spotted Johnny's car. Then just as we were getting out in front of the garage, we heard a shot. Phil called in for help, and I went in. I found Johnny, then I heard voices. Just as I got to where I could see what was going on, I saw you. I saw him raise the gun."

"If you'd been a second later . . ."

He didn't say what would have happened if he'd been five minutes earlier, but I could see it in his eyes.

"A cop. A perfect guy to run the show," he said bitterly. "That's why they dumped you downtown the night you were grabbed. So the jurisdiction would be shared with the Central Division cops. Tolen could check and see if Phil turned up anything that led to the gang. All the blackmail payoffs we know about were downtown, too. He could find out if the vice cops were set to move in. If they weren't, he knew the drop was safe."

"Where was he when Maritski was killed?"

"On his dinner break."

"That's how they got Maritski out of the hotel."

"Yeah. Tolen just flashed his badge and walked him right out the back door. He made it easy for them to get the make and license number of Maritski's car. Once they found it, all they had to do was watch it. Nobody in L.A. goes without his car for long. They followed Maritski back to the hotel. They watched it. They saw him in his front room and started figuring out how to get him."

"But how did Tolen get into the hotel? He couldn't have just walked up the stairs. The desk clerk would have stopped him. And the desk clerk didn't recognize him later."

"A disguise. And he could easily have hired a hooker to get him in while he hung back in the shadows. The desk clerk doesn't care about the johns. Only his piece of the action. Tolen got in, sent the hooker away before she got too good a look, and found Maritski. But once he got him outside, something went wrong. Maritski got suspicious for some reason and tried to get away. They had *r 'him there."

"Maybe he saw Jack."

"No, they wouldn't let Jack in that close. Maybe it was Deegan. Whatever the reason, they had to kill Maritski fast. But they weren't prepared to transport a bleeding body, so they dumped him into that trash can to give Tolen enough time to get back to work and try to get himself assigned to the case."

"Why use the garage?"

"Deegan's car would be out of sight. And nobody would hear him if he came to and started kicking on the trunk lid. George went to give Jack the word to get out. Then he went back to the garage and drove in. That way, if anything had gone wrong, he'd have the advantage of a set of wheels if he had to get away fast. Nothing had happened, so he checked to make sure Deegan was still knocked out, then parked his own car in a side street and went back for the Cadillac."

"Where did they find the Remington?"

"They haven't."

"What? I don't understand. I thought all this was a plan to blame Don for everything they thought we knew about—the blackmail and the killings. I thought they were going to plant the Remington on him and push his car over a cliff or something."

"He's a perfect fall guy. He had a provable connection to Jack. And I told Tolen that he was one of the people Maritski might have been afraid that you'd go to for money."

"But?"

"tied him up. Ropes leave bruises. When a guy cliff, he doesn't have bruises on his wrists. ovel in the trunk. It looks like they were m."

"Then why was he still alive?"

"Rigor starts setting in pretty fast. It's a lot easier to get a live body out of a trunk than a dead one. And it could be they needed him to walk a while before they got to the spot where they planned to bury him. If I'd been them, I'd have set Deegan up as a suicide, with a nice, convenient confession and the Remington. I don't know why they didn't."

"Maybe because it wouldn't have given us the whole gang. They knew we were looking for at least three men — the ones who waylaid me. Dean couldn't have been one of them because he'd been sick that night. We had identified Jack, but Don would only give us two."

"Could be. But handing us Deegan, a confession, and the gun would have taken off plenty of heat." He stood up. "The DA doesn't want any reporters to find out about you. You're admitted here under a phony name. You won't be bothered. I'm going back up to Johnny."

"Of course."

He picked up his hat from the sill and went out.

Juanita had brought a newspaper. The headlines were an inch high. POLICE DETECTIVE DIES IN SHOOTOUT. MARATHON DIRECTOR MYSTERY. Marathon Studios director Don Deegan was hospitalized, it said, following an incident in a parking garage downtown, possibly an attempted kidnapping. Detective Sergeant William Tolen was dead, along with another man, who was as yet unidentified. A third man, John Winslow, believed to be an employee of a private security firm, was in critical condition. Peter Winslow, identified as the man's brother, was being questioned by police. His part in the tragedy was unclear.

After I dressed, I took the elevator to the surgical recovery ward. The nurse wouldn't let me in. Famil...

only. I left a note for Peter, telling him I would be at home, signing it only with an "L" in case a reporter saw it.

My Lincoln was still parked at Central Division, and Juanita was not about to let me drive anyway, so she drove me home. As we were getting out, a convertible screeched out of the street, roared up the drive, and dipped forward sharply as the driver slammed on the brakes. Franklin leaped out.

"Lauren! What's going on? I just came from the— Good God! What happened to your face?"

"I'm fine. It's not serious. Calm down and come inside." I took his arm and guided him to the front door. "Juanita, would you make us some coffee?"

"I'm going to make you some breakfast," she said staunchly, and went off to the kitchen.

I took Franklin into the study, and I sat down, feeling suddenly a little shaky.

He planted himself in front of my chair. "The studio called me at dawn to tell me we're not shooting today, that Don was in the hospital, and it might have been a kidnapping. Then I opened the paper, and I saw some guy named Peter Winslow's been arrested for it."

"He wasn't arrested."

"I tried calling here for hours."

"I was at the hospital."

"So I found out. I went over there to see Don, and there was a policeman in front of his door. He wouldn't let me in. Then I ran into Winslow in the elevator. He looked like he was under arrest. There were a couple of policemen with him who didn't look happy, and it somebody'd broken his nose for him. I asked where you were, and he said you'd gone tell me you were hurt." He pointed to the cut on my cheek. "Did he have anything to do with that?"

"He didn't hit me, if that's what you mean. It happened last night."

"How? Good God! Were you there? At that garage?"

"Yes. I can't talk about it. I promised the police."

"You can't say something like that and just leave it! Who the hell is Winslow? He sure as hell's not in insurance!"

"He's a private detective. I hired him. I can't tell you anything else. I gave the police my word."

"What happened to Don?"

"I'm not sure. They found him unconscious in the trunk of his car.

"And if you were sure, you still wouldn't tell me."

"Stop it. I've told you all I can."

He stood there, his face working, his hands thrust into his trouser pockets, but after a minute, he said more gently, "Are you in any trouble?"

"No."

"Are you sure?"

"Yes. I'll tell you all about it as soon as I can."

"How much trouble is Winslow in?"

"He didn't do anything wrong."

"Is it business with you two or something else?"

"It's something else, I think."

"I see."

"I need a few minutes. I have to make a phone call. Then we'll have some breakfast."

"Calling Winslow?"

"No."

"I'll be out by the pool."

"Thank you."

"Yeah." He went out and shut the door.

I called Helen. Sam had gone to the studio, she said, to meet with the police. She said Sam hadn't recognized Peter's name in the paper, but he might remember it later.

I told her that, because of the deal I had made with the DA, I couldn't say much, but we thought we'd found most of the gang, and she wouldn't have to worry about her name coming out. Johnny was holding on.

I called Alex. I told her most of the same things. Except that I didn't tell her that I had given her name to the police. Maybe she'd never have to know.

Franklin made me eat, then he went home, and I undressed while Juanita ran me a bath. There was a large purpling bruise on my hip, and my elbow was painful to bend. The stitches on my cheek had been done well, but there would probably be a scar. After I soaked for a while, I shampooed my hair and rinsed it carefully under the shower head, holding a dry washcloth over my cheek. I dried my hair with a towel till it was just damp, combed it out, and climbed into bed. The pillow was cool. The room, with the curtains drawn, was dark. Four weeks ago, I had lain here, bruised and stitched and ill. Four weeks ago, when five people who were now dead were still alive. Four weeks ago, when I thought it was just robbery.

I was drifting somewhere between sleep and consciousness when the phone rang. I picked it up automatically and said hello.

"Lauren? Were you asleep?" Peter asked.

"Uh. I guess so. No. I'm awake now. How's Johnny?"

"Not any worse. Guess who called and wants to talk?"

"Who?"

"Deegan. They've let him go home. Want to come along?"

"We're not supposed to discuss the case. Especially not with Don."

"You won't be, but I've got to find some hard evidence to prove Tolen was running the show. They might not find his prints in that warehouse. If I don't give them something, the cops will make sure I never work in this town again. They've got my house staked out, so I'll have to slip out and use a borrowed car. They might be watching your house, too, so at nine, go out the back way. Go through the yard of the house behind yours. I'll pick you up."

Don lived in a thick-pillared colonial set well back from the street on a knoll of lawn in Bel Air. Enormous willows dusted the way up the drive. A couple of private guards were posted by the gate to keep the reporters from getting any closer. They were expecting our car and waved us right through. One of cars parked along the curb had to be a police car, but it was dark, so no one could see our faces.

We pulled around the back to the garages, and a Japanese manservant opened the back door. "Yes, sir," he said in a whispered staccato, "Mr. Deegan is expecting you."

He escorted us through the kitchen and out to the main foyer. He knocked on the door on the far side and opened it. Beyond was a railed landing and steps that led down into Don's study. It was paneled in pine with a fieldstone fireplace and Navajo rugs. Don and another man were sitting in scarlet leather chairs.

Don set down his drink and stood up. "Laurie," he said in uncomfortable surprise. The other man rose, too, but more slowly.

"How are you, Don?" I asked.

"Better. Come in. Come in. Both of you. This is my lawyer, Sheridan Marsh."

Marsh was wearing a yellow cashmere sweater, tan slacks, and handmade shoes. "Good evening, Mrs. Atwill," he said stiffly.

"Sit down. Sit down," Don said. "Somethin' to drink?"

"No, thanks," Peter said. I shook my head.

Don loaded fresh Scotch into his glass and sat down.

Marsh pressed his manicured fingertips together. "I'm sorry that you've gone to the trouble of coming all the way out here, Mr. Winslow, but I've advised Mr. Deegan not to discuss this case."

Peter said, "That advice wouldn't have anything to do with Mrs. Atwill being here, would it?"

"Of course not," Marsh replied evenly.

"Then, I'm a little confused. Mr. Deegan's got a lawyer. One of the best. This lawyer knows Mrs. Atwill's my client, so he knows he can't hire me. Besides, he's already hired Tom Crane's boys. I checked. By now, they must have found out that I'm in trouble with the cops and that I might be looking for something to give them. But this lawyer still lets his client set up a meeting. Why would he do that? Maybe because Crane's boys also told him that I spent plenty of time talking to the cops last night. And this lawyer might think that, for the right price, I'd tell him what the cops know."

Little mottled patches broke out on the side of Marsh's neck, but the voice was still smooth. "Mr. Deegan told me about this meeting. I came here to prevent it. You have taken it as an opportunity to put on a cheap show for your client."

"You know, Mr. Marsh, when I'm insulted, I sulk, and when I sulk, I don't talk. That's the last thing you want right now."

One corner of Marsh's mouth lifted, but it didn't look much like a smile. "Good night, Mr. Winslow."

"Is that the way you want it, Mr. Deegan?"

"Good *night*, Mr. Winslow," Marsh said again.

Peter started to rise, but Don stopped him. "Hold on a minute. Hold on. Throwin' him out won't do any good. Sit down, Mr. Winslow. Please. I didn't think you'd go for it, but Sherry thought it was worth a try."

"Don," Marsh cautioned, "I remind you that he has problems with the police."

Peter turned to him. "I don't know what you've been telling your client about his chances, but he can't pass this off as a kidnapping. The cops know all about him getting Jack Logan into the studio, and Logan's connected to a warehouse full of heroin and the murder of Dean Cummings."

"Oh, God," Don said, his face clinched in pain.

"If you're in this up to your neck," Peter said to him, "I can't help you. If you're not, there might be a way out."

Marsh pressed his fingertips together again, but the gesture didn't look nearly as smooth as the last time. "My client had absolutely no knowledge of any crimes."

"Fine. Then he doesn't need me." Peter started to get up again.

"Sit down, Mr. Winslow. Your theatrics are becoming monotonous. We both know you didn't come out here to help Mr. Deegan. You want something. What is it?"

"A way to prove the cop I shot was running drugs and killing people."

"And my client is supposed to help you do that."

"First, he has to convince me that *he* didn't kill anybody."

"And you would give us your word that nothing you heard would be repeated outside of this room."

"No."

"I think we will have to pass on your offer."

Don was moving his glass around on the table beside his chair, smearing the wet circle beneath it, watching it closely. He said, "No, Sherry, I can't do it. I'd be dead if it wasn't for him."

"Don—"

"If you want, you can go. You won't be responsible."

"Don—"

"I've made up my mind. If you want to go, go."

After a moment, Marsh said, "You know I'm not going to do that."

Don gave him a brief smile. "Thanks." Then he looked across at Peter. "What do you want to know?"

"Whatever you knew to end up in that trunk."

Don took a long draw on his Scotch and held on to the glass. "I used to have a production company. Maybe Laurie's already told you. When it went under, I was busted. I sold about everything I had. The ranch, the house in Connecticut, cars, stocks. I took care of the loans, but I was cleaned out. An' I had two ex-wives waitin' for alimony.

"Then one night, George Scarano came up to me at the club, asked if we could have a talk. I figured we were gonna go see Elizondo. I had a tab there, too. A few thousand. I figured Elizondo wanted to know if he was ever gonna get his money. But Scarano took me out to that garden they got. We were all alone. I got a little nervous. I know Elizondo used to be a pretty tough guy in this town. Scarano said he'd heard I was in trouble. He said he might be able to help. It'd just be between us. Not Elizondo. All I had to do was get somebody on the extras list, get someone onto the studio grounds whenever I did a movie. I'd get the casting directors to put Jack Logan's name on their lists when we were ready to shoot the extras' scenes, an' they took care of it, called him, whatever they needed to do. An' Scarano asked me to get Logan on the lot at least once a month with a visitor's badge, too. That's all I had to do. Look, Scarano told me that it was gamblin'. The actors, the crew, they all like to play the horses, bet the fights. Some of 'em bet plenty. I was busted, an' a few thousand from time to time helped get me back on my feet."

"When did it start?" Peter asked.

"I don't remember. Some time in '43. In the fall, maybe."

"That warehouse has film equipment in it. Sixteen millimeter. Is it yours?"

"All the stuff I had went with the bankruptcy."

"When was that?"

"Late '42. If any of that stuff belonged to my company, they bought it at auction. I didn't sell it to 'em."

"Tell me what happened last night."

"I was down on my boat. It was maybe ten-thirty. A man came on board. He showed me a badge, said he wanted to talk to me about Logan, said we had to go downtown. We got in his car, an' that's all I remember."

Peter took a picture out of his jacket and handed it to Don. It looked like a copy of Tolen's police identification picture.

"That's him," Don said. "I recognized him from the picture in the paper this morning. It's the same guy that was killed last night."

"Where were you the night Cummings died?"

"I don't have an alibi if that's what you mean," Don said, with a trace of his old irritability.

"Where were you Tuesday after you left the studio?"

"What happened Tuesday?"

"Where *were* you?"

"Mr. Winslow—" Marsh began.

"I'm not half as tough as the cops'll be."

Don said, "I was here. Workin'."

"Anybody see you?"

"When I'm workin', I don't like to be disturbed. My man came to check on me 'bout eleven, maybe. What happened Tuesday?"

Peter took out the picture of Maritski that I'd got from Central Casting. "This man was murdered. Recognize him?" Don said he didn't. He said none of the aliases sounded familiar, either.

Peter said, "How did Cummings fit into this?"

"I don't know. I hardly knew him."

"How many times did you meet with Cummings and Logan?"

"I never did."

"You never saw them together?"

"No. Not once."

"What do you know about that warehouse?"

"Nothin'. An' nothin' about dope either."

"Where were you the night Mrs. Atwill was robbed?"

"What was that, a Saturday? I must have been on my boat."

"Alone?"

"Yes."

We went over it all again several times, but Don's story didn't change. He didn't have any idea where Jack might be. He'd only spoken to him a couple of times and never about anything that could help us.

When he finished, Marsh said, "What do the police have?"

"At the moment, nothing except that your client hired Jack Logan. They can accuse him of plenty, but they can't prove it. Not yet. Not based on anything I told them."

"You said there was a way out."

"I said there *might* be a way out, provided your client was relatively innocent. And provided I can find some solid proof against Tolen. If I do, the DA'll leave your client alone, because a trial would drag the police department into court, too. If the DA decides to go along with the story, so will the studio. They won't go looking for scandal. Wish me luck, Mr. Marsh."

Peter stood up, and Don did, too. He started to offer his hand, but thought the better of it. "I'm sorry about your brother," he said.

Peter only nodded, and we went out without waiting for the manservant. When we got into the car, I said, "You don't believe him, do you?"

"No. I think gambling was probably part of it. A studio would be a playground for a bookie. That many people in one place, most of them with plenty of money. And Jack could put personal pressure on them to collect. If Deegan's telling the truth, it means George had thrown in with Siegel's bunch. Gambling at the studios is their territory. Deegan was at the Rosses' party, and that night somebody called Jack and told him to disappear. Maritski saw someone at the warehouse he thought you knew. And so far, none of the bodies that have turned up fit that description. Deegan drinks Scotch. So did Cummings's killer."

"So do thousands of people."

"And he smokes Raleighs. There was a pack of them on his desk." He started the car.

He took me home and went back to the hospital.

Although I slept soundly, I woke up exhausted. My

head and body ached. I soaked in a cool bath with an ice pack over my eyes, but it didn't help much.

No one answered the phone at Peter's house, so I called the hospital. He wasn't there, but the nurse on duty remembered me from the day before and told me that Johnny was still holding his own.

I took my coffee out to the pool and read the newspaper.

George Scarano's name had been released. Next to the story was an unflattering sidebar on Elizondo's Prohibition and gambling ship career.

Jack Logan/Hochauser's picture was just above the fold, along with a request to the public for assistance in locating him.

All the police would say about Tolen's death was that it was under investigation. There was a picture of Peter leaving the hospital. With the bruises still under his eyes, he looked sinister.

I tossed the paper down. I didn't feel like reading the rest of it. I didn't feel like eating breakfast. I didn't feel like staying home. I got out the Hudson.

There were three squad cars and a half dozen gray Fords parked at random angles along the street in front of the warehouse. I gave my name to one of the officers standing outside and asked to see Sergeant Barty. After a few minutes, he came out, an unlit cigar stuck in his face.

"I'll be glad when they're through so I can light this thing," he said. "Come on upstairs. How are you?"

"Better."

"Don't touch anything or go beyond those ribbons, okay?"

The ribbons were strung across the doorways and across the opening to the storage area, where two men were down on their knees in front of the elevator cage. All the door frames and knobs were covered in gray powder. There were plenty of fingerprints.

Peter was standing, one hand in his trouser pocket, outside the pebbled glass door. When he saw me, he looked briefly, but pleasantly, surprised before a pained line formed between his brows. "Johnny," he said softly.

"No, he's all right. I talked to the hospital before I came."

Barty said, "How'd you know we'd be here?"

"It's the best place to start looking for evidence."

"Nosing around gets to be a habit, doesn't it? Be careful. You could turn into a shamus."

He eyed Peter with an expression that wasn't entirely amused and walked away.

Peter and I stood there, looking at each other. I wanted nothing more than to lean my body against his.

I said, "Do you have to stay?"

"They want to keep an eye on me."

"They don't know you slipped their stakeout last night, do they?"

"No."

"Any news about Jack?"

"Not yet. If he's still in the country, he'll have to lay low. He's got a face people would remember."

"Have they found anything here?"

"Nothing we didn't see Thursday night." He took a notebook out of his jacket. "I've been checking out alibis. Trying to figure out who could've done what."

"Any luck?"

"A little. First, there's the attack on you."

"I'm pretty sure Jack's the one who grabbed me. He's the right height."

"And George and Tolen may have been with him. George didn't come in to work that night, said he had that flu. Tolen was off duty. Fridays and Saturdays were his nights off."

"Dean was killed on a Friday, and Helen's pictures were taken on a Saturday."

"He could've done both. He fits Mrs. Ross's description of the man with the camera. Jack was probably the driver. But Tolen's clean on the desk clerk's murder since he was with Phil. Jack could've done it easily since he didn't show up at the Courts again till four o'clock. George is clean on all three killings. He was at the club those nights and couldn't have slipped away long enough without someone noticing."

"Then Maritski wasn't trying to say 'Elizondo's body-guard.' "

"No."

"Do any of them smoke Raleighs?"

"Not usually. That leaves Deegan as the lookout at the club. They found a couple of army surplus radios in Tolen's garage. There could be fingerprints."

A man came over carrying a fingerprint kit and took down the ribbon across the office door. "You finished in here, Menendez?" he shouted toward the men by the elevator.

"Yeah, I'm done," one of the men yelled back.

The first man went in, tossing us a sour glance first.

I was unnecessary and underfoot. "I guess I'll go home."

"I'll walk you out."

There was a knot of uniforms gathered in the shade of the arches, smoking. As we passed, one of them spat.

"Not too popular," I said.

"Cop killers are never too popular, even when the cop's no good. If we're lucky, they'll find his prints upstairs."

He put me in the car.

"Come to dinner tonight," I said.

"I'd like that."

I touched my fingers to my lips, then rested them on his. He was smiling when I pulled away.

Chapter 16

Los Angeles was sitting in the hot lap of the afternoon, and Pasadena wouldn't be any cooler. I skirted north of downtown, drove through Hollywood to 101, and out from under the porcupine cloud of industrial smoke to Elizondo's.

Even though it was Saturday, it was much too early for anyone to be there, except perhaps the kitchen staff. The customer lot was empty. I parked just past the portico and shut off the engine. Except for the soft brushing of the wind in the eucalyptus, it was very quiet.

I got out. At the angle of the hedge where it cut away to the rear of the club, there was a break just wide enough for me to squeeze through. I walked back along the hedge until I found the spot where I had discovered the cigarette butts two weeks ago. I didn't know if the police had been there yet, but there was nothing to see. The cigarettes had disintegrated.

Had someone stood here with one of those surplus radios from Tolen's garage, smoking cigarette after cigarette, waiting to call his friends and tell them Helen was on her way? Had he dropped a cigarette and taken his time to crush it to make sure he didn't set the field on fire? When he looked up, had there been a tall blonde in a white dress standing in the shadows under the portico, and before he could adjust a pair of binoculars, had she got into a light-colored Lincoln? I told myself it could have been Tolen or George with borrowed Raleighs. It couldn't have been Don. Not Don.

I picked my way back, telling myself the brand didn't mean anything.

But if it wasn't Don, who had Maritski recognized at the warehouse?

I stepped through the break in the hedge and instantly stifled a cry of alarm.

"Mrs. Atwill, what an unexpected pleasure." Ramon Elizondo was leaning against the fender of my car, his arms crossed, the expression in his eyes concealed in the hard shadow of his hat brim. "I do not allow my staff to park in this lot. I came out to see who had transgressed my instructions. What a surprise to find you here."

"I can imagine," I said lamely. There was absolutely no adequate excuse for my being there.

He glanced down at my dusty feet. "You must be tired after your walk. Won't you let me offer you some lemonade?"

"That's very kind of you, but I must go." I reached for the car door. He put his hand on it.

"I have spent many hours in the last two days trying to convince the police that I am not a murderer."

"I know."

"Do you think that I am?"

"No."

"When one of the victims died in your arms saying my name?"

"Are you trying to frighten me?"

"I would like to know what you are doing here."

"If you're the murderer, you know what I was doing. If you're not . . ."

"I have nothing to fear? Do not be naive, Mrs. Atwill. Have you seen the newspapers? No one will believe I was not part of this."

"I know. It's one of the reasons I didn't go to the police right away."

He leaned toward me. "Is that true?" His eyes were very dark.

"Yes."

"You will not tell me what you were doing?"

"I found nothing to implicate you."

"Are you certain this man was saying my name?"

"No. It sounded like your name. Weren't you here the night Maritski died?"

"Not until very late."

"And your alibi is married."

He smiled. "I have always thought myself so mysterious. You see through me too easily." Gallantly, he stepped back and opened the door for me.

"On the contrary, I've decided I can't see through anyone."

The traffic was crawling. For once, I didn't mind. I didn't want to go home. But I didn't have anywhere else to go.

I found the Lincoln sitting in the drive. Two policemen had brought it, Juanita said.

I went upstairs to shower. As I was toweling off, the phone rang; I answered it.

"Lauren—"

"Peter, I—"

"I can't talk. Johnny's in trouble. They're going to have to operate again. I'm going to the hospital."

"I'm coming, too."

"There's no need. Not yet. I'll call you when I know something." He hung up.

I took a long time getting dressed. Nothing I did seemed worth bothering about. In the chest of drawers, I found the envelope of money that I had taken to the Whately Hotel. I took it down to the study and locked it back in the safe. Lethargically, I sat down at the desk and looked with loathing at the drawer where my book was stored. My neat, clean, antiseptic story with no guts, no terror, and no hopeless dread that someone I cared about was going to die.

Juanita came in with a tray of egg salad sandwiches and iced tea. "Did you eat today?" she asked.

"I'm not hungry."

"Eat. Or I will stand here until you do."

I managed a smile and picked up half a sandwich. "Thank you," I said humbly.

She nodded in satisfaction and pulled a dust cloth out of her apron, running it lightly over the immaculate furniture while she watched to make sure I ate.

I swiveled the chair to face the wall so she wouldn't see my face. I didn't want her sympathy.

If I hadn't been so damn willing to jimmy that lock, if I had refused, Johnny and I would have been outside when Tolen arrived. Johnny would be safe.

But Don would be dead.

When George came out of the garage driving Don's Cadillac, Tolen would have pretended to follow him, pretended to lose him.

Don would be dead, and George and Jack would both have escaped.

And eventually, Tolen would have killed Peter as well.

Because Peter wouldn't give up until he found the boss, the man most responsible for Christina Winnack's suicide.

Why hadn't they made Don their fall guy? Why hadn't they handed him to us as the boss?

We knew now that Tolen had found Don alone on his boat. He could easily have forced him to sail out in the dark to some secluded bay, shot him with the Remington to make it look like suicide, planted a remorseful confession and evidence, then escaped by having George pick him up in a skiff.

They could have handed him to us. Not only as the boss, but also as the man Maritski was afraid I would call for help. He had Don. Handing him over would have taken plenty of heat off. Why hadn't he done it? Why else would the gang hang on to the Remington?

It didn't make sense.

Unless.

I sat there, staring at the wall, my sandwich in midair.

It made sense if there was someone else.

If Don was telling the truth.

It made sense if there was someone else we had not seen yet.

Someone who still had the gun.

And had not blamed Don for a very important reason. He was going to blame someone else.

Don had suddenly become dangerous. He had to be removed quickly to keep him from giving Peter the connection to George. When the gang grabbed him, they thought we had only identified Jack and Dean, but they knew we were looking for at least two other men. The two men who were with Jack the night I was attacked.

They kept the gun. Was their plan to frame someone?

A final frame that would give us the last of the four gang members?

Dean, Jack, Don, and the fall guy.

Jack would disappear. The case would go cold. Then Tolen, George, and the boss could go on selling dope.

I started to reach for the phone. But I couldn't call Peter. He was on the way to the hospital. I could call Barty, but what would I say? That I had a hunch there was one more member of the gang out there somewhere with the Remington? What could he do? I didn't know any more than I did yesterday.

If I was right, it had to be someone Maritski was proud of recognizing. Someone he was afraid would find out if I started calling around for money. Someone who had a connection to Alex's list. Someone Maritski tried to name. Someone whose name sounded like . . .

My heart jolted painfully, a stabbing blow that knocked the air out of my body. For a moment, I could hardly catch my breath. I closed my eyes, squeezed them shut, and slowly, I drew a long, thin ribbon of air back into my lungs.

Maritski had named his killer.

There *was* someone else.

Someone besides Dean who had been able to point out potential blackmail victims. Someone who knew by the night of Helen's party that I had found Peter and told Jack to disappear.

Someone who had stood behind that hedge at Elizondo's club, carefully grinding out cigarette after cigarette, waiting. Waiting for me.

What a fool I'd been. What a damned egotistical fool. So flattered to think that I could be mistaken for Helen Ross. So flattered that Peter thought I was beautiful that I couldn't see what was right in front of me all along.

The gang had gotten exactly what they were after the night they waylaid me. Pictures of Peter and me. But not to use for blackmail. Never for blackmail. For murder. Mine.

There was someone else.

Someone who had very much to gain if I died.

I turned my chair back from the wall.

"Juanita," I said.

"Hmm?"

"Have you ever heard of the Ellice Islands?"

"Yes. It is in New York."

"No, not Ellis Island. The Ellice Islands."

"No."

"They're in the South Pacific. Near the Dateline, I think."

"Why do you want to know?"

"I didn't. I wanted to know if you'd misunderstand me. Sometimes when a person says one thing, you think it's something else entirely."

She came over and stood on the opposite side of the desk, looking down at me, maternal and troubled. "I thought this was over."

"No. I'm afraid not. Would you leave me alone for a while? I have to think. And I'd like you to go back to your sister's tonight."

"What are you going to do?"

"Nothing foolish."

She didn't believe me for a second, but she left.

I went upstairs and took my copy of Alex's list out of my handbag, then I went back to the study and shut the door. I opened my address book, thumbing through the worn pages until I found the Ps and the number. I dialed.

"Hello, this is Lauren Atwill. Frank Atwill's wife. Is Miss Parsons in?"

In a minute, Louella was on the line, chirping cheerily. "What have you got for me? What have you heard from Frank? There's a rumor going around that there's more to this Don Deegan kidnapping story."

"I'm afraid they haven't told Franklin a thing. I need to ask a favor, Lolly. A name. Do you know Forrest Barlowe?"

"Of course," she said, suddenly bored.

"He had a daughter. Stella. She died before the war, but I remember that she was an actress."

"So?"

"Do you remember if she had a stage name?"

"Why don't you ask Forrest?"

"He's out of town. I wouldn't bother you if it weren't important."

She sighed. "You owe me."

"I know."

I don't know where she went, what file she looked into. When she came back, she said, "Palmer. Stella Palmer."

There she was. The fourth name on Alex's list.

I took a breath before I said, "Thank you."

Ten minutes later, I picked up the phone again and called the sheriff of San Diego County, where Forrest was spending the week at his house near La Jolla.

It was just dusk when I reached the fringes of Hancock Park.

The house was a lovely Tudor, considered old-fashioned now, but Forrest had never remodeled it. It was just as well. Tradition suited him.

There was a single light on upstairs in one of the windows toward the rear. Forrest must have left it on when he went to La Jolla. No one was home.

I parked around the corner in front of a house with an empty driveway and waited. The smell of charcoal and lighter fluid floated over from the backyard barbecues. People came home from the beach, cranky and sunburned, carrying children and damp towels. The sun went down. The streetlamps came on, along with more lights in the houses. The air got cooler. Some of the neighbors dragged sprinklers into their front yards, but nobody gave me a second look. No patrol car pulled up and threw a light on me.

I got out and walked quickly down to Forrest's house. The driveway ran beneath a side portico and on back to the garages. I followed it and went through the wooden gate into the backyard and up the flagged path to the back door. It took only a few seconds to jimmy the lock; the door glided open.

I relocked it and turned on my small flashlight. The air was stuffy, but underneath, it smelled of lemon oil. I guided the light through the silent house and up the curving staircase. At the top, it was easier to see because of the light from the open door of the bedroom down the hall. Immediately on my right was another bedroom. I went in, leaving the door half-open.

The drapes had not been closed, and the shades were slanted behind the sheer curtains between them. The windows faced the street, so there was enough spill of blue light from the streetlamps for me to see. I switched off the flash, turned one of the winged chairs toward the window, and sat down. I laid the flashlight in my lap and waited. Ten o'clock passed and ten-thirty. I didn't have to look at my watch. The silver clock by the bed had illuminated hands. A few cars whooshed past. The neighborhood grew quieter and darker. The front porch light of the house across the street went out. Eleven. A few more cars passed. Whoosh. Whoosh. It was such a soothing sound, like the breeze that droned against the windows. I remember the clock said eleven-fifteen.

I jerked awake. For a moment, I did nothing but stare into the semidarkness, trying to focus, then I ran my tongue around a gluey mouth. My head felt full. My eyes watered. How the hell could I have fallen asleep? I didn't even remember closing my eyes, hadn't realized how exhausted I was. I tried to stretch my legs, but I had gone to sleep with them crossed, and the right one was full of electric needles. I started to get up, then froze, one hand on each armrest. The needles scampered up my spine.

Someone was coming up the stairs. The old stairway creaked under the weight. Someone was in the house.

The footsteps paused, then headed away down the hall. My heart started beating again. Very hard.

I crept to the door. At the other end of the hall, a bar of soft light glowed from the barely open door to the study. I stood there with my hand on the doorframe, unable to move. The wave of fear was almost incapacitating. Weakness rushed into my legs, and they started to tremble.

It was a very long walk to the other end of the hall.

From inside the study came the muffled clattering of a typewriter. I waited until it stopped. I kept waiting until I was sure that it was not going to start again. Then I touched the knob and pushed. The door opened silently. There was no creaking of the hinges, no brush against the carpet, no sudden suction of air pulling on the tightly closed drapes.

There was only one light on, the copper-shaded desk lamp. Beside it, on the blotter, was a flashlight, two large Manila envelopes, and a ledger book. The figure seated behind the desk was turned away, concentrating on reading the letter in the typewriter that sat on a small rolling metal table.

I took a step. The longest of my life. "Trying forgery now?"

Alex whipped around so fast that the swivel chair crashed into the table. But she recovered admirably. "Oh, Lauren, you frightened me." She pressed her gloved hands delicately to her chest. The voice was level enough, but the eyes were searching past me into the hall. "What are you doing here? Forrest didn't tell me you were coming by."

"You've talked to him, then?"

"Well, of course. You didn't think I—? My goodness, he gave me a key. It's right here."

She stretched out her hands for her bag, but I was quicker. I jumped for the desk and yanked the handbag from under her suddenly grasping fingers.

"Heavy," I said. I opened the clasp and looked inside. It was the Remington, shining against the black satin lining. "My, my. This wouldn't be the gun that killed Dean Cummings, would it? Ooh, and I recognize *these*." Out of the bag, I took a couple of thin strips of lock-picking wire. "Maybe Forrest didn't give you a key after all."

She ripped the paper out of the typewriter and folded it away into the waistband of her slacks suit. "I think you must have been drinking." She stood up and put her hand out. "Will you please give me my things?"

"Certainly." I replaced the wires, but I took out the Remington. I tossed the bag to her. "Here you go. Leave the other stuff, all right?"

Her eyes darted to the items on the blotter. "Those aren't mine."

"Fine."

"I'm leaving," she said.

"Go ahead."

With a snap of her head, she snatched the flashlight off the desk and went out. I heard her going down the hall and down the stairs. I parted the drapes just far enough so that I could see her come out the back door and go across the lawn to the garages. The side door to them wasn't locked. She disappeared inside for just a few moments, then she came back out and reentered the house. Five minutes later—and it seemed like forever—I heard her on the stairs. She opened all the doors along the hallway and searched each room with her flashlight.

Finally, she came back into the study.

She dropped her bag on the chair and began searching for the extra wires that go with microphones. She checked around the desk and all the chairs. She lifted the rug and ran the light around the baseboard. She knew what she was doing. She unplugged the radio on the table beside the desk. She looked into the bookcase and behind the pictures, the drapes, and the small blue steel safe in the corner. She examined the desk lamp and lifted the blotter. She unscrewed both ends of the telephone receiver and looked inside. There was nothing there, but she dropped the phone into the deep side drawer anyway. Then she picked up her bag.

"If you don't mind," I said and held out my hand. The other one had the gun in it. After a moment, she gave me the bag. Inside was a wide-bladed kitchen knife. "And we both know you've had practice using one of these," I said. I closed the bag and put it on a shelf in the bookcase behind me.

She started to sit down. "One minute," I said. "Open the jacket. Just in case the first was a decoy."

Her mouth twitched in a contemptuous smirk, but she held the jacket open. "Lift it up and turn around," I said. There was nothing tucked into the waistband of her slacks, and there were no pockets big enough to hold another knife. "Thank you. Have a seat."

She did, positioning the chair so that she could see down the hall. I pulled a side chair from against the wall and set it on the opposite side of the desk toward the end, so she was far enough away, but I could still see most of her. I sat down and cradled the gun in my lap. "It was very well done, Alex. Very well played. You completely took me in."

The lamp cast sharp shadows on her face and dark halos around her eyes. Still, she didn't look sinister. If it hadn't been for the hard set of her mouth, she would have been the sweet, shy girl I had felt so sorry for.

"Where is Mr. Winslow?" she asked.

"At the hospital with his brother. They had to operate again today."

"I can't believe you'd come here alone."

"You're not the only one who's full of surprises. Seen Jack lately? You haven't killed him, have you?" I sniffed the gun. "Well, not within the last few hours, anyway."

"I haven't killed anyone."

"I wouldn't take any bets on that. What was it like to destroy your own sister? Did you hate her that much, or was it just for a bigger piece of your father's fortune?"

She didn't say anything. Neither did I. Slowly, indifferently, she took off her gloves and smoothed them out on the blotter. And waited.

Finally, I said, "Let me tell you a little story. You correct me if I get anything wrong. You had some problems. You wanted Dean, Peter, and me all dead. But that would leave three unsolved murders. Dean's parents would put pressure on the police. Peter's boss would assign his own men to investigate. And if you killed me, the police would naturally start by looking at the one person who stood to gain the most. Franklin. Three million dollars. Imagine the stories in the papers and the fan magazines—FRANK ATWILL'S WIFE MURDERED. HE INHERITS A FORTUNE. You couldn't have that.

"You're no fool, Alex. You know Franklin wants to be married. He likes it, even if he has trouble with the vows. But he wasn't getting a divorce fast enough to suit you. With me out of the way, you'd get him by default. And nothing has ever stood between you and what you want. Wouldn't it be nice if you could find a way to kill all three of us and hand the police the killer at the same time? Now, *that* would be a plan.

"You'd have to shut down your blackmail operation, but I think you'd already done that. Maritski—I think you know him better as Paul Kovak—Maritski told me that a long time passed between the day he found out about the blackmail Jack was involved in and the day he found the pictures of me. I realized today that he meant months. He said the woman in the first set of pictures he found had been wearing furs when he saw her pick them up in the library. That means winter in L.A. That's a long time for a gang as active as yours. But blackmail was getting too dangerous. Tolen got your sister's death declared an accident, but Peter started asking questions. Too many questions. Tolen's captain had gotten involved, too.

"What if you could make the fact that the police already knew about the blackmail work to your advantage? You'd frame someone for the blackmail and the murders you were going to commit. The police would get their man, and you'd get to keep smuggling dope.

"First, you waylaid Peter and me and took pictures of us. You needed a man for the pictures, and you couldn't use one of your own. Then you were going to kill him. Get him out of the way first. He was the most dangerous. Then Dean would die. Then I would turn up dead, of course in Tolen's jurisdiction. Very quickly, before there could be any rumors about Franklin, Tolen would say that he'd got a tip from one of his snitches. I was killed because someone was trying to blackmail me, and I had figured out who it was. Tolen would start investigating the fall guy you picked, who would then conveniently kill himself, leaving behind a remorseful confession and lots of evidence, including the Remington that killed us all. Dean's dead, Peter's dead, I'm dead. And the police have the bad guy. Very neat.

"But a couple of things went wrong. First, Peter escaped, then Maritski stole the pictures.

"I turned up at Maritski's, which might have worried you a little, but you must have figured that Tolen would find him long before I did. But when I showed up at Helen's party with Peter, that must have given you quite a turn.

"You had to make sure Jack disappeared. Peter would trace him in no time. Even with Jack gone, Peter might still discover Jack's connection to Don, who would implicate George. Don might have to be eliminated. So, first, you had to find out how much we already knew. The only way to do that was to pretend to be a victim yourself. Luckily, Peter wouldn't let me tell anyone very much. *I* would have told you everything.

"As it was, I let it slip that we thought my pictures were a mistake. You must have been relieved to hear it. Peter thought your gang had been after Helen that night, so they could use pictures of her to keep Dean quiet. He thought the gang had only taken pictures of me on the chance they might be worth something. You can't blame him. Otherwise, the pictures didn't make much sense.

"How did you find Maritski at the Whately? Did you find his car first? Did you play the hooker who got Tolen into the hotel? That's why the desk clerk had to die, isn't it? He'd had a good look at you. And it's why Maritski died in that alley. He tried to get away because he recognized you. He had seen you before. He knew your face from the society pages with Franklin, and he saw you at the warehouse with Jack and Dean. When he tried to blackmail me, he told me not to call anyone I knew. I thought the person he saw at the warehouse was a friend of mine. But he was afraid I'd call Franklin for help, and you would find out.

"After you stabbed Maritski—it had to be you, Tolen couldn't get blood on his clothes—you and Tolen dropped him in that trash can to give Tolen time to get back and be assigned to the case. Then you and Jack followed the clerk home and killed him. The witnesses were dead, and Tolen was in charge of the Maritski case."

She smiled. She pulled her lips back, anyway. It made her face flat and masklike.

I went on. "But you made one small mistake. Not making sure Maritski was dead. When we pulled him out of the can, he tried to name his killer. We thought he was trying to say 'Elizondo.' It sounded like Elizondo, if you didn't listen to those little coughing, choking sounds. When you hear someone dying, you try not to listen to them. But it wasn't Elizondo. It was Alexandra."

The smile did not change.

"You're very clever," she said, not without a trace of sarcasm.

"Clever enough to find you here."

"You haven't been following me," she said. It wasn't a question.

"No. But once I decided it was you, I wondered if you were still planning on using the Remington to set up a frame that would keep the police and maybe even Peter away from you.

"I started thinking about that list you gave me. The party had to have been real. You couldn't lie about that when you'd given me the names of some of the guests. It was probably the one where your sister's blackmail pictures were taken. But I wondered why you'd put evidence that you were at an orgy in my hands. Were you afraid that, if you didn't give me something, I'd start to wonder? Or was there some other reason? Was it all part of a plan to set someone up? I looked over those names in a way I hadn't earlier, when I had only been interested in Dean Cummings and your sister. And then I saw her. Stella Palmer. And suddenly the name seemed very familiar. Using her stage name was a nice subtle touch.

"Forrest has been your fall guy all along, hasn't he, from the moment you decided Peter, Dean, and I had to die? Franklin must have told you about my affair with Forrest and that I left him money in my will. It bothers him more than he likes to admit.

"You lost your gang, but you could still blame Forrest, kill Forrest. That would be *some* revenge against me for ruining everything.

"You knew that he was all alone in La Jolla. You'd heard him tell me about it at Dean's funeral." I gestured to the empty typewriter. "I thought that, if you decided to kill him, you might come here first to type the confession. He might not have a typewriter in La Jolla."

Her eyes searched down the empty hall, then she

flexed her fingers and laced them carefully together again. "And what if I'd gone straight down there?"

"Oh, I called the San Diego County Sheriff's office and got Forrest's address from them. I hired someone— not from Paxton's, but tough enough—to go down there and keep an eye on the place. Forrest doesn't know he's being watched. There's no need to involve anyone else. Yet. What did Dean have on you? An assistant at Marathon overheard him on the phone. Something about a letter."

After a moment, she said, "Just some things he shouldn't have written down."

"So you had Jack and Tolen take pictures of Helen and Dean to keep him quiet till you found the letter. Was that what was in his parents' safe?"

"His mother's an even bigger fool than he was. I took her an envelope and told her it was a list of people I'd heard making remarks sympathetic to communism while I was at Hollywood parties. I mentioned that Dean said he had given her something to keep and that he felt it was very safe. She said that he had. I made her swear not to tell anyone that I had been there, even him. I said that sometimes he did talk a bit too much. She understood. She said that there were several people like me who had come by to leave lists and not to worry. She wouldn't say a thing. She let me stand right there and watch her open the safe."

"Surely, he wasn't threatening to go to the police. He would have ruined himself."

She shrugged, a bored, scornful shrug. "It was a game to him. George and I would tell him who to play up to. Women loved to talk to him, and they always talked too much. He liked that part. He thought he was clever. And he liked the money. But he thought it was a game."

"Until you moved on to heroin smuggling. Or was it when your sister committed suicide?"

She shrugged again.

I said, "What would happen if I told your father what you did?"

"Do you think he'd believe you? Nothing here is in my handwriting. Neither is the list I gave you. Did you think it was in my handwriting? And it doesn't have my fingerprints. Neither does the gun. You don't really have a thing."

"Do you think you'll get Franklin if I tell him?"

"If you were going to tell him, you would have brought him with you."

"You're very clever, too, Alex. You're right. I couldn't tell him, because I know what he'd do. He might love you. I think he does. But he would have gone to the police. Your father's a powerful man. He'd get you the best lawyer money could buy, and the lawyer would blame everything on the absent or the dead. You'd be the poor little rich girl who just fell in with the wrong crowd. You might do six months, then you'd be off to Europe, where you'd stay until nobody gave a damn anymore.

"But they'd give a damn about Franklin. You're rich. You're society. You'd get ink. Plenty of it. Enough to float this house to Nevada. His career would never survive. Drugs, smut, blackmail, murder. No one would believe he didn't know what was going on. I know how the studio would react. Their press releases would back him to the hilt, but they'd shove him out so fast his eyes would rattle. I know this town. I know how it thinks. As long as the dirt's under the rug, fine. But if it comes out, nobody gets higher and mightier faster than a studio boss. I'm not going to let you do it."

She almost fluttered her eyelashes. "You'd let me get away with it? All for Franklin?"

I got up and glared down at her. "Don't push me, Alex," I said fiercely. "I saw Dean and Maritski when you were through with them. Don't push me. Tomorrow morning, you're going to tell Franklin you want to think about your engagement, then you're going to get out of the country. Out of the way and out of his life. Eventually, Peter is going to figure this out. By that time, I'll have put some distance between you and Franklin. Stay away from him, Alex, or I'll make you sorry for the first time in your life."

"How? Look at you, trying to be tough. You should have seen yourself trying to play detective. Patronizing poor little Alex. You loved that, didn't you? 'We're going to find these people, Alex. We're going to make them pay, Alex. My marriage is over, Alex. Franklin's going to marry you, Alex.' Did you think I was that stupid? You're not about to give him up."

I didn't see it coming, had no idea what was going on behind those cold, sneering eyes. She leaped out of the chair, driving her shoulder and forearm into my stomach with her full weight. The air rushed out of my lungs. Cold nausea enveloped me. My astonished muscles, instinctively more interested in maintaining my balance, dropped the gun. The force of the blow carried me back and back and back. She slammed me into the wall. Light exploded in my eyes. My knees collapsed. I was sliding sideways down the wall. I tried to grab something, anything. I snatched her hair and held on.

I landed hard on my injured hip; the pain shot through my entire body. She fell on top of me. Her head struck me in the stomach. I locked my hands in her hair and clutched her head to me while my heels worked in the carpet and kicked the baseboard, desperately trying to get some leverage so I could use my greater weight against her. I had to keep her away from the gun. I had no idea where it was.

She arched her neck and strained, trying to get away, but I held on. Her fingernails dug into my arms as she tried to loosen my grip. The skin broke. Madly, she jerked her body back and forth like a wild animal. Her shoes tore at my ankles, shredding my stockings, flaying the flesh. Still, through the pain and the vicious sickness, I held on.

She began to make weird sounds in her throat, half between a pant and a groan, but with a sharp, frantic edge that was chilling—and quite mad. She stopped tearing at my skin. She stopped trying to get away. Instead, she clutched the front of my dress with one hand and pulled. Dug into the fabric and the flesh and pulled. She used her strength to crawl up my body. I tried to hold her back. Her white face was coming closer, the skin drawn back, the cords of her neck standing out boldly, the eyes wide, unblinking, and full of murderous fury. I let go of her hair with one hand and struck her in the face, but I couldn't get much force behind it. Even if I had, I doubt it would have stopped her. Her right hand clutched my throat. I grabbed that wrist with one hand and with the other, I struck her again. Her left hand wrapped around my throat. Both thumbs pressed hard into my larynx. I went for her eyes. I tried to find her eyes.

A hawk's shadow moved over us, hovered, and suddenly swooped. With a scavenger's strength, he plucked her off effortlessly and held her above me. Her fingers jabbed out, raking the air. Her head twisted from side to side. She moaned and shrieked and clawed at me. Then she flew straight into the wall.

Something glinted briefly and came to a rest beside her temple.

"Don't try anything. I could blow you through the wall and not bat an eye."

The floor trembled beneath me, and Sergeant Barty rushed into the room. "All right. Easy, Pete. Put it away. She's not going anywhere.

I struggled up onto my hip. The room bobbed and settled. "Peter. Please."

Slowly, the gun disappeared inside his coat, then with her collar still in his fist, he marched her to the desk and thrust her into the chair.

"Back off, Pete," Barty said. "I mean it. No more rough stuff. It's over."

The overhead light came on, and the doorway was suddenly full of suits and uniforms.

Peter knelt beside me. Gently, he took me by the shoulders and propped me against the wall. "You okay?"

"I'm glad you didn't wait for the bell to end the round."

"Jesus," he said softly as he examined my flayed arms and legs. Several of the slashes were actively bleeding.

Barty bent over and stuck a pencil through the trigger guard of the Remington. "What have we here?"

Alex wiped a hand across her wet face. She was still very white, but her voice was under control.

"What just happened here was very ugly," she said softly. "I'm not proud of myself, but I was only acting in self-defense. Mrs. Atwill called me and asked me to meet her and Mr. Barlowe here this evening. She said it had something to do with Franklin. When I arrived, she was acting very strangely. She threatened me with that gun and accused me of all sorts of things. I know she must have asked you to come here so she could repeat these accusations, but . . ." There was a little throb in her voice. She pressed her fingers to her lips and turned away.

"You're good, Alex," I said. "You're real good."

"I don't know what Mrs. Atwill has told you—"

"Well," said Barty, "she seems to think you're a blackmailer, a smut-peddler, a dope-runner, and a murderer. You wouldn't think a woman like you could get into that much trouble."

"I haven't," she said, with quiet sincerity and a brief, pitying glance at me. "I give you my word."

"We might need more than that, Miss Harris. You see, Mrs. Atwill thought you might be after Mr. Barlowe, so she got hold of him this afternoon through the San Diego County sheriff and told him to get out of his house, then she came to see us. We got in touch with him at the sheriff's office, and he agreed to go back out and stay there, with some of the local police and some of Mr. Winslow's boys watching. Just in case she was right, and you showed up. And he gave Mrs. Atwill permission to occupy this house while he was gone." He turned to me. "Mrs. Atwill, did you invite this woman here?"

"No."

"Alexandra Harris, I'm placing you under arrest for breaking and entering. The other charges we can sort out when we've been through this ledger. And, of course, gone over the transcript of your conversation." He patted the table radio. "Real clever, those army boys. Came up with this during the war. Never seen one of them myself before today. These shamus outfits got everything. There's a shortwave inside. No wires necessary. We've been down in the garage of the house next door with a stenographer, taking down every word."

Alex's face twitched. "I have not—"

"If I were you, I wouldn't say anything else till I talked to a lawyer."

"She's got a piece of paper in her slacks," I said. "Whatever she was typing."

"Let's have it," Barty said, and held out his hand. Alex didn't move. "Put it on the table, Miss Harris. I can get a policewoman to search you."

Her fingers jerked spasmodically before she reached into her waistband and pulled out the paper. She set it on the desk.

"Thank you. Okay, let's go."

Alex pushed herself back into the chair. Her body got very stiff, her fists clenched. Something of the wild look came back into her eyes. Barty waited patiently, his hand out for her arm. "No cuffs, if you come quietly."

Finally, she got to her feet. She drew her arm away when he tried to take it.

"Suit yourself," he said.

Chapter 17

I took my stockings off in one of Forrest's bathrooms and washed the blood off my arms and legs. Peter drove me back to Central Division in the borrowed Plymouth that I'd used to drive to Forrest's house. We hadn't wanted to risk Alex recognizing my car.

I sat beside Barty's desk while he called the San Diego County Sheriff's Office and told the deputy on duty that it was over. When he finished, he handed me the receiver and went off to book Alex. How was Mr. Barlowe, I asked the deputy? Fine, just fine, he said proudly. The sheriff and those private detectives were out watching the house real careful. He'd call them on the radio. He knew just what to do. I could rely on him. I thanked him and hung up.

Peter appeared beside me. "I called the hospital. Johnny's still asleep."

"Do they want me to make another statement?" I asked, and stood up. The room looked awfully smoky.

"I think we should get you home."

I took a step, and suddenly all the feeling went out of my legs. The only thing that kept me from dropping straight to the floor was Peter's arm, which caught me around the waist. He deposited me back in the chair and knelt in front of me.

"It's a delayed reaction, that's all," he said. He turned and shouted over his shoulder. "Hey, could someone get me some water?"

"This is stupid. I keep falling down. I never do this. I don't faint."

"You never used to catch killers, either. We never should have let you go in there."

"So you kept saying this afternoon."

There was a discreet cough, and Evans handed me a paper cup of water.

"She's not feeling too well," Peter said. "Do you need a statement tonight?"

"Tomorrow'll be fine."

Peter took off his jacket and wrapped it around me. I shook hands with Evans and thanked him once again for remembering the location of the parking garage.

Peter took off his holster and carried it out in his hand. As we went down the steps, a dozen men, suit jackets flying, dashed up past us. Half of them were carrying flash cameras. Someone had put the word out.

When we got to my house, Peter said, "Go up and wash those cuts."

"I have to call Helen first."

"When you're finished, go wash them. I'll make you something to eat."

I called Franklin from the study. My agreement with the DA had been canceled. I had insisted that, if I was right about Alex and we caught her, I would have to be able to explain to Franklin and Helen.

Franklin wasn't home. I told the groggy maid that it was urgent, very urgent. She swore she didn't know where he was. I said, "Have him call me the minute you hear from him. Before he talks to anyone else. Anyone." She promised she would.

I called Helen.

"We found the boss," I said.

I could hear her sitting up in bed. "What? What do you mean?"

I heard Sam in the background, his voice clouded with sleep. "What is it? What's wrong?" he was saying.

"Can Sam hear me?" I asked.

"No," she replied cautiously.

"Tell him I have to see you. Tell him I wouldn't say what's happened, but it's important, and I'm very upset. You can call him later and explain."

"Now? Come over now?"

"Yes. I can tell you everything."

I put the phone down. When I looked up, Peter was standing in the doorway.

"Helen's coming over," I said.

"What did your husband say? You called him, didn't you?"

"He wasn't home. I never thought he wouldn't be home."

"You didn't learn much from being married to him, did you? You don't have to sit there and wait for him."

"I wasn't going to."

"Good. Go wash those cuts." He turned abruptly and went out.

Upstairs, I stuffed my hair under a cap and turned on the shower, letting the warm water massage my chilled, aching body, then I dried off and smeared medicine on the scratches. My arms and legs were relief maps of Merthiolate. I put on some slacks and a long-sleeved sweater.

There was a plate of sandwiches and a pot of hot chocolate waiting on the coffee table in the study. Peter handed me a cup.

The doorbell rang; I went to let Helen in. She was wearing hardly any makeup and a sienna slacks suit that drained what color there was from her face. I settled her on the sofa and gave her some brandy.

While I sipped my chocolate, Peter told her about Alex and everything else that we had discovered in the last week. Then he told her what had led me to Forrest's house. "We didn't know if she'd make a move, but if she did, we were pretty sure she'd do something fast."

"And you went in there with her alone?" she asked me, astonished.

"I didn't think I was being all that brave. I thought that, if she decided to go through with it, she'd go straight down to La Jolla. Forrest is the one who was brave. He agreed to go back to his house and sit there, knowing she might be coming down to kill him."

"We had plenty of men around him," Peter said.

"Still . . ."

Helen asked, "How did you get the police to agree to help you?"

Peter said, "We told the DA that we had Barlowe's permission to set up a microphone in his study where the safe and the typewriter were. Phil said he'd come along. The DA sent some of his guys, too, but only to make sure I didn't do anything illegal. He didn't believe us for a minute."

"If this man Maritski saw Alex at that warehouse, why would he think you'd call her for help?"

"He didn't," I said. "He was afraid I'd call Franklin, and she would find out. He knew her face from the society pages and fan magazines with Franklin."

Peter said, "We think she was the one who acted as the lookout the night Mrs. Atwill was attacked." He told her about the cigarette butts I'd found outside Elizondo's. "No lipstick, but there wouldn't be if she used a holder. And there weren't any signs of a holder because she crushed the butts completely to keep from starting a fire."

"I saw a holder in her apartment the day she gave me the list," I said. "The police found Raleighs in her cigarette case."

"She must be crazy." She was silent for a while, staring into her cup, painfully inventorying everything that Alex Harris had cost her. "What was Dean doing for them?"

"Setting up blackmail victims. But not you," Peter said. "That was the gang getting something to keep him quiet. He wanted out."

"Do you think she killed Dean?"

"He felt safe enough with his killer to pour a drink. She'd look a lot safer than any of the others."

"Can you prove she did it?"

"We can prove she was in this up to her neck, but not that she actually pulled any triggers, no. If we find Jack— and he talks—maybe."

"How much does Don know about all this? I think Sam has a right to know."

Peter said, "There's no proof that Deegan did anything but get Jack Logan onto the lot. He says it was for a little gambling, and I think he's telling the truth. I'm sorry we haven't been able to find your pictures yet."

"You've done more than I thought possible. I'd better go call Sam. There'll be plenty for him to do. I'll tell him what you said."

"Mrs. Ross." Peter's voice stopped her at the door.

"Make sure your husband understands that Mr. Atwill had nothing to do with any of this. The transcript of what Miss Harris said tonight will prove it."

"Of course." She glanced at me and went out.

"I'll take care of the dishes and lock up," he said. "You need to get some rest."

"I'm all right. I'll get you some fresh sheets."

"I can find what I need. If anyone calls, you can hear the phone up there. Go to bed."

For once in my life, I was too tired to argue.

The phone rang just after five.

"What's going on?" Franklin said. "There are reporters all over the place. I had to drive around the block and come in through the Stewarts' yard."

I didn't ask him where he had been. "Have you talked to anyone?"

"The maid said to call you first. What's going on?"

"It's Alex. She's been arrested."

"What are you talking about?

"She's been blackmailing people. There's a chance she killed Dean Cummings."

"Are the police out of their minds? Is this what they told you not to talk about?"

"I swear I didn't know it was Alex then."

"Is Winslow responsible for this?"

"Franklin, listen to me—"

"Is he?"

"Please, don't try to see her. The police won't let you, and the reporters will be all over you. Call the Harrises. They can tell you where things stand. After you talk to them, call Sam Ross."

"Why?"

"Just call him. He knows what happened. Then call your press agent."

"I will not!"

"Franklin! Alex is in jail, and it's not a mistake. I don't want her dragging you down with her."

"I am not calling my press agent!"

"All right. All right. But call Sam. Please."

I put on a robe and went down through the silent house to the kitchen. I got out the percolator and filled it with water, then I turned around and went straight to the phone. When I finished my call, I hurried upstairs, pulled on some clothes, and dragged a comb through my hair. I closed my bedroom door on the way out, but if I were lucky, I'd be back before Peter woke up. I got out the Hudson, closed the garage door, and drove over to see Sam Ross.

When I got home, it was just after seven. I came in through the back door and found Juanita in the kitchen, rinsing out a coffee cup. She looked up, surprised.

"I thought you were asleep," she said.

"I had some business to take care of. Mr. Winslow's upstairs—in the front guest room."

"He's gone. I gave him some coffee. He said when you got up to tell you that he called the hospital, and his brother is doing better. He said he had things to do before he went to see him. I came home when I saw the newspapers." There was a copy of the *Times* on the table.

HEIRESS QUESTIONED IN ACTOR'S MURDER. There was a society picture of Alex, looking about as innocent as a girl could. And one of Franklin. There was a paragraph about their romance.

Below the fold were equally large headlines: POLICE RAID DRUG WAREHOUSE. There was a picture of the DA and the police chief looking suitably serious over the boxes of dope. There was no connection made to Alex.

I told Juanita the whole story.

Reporters called, trying to find out if I'd seen Franklin or talked to him. I was very polite. Yes, I had talked to him. He was very upset, of course. But he was the only one who could answer their questions.

Louella Parsons called. I had to tell her the same thing.

At noon, Forrest called. He had just gotten back from La Jolla. I thanked him for what he'd done for us.

"This is the most excitement I've had in a long time," he said. "Come on over, and I'll make you some lunch. You can tell me everything."

When I returned home, Juanita had a message from Peter. He'd called to say he had to leave town for a few days. He hadn't said why.

By the next morning, the *Times* had dug out more of the story.

GUN RECOVERED IN HEIRESS'S ARREST LINKED
TO ACTOR'S MURDER
DEEGAN KIDNAPPER OWNED DRUG WAREHOUSE

That afternoon, the DA called the press, radio, and newsreel reporters together to confirm the story. I listened to it on KHJ.

Tests conducted on a gun recovered by police in the possession of Miss Alexandra Harris had revealed that it was the weapon that killed actor Dean Cummings last week. Police had also discovered that George Scarano, who had been killed after attempting to kidnap Marathon director Donald Deegan, was the owner of the warehouse in which a large amount of heroin had been found. Then he said that the district attorney had sufficient evidence to hold Miss Harris on charges connected with the smuggling and the murder.

The reporters went crazy, shouting over each other in a frenzy of questions. Did she kill Cummings? Why was he killed? Who killed Sergeant Tolen? What really happened in that garage? Why was Deegan abducted? Were any other people at Marathon involved? What about Frank Atwill?

It took a full minute to restore order.

Then he said that it was his sad duty to announce that evidence developed by the Los Angeles Police Department indicated that Detective Sergeant William Tolen might have been involved in these activities and might have been responsible for the shooting of Mr. John Winslow, whose firm had been hired by a private citizen to look into Mr. Cummings's death. A full report was being prepared.

He did not answer any of the second furious volley of questions. He thanked the reporters and left quickly.

Franklin—through his press agent—issued a statement saying that he was confident the charges against Miss Harris were a terrible mistake. Meanwhile, the studio issued its own. Marathon was certain that Frank Atwill had absolutely no knowledge of these crimes and that, should any of the public doubt it, the studio had been assured by parties connected to the investigation that there was irrefutable proof to that effect. Frank Atwill was a man of strong character and convictions. Of course, he would stand by Miss Harris. He would not desert her in her hour of need.

It made Franklin sound noble and, at the same time, began to separate him from her. It was the first step in our strategy. The nagging question was whether the transcript of my conversation with Alex could be made public before the scandal tainted Franklin with the fans and did irreparable damage. All it took was a small shift of loyalty. A few parents wouldn't let their daughters see his movies. They'd write letters to their newspapers complaining about the lack of morality in Hollywood as exemplified by Frank Atwill, A married man, engaged to another woman. How could he not have known what she was doing? The word would come back from the exhibitors: Box Office Poison.

The press release about Don was more guarded. It said the studio had Mr. Deegan's word that he knew nothing about the crimes. It said that the studio was confident that the investigation would clear him. *The Final Line* would start shooting again in two weeks.

I called Myrna Pearl. The police had been all over Central Casting, she said, asking questions about Jack Logan. I told her not to worry. The police knew all about me. I was the private citizen who had hired the detective. Dean Cummings had been a friend, I said. It was terrible that the investigation had led to Alex. I'd had no idea, of course. I told her that, when things settled down, I'd take her to that lunch I'd promised and explain it all. I asked her not to talk to reporters. She said the little creeps wouldn't get a thing out of her.

Johnny's second surgery seemed to have taken care of his internal bleeding, and the hospital allowed me to visit him for a couple of minutes. He didn't have any idea where his brother had gone or what he was doing, but he knew Peter would call him. He called every day. I asked Johnny to give him a message: I had to talk to him.

Peter didn't call.

I stayed home, thinking too much. By Thursday, Juanita was steering clear of me, venturing into the study only long enough to tell me she had left my dinner in the oven and was going to her sister's for the evening. After I had moved the food around on the plate, I switched on the radio. There was a comedy about a marital misunderstanding. He thought she was seeing another man. She thought he was seeing another woman. The audience thought it was hilarious. I growled at all of them before I turned it off. I got out a book and, in a perverse mood of martyrdom, drank far too much brandy while I didn't read it.

The next morning, nursing a hangover and having absolutely nothing useful to do, I dragged out my novel and thumbed through it. The hero was a prop. Maybe, I decided, it was because I didn't know a damn thing about men. None of the people stomping around in my head disagreed with me. So, with the dispassion that only a don't-give-a-damn headache can make possible, I began a new outline. What I needed was someone I did understand. A woman. A little spoiled, a little naive, and more than a little stubborn, who falls in love with a tough private eye. After they've solved the case, they've both changed, but probably not enough. Not when the man disappears for days and has girlfriends who wear cheap perfume and stay only one night.

Somewhere about one, Juanita brought in lunch. About seven, dinner.

As she was setting down the tray, the doorbell rang. I went out to answer it. Franklin was standing on the porch, furious. "You've known about this all along, haven't you?" he demanded. "Haven't you?"

"Known about what?" I asked, not quite as ingenuously as I might have.

He stormed past me into the study. I followed him. Juanita spread a napkin over the tray and went out. He slammed the door after her. "Jesus Christ!" he exploded.

"Do you want to tell me what's happened, or do you just want to yell at me?"

"Sam asked me to come see him. 'Louella's been hinting about you and Lauren for weeks,' he said. 'We can use that to our advantage,' he said. 'I think we can get Lauren to cooperate. He thinks! You've known about it all along!"

"Sit down, Franklin," I said gently.

"Do you know what this will make me look like?"

"The studio's trying to save your career."

"By telling me to walk out on Alex?"

"By trying to put some distance between you."

"Jesus Christ!"

"Louella will cooperate. She loves it when she gets something right, and she's always liked you."

"I don't need any help. Alex didn't do anything."

"She had the gun."

"It's not her gun."

"Did she tell you that?"

"I can't see her. They won't even let me see her. But her father told me that Elizondo's got plenty of cops and politicians on his payroll. And that Winslow's an old friend of his. Did you know that?"

"What are you saying? That Ramon Elizondo hired Peter and paid off the cops and the district attorney to set up Alex? The daughter of one of the most powerful men in the state? If her father believes that, he's crazier than she is." I caught myself, but not soon enough. "I'm sorry. I shouldn't have said that. Please sit down. I have a lot to tell you."

He glared at me for a while, but he finally sat down.

I told him the whole story, every detail, then I went into the dining room and brought him back a strong Scotch.

"I'm sorry" seemed the most inadequate thing I could possibly say.

The doorbell rang.

After a moment, Juanita knocked on the study door. I opened it. Across the foyer, I could see Peter standing in the front door, his hat in his hands. I went out to him.

He looked terrible. His eyes were raw. There were deep lines across his forehead and at the edges of his mouth. The skin beneath his eyes had a yellowish cast where the bruises were fading. He hadn't shaved. His trousers were dusty, and his shoes had a layer of dried mud on the soles.

"What happened?" I asked. "Are you all right?"

"It's not as bad as it looks," he said with a swift half smile that didn't come anywhere close to his eyes. His breath smelled of bourbon.

"Come in."

"I'm dirty."

"I don't care."

"Your husband's here."

"I just told him everything. Please come in."

"I guess I better. I have something to tell you."

He followed me into the study. Neither man offered to shake hands.

"Would you like some coffee?" I asked Peter.

"A bourbon," he said crisply. He sat down in the chair I had been using.

"Where have you been?" I asked.

"Up north."

"I left messages."

"I got them."

I didn't know what to say, so I went to get his drink. When I came back, Franklin was on his feet. "Maybe I should go. I've got to call Sam. I'll call you tomorrow."

"Sit down," Peter said. "You should hear this. As long as you're here."

Franklin and I looked at each other. He sat back down.

Peter knocked back about half the bourbon. With his rugged, weary face, he couldn't have looked more like a tough guy if he'd been trying. Or maybe he was trying.

"I've been looking for Jack," he said. "Miss Harris owns a house up near Monterey. I took Jack's picture up there and asked around. The woman who does the cleaning thought he looked like a man she'd seen there once, but she wasn't sure. Her eyes aren't too good. I got inside the house. The only signs that anyone had been there recently were ashes in the fireplace and some tire tracks in the back. The ground was soft, so they were pretty clear and just a few days old, judging from the debris in them.

"One of the county deputies knew where to find some dogs, and Phil brought up one of Jack's pillowcases from the San Marcos Courts, where Jack was hiding out before he disappeared. The dogs picked up the scent near the tire tracks, but it didn't lead anywhere. So we laid out some maps and tried to figure out where you could get rid of a body up there—the most deserted areas that are still accessible by car. There's about a hundred acres of undeveloped land bordering the national park up there that belong to Miss Harris's father. She wouldn't have to worry about campers finding something the animals dug up. I thought it might be a good place to start.

"We spent the last three days up there. This afternoon the dogs turned up something. It wasn't buried deep enough. It takes a long time to bury a body deep enough, and it's hard work. We found Jack. There was a bullet lodged in his brain. It didn't go through. It was the Remington. She should have stood closer."

"Peter!" I said.

"Or used a bigger gun."

"Stop it!"

Franklin stood up.

Peter said, "Going to ask me to step outside?"

"I'm not going to fight you. I know you could take me. Is that what you want to hear? You want to hear me say you could take me in front of Lauren?"

Peter looked at him for another moment, then set down his drink and stood up. He picked up his hat and started for the door.

I said, "I don't think you should be driving."

"I'm all right."

Franklin said, "Look, Winslow, I don't like you, and you don't like me. That's fine. But you saved Lauren's life, and that's worth a lot, so I'm not going to let you kill yourself. I'll tell Juanita to make some coffee." He turned to me. "I'll call you tomorrow." Then he went out. I heard him calling to Juanita. A moment later, the front door slammed.

I said, "How could you say those things to him?"

"I was out of line. We found some stuff buried with Jack. It looked like what was left of her burning all the pictures and negatives. You can tell Mrs. Ross that she probably won't have to worry about her pictures turning up."

"Why didn't you call me? I told Johnny it was important."

"What was it? You can tell me now," he said coldly.

I explained about Sam's plan. "It'll start in a few weeks. I wanted you to know before anything showed up in the papers. It'll say Franklin and I were getting back together all along. We'll have to be seen together for a while. It's just a story the studio's invented. It doesn't mean anything."

"No, it's a story *you* invented. That's where you went Sunday morning, to set it up. When I left, I saw the garage door was closed, but the Hudson was gone."

"I can't stand by and let her ruin him. You don't know how easily a career can go under. I have to help. You were willing to go to jail for Elizondo."

"There's a difference. I'm not in love with Ray."

"I'm not—"

"He was the first one you thought about. You marched right over and offered to do anything they needed."

"I had to."

He looked at me with sober eyes. "I guess it's just as well. It never would have worked out."

I stood there, very, very still. My heart was punching my ribs.

He went on. "Even if you weren't still carrying a torch for him, it wouldn't have lasted. You've seen what I do. The people I get to know. It might be exciting for a while, but it'd get old fast. Me gone for days, coming home smelling like some other woman's perfume. How long before you stopped believing I was just doing my job? How long before you'd get sick of my job? And I'd be plenty of laughs at a party when one of your friends realized I was the guy who cost him his kids. You've never known anyone like me before, but you weren't brought up to it, and you wouldn't like it for very long."

He put on his hat and turned to walk out of my life.

I picked up the first thing I could get my hands on, which happened to be his bourbon, and smashed the glass

into the fireplace. "How dare you! After what I've done—
After what I've been through, don't you ever, *ever* tell me
that I'm not tough enough. If you want out, then go. Get
the hell out of this house. But don't blame me because
you can't stick it. Because you'd rather have a woman
whose name you don't have to remember in the morning.
If you don't love me, say it! Godammit, you're going to
have to say it to my face!"

I didn't dare say anything else. I knew if I did, I'd start
to cry.

Then, suddenly, my eyes were stinging. I covered them
with my hands.

"Lauren," he said in a clouded voice. I heard him
move, and then he was beside me, drawing me to him, a
slow, gentle enclosing into his arms.

I laid my head on him. "You were going to walk out."

"There for a minute, I was afraid you were going to let
me." He laughed softly into my hair and pressed his lips
into it. "Christ. All week, I kept telling myself it was the
right thing to do. It would never work. Funny thing. I kept
having to tell myself every morning, every night, every
minute I wasn't working, even though I knew you'd get
tired of apologizing for what I did. Even though I knew
you'd wake up one morning, take a look at me, and go
back to that smug son of a bitch."

I reached into the pocket of my slacks and pulled out a
handkerchief. I leaned away from him just far enough to
use it loudly. "You're the smug son of a bitch. Thinks he
knows so much about women."

"One thing, for future reference. Are you going to
throw things when we fight?"

"I've never done that before. Never anything break-
able. Never with someone else in the room."

"Never threw a glass at him?"

"I didn't throw it *at* you," I pointed out. I used the handkerchief again, this time to wipe my eyes. "I look pretty tough now, don't I?"

"You look fine. Just fine."

"How long do you think it'll take before the reporters find out I hired you?"

"Maybe a month. No more. Too many people know."

"They'll be all over this place."

"Yes."

"I'll probably need a bodyguard."

"Yes."

"He'd have to be willing to stick awfully close."

"Yes."

I opened my mouth. I think I meant to say something else, but his lips brushed over mine and began to savor them, first individually, then together, then with purpose. Urgently, he whispered my name and crushed me against him.

I pulled away again. "Peter."

"I'm sorry. You're right. I'm dirty. I must smell like a bar. Like a goddamn brewery. I'm sorry. I'm going way too fast."

"No," I said. I took his hat off and tossed it away. Then I opened his jacket. "But if you're going to sweep a girl off her feet, you might at least take off your damn gun first."

CHAPTER 1

New York City
October 1946

The elevator doors opened and I stepped out. Ahead of
me was a wall of glass and beyond that, the point of no
return.

I stood there for a moment, fake glasses perching on
my nose and a smart little blue hat nesting in my
brunette dyed hair. I swallowed and thought about the
possibility that I was putting my life in danger again, this
time for a woman I had known for two hours and twenty
minutes.

Then I pushed open one of the glass doors and
went in.

It wasn't the sort of place in which you'd expect a
murder to have been committed. The reception room
was paneled in gleaming cherry wood and carpeted in
thick burnt umber. The sofa was upholstered in syrupy
gold, the chairs in muted copper. The floor lamps had
saucer shades of frosted glass that breathed soft light onto
the ceiling.

The receptionist was sitting in the center of the room
behind a cherry-wood desk. I walked up and gave her a

trying-to-be-confident smile, which under the circumstances, wasn't hard at all.

She was past the age you see on most receptionists—by maybe half a century—with hair so densely black that it could not possibly have been natural. She had a roll of bangs that stopped mid-forehead; the rest was parted down the center and folded back onto her neck, framing a leathery, square-jawed prune of a face. There was not a quarter-inch of her skin that didn't have a crease, seam, sag, bag, pouch, line, or furrow.

"May I help you, dear?" she croaked at me with a smoke-scarred, gravelly frog-groan of a voice.

"I'm here to see Mr. Benjamin," I said. "I have an appointment."

"Would you be Mrs. Tanner?" she asked without consulting her book.

"Yes. I'm sorry."

"No problem, dear. I'll tell him you're here. Have a seat."

"Thank you."

"Take the sofa. The chairs are bricks."

She picked up the intercom phone.

I sat down on the sofa and laid my handbag beside me. Not far away, against the rear wall, was a vintage Kent cabinet radio of burled mahogany; its doors were open, revealing the gold silk over its speaker. The source of the Kent family wealth.

Along the walls were lithographs of the radio programs produced in these offices. For the soap opera *Love Always*, there were men and women in chaste romantic embraces. For *Adam Drake*, there was one of the detective disarming a gunman and another of him holding the wrist of a beautiful woman, bringing the match in her hand up to his cigarette. Drake's face was turned away so there was just the hint of a terrific profile.

I opened my handbag and took out my compact. It was a new one of plain enamel, not my silver one, which had L.A. engraved on it for my real name, Lauren Atwill. I adjusted my hat and glasses and checked my make-up. Geoffrey, who had reluctantly agreed to dye my hair, had been right. I looked terrible as a brunette. I put the compact away. I was not here to worry about my appearance.

Through the glass wall I could see both elevators and the door beside them, which I knew led to the service elevator and stairs. These were the only means of escape the killer could have used. Somehow, he had figured out how to conceal himself inside the offices at the end of the day so that no one had noticed him. Then he had waited, again unobserved and committed a violent murder, with four people not forty feet away, without raising any alarm.

But then his plan of escape had depended on the chance that, when the body was discovered, everyone would desert the reception area and allow him to bolt unseen.

It was a madman's plan.

And yet, it had apparently worked.

I never imagined that I would be involved in another murder.

Until the first day of summer, I'd never been closer to a crime than my typewriter. Then for the next six weeks, I was closer than I ever wanted to be again.

But that was before I met Hazel Kent and before I knew that I would have to leave Los Angeles.

As it turned out, both events occurred on the same day.

Friday, September 13.

At eight o'clock in the morning, I was sitting at my desk in the study in my home in Pasadena, having been awakened an hour before by the first of the phone calls. I was staring into an empty coffee cup beside my typewriter, waiting for inspiration.

The door opened. A man with a gun walked in.

He closed the door after him and walked over to me. I wasn't hard to spot. I was the only person in the room.

He was dark and fit, in his late thirties, about six foot two of the kind of trouble most women like to get into.

I swiveled my desk chair to face him, crossed my legs, and regarded him steadily. "Who the hell are you?"

He took a good look at what he could see of my bare legs beneath my summer skirt and said, "I heard you might need some help."

"And you think you're the man for the job."

He pulled me to my feet and spent a little time proving that he was.

When he finished, I took out my handkerchief and started wiping the lipstick off his face. I said, "Some bodyguard you are. I haven't seen you for a week."

"I've been working a case."

"Hmm."

He kissed me again. "It's getting worse."

"I'm out of practice and whose fault is that?"

"I meant outside."

"Ah."

Reluctantly, I eased out of Peter Winslow's arms and went over to the study windows. I pulled the draperies aside a couple of inches and took a look at my front lawn.

He was right. He usually was.

Dozens of reporters, some with cameras and all with determined faces, were teeming on the sidewalk and creeping up cautiously to infest my lawn. Radio, newspapers, newsreels, news services, news magazines, fan magazines, and probably foreign press as well.

The last time I'd looked out, there had been six.

He took the drape out of my hand and closed it over the window. "Don't let them get a shot of you. It makes you look furtive."

"Furtive?"

"I like to use a dictionary once a month."

He unbuttoned his suit jacket and took off his hat. He tossed the hat onto the sofa, giving me a glimpse of the Colt M-1911 under his left arm. It was a large gun for a man to carry concealed. It was the sort of gun a man wore when he wanted people to know he was carrying it.

"Are all the drapes closed?" he asked.

"Yes, as soon as they showed up."

"Upstairs, too?"

"Yes."

"Good."

"We had to take the phones off the hook," I said.

"Johnny told me."

Johnny was Peter's twenty-three-year-old brother, who was finally able to work again after spending almost two months recovering from bullet wounds he had suffered in an attack that had nearly cost me my life as well. I carried a small scar on my cheek from it. He was my regular daytime bodyguard now, protecting me from the possibility that the killer I had caught might want both to take revenge and eliminate a witness.

"We're using Juanita's phone," I said, "but they'll get that number, too."

"We'll get someone to answer the phones," Peter said calmly. "They'll stop calling so much when they can't get through to you. I brought two more men over. I've put one out front with Johnny. The other'll stay out back. They'll keep them off the yard and out of your trees."

"My trees?"

There was a knock on the door.

I gave Peter's face another pass with my handkerchief and said, "Come in."

My housekeeper, Juanita, entered, carrying a tray with a china coffee service on it and the appropriate cups, saucers, spoons, and neatly folded linen napkins. She set it down in front of the sofa.

"Have you had breakfast?" she asked Peter.

"I'll get something later."

"I haven't eaten either," I said to him, then to Juanita, "Would you fix us some eggs?"

She said, "I'll need to go to the market today to buy some more food."

"Don't worry about me and the men," Peter said.

"There'll be five for dinner," she said to me.

"Fine," I said. "Get what you need. Don't go alone."

Juanita nodded and went out, closing the door after her.

Peter said, "I like the way the women in this house pay attention when I say something."

"We're good at it."

I sat down on the sofa, poured a cup of coffee, and handed it up to him.

"We knew this was bound to happen," he said quietly.

"I know."

"I'm surprised it took them this long."

"It means you might have to show up more often. No more excuses, buster."

He sat down beside me, put the cup on the table, and we made up a little more for lost time.

Then Peter went back to work.

He sat down at my desk and started making the new arrangements for my life. There would now be *two* men on each of the three eight-hour shifts. I thought it was interesting that one man had been enough before, when we were only worried about my life being in danger.

He called Sam Ross, who was a producer at Marathon Studios, which our investigation had tossed into a scandal and then saved from the worst of it. Sam was also married to my best friend, Helen. From the night the killer was arrested, he had known that I was involved in the case, and he held a copy of the press release that I had created for this eventuality. It was time for him to get it out and call his publicity chief.

Sam agreed to send over a secretary, at the studio's expense, to answer my phones, take messages, and be the villain who wouldn't let reporters talk to me.

Then Peter handed me the phone. "He wants to talk to you."

As he usually did, Sam shot me a list of questions before he paused for an answer.

"Hey, how are you? You holding up? Got a question for you, okay, nothing to do with this. We're thinking about doing a picture with that radio detective, Adam Drake, you know the show? What do you think? Ever listen to it? Think you might be interested?"

He took a breath. I stepped in. Yes, I said, I knew the show, liked it, listened to it on Thursday nights whenever I could.

"Good. We brought the producer out here. Hazel Kent. She wants to talk to some writers. She wants to meet you."

"You want me to audition for a radio producer?"

"No, no. You meet with her. It's a meeting. That's it. That's all. Call her. She wants to meet you."

"I'm having a little trouble getting out of the house, Sam."

"We'll work something out. You can meet here. We can get you a bungalow, some lunch. It's a meeting. That's all. Call her. She's at the Beverly." He rat-tatted a phone number at me and hung up.

I set the receiver in the cradle just long enough to disconnect the line, then I set it down on the desk top.

I told Peter what Sam had said.

There was a tap on the study door, and Juanita rolled a chrome bar cart into the room. On the top shelf, she had arranged a crystal pitcher of orange juice, chilled glasses on small plates, a china serving dish piled with ham and bacon, a silver rack of toast, and a small chafing dish with a fluffy, lightly browned omelet stuffed with cheese and onions. Peter's favorite.

"Thanks," I said.

When she had gone, he asked, "Does breakfast always look like this?"

"She likes you."

"That must be why she scowls at me."

"She's naturally suspicious of men, but she appreciates one who saved my life. Twice."

I loaded plates for us, and we sat there and ate like a couple of ordinary people, not a private detective and his client who had fallen in love while solving a case that, given the identities of the participants—guilty and innocent—was proving to be one of the biggest in California history.

At the end of July, the case that brought us together had ended. At least, the killer had been captured. For the last six weeks—through the delays contrived by the defense attorneys—the D.A. had tried to keep my identity secret, which meant that Peter and I had not been able to see each other often. The reporters knew he was involved. He didn't want to lead them to me.

But too many other people knew that I was the woman who had hired him.

It was inevitable that the press would find out.

Apparently, they didn't yet know the extent of my involvement—that I was the one who had in fact identified the killer—but I was still technically married (although separated for over a year) to Frank Atwill, one of Marathon's biggest stars, who had managed to get himself into some trouble in connection with the case, and that was plenty.

Morty Engler, who was head of publicity at Marathon, showed up two hours later with a secretary, who immediately took over the phones. Morty had enjoyed too much of everything that wasn't good for him: rich food, straight gin, and bad temper from his bosses. Despite those indulgences, he still had the moist, small-pored skin of a baby. He wasn't that short, but it wasn't easy to tell: he was perpetually bent forward, ready for the next crisis. He made up for any lack of height with handmade shoes with lifts, and for a natural nervous dampness by never taking off the jackets to his expensive suits.

He lit a cigar and went straight to work.

He handed me one of the mimeos of the press release he had brought with him. He had made a few changes to my original, but they were good ones, and I told him so. He grinned around the cigar. Working for a studio, he wasn't used to people telling him that his work was good.

He threw back two fingers of gin from my bar, straightened his tie, and smoothed his hair in the hall mirror, then went out to meet the crowd Johnny was keeping to the sidewalk.

The district attorney had instructed Mrs. Atwill not to comment on the case, he said. She would, therefore, be unable to meet with them, as she could not answer questions. She understood, however, that they had stories to write and deadlines to meet, and she would give them as much information as she could, which was to explain how she had become involved in the case.

Morty told the reporters, in essence, what was in the releases that the secretary handed out. Mrs. Atwill had hired Mr. Winslow through Paxton Security, the company for which he worked, following the death of the actor Dean Cummings. Mrs. Atwill had known Mr.

Cummings, having met him through her work as a screenwriter at Marathon Studios, with which he had a contract. She had found him to be an engaging, talented young man, and she had been distressed at his murder and determined to make sure that his killer was found. When she had hired Mr. Winslow, she had no idea where the investigation would ultimately lead. It had taken her, as everyone else, by complete surprise.

That part of the press release was absolutely true.

Morty thanked them for their restraint and said that they would have to direct any questions to the district attorney.

Of course, as soon as he turned around, they began to shout those questions: "What does she know about blackmail? Is it true there was blackmail? Was she involved with Cummings? What is Frank saying? When can we talk to Frank?"

Morty reminded them about the district attorney, thanked them again, and went inside. He tossed back another gin, passed on my offer of lunch, and went back to the studio.

The newspaper reporters lucky enough to have assistants with them scribbled out stories and sent them and the press release off to their editors. The rest went to call in. The radio men, who did not yet have hook-ups, packed up and took their stories back to be broadcast. The newsreel men, perched on their trucks, stayed where they were. So did the magazine reporters.

In all, about half of the gathering moved on. But only half.

We set the secretary up at a card table beside the telephone that was in the hallway alcove. I replaced the receiver in the study. Out in the hallway, the ringing began immediately.

"Let me get you a drink," Peter said.

"A light one." The usual strength of Peter's cocktails would render me incapable for most of the day.

He brought me back a mild gin and tonic, full of ice.

I thought it would make a perfect afternoon if I could spend it in bed with him and some iced cocktails. But it wasn't possible, so I went up to my bedroom alone and took off my clothes. Alone.

I put on my dressing gown and started running a bath. If I closed the bathroom and dressing room doors and put a pillow over the phone, I wouldn't hear it ring. I poured some salts under the tap, and while they were foaming, I went back out to the bedroom. I eased the receiver out of the cradle. When I heard the dial tone, I pulled the number Sam had given me out of the pocket of my skirt and called the Beverly Hills Hotel, that grand old lady. She had fallen on hard times during the Depression but was now refurbished and fashionable again. I asked for Hazel Kent.

She answered the phone herself. She sounded a little breathless. "I hope this isn't a bad time," I said when I had introduced myself.

"I was halfway down the hall when I heard the phone ringing. I was headed to the beach. How do you stand it out here? No soot. Clean water. Sunshine every day."

"It toughens you up."

She laughed. She had a wonderful laugh, a wonderful voice, warm and low-pitched; if she was a native New Yorker, she had made a determined effort to get rid of her accent. Every once in a while, as we talked, a vowel that should have been "ah" veered toward "aw," but that was it.

"Why don't we get together?" she suggested. "I've heard a lot about Chasen's. But I won't be back before lunch."

"Chasen's isn't open for lunch."

"Then we better make it dinner."

I explained about my constant companions

"I saw the papers. Hell with them. Come have some dinner. I promise not to ask you any questions. I'll get Marathon to make the reservations. We'll need them, won't we?"

"Yes. Do you have an escort?"

"I'm here by myself, but I'm sure the studio can take care of that, too. Unless you know somebody."

"I'll bring the man. One will be enough."

"Good. I'll have the studio make the reservation under my name. Don't worry about people staring at you. I'm so gorgeous, they won't give you a second look."

I laughed. "All right. I'll be the one with the reporter wrapped around her ankle."

"I'll be the redhead in the scarlet suit."

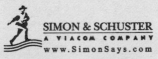